I0788715

BOOK DESCRIPTION

Lana

I knew it would end in disaster, but I didn't listen to reason. I didn't care. Because I loved him so much.

Kalvin Kennedy ruled my heart.

Until he destroyed it.

Shattered it so completely that I became someone else. Someone I loathed. Someone who repeatedly lied to her loved ones.

So, I ran.

From him. From myself. Desperate to hide my new reality.

But I could only run so far.

When he reappears in my life, I'm terrified. Unbelievably scared of facing the consequences of my actions.

Never mind that I still love him and want him so badly—there's too much at stake now.

How can I trust him with the biggest secret of all when he's likely to rip my world apart again?

Kalvin

Lana was always far too good for me. Everyone knew it but her.

I tried to stay away, but I was weak.

And I hurt her.

Crushed her until she barely resembled herself. Forced her to follow
a path she would never
have willingly chosen.

And then she was gone.

And my world has never felt as empty, as lonely.

She begged me to stay away. Not to find her. To forget she ever
existed.

But that's like asking me to slice my heart in two and toss half aside.

I've never believed in fate, but when I rock up to the University of
Florida, I'm ready to eat my words.

Because she's here. Like I hoped she would be. And I'm determined
to prove I deserve a second chance.

Note From The Author

While you do not need to have read **_Finding Kyler_**, **_Losing Kyler_**, or **_Keeping Kyler_** to enjoy **_Loving Kalvin_**, it is highly recommended as that is where we were first introduced to our two main characters and some of the supporting characters.

I would like to set the scene so there is no confusion for readers who are up to date with the series or those who are new to the series. The prologue in this book takes place on the morning of the trial (from **_Losing Kyler_**) which occurred on November fifteenth, and then our main story starts eleven months in the future, or three months after the epilogue in **_Keeping Kyler_**.

When we meet Lana and Kalvin, they are both attending the University of Florida, and they are two months into their freshman year.

LOVING
KALVIN

Prologue
Lana

November Trial

I used to think I was a decent person.

Kind, mostly selfless, with a good sense of morality, a good heart.

But I was clearly mistaken.

Because a good, kind, selfless person doesn't do the things I've done these last couple months.

A good person wouldn't continue to lie.

A good person wouldn't accuse the only boy who's ever mattered of such a horrible thing.

"Lana, we need to leave in thirty minutes to ensure we get parking outside the courthouse," Mom says, poking her head through the door. She checked us into adjoining rooms in the hotel because she's terrified to let me out of her sight these days.

I look up from the desk, chewing on the corner of my pen. "Okay. I'll be ready."

Her expressive hazel eyes—so similar to my own—flit to the handwritten page in front of me. Straightening up, she levels a stern look at me. "What are you doing?"

"I'm writing Faye a letter," I lie with the confidence of an expert deceiver. The lies just flow off my tongue like warm butter sliding off a knife these days.

I'm a total fraud, and I couldn't hate myself any more if I tried.

I swallow the painful lump in my throat as I offer her a brittle smile.

"Why? You don't owe that girl anything." Her lips pull into a tight line.

"Don't, Mom." I shake my head. "She was my friend, and I owe her an explanation."

"I beg to differ." Mom crosses her arms over her chest. "Today is all the explanation she needs. Once you testify, she'll understand exactly why you left without clarifying what happened. It was better that way. Leave it alone, darling."

Nausea swims up my throat, and I doubt I'll get through today without hurling. I could continue arguing with her, but then I won't get my letter finished. And it's too important to rush. "Mom, please. I don't want to fight. Not today. I'm writing my friend a letter, and then I'll put my suit on"—I gesture toward the black, shapeless monstrosity she laid out on the bed earlier—"and meet you in the lobby before we need to leave."

Clearly noting the resolve in my tone and my expression, she backs down. "I don't want to fight with you either, honey. I know how difficult today is going to be. I'll leave you to write your letter in peace." She closes the door quietly behind her.

I collapse in my chair, exhaling loudly.

Yes, today is going to be difficult.

But not for the reason she thinks.

Shaking aside those thoughts, I refocus on the task at hand. I examine the heap of crumpled pages in the trash—testament to more epic failure. For someone who aspires to be a writer, it's pathetic that I can't find the right words to tell the boy I love how sorry I am. I know him inside and out, so this should be uncomplicated. Shoot straight from the heart. *Cakewalk, right?*

So, why is this one of the hardest things I've ever had to do?

Glancing at the half-written page in front of me, I scan my latest effort with a frown. Frustrated, I scrunch the page into a ball and toss it clear across the room.

Ugh. Propping my elbows on the desk, I drop my head into my hands and shut my eyes.

His hauntingly beautiful face dances across the fields of my imagination, and a deep pang of yearning punches another hole in my heart.

Gosh, I miss him so much, and I'm not sure I have the strength to do this.

The problem is simple really.

I *could* write this letter, but I don't want to.

That's what's holding me back.

Even though I know it's for the best, there's a romantic, nostalgic part of me that still sees Kalvin Kennedy as my Prince Charming. My Mr. Right. My future.

The issue with that picture isn't Kal. Not really. Although, I'm sure he must hate me now, but this one is on me.

It's all my fault.

I wish things were different.

I wish I could rewrite our story, but I can't. The damage is done, and there's no going back.

The usual panic waylays me. I take deep breaths. In and out. Reminding myself I'm doing the right thing. And I can do this.

I'm strong enough.

I'll have to be.

I rub a tense spot between my brows, picking up the pen and a new piece of paper. I squint at the clock. Time is ticking. It's now or never.

Kal,

Writing this letter has been one of the most difficult things I've ever done. I never thought the time would come when words were the obstacle lying between us.

I'm sorry has never seemed more inadequate than it does in this moment. I could fill this page with row upon row of apologies, and it still wouldn't come close to making up for what I have done to you, so, I won't go there. Just know there is no word in the English language that can convey how truly regretful I am.

I don't think a day will pass where you aren't hijacking my mind because you live there—in my thoughts and in my dreams. Sometimes, in my nightmares.

You are all I think about, even when I'm trying so hard to forget you.

Even now. Even after all the hurt and the pain, I still love you so much. Probably too much for someone my age. I used to believe it was because we were made for each other. That we had a special kind of love most people never find. Now, I wonder if it's the opposite. If we were put together to show the destructive side of love.

You have always been my light and my dark.

My sun and shadow.

My strength and weakness.

You bring out the best and the worst in me.

Your continual rejection over the years hurt me more

than you know—yet it was nothing compared to the pain I endured when Addison showed me that video.

It hurt, Kal. It hurt so much.

I've never experienced that kind of soul-crushing pain before. Not even when you first brushed me aside, and I thought I wanted to die.

It's not an excuse for how I've behaved, and I'm not presenting it as such—I'm merely stating the facts, so you can try to understand where this stemmed from.

I've gone over and over it in my mind, and most days I struggle to connect my actions with the person I know I am. It's like a stranger inhabited my body, and I allowed her full control. Unbearable pain blind-sided me, separated me from my soul and my heart, and I trusted in someone who manipulated me. I should have known better. I did know better.

I've rewritten this letter a hundred times, and it's tempting to leave out the most important fact, but there's no point in writing a letter without honesty. I knew it would hurt you, and I wanted you to hurt as much as I was.

There. I've said it. Now you know how truly awful I am.

I don't feel that way anymore, and I'm ashamed I acted so rashly, that I caused so much pain, but I can't undo what I've done. I can only try and repair the damage and hope that, in time, you can somehow find it in your heart to forgive me. Because the thought *of you living the rest of your life hating me is worse than the prospect of living mine without you by my side.*

Mom claims I have an old soul. Maybe that's why I was always so sure about us. Why our age never made a difference. Why my love felt like it was born of decades not years. Perhaps that illusion of love shielded me from facing reality.

You and I aren't meant to be.

I will never regret the time we spent together. Precious childhood memories will remain untarnished in my mind, but that future we both dreamed about as kids was a fallacy created by fertile imaginations.

It's got to be. Because otherwise we would not have ended up here.

A sneaky tear slips out of my eye, rolling in slow motion down my face. It lands on the page, blurring the ink a little. I swipe under my eyes with my thumbs, glancing at the clock. I resume writing before I run out of time or my nerve fails.

I love you. I always have and I always will, but I'm letting you go. It's best for everyone involved.

Dream big, Kal, because you are destined for great things.

Don't look for me.

If you've ever cared for me, you will do that one thing. You will stay away. Leave the past in the past, and pretend like I never even existed.

But remember this much—you are the only boy who

ever owned a piece of my heart, and that piece will always belong to you.

I will never forget you.

Be happy.

Lana.

The tears return as I fold the page, fit it into an envelope, and write his name on the front. More quiet tears fall as I shuck off my pajamas and pull on the austere jet-black skirt suit. I button the crisp, white shirt all the way up to my neck as I toe on my ballet flats. Tucking the letter safely into the inside pocket of my jacket, I vow to find some way of getting this to Faye before the end of the day. She's the only one I trust to deliver it to him.

I smooth my long, dark hair into a tight ponytail, taking one last look in the mirror before I leave.

I look like I'm attending my own funeral.

Which is pretty ironic, because that's exactly what it feels like as I vacate my hotel room for the final time.

Chapter One
Lana

October of the following year

My head is buzzing, and it feels good. Feels great.

I'm doing it.

Thrusting my bottle of beer at Olivia, I stride toward the bar on slightly shaky legs, determined to properly let loose. This is the third time we've attended the Kappa Sigma Friday night party, and every other time I've wanted to do this, I've chickened out.

Not tonight.

Tonight, I have my big girl pants on.

The few beers I downed earlier at the Gator Growl—UF's flagship event which marked the culmination of all the homecoming week activities—have helped loosen my inhibitions, too.

"Lana?" Olivia tugs on my elbow. "What're you doing?"

"I'm dancing," I confirm, kicking off my shoes. My roommate gawks at me, and I flash her a crooked grin.

Friday night is the only free time I have during the week, my one and only opportunity to cut loose, and I'm determined to make the most of it tonight.

I skip toward the bar area at the rear of the basement. This whole space was purpose-built a few years ago from a generous ex-frat alumni donation, if rumors are to be believed. The other side of the basement houses a few pool tables, a foosball table, a bunch of bean bags and low couches, and a top-notch stereo system. I stuck my head in that room one time and almost passed out from the pungent smoke infusing the air. This section is where most of the drinking and dancing takes place, and I'm way more comfortable out here.

I've never been a big drinker, but I allow myself a couple drinks on Fridays, as a reward of sorts for working my ass off all week.

A large counter runs the length of the wall at the back. Rows of shelves are built in behind it with designated space for kegs and cubbyholes stacked full of cups and other drinking paraphernalia. It's not a functional bar, but it's the next best thing.

These parties are legendary, and everyone wants an in. Riley— the junior Liv recently started dating—lives here, so we're an automatic shoo-in now.

The dancing on the bar tradition was started a couple years back by a few seniors—girls from a nearby sorority—who gatecrashed one night. They started a trend, and now it's almost as legendary as the parties themselves.

The old me wouldn't have dreamed of doing anything so wild.

The new me can't wait to get my ass up on that counter. Tonight, I'm joining the honorary roll call, consequences be damned.

I haul myself up on the bar, rather inelegantly, staggering a little until I find my balance. A loud cheer erupts from the packed crowd when I remove my shirt and toss it in Olivia's direction. My white tank top is tight with thin straps and a sheer lace overlay which touches the edge of my short jean skirt. My usual pale skin is tan from a summer spent by the pool on the grounds of my grandparents' lavish property.

My hips move of their own accord, and I glance sideways, sharing a blinding smile with the petite redhead dancing alongside me. We grin at each other as the slick beats pump out. Flinging my hair over my shoulders, I do a little shimmy up and down, earning a few catcalls in the process.

I notice a couple of guys watching my every move, and my skin heats up. My moves become a little more provocative, a little sexier. Out of the corner of my eye, I catch Liv smiling in my direction. She gives me a quick thumbs-up, and I laugh, continuing to bump and grind to the sultry rhythm.

Surprisingly, I'm enjoying this.

The old Lana would never have been so uninhibited.

But that girl no longer exists.

Along with her scandalous past.

I'm not Lana Taylor anymore. Courtesy of my wealthy grandparents, and a recent circuit court petition, I'm now Lana Williams. A new name deserves a new outlook on life, and I'm determined to forge a new path. To forget the boy who forever captured my heart on a beach in Nantucket.

A surge of guilt washes over me. It's the same any time I think of Kal. Which is mostly every day, so, obviously, I haven't been entirely successful with banishing my past, but it's a work in progress. I'm determined to move beyond it.

Otherwise, what was the point of it all?

The redhead nudges my hip, and I realize I've stopped dancing. Forcing all thoughts of Kalvin Kennedy from my mind, I immerse myself in the song, dancing my punctured little heart out.

Sweat trickles down my spine, and my mouth is dry as sandpaper. I'm thinking of calling it quits when I'm distracted by the sound of roaring and clapping coming from the far right-hand side of the room. A group of football players are huddled in a circle, raising their beers in a united salute. As the crowd disperses, I notice the boy and girl descending the stairs into the basement, and my heart stutters in my chest.

She is model beautiful with thick, glossy blonde locks, killer curves, and long limbs. More than a few heads turn in her direction, but I've stopped noticing her because the boy beside her has just sent my world into a tailspin.

"No!" I gasp, and my knees turn to Jell-O. With my stomach lurching, and my legs almost buckling, I sway precariously on the counter as everything crashes down around me.

I'm going to be sick.

His head is angled toward the bar, and my mind switches off. I dive off the counter, uncaring how or where I land. I just know that I need to get out of his line of sight before he spots me.

My heart is jackhammering against my ribcage as I flail about in the air. A pair of strong, muscular arms catch me before I face-plant the ground. "Whoa there, pretty lady!" a deep, rich voice says. "You fall or something?" my savior asks, repositioning me so I'm cradled against his very broad, very warm chest.

I peer into lush chocolate-colored eyes, blinking profusely. "Sorry!" I attempt to wriggle out of his hold, but he tightens his grip on my waist.

"You sure you're okay?"

"She's fine," Liv says, materializing alongside us. "You can release her now, Chase."

Chase frowns as he carefully places my bare feet on the ground. Olivia hands me my shoes, eyeing the guy suspiciously. With her abnormally tall frame, flawless dark skin, striking eyes, and thick jet-black hair, Olivia can command a room like no other girl I know. She's like this fierce Amazonian warrior, reminding me of those stunning female vampires from *Twilight*.

I'm dwarfed when I stand beside her, scrawny and small, the contrast between us never more transparent. Perhaps that's why she's taken such a protective stance. Why she looks out for me even when I don't ask her to.

Chase regards her warily, scrubbing a hand over his stubbly jaw. "Do I know you?"

"Nope, but your rep precedes you."

He grins, showcasing a set of cut dimples. "Don't believe everything you hear."

"Uh-huh." My roomie pins him with a wary look.

Chase chuckles, raising his palms in the air. "Hey, I was just doing my good deed for the night. No ulterior motives." He turns to me, his eyes roaming up and down my body as I toe on my shoes. "None, whatsoever." He winks, and heat floods my cheeks. I'm unaccustomed to such shameless flirting, and it throws me for a loop. "Not like I was watching your pretty friend rock that counter like she belongs on stage or anything." His grin widens, and my cheeks burn brighter.

Straightening up, I clear my throat. "Thank you. For catching me."

He takes my hand in his meatier one, drawing it to his mouth. "The pleasure was all mine. Anytime ..." He quirks a brow.

"I'm Lana."

He plants a soft kiss on the back of my hand. "Nice to meet you, Lana." Leaning in, he presses his mouth to my ear. "I definitely hope we meet again." A slew of shivers ripple over my skin as his warm breath tickles my neck.

He sends me one final cheeky wink before disappearing into the heaving crowd.

"That one is trouble," Liv warns.

Mention of trouble brings me back into the moment. Grabbing my shirt and purse, I tug on her arm. "Come on. We need to leave. Now."

"Where's the fire?"

I risk a quick peek over her shoulder, emitting a high-pitched shriek. He's heading our way, and if we don't get our butts out of here right this second, everything I've worked for will be shot to hell. Olivia turns to look at the object of my distraction. "No! Don't look at him. He'll see you!" I yank on her arm again.

"What the hell, Lana?" She slants a puzzled look my way.

"I'll explain everything when we get back to the dorm, but we have to go. Please, Liv. I'm begging you. We have to go *now*." Hysteria is bubbling to the surface as the words leave my mouth, and butterflies are running amok in my chest.

"'Kay. Quick."

We start pushing our way through the crowd. My tank top is glued to my back, and tiny beads of sweat have formed on my brow.

He can't see me, he just can't.

Olivia guides me to a side exit at the back of the bar. We shove through the door, barreling out into a narrow alleyway at the back of the building. I run toward the steep stone steps, ignoring the sounds of heavy make-out sessions happening all around us.

"Lana!" a familiar voice calls out, and I whimper. Dammit all to hell.

"Keep running," Olivia commands, racing hot on my heels. Fueled by adrenaline, I bound up the stairs, pushing my limbs harder than ever before, such is my desire to outrun him.

"Lana! Wait!" The voice is distant, but it won't take him long to catch up.

We race around the corner of the building. "Follow me." Olivia veers off to the right. I give chase as she maneuvers a curved path through the shrubbery in between various frats, weaving in and out of houses like it's her own personal obstacle course. Under the dark blanket of nightfall, I stumble several times as I struggle to keep up. My breath hisses out in panicked spurts, but I resist the urge to look over my shoulder as I race after Liv.

We emerge on one of the main roads, a few yards from a bus stop. "Hold the bus!" Liv screeches as the last passenger ascends the vehicle parked at the curb. We tear down the sidewalk and hop onto the bus in the nick of time. Panting, I scan my card and scurry behind Olivia, dropping into a seat alongside her.

"That was cutting it close," I pant, desperately trying to get my breathing and my heart rate under control.

"I'll say." She shoots me a curious look, before glancing out the rear window of the bus. It takes considerable willpower to keep my focus straight ahead.

A couple of minutes pass in silence, as we both bring our breathing back in line.

I sigh. My head is a mess, and my slightly inebriated state isn't helping either. Anxiety is holding me hostage, and I can't think straight.

What the hell is he doing here?

Olivia bumps my shoulder. "You said there was a guy."

"Yes."

I told her there was a guy, but I deliberately avoided divulging the details. I had good reasons not to. Plenty of them. Liv and I gelled the instant we met, and I didn't want her thinking any less of me. Now, there's no avoiding it. I owe her an explanation, and I'm not going to lie.

I've already told a lifetime of lies.

Liv isn't prone to rash judgments, and I know she'll give me the floor to explain. I hope it's enough. Wetting my dry lips, I study her calm expression.

"When were you going to tell me it was Kalvin Kennedy?" she asks.

Chapter Two
Kalvin

"**G**oddammit!!" I yell in frustration, coming to a halt as I watch the bus pull away from the curb. Dropping onto a nearby bench, I rest my head in my hands. Adrenaline is coursing through my body, and my heart is thundering in my chest.

She. Is. Here!

When I first caught a glimpse of the crazy girl nose-diving off the bar, my heart stuttered at the mere possibility that it might be her. Well, that and the fear that she'd go splat on the floor. Then I lost her in the crowd, especially when Shelby stopped to talk to some jerk from her anthropology class. It was only when Lana's considerably taller friend started rushing her out the side exit that I got another look. I only saw her from behind, but I knew. I knew it was her, even if her hair is longer than I've ever seen it and the clothes she was wearing were nothing like my Lana used to wear.

I only needed that teeny, tiny glimpse to know it was her.

You never forget the girl who claimed your heart. Even if she did it without me realizing.

It took our lengthy separation for me to see her in the right light.

To know I loved her more than I loved anyone or anything in the entire universe.

I didn't know love until it tore up my heart. Until I was all cut up inside. Until the loss consumed me, and I could barely breathe without her. It's only then I realized I'd do anything to get her back.

Kill. Maim. Injure. Beg. Borrow. Steal.

There isn't anything I'm unprepared to do to win Lana back.

Fuck me. I'm turning into my pansy-ass brother. Lying flat on my back on the bench, with my knees bent, I laugh my ass off as relief cascades over me like a waterfall.

She enrolled, after all. Thank fuck.

My laughter dies off, replaced by a heady surge of longing.

I can hardly believe it.

I've been on campus for two months now, and I spent the first few weeks scouring the place for any sign of Lana. I had no idea how vast the University of Florida was or how trying to find one girl on a two-thousand-acre campus was virtually impossible. Although, it doesn't seem as big now that I know my way around a bit better. After weeks of roaming the campus like an aimless idiot, I finally succumbed and called my brother. Keven has mad IT skills, and it didn't take him long to hack into the college servers and search the considerable student database only to draw a blank.

My heart had sunk when he confirmed there was no Lana Taylor registered.

I'd been so sure she'd come here. I knew she had enough credits built up to skip senior year, like me, and she'd had her heart set on UF. I remembered the times we'd talked about it, and it had played no insignificant part in my decision to come here instead of attending Harvard with my brothers and my cousin.

Although this is one of the top universities in the country, and their architecture program is dope, I came here for *her*.

A goofy smile appears on my lips.

For the first time in over a year, I feel alive. The urge to pull a Leo and shout "I'm the king of the world" is riding me hard. Damn my wacky Irish cousin Faye and her stupid *Titanic* fixation. That girl has messed with my brain in a big way.

If anyone found me now—lying on a bench, in the pitch dark, in the middle of the night, laughing to myself—they'd have me carted off to the nearest psychiatric ward before I could draw a breath.

My knee bounces up and down, and I'm chock-full of nervous excitement. I desperately need to track Lana down. If I knew where to begin, I'd be on it in a flash. It feels like an eternity since I last spoke to her, and I crave her company as intensely as a druggie craves his next fix.

To have come so close is killing me.

However, I refuse to feel anything but pure excitement.

Lana is here. That is all that matters.

This changes *everything*.

I may have lost her just now, but I'm not giving up until I find her. Until I speak to her and convince her I'm finally in the right place. Ready to give her a commitment and mean it this time.

I haul myself upright and make my way back to the frat house.

"Hey, is everything okay?" Shelby asks, the second I reappear in the room.

The music is blaring and the crowd is getting rowdy. Most of us have been partying since the event earlier, and things are turning messy. I've been making a concerted effort to keep my nose clean. Party-boy Kal is a thing of the past, and I'd rather not hit a speed bump.

Shelby palms my face in concern. That's another thing I'll need to deal with but not now. Now, I need to drag Brett's ass out of here and force him to help me.

"Who was that girl?" she asks, peering up at me through her gorgeous big blue eyes. Shelby is every dude's wet dream, and I know I'd only have to say the words and she'd be mine, but that was never my intention. Even less so now. In the past, I wouldn't give two shits about screwing a girl one minute and ignoring her the next, but I'm not the same person I was. All the stuff that went down changed me. I'd like to think for the better.

"Someone important." That's as much as I'm saying on the subject.

Little lines crease her forehead. "Oh." She's not pleased.

"Look, I need to get out of here, but wanna meet for lunch tomorrow?" She deserves to be let down gently.

She perks up, and I feel like a dick. "Awesome. It's a date."

Double shit. "I'll text you in the morning."

She leans in to kiss me, and I twist my head at the last second so her lips meet my cheek instead of my mouth. Hurt flickers in her eyes, and I feel like a dick again. Over her shoulder, I spy Brett entertaining the adoring masses, and I catch his attention, gesturing toward the door.

My roomie nods, draining his beer and making a dash for it. "Please tell me we're not calling it a night, bro." He slaps me on the back. "I'm only getting started."

"We're not, but I need to talk to you. You want to shoot some pool?"

He steers me out of the room. "Lead the way, dude."

We grab an Uber to the local town and hop out in front of the combination sports bar and tavern. One of Brett's brothers attended UF a few years back, and he told us about this place.

They happily accept our fake IDs as the real deal, so we grab a couple of beers and slip into a booth while we wait for a pool table. Most Friday nights, this place is hopping, but it's quieter than usual tonight. The majority of the college crowd is still on campus, hitting up parties and enjoying the last festivities of homecoming week.

"What gives?" Brett asks, sipping from his beer.

"I found her. I just found Lana."

His eyes pop wide. "No shit."

"She was at the party, but she ran off before I could talk to her." I raise the bottle to my lips, enjoying the cold, bitter taste as the beer slides down my throat.

"What's the plan?"

"I'm going to get my brother on the case again. If she goes to school here, she must be registered under a different name." I lean my arm along the top of the booth. "Now that I know she's here, she can't hide from me."

"What if she was only visiting? She could have a friend here."

It's a legit argument, but it carries no weight. "She doesn't have any friends here. She grew up, with me, in Wellesley. Besides, it was always her dream to come here. She's enrolled at UF. I'm certain of it."

He props his arms on the table. "I still can't believe you traded Harvard—*Ivy League, dude*—for UF, on a hunch that some chick might attend."

"It was more than a hunch, and she's more than some chick." Brett isn't a fan of my girl, and he's starting to get on my last testicle. He's judging her—like the rest of the country—before he's even had the chance to know her. I take another quick glug of my beer. "The summer before we started high school, we discussed it. She told me she had her heart set on the University of Florida because she wanted to attend college in a sunnier climate and she wanted to connect with her grandparents. Her Mom never let her visit them."

"What's up with that?"

I shrug. "No idea, but it was important to her to be close to them. She had no other family."

He scratches the top of his head. "Dude, it's still weird. Who leaves their family behind to go on a wild goose chase? Just 'cause you discussed it a few years back was no guarantee she'd actually be here." His lips curve up. "Knew you had more than a little reckless in you."

I grin wickedly. "Dude, whatever, you're totally missing the point." I cock my head to the side. "I was right, because she *is* here, and that's all I give a crap about now. I *knew* she'd be here. Maybe my cuz is right." He arches a brow, waiting for elaboration. "Faye sa—"

"That's the hottie Irish chick you told me about? The one who's fucking your brother?"

I roll my eyes. "Yes, and yes, but you know it's not like that. Ky's my half-brother, and they're not actually blood related."

"It sounds much hotter the way I tell it." He smirks.

"Whatever gets you going, bro."

"You have any pictures of her?"

"Faye?"

"No, dipshit!" He taps his bottle against mine. "Your girl."

"Yeah." I remove my cell from my back pocket and hand it to him. My screensaver is a pic of Lana and me. It's the last happy image of us before everything turned to shit.

Brett whistles low on his breath. "She's pretty."

I grab my cell back, scoffing. "She's fucking gorgeous, but I don't expect you to understand everything she means to me."

He taps his fingers off the tabletop. "Enlighten me."

I pick at the label on my bottle. "I told you I spent years acting like a jerk. Pushing her away and pretending I didn't have feelings for her. Then I lost her, and my world lost all its color. When I get her back, I'm going to treat her like a fucking goddess."

"Pussy-whipped already," he murmurs, "and you don't even have the girl."

"Semantics, dude. That's all it is."

"Or a nasty case of overconfidence." His grin is teasing.

"I fucked up before, but I'm not going to do that again. I just need to make her understand that. She told me not to find her, so she's bound to be a bit pissed, but I'll use some of the ole Kennedy charm to win her around to my way of thinking." I'm spouting the biggest load of bullshit, but maybe if I say it out loud, I might start believing it. Truth is, I'm scared shitless that Lana will refuse to have anything to do with me. Can't say I blame her. Not after the years I spent acting like a complete moron.

And let's not forget how spectacularly I messed up with that bitch, Addison.

"You're a nice guy, Kal," Brett says, in a more serious tone of voice. "I'm not sure I'd be so understanding."

There'd been no need to tell Brett my story. When I rocked up to the dorms and met my new roomie, he recognized me instantly. That's what happens when your mom spearheaded one of the most prestigious, most recognizable fashion brands in the country. There was no such thing as privacy. My six brothers and I had grown up under the glare of the world's media. Last year was definitely one for the record books, though. Between my trial, my brother's arrest, my dad's affair, my cousin almost being killed, news that my three eldest brothers had a different father, and my mom's admission that she had lied to build her business empire on a falsehood, we were rarely off the airwaves. The media lapped the scandal up, and we were virtual pariahs at school.

Brett knew everything, which, to be honest, was freaking awesome, because it meant I didn't have to explain the shit show that is my life. More than that, he was understanding.

Except when it comes to Lana. That's where he draws a line.

When she came clean at the trial, she put herself in the spotlight, and it didn't present her in the most flattering light. Come to think of it, no wonder she registered under a different name. She probably didn't want anyone to know who she was. I'm sure she's picked up her fair share of enemies. That thought kicks my protective instincts into overdrive, accelerating the need to find and shelter her.

"She isn't how she was portrayed," I explain. "If anyone's to blame for what happened, it's me. Me and my brother's ex. Lana is a total sweetheart, and it was completely out of character for her to lie."

"I can tell you mean that. Like I said, you're one of the good guys."

"She means everything to me, man, and I let her down when she needed me most. It wasn't that difficult for me to forgive her. Fact, friend," I tag on the end, chuckling as I repeat Brett's catchphrase.

"She's a damn fool if she turns you away."
"It's not as simple as that."
I'll say.
Convincing Lana I forgive her for what she did is the least of it.
I have years of stupid mistakes to make up for.
And I can't wait to get started.

Chapter Three
Lana

"Okay, spill, girlfriend. I want to know everything," Liv says. We didn't talk much on the bus, and when we got back to our dorm, I went to use the bathroom, while Liv fixed our usual nightly drinks. Now, we are both in our pajamas, our faces scrubbed clean of makeup, sitting across from one another on our twin beds, sipping chamomile tea.

I knew this was coming. That it was time to fess up, but it does little to ease my nervousness. Placing my cup on my bedside table, I wipe my sweaty palms over the front of my sleep shorts. I attempt to clear my throat. "Before I start, I need you to know that I was evasive on purpose, but I had every intention of telling you the full story once we got to know each other."

She bobs her head, urging me to continue with her eyes.

"I was scared when we met and you told me you were from New York because I figured you'd definitely know all about the Kennedys and last year's trial." The trial was front page news on every paper and the main item on every news channel that whole week. The nation was glued to the drama.

Leaning forward, she cups both hands around her drink. "Girl, *everyone* knows who the Kennedys are. Kennedy Apparel was *the* fashion brand to be seen in. I've got a bunch of their dresses in my closet, and I'm still mourning the demise of the label."

Last year, Alexandra Kennedy shocked the fashion world when she stepped down as CEO and sold the label to her main competitor. The KA brand has since been swallowed up by the new parent company, Accardi.

My heart falters. "Great, now everyone on campus is going to know."

"Is that why you changed your name?" she asks, confirming she's figured things out.

"Partly." I rub the back of my neck. "Initially, switching to my mother's maiden name was one of my grandparents' conditions. My college application was made at the eleventh hour, and they used their connections to help me get in. But it made sense on another level because my name is tainted."

And, honestly? It's no less than I deserve.

She sends me a sympathetic look, but I toss it aside. I don't warrant anyone's pity, but I also refuse to dwell on it. There are more urgent demands on my headspace these days.

"I'm sorry I kept this from you. Truly, I am," I admit. "I was sure you'd recognize me and judge me before you'd even had a chance to know me."

She takes a sip of her tea. "I didn't recognize you. Not at all. Most of the press coverage focused on Kalvin."

At the time of the trial, yes. But afterward, the media enjoyed plastering my face everywhere and slandering my previous good name. In most other states, as a minor, I would've had some privacy but not in Massachusetts where they have this weird law which meant there was little I could do to stop them from revealing my identity. Add the Kennedy celebrity factor into the equation, and public exposure was guaranteed. It was a relief to leave the north behind for the Sunshine State. At least, in the early days.

"Tell me about him." She tilts her head to the side. "Tell me about you, and let me hear your side of things because I know what was reported wasn't the truth. I know you, and you aren't capable of the things they said you did."

I can scarcely swallow over the bitter lump in my throat. "That's the awful truth, Liv. I did most of what they said I did." I hang my head, not wishing to see the disgust and disappointment in her eyes. I've had to face that same look on my mom's face every day since my testimony. Every day since I dropped the bomb.

"Hey." The bed dips as she plops down beside me. "I'm not going to judge." She wraps her arm around my shoulder. "We've all done things we're not proud of, and I know you're a good person, Lana."

"Would you have felt that way if you knew immediately who I was?"

She spears me with honest eyes. "I don't know. I'd like to think I would've given you an opportunity to explain your side of things."

Not for the first time, I count my blessings for whatever cosmos deemed to pair me with Olivia. We just click. Maybe it's the fact we're both an only child, or she's just one hell of an awesome human being. Whatever the reason, I'm glad she's my roommate, my friend.

"Do I need to give you more alcohol to get it out of you?" she jokes with a smirk.

I scoot farther up the bed, resting my back against the wall. "It's late. You sure you want to do this now? If I'm going to do this right, I need to tell you from the start. It could take a while."

She twists around, pulling her legs up off the floor. "I don't have much to do tomorrow, and I can sleep in. I'm ready and willing to listen if you're up to it."

I nibble on the corner of my lips as I prepare to open the doors to my heart. "I was two when my parents landed jobs with the Kennedys. Mom was their housekeeper, and Dad maintained the gardens surrounding the Wellesley property. We moved into a guest bungalow at the edge of the forest that backed onto the estate. Not that I remember too much of that time." Those early memories are scarce.

"When I got a little older, I used to play outside with the boys. Alexandra didn't seem to mind in those days. Kal was only a little younger than me, and we gravitated toward one another from the very start. Soon, we were basically inseparable, and we did everything together. We didn't go to the same schools, but we would meet in his kitchen after school every day, and Mom would fix us a snack and her legendary pink lemonade, and we did our homework together every night. In the winters, we'd watch the latest movies in their home theater or swim in the indoor pool, and I went to all his Little League games. I showed him all my stories"—Liv knows my lifelong dream is to be a writer and that I've written a ton of books, all currently lurking undiscovered in the hard drive of my computer—"and he was my most avid fan. He loved everything I wrote, even when it was crap." I smile at the memory. "He used to draw these pictures to depict scenes from my stories, and he helped me create homemade books." A tender smile graces my lips as countless memories replay in my mind.

"During the summers, we'd spend days hanging out by the pool, and he was always the one protecting me from his brothers."

She arches a brow.

"You know he has six brothers?"

"Girl, everyone knows the Kennedy boys. I can't believe you grew up surrounded by all that hotness." She fans herself. "Damn, I'm wet just thinking about it."

I throw a pillow at her head, laughing. "Stop it! They're like my brothers, and that's grossing me out. Except for Stinky."

She splutters. "What the what?"

I laugh again. "Stinky. That's what I called Kal when we were younger because he used to let rip with the worst farts known to man." I double over, clutching my stomach. "If I want to annoy the fuck out of him, all I have to do is call him that name and watch him go crazy." I chuckle to myself.

"He's not the only crazy one if you ask me," she quips.

"All his brothers are crazy," I retort, pretending to ignore her little jokey dig. "They were always trying to dunk me in the pool or pull my bikini top off. Kal would get so mad at them, and I'd have to pretend to be furious because the truth was I didn't mind. They were fun to be around, and I knew they were only teasing. It was always so quiet in our house, and I enjoyed spending time with them. I looked forward to our summers so much."

"It sounds like you were a part of the family."

The sheen wipes off the edge of my reminiscence. "I used to think so, too, but Momma Kennedy made it very clear I wasn't."

Liv falls forward onto her stomach, propping up on her elbows, and resting her chin in her hands. "What happened?"

"We grew up." I drill her with earnest eyes, as the usual hurt resurfaces. "The Kennedys bought a vacation house in Nantucket, and for the first few years, we went with them for extended periods during the summer. It was bliss. Mom and Dad were working, and I spent the days with Kal and his brothers on the beach or out on our bikes. At night, there were BBQs and parties, and we always got to stay up later because the adults lost track of time. The house was exquisite, and it had the most gorgeous infinity pool and—"

"Okay, now you're making me jealous on purpose."

I laugh. "Seriously, I loved that house. Loved those summers, which is why it hurt so much when it all came to an abrupt end."

"Come on, Lana," Liv groans. "Stop keeping me in suspense. Get to the juicy stuff."

I fling my pillow at her. "Hey! This isn't the latest soap opera we're discussing. This is my life!"

"Your life with the Kennedys," she swoons, tossing the pillow back at me. "That sounds like a soap opera I'd watch."

I roll my eyes, though I appreciate her attempts to keep this light-hearted. "The last time I was in Nantucket was the summer before I turned fourteen. Kal had been acting really weird the whole time, and I was worried I'd done something to upset him. I kept asking him what was wrong, and he kept saying everything was fine." My heart starts fluttering at the recollection. "I was in my room packing the day we were due to return to the mainland when he came barging into my room and kissed me. No warning. Nothing. He just walked right up to me and planted one on me." My heart is pounding in my chest. "I can still recall it in vivid detail, as if it was yesterday." My hand moves of its own accord, and I run my fingers across my lips. "As first kisses go, it was pretty damn magical."

"Wow."

"I know." My smile deepens. Irrespective of where we've ended up, no one or nothing can take that memory away from me. I grab a hair tie off my nightstand and twist my hair into a messy bun. "Of course, Kal's mom had to choose that exact moment to bust into my room, and she caught us in the act."

"She flipped out?"

"Totally, not that you would've known it at the time. She pretended not to notice, quietly insisting that Kal go to his room to finish packing. No one ever said a word about it again, but I was never invited back, and from that point on, Kal started acting weird around me."

"She must've said something to him," Liv deduces. "What a bitch."

"I think so. Alexandra is a snob, and there's no way she'd ever consider me good enough for her son, but at the time, I didn't understand it. I thought I was a horrible kisser and that's why he didn't want to hang out with me so much."

"Wait. What?" She pulls up on her knees. "He just kissed you and that was it? *He* didn't bring it up?"

I shake my head. "Nope. He never spoke about the kiss or why I was banished. He just kissed me and then never mentioned it again."

"And how did you feel?"

"Oh, I was head over heels in love with him. Think I probably always had been, but I didn't know what I was feeling." She nods vigorously. "I was hurt when he stopped hanging out with me so much but not enough to stop loving him. God, when I look back on it now, I was so pathetic."

Loving Kalvin

I lean my head back and stare at the stark white ceiling. "My friend Zoe used to say I had obsessive compulsive disorder when it came to Kalvin Kennedy, and I argued nonstop with her about it, but she was right. I see that now. There was nothing healthy or normal about the way I crushed on him. I had no interest in slapping 1D on my walls when the hottest boy on the planet lived in the house next door."

"Were you hanging with him at all, or had he completely frozen you out?" Liv is frothing at the mouth for further intel.

"Oh, we always hung out, just not like before. We still spent time together almost every day just not in public. We were always alone. Either he came to my house when my parents were at work or we hung out in the cabin at the back of the woods."

"Kinky!"

I snort. "I wish!"

"You mean there was nothing going on?" She sounds outraged.

"No, not until last year."

"What the heck did you do?" A puzzled frown furrows her brow.

I crank out a laugh. "Jeez, Liv. There are other things to do with boys besides sex."

"Boring!" She throws another cushion at me.

I catch it with both hands and stuff it behind my head, sticking my tongue out at her. "We did all the same old stuff, and we talked a lot. About everything and anything. Kal is a real jokester and sometimes it was a chore trying to get him to act serious, but we talked about a lot of deep stuff too, and he opened up to me as I did him. We shared our innermost secrets, and that kept me going, you know? When he was off screwing anything in a skirt, I took some comfort knowing I was the only one he was sharing his dreams with."

"I gotta tell you, Lana, your boy isn't sounding like much of a dreamboat."

I shrug. "It was like there were two sides to him. In public, he was the teasing, charming player every girl in Wellesley wanted to hook up with, and a lot did, trust me on that." Bile coats the inside of my mouth as years of hurt and rejection attack me from all sides. "But, in private, with me, he was sweet and vulnerable and thoughtful, and it made it extremely difficult not to crush on him."

I stare off into space. "And he didn't hesitate to jump to my defense in public if the situation warranted it." I fiddle with the hem on my shorts. "There was this one time I remember." My heart skips a beat as I recall the incident. "It was sixth grade, and all the Kennedy boys had come with their dad and my parents to the school play because I had one of the lead parts that year. I knew my lines by heart, but the second I got up on that stage and saw the crowd and felt the heat of the lights, nerves got the better of me, and I was fluffing all my lines. Jasmine Reed was one of the other leads, and she was also the biggest bully in our year. She got mad at me and pushed me mid-scene. I fell over, and some of the other girls laughed. I was so embarrassed."

"What did boy wonder do?"

I chuckle. "He stormed onto the stage and helped me to my feet. Tucking me under his arm, he turned around and yelled at Jasmine before the teacher dragged him away." I sigh dreamily. "He was my hero that day, and, funnily enough, I didn't forget any of my lines after that."

"Cute story, but let's get back to more recent times." She's practically salivating, and I roll my eyes again. "Something obviously changed between you, though, or last year wouldn't have happened."

My chest heaves painfully. "Something snapped inside me last year. Or maybe Zoe finally got through to me. I'm not sure, but all I knew was I couldn't go on any longer trying to deny my feelings for him. I had tried to move on. All through high school, I dated other boys, and I even had a couple of boyfriends. At first, I did it because I thought it'd make Kal jealous, but it never seemed to bother him. Then, I went through periods where I hated him because I was sick of hearing about him with other girls. And I had girls latch on to me continually when they heard I lived on the grounds of the Kennedy estate only to drop me like a hot potato the minute they realized I couldn't help them into his bed. I'd continually promise myself I was going to forget about him and find a boy who liked me as much as I liked him, so I went out with a few guys, hoping they could help erase Kal from my mind, but it never worked. I was hopelessly smitten. While I did plenty of stuff with my boyfriends, I never let it go beyond that. I always broke the relationship off before it got serious."

"Before you had sex, you mean?"

"Yeah. It was stupid, but I was saving myself for him."

"That's not stupid, Lana. I wish I'd waited for someone special my first time. My first time was … ugh!" She shivers, making a gross face. "Anyway, we're not talking about me. This is the Lana and Kalvin show. What happened next?"

I fight another eye roll. "I found the courage to tell him I loved him, and he deflected. Tried to laugh it off, like my feelings were some kind of joke. I got mad and told him to get out. A few days later, he came back. Said he was sorry for how he'd reacted and he had feelings for me, too, but he didn't know if he could commit to one girl."

"What an asshole." Indignation is ripe in her tone.

"What a pity I didn't get that memo." I chew on the inside of my mouth. "I focused on the only part of his admission that I wanted to hear—he had feelings for me too. I suggested we take things slow and casual, no labels or explanations, no exclusivity, just see where things went."

"You didn't." Her mouth is hanging open.

I cringe a little. "I did mention I was obsessive and stupid, didn't I?"

She jerks her head at me. "Go on. I sense we're *finally* getting to the juicy stuff."

Only someone who wasn't there could refer to what went down as the "juicy" stuff. "I was in cloud cuckoo land for a couple of months. We met up in the cabin at least three or four times a week, like usual, but instead of just talking, we were making out like we needed each other to breathe, and it was like nothing I'd ever experienced before. Seriously, none of the guys I dated made me tingle all over like Kal did. I was walking around in a daze, completely infatuated and daydreaming about our future home and our kids and everything." I shake my head sadly. "I was so stupid, but, in my defense, I was crazy in love, and he made me feel so much. Too much, really."

"That's the way first love should be, right?"

"Who knows?" I shrug. "I'm like the biggest screw-up when it comes to love. You should take anything I say with a pinch of salt. Honestly, I'm like an anti-love remedy. Listen to what I did, and then do the opposite."

"Stalling, girlfriend. Move it along."

"Move that along." I show her my middle finger, and we both grin.

I do a belly flop, landing alongside her, mirroring her position. "If I'm the anti-love remedy, then Zoe is like the anti-love cure times a thousand. She was totally anti-Kal, and when she found us kissing one night, she went ballistic. She yelled at me until her face looked like it might explode, and, of course, I told her to fuck off and continued to wallow in ignorant bliss. Then Kal hooked up with this girl from my school at a party, and on Monday she regaled the whole cafeteria with a blow-by-blow account of"—I curl my fingers in the air —"'the best sex of her life.' That brought me back to earth with a bang."

A painful ache ties my stomach into knots. Even now, it still hurts so much. "I don't know how I ever thought I'd be able to handle him kissing me and hooking up with other girls at the same time. It was a recipe for disaster from the outset. I poured my heart out to him that night. I told him how much I loved him and how I'd been saving myself for him but I couldn't do it anymore. Couldn't be his girl on the side. His dirty secret to hide. I told him I wouldn't share him with other girls, and if he wanted to continue to see me, then he had to commit and promise to stay away from other girls—to be exclusively mine."

Liv nudges me in the shoulder. "Good for you."

"It was about time I stood up for myself. Honestly, I let that boy walk all over me, but I'm glad I had some sense of self-preservation, and he surprised the hell out of me by agreeing."

Tears prick my eyes. "He told me he loved me, that I was the only girl for him, and he would commit to me. He promised." Tears roll down my cheeks now. "I was deliriously happy, and a few nights later we slept together. It was the most incredible night of my life." My tears turn to full-blown sobs, and I break down, burying my head in the comforter and crying my eyes out.

Liv smooths a hand up and down my back, but she doesn't interrupt. She lets me vent. I roll onto my back, wiping my moist eyes with the corner of my pajama top. "It still hurts so much. I don't think the pain will ever go away. Even though I hurt him way more, it does nothing to dampen the constant ache in my heart." I clamp a hand over my chest.

"It's him, isn't it?" she asks quietly. "He's the one."

Everything locks up inside me, and immense terror has a vise-grip around my heart.

This is my worst fear come to life, but I can't lie to her. Not about something like this. Not when she already knows so much.

Slowly, I nod.

Her lips pull into a grim line. "He doesn't know, Lana, does he?"

Chapter Four
Kalvin

"I'm very disappointed in you, Kalvin," Shelby says, stirring her coffee way too fast. Droplets land on the Formica tabletop as I look everywhere but at the girl sitting across from me. The diner is jammed. It seems everyone's in need of a caffeine injection after the excesses of last night. "I thought you liked me." I can hear the pout in her voice. Girls like Shelby aren't accustomed to getting the brush off. Rejection isn't sitting well with her.

"It's not like that," I protest, manning up and raising my eyes to meet hers.

"Please don't give me the 'it's me not you' speech. Don't insult my intelligence." She glares at me.

"Shelby, you're beautiful, smart, and cool to hang with. Any guy would be lucky to date you, but I came here determined to stick to my goals. We went on a couple of dates, and it was casual. It was never leading anywhere for me. I'm sorry if I gave you the wrong impression." I'm not trying to be a dick, but my lack of honesty has gotten me in trouble in the past, so I need to be blunt now.

I never should've hooked up with her that first night, but it'd been over a year since I've done anything with any girl, and I was depressed after my call with Kev. He'd only just confirmed that Lana wasn't enrolled in UF, and my mood was low. I thought I'd lost her forever. Brett convinced me to go to the frat party with him, and when Shelby approached me, I didn't turn her away. Empty inside, I'd needed to feel *something*. To know I wasn't completely broken. We'd hooked up and then parted ways with no plans, and that suited me fine. When I'd bumped into her the following week, she'd convinced me to meet her for lunch. At some point, from then until now, it had turned into several dates, and she was starting to get clingy. I hadn't slept with her again, and I sensed it was going to blow up in my face. Even if I hadn't found Lana last night, the writing was already on the wall for Shelby and me.

Even thinking that—Shelby and me—feels wrong on so many different levels.

"This is about that girl last night, isn't it?"

She's way more observant than I gave her credit for.

She flings her blonde hair over her shoulder with noticeable defiance.

"Leave her out of this." There's no way I want Lana dragged into any more of my drama. I stand up, tossing a twenty on the table. "I'm sure we'll bump into each other from time to time. I'd like to stay friends."

"Screw off, Kalvin. It's not like you're anything special. I've been knocking guys back left and right, so I won't be short on options." She flicks her fingers in the air, swatting me away like an annoying gnat. "You've some nerve turning me down. Half the girls on this campus hate you. I was doing wonders for your rep."

Wow.

What a dreamboat.

It's a side of her I haven't seen before, and my gut's telling me this is the real Shelby. My bitch-o-meter is usually more reliable than this. I think I've been played.

Shoving my hands in the pockets of my jeans, I wonder how I misjudged her so badly. "Okay, then." She glowers at me as I walk off, but I couldn't give two shits. My shoulders loosen up as I step out onto the sidewalk.

Back in the dorm, I change into my track shorts and shirt and rest on the edge of the bed to call Kev. "Dude," he greets me.

"Bro. She's here."

"No shit."

"I need you to hack into the college system again." He mumbles something incoherent under his breath. "Please. She must be registered under a different name. Can you do a search for anyone named Lana and see what you find."

"Okay. Consider it done."

"Thanks, man. I owe you."

He snorts. "Yeah you do."

I hang up, feeling wired. I need to run this excess adrenaline off, so I head out to the track. After stretching, I start off at a leisurely pace, building my speed with each lap. My mind churns a million miles an hour. Finding her is only step one. I need a plan of action to win her back. Shelving Shelby helps. My track record with other girls is abysmal, and winning Lana's trust is key. She needs to understand I want the whole shebang with her. I'm invested. Lock, stock, and barrel. I'm ready to take our relationship to the next level, and I think we're finally on the same page. I want to commit to her exclusively. Now, I just need to convince her I'm genuine and pray that she hasn't moved on.

I'm spread-eagled on the bed in fresh sweats, bare-chested, and listening to Bono rock it out on my iPhone when Brett graces me with his presence. He must have a new girl on the scene because he's barely been here all week. Last night was the first time I'd seen him in days.

"What's up, asshat?" he asks, dumping his gear bag on the ground. Crossing to the refrigerator, he removes two bottles of water, tossing one to me. A musty, sweaty smell filters through the air.

My nose wrinkles as I pull my earphones off. "Dude, you're polluting the environment." I point at the offending bag, adding in some gagging sound effects for good measure.

He shrugs. "And you're insulting my manly smell. I'm wounded." He pulls a chair over, swinging it around and straddling it. "You're hardly in a position to throw stones. You leave your smelly shit lying all over the place." He points at my damp running outfit, currently occupying center stage in the middle of the floor.

Valid. Not that I'm admitting it.

My nostrils flare in disgust as I jump up and open the window. "The difference is my sweat rocks. Yours reeks like hundred-year-old granny panties."

He laughs, shaking his head. "Delusional much, Kennedy? Your shit smells the same as the rest of us." Can't deny that. "What you listening to?" He gestures toward my phone.

"Do you really have to ask?" I stick my head out the window and promptly retreat. I keep forgetting I'm not in Massachusetts. No gentle breeze offers relief from the noxious smells wafting around the room. The sticky humidity takes some getting used to; although, I've detected a slight change in the weather this last week. Apparently, the weather rarely dips below sixty here, and the humidity lingers like a bad smell, but it does get a little cooler during winter. My body temp is cranked to toasty all year round, and I never thought I'd hear myself complain about the heat, but the climate in Florida is fucking up my internal wiring. If I could get away with walking around naked, I'd do it.

"U2 is the shit, but you could vary it up. Your taste in music is a lot like your taste in women—singular and a bit on the boring side."

I flip him the bird. "Don't insult Lana or Bono and the boys. I'll stick my dad on you." Dad hails from Ireland, and the members of U2 are living legends in the Emerald Isle. I grew up indoctrinated. Dad rarely played anything else, and he's attended every major event U2 has played in the States the last ten years, without fail. Once I turned thirteen, he brought me with him. None of my brothers understand our U2 obsession, and I love that it's something I get to share with him alone. When we vacationed in Ireland last summer, we saw them live in Croke Park, and there's nothing like watching living legends perform on home soil. The crowd was electric, the atmosphere was out of this world, and it was the experience of a lifetime.

"I can take Daddy Kennedy any day." Brett flexes his fists. "Bring it."

I roll my eyes, swigging from my bottle. "Where you been all week?" He makes a disgusting gesture with his hands, and I laugh. "Figured. Who's the flavor of the week this week?"

"Sydney. She's a senior. Met her at the party last week."

"A senior, huh?" I'm impressed.

"Perks of playing college football." He winks, puffing out his broad chest.

"You seeing her tonight?"

"Nah. Think it's time to broaden my horizons."

I chuckle. Brett has a short attention span. "She know that?"

"She's cool, man. She knew what this was."

"If you say so." I'm remembering the last girl who turned up at our door, sobbing her heart out. "One word. Hayley."

"Oh shit, man. Why'd you have to go and ruin my good mood. You know I feel bad about that."

"Just looking out for you, bro. You forget, I've been you, and it's not all it's cracked up to be."

"Says the born-again virgin," he teases, and I give him the finger. "A few of us are heading to a party in Gainesville. Wanna come?"

"I'm down." I need something to take my mind off Lana, and you never know, maybe she'll turn up at this party too.

The party was a dud, but at least it was time suckage. Shelby spent half the night shooting daggers my direction, but she wasted little time moving on. She worked the room like a pro. Think she went home with one of Brett's teammates. At least she's no longer my problem. Thank fuck.

Sunday turns into Monday, and there's still no word from Kev. I'm not known for my patience, and he cusses me out when I call him for the umpteenth time Monday night. It works. He emails me a list a couple hours later. I'm disheartened to see over twenty names on the list. Fuck me. *Who'd have thought Lana was such a popular name?* Guess I shouldn't be all that surprised in a campus of over fifty thousand, but I'm overdue a break, and I thought Lady Luck was finally shining on me.

Due to some current system upgrade the college is undergoing, Kev wasn't able to search by photo ID, so I'll have to do this the old-fashioned way and call on every girl on the list until I find her. That doesn't mesh well with my rapidly diminishing patience supply. I'm going out of my mind knowing Lana is so close but still so far out of my reach.

Tuesday and Wednesday come and go. I attend my classes, spend a couple hours at the track, and the rest of my time is spent checking out the names on the list. I'm growing more disheartened as each girl turns out not to be her. *What if she registered under a completely different name altogether? How the fuck am I expected to find her then?*

I'm sitting in the bleachers at the Sanders Football Field Thursday evening watching Brett's practice as I mull over my options. I have seven addresses left to investigate. Seven girls. If one of them isn't *my* Lana, I don't know what I'm going to do. Unless I happen to bump into her again, I don't see how else I can track her down. The chances of lightning striking twice are slim, but I can't contemplate failure. Not when I've come this far. This close.

Shouting on the field rouses me from my depressive inner monologue. Brett and the douchebag supremo on his team are shoving one another as the coach repeatedly blows his whistle, calling for a time-out. Another coach races onto the field, and between them, they manage to separate the boys. Words are exchanged. It looks heated, but I can't hear what's being said from here. Douche pants throws his helmet on the ground and stomps off. Hanging his head, Brett walks in the opposite direction, toward the locker room.

The douche reaches my section of the bleachers and scales the steps two at a time. The man is a beast. And a grade A asshole. He seems to have it in for Brett, and this isn't the first time they've clashed.

I narrow my eyes as I watch his ascent. He's red in the face, and his hands are clenched into tight fists at his side. He sees me watching, and his lips twist into a snarl. "What the fuck you looking at, Kennedy?"

"Not a hell of a lot." I lean back casually, locking my hands behind my head.

"Screw off. Go find some new girl to rape."

I'm out of my seat before I've had time to process the move. Never mind that he's built like a brick house, I'm not taking shit from no one. Especially not about that. I fist my hand in his shirt. "I didn't rape anyone, fucktard, and I'll kick your ass into next week if you insinuate that again."

He snorts, pushing me away, and the urge to punch him until he bleeds is riding me hard. It would almost be worth the beating I'd get, except I can't risk my place here. They're big on safety, and violence on campus is a major offense. I need to maintain a squeaky-clean record. "Do I look like I give a shit? Give it your best shot, *pervert*."

Rage pummels my insides, and I grind down on my molars. He may be broader than me, and packing more pounds, but I bet I could go a few rounds fueled by rage alone. Man, I want to hit this dude so badly. Lana's face drifts in front of me, and I take a step back. I need to calm the fuck down before I ruin everything. "Whatever, douche. I've way better things to do with my time."

He sends me a gloating smirk, and my eyes narrow to slits. Coach blows his whistle, purposely looking up here as he barks out a rough demand. "See ya later, perv." Chase flips up his middle finger as he leaves. I sit back down, resting my head in my hands, mentally talking myself off the ledge.

That's how Brett finds me twenty minutes later. I'm still brimming with pent-up frustration. "Let's get out of here," he says, slapping me on the back.

I crank the A/C to the max when we buckle up in my truck. "You in a hurry to get to the dorm?" I ask.

Brett's jaw hasn't relaxed since we left the practice field. "Not especially. You fancy a game at the Reitz?" The Reitz is the campus union, and it's a sprawling building with a bunch of resources for students including a kick-ass games room we're quite attached to.

"I wanted to check out a couple more addresses if you don't mind tagging along?"

"Not like I've anything else to do," he murmurs, and I know better than to go there. He's pissed over what just went down, not that I'd blame him. You don't want to draw attention as a newbie on the team for all the wrong reasons. It's why I'm not telling him about my run-in with douche face yet. No point in riling him up further.

The first two addresses are in the same building, which is a gift. I work my usual charm—sweet-talking whichever girl happens to be at the entrance into letting me into the building—and then I knock on the relevant door, trying to temper my expectation. I come up empty on both occasions. Neither Lana is my Lana, and I make a hasty exit.

Brett sends me a sympathetic look when I haul my grumpy ass back in the truck. He slaps me on the back. "Chin up, my man."

I drive to Broward, which is next on my list, pulling up on the other side of the road, across from the dorm. I cut the engine and stare out my window, squinting in the dark night at the historical building. The campus here is a mix of old and new, with legacy redbrick buildings residing alongside newer structures. Centuries-old oak trees and tons of green areas line the spaces in between. I love how the newer buildings have been designed with a unique and complimentary architecture that also considers the environmental impact.

I jump out of the truck and hoof it over to the dorm. A cute girl with rapidly reddening cheeks lets me into the building, and I quickly find my next target. Rapping loudly and successively on the door, I wait a good five minutes before accepting no one is home.

Back in the truck, I'm slow to move on. Call it instinct, or wishful thinking, but something is urging me to hold position. "You mind waiting a while?" I ask Brett.

He shrugs. "Go for it."

Synching my iPhone, I line up a few U2 tunes and settle back to wait.

Chapter Five
Lana

My heart-to-heart with Liv ended in a humdinger of a row after I confirmed her suspicions about Kal. She doesn't agree with my decision, and I refused to get drawn into discussing it. I can't deal with that. Not when my brain is struggling to grasp the fact he's here. So, we both went to bed mad.

She's still pissed at me, so I've been avoiding her all week.

It's not actually that hard. Between classes, study, yoga, and my volunteer work at the center, I have minimal downtime Monday through Friday so avoiding my roommate has been a breeze. Doesn't help with the horrific guilt though. I don't want to fall out with the best friend I have here, but I'm not ready to delve into all that other crap yet.

I know I can't avoid the conversation forever, but I need to psych myself up for it. Truth is, I agree with her, and I can't believe I allowed myself to be *coerced* into something I knew was wrong, *again*. You'd think I'd learned my lesson, but it's hard when the coercers are your parents—the two people I've loved and admired for so long.

All week, I've been looking anxiously over my shoulder,

expecting to discover Kal lurking in the shadows. I know it's only a matter of time before he finds me, and that thought has my body on high alert. My appetite is virtually nonexistent, and I've had trouble sleeping. I look like death warmed up, and I can feel the beginnings of a cold starting.

It's late when I leave the library on Thursday night. Yawning, I make the short stroll to the bus stop, almost buckling under the weight of my bag. I've taken on extra classes this semester as I'm determined to graduate as quickly as possible. I need to get my business degree and find a job, pronto. I can't indulge in the usual college lifestyle because the choices I've made demand sacrifices, and I'm okay with that. It's not just about me anymore. My parents have made the ultimate sacrifice so I can come here, and I need to make it up to them.

I'm lost in thought, so I don't notice the rust-colored truck idling at the curb. "Hey, pretty lady," a baritone voice booms, extracting me from my head. I lift my chin up, coming in direct contact with a pair of rich, luxuriant brown eyes I've seen before. It's the guy from the frat party last Friday. The one who caught me mid-flight. Chase, I think Liv called him.

"Hi." I wave, shooting him a cautious smile.

"Need a ride?"

"I'm good. The bus will be here any minute."

Leaning across the seat, he opens the door with a loud creak, his shirt stretching tight across well-defined shoulders and biceps. "I don't mind. It would be an honor." He shoots me a lopsided grin, and strands of dirty blond hair fall into his eyes.

I don't move position. "My mom always told me to never accept rides from strangers." This guy is massive, his body dwarfing mine, and it wouldn't take much for him to overpower me. I also haven't forgotten Liv's warning. She said this guy was trouble, and I don't need any more of that.

He chuckles. "Your friend is dating Riley, right?"

"You know Riley?" I'm highly skeptical.

"We're buds." He removes his cell phone from his jeans pocket. "I'll call him. He can vouch for me."

"Look, it's fine. The bus will be here shortly," I say, but he's already punching buttons on his phone.

"Yo!" he hollers into the handset. "Bro, I need you to talk to Lana for me. She's refusing to accept a ride home." He thrusts the cell at me, and I reluctantly step forward, taking it from his hand.

"Hey, Riley."

"Hey, Lana. I didn't realize Chase was sniffing around you."

"He's not, I mean, I don't think he is." I look over at him, noticing the spreading scowl.

"The guy's a bit of an idiot, and a total player, but it's safe to ride home with him if that's what you want," Riley confirms.

"'Kay. Thanks."

"Lana?" His tone makes me falter.

"Yeah?"

"I don't know what caused the argument between you and Livvie, but she's upset you guys aren't talking. I know it would mean a lot to her if you could smooth things over."

"I am too, and I'll fix it."

"Cool. I know that'll make her happy."

"Bye, Riley. And thanks."

I land the cell in Chase's outstretched palm. "Well?" he asks. "Am I Ted Bundy's reincarnation, or is it safe to ride with me?"

"Wow. Way to sell it."

He chuckles. "Come on, sweetheart." He pats the ripped leather passenger seat. "I'm trying to be chivalrous, and you're not making it easy."

"Nothing in life is easy," I deadpan, dumping my bag on the floor as I swing myself up into the cab. I pull the creaky door shut and strap myself in.

"Wow. Cynical, much?" He checks his mirrors before easing the truck out onto the road.

I shrug, folding my hands in my lap as I look around. The cab is old and well-worn, but it's clean and smells like peppermint and smoke. The engine is a little on the noisy side, but it moves solidly, feeling more heavyweight than modern trucks. It has a certain charisma, a certain charm. "Cool truck."

I catch a hint of a scowl before he smiles, glancing at me briefly. "Thanks. It was my grandfather's. Been handed down through the generations."

"That's awesome. It's like a piece of moving history."

He looks skeptical as he shrugs. "I guess." His mouth puckers, and I fall silent. "Where to?" he inquires a minute later.

"Broward."

He chuckles again. "You don't give much away, do you?"

"Funny. Everyone usually says I'm an open book." Or at least I used to be.

"I haven't been in your company enough to comment intelligently on that statement," he replies. "But I'd like the chance to."

I stare straight ahead, wondering what to do with that. He is so hitting on me. I've given guys a wide berth this last year, with good cause. "I'm not into random hook-ups, so if that's why you offered me a ride, you can just let me out here." I don't even look at him as I speak.

He busts out laughing. "Whoa, Lana. Cool your jets. I'm only asking if you'd like to hang out sometime. There's no other agenda."

I swivel in my seat, the leather squelching with the movement. I eyeball him, and he turns his head momentarily in my direction. "Why?"

"Why what?" His forehead creases.

"Why do you want to hang out with me?"

His lips curve into a lopsided grin. "Because you're an enigma. You're not like the other girls I've met here, and I like that."

My eyes showcase my wariness.

"And it helps you're pretty." His grin turns wolfish.

"No agenda, my ass." My eyes drill holes in his skull, and he laughs again.

Stopping in front of my building, he cuts the engine, and the truck comes to a juddering standstill. He turns to face me. "Look, I know I've got a bit of a rep already. I may have been a little overeager when I first arrived, but that's not who I am. I think you're a nice girl, and I'd like to get to know you." He holds up his palms. "I swear that's the extent of my agenda. I can tell you're different, and I like that."

"I don't have time to hang out let alone date," I reply truthfully, reaching down for my bag.

"Ah, come on, if you're going to give me the finger, at least be original."

This time I laugh. "I'm being honest, Chase. I've a very full schedule during the week, and I go home every weekend."

"You do?"

"Yep. I have family commitments." I swing my bag over my shoulder and open the door. "It's sweet you asked, but I don't really see the point." I jump out, walking around the front of the truck. Chase is out on the sidewalk by the time I reach it. "Thanks for the ride."

"Anytime, Lana." He runs a hand through his hair, messing it up in a way that makes him appear way sexy. "Look, why don't we swap numbers and meet for a quick coffee next week? Everyone's got time for coffee with a friend." He pins me with a puppy dog expression. "Pretty please?"

I roll my eyes, fighting a smirk as I remove my cell from my bag. I hand it to him. "Add your number, and then I'll text you back so you have mine."

"Cool." He winks before inputting his digits.

All of a sudden, little prickles of precognition dance across my skin. My head whips around, my eyes narrowing suspiciously. It's been the same all week. Either lack of sleep or my epic fear of running into Kal is behind it. I shake it off, accepting my cell from Chase's outstretched hand. He's watching me with amused curiosity. Great, now he probably thinks I'm a freak.

I pocket my phone, gripping my bag tightly. "I'll see you around, Chase."

"Until we meet again." He lifts my hand, drawing it to his mouth. His lips sweep softly and quickly across my skin. "See you soon, pretty lady," he quips, climbing back into his truck. He waves as he maneuvers away from the curb.

Frowning, I take the steps, two at a time, wondering what the hell I've just gotten myself into.

Liv isn't home, and I'm relieved. I'm exhausted and not up to broaching the subject with her tonight. But there is something I need to do, and I'm not putting it off any longer.

I haven't talked to my friend Faye since orientation week. I assume she's as busy settling into life in Harvard as I am here, but this conversation can't wait. It's been on my mind all week.

Belly-flopping on my bed, I dial her number, and the phone rings a few times before she picks up.

"Howdy, stranger," she answers cheerfully. "Long time no hear."

"Hey, Faye. How are you?" My tone is off, and she can tell.

"Hang on a sec, Lana. Let me get rid of the others." Muffled voices filter through the line, until she returns a couple minutes later. "Sorry about that. I have a feeling we need privacy for this conversation."

"Did you tell him?" I can't disguise the hurt and disappointment in my voice.

"Back up there, Lana. What exactly are you asking?"

"Did you tell Kal I was enrolled in UF?"

"I have never discussed our phone calls with Kal. Never." Her tone is chilly, and I know I've just offended her. "And I'm annoyed you've jumped to that conclusion."

"I didn't mean to accuse you. I swear."

She sighs. "Look, for the record, I didn't tell Kalvin you were going to UF. I'm guessing you guys bumped into each other?"

"Yeah, but if you didn't tell him, how did he know I was here?"

"He didn't."

Now I'm confused. "You can't mean to tell me it's a coincidence?" I know I've been naïve in the past, but I'm not that damned naïve.

"It wasn't a coincidence." She sighs down the line. "I want to level with you, but I don't want to get caught in the middle. You're my friend and he's my cousin. I've tried to respect both of your privacy and not get involved. He didn't even know we were in contact. He keeps most things bottled up inside, but he has spoken to me in the last year about you a little. However, I can't tell you what he said. You need to hear it from him."

"I respect that, Faye. I do, and I don't want to put you in an awkward position."

"I'll tell you what I can. Kal informed me and Ky in July that he wasn't coming to Harvard with us—that he was going to UF. I was instantly suspicious. I figured you two had discussed it in the past and he was hoping you'd be there. I had to come clean to Ky, and he wasn't pleased."

She snort-laughs, and I can only imagine the argument that must have caused. I'm still reeling at the confirmation that Kal is going to school here. One part of me thought he might have been visiting on the off chance I was here, but now I know he's enrolled, I'd like to know why.

"I've been talking to you in secret for months, and my boyfriend didn't know," Faye continues. "We made a promise never to keep secrets from one another again, and he was totally pissed off at me, especially when I made him swear not to tell Kal. And he didn't, Lana. That's not how Kal discovered you were there. Ky and I have been arguing furiously over this—he wanted to tell his brother, but I forced him not to. I've gone out on a limb for you, but I can't do that anymore. I love Ky, and I love my cousin, and I'm not comfortable hiding the fact we are in touch anymore. Moreover, if you tell me important stuff going forward about Kal, you can't expect me to keep that to myself. It's not fair. I'm trying to be your friend, without being a shitty girlfriend and cousin."

"I'm sorry, Faye. I never thought about the position I was putting you in."

"It's okay, I get that." There's a pregnant pause. "So, did you two talk?"

"Not exactly. I ran away." Her disappointment filters down the line. "You don't have to say it. I know I can't ignore him forever. Waiting for him to approach me has me on edge. I ... I don't know what to do with this, Faye. He's here, and I'm a mess all over again."

"Oh, Lana."

"You know I've always been an idiot when it comes to him."

"I can relate to that, more than you realize." There's another pregnant pause. "He still loves you, Lana. He hasn't said it outright, but he doesn't need to. Actions speak louder than words."

"Don't," I whisper. "Don't give me false hope. Nothing can happen between us."

"But you still love him, I know you do. You don't have to say it either. The kind of love you have for him is not the type to disappear overnight."

"Whether I love him or he loves me isn't important anymore," I say, the words cleaving a line straight through my heart. "It's too late. He shouldn't have come here. I wish he hadn't."

Chapter Six
Kalvin

"**I** still want to kill him," I tell Brett, leaning over the pool table and lining up my shot. I imagine the ball is Chase's face, and I thrust the stick with more force than necessary. My aim is off and the ball narrowly misses the pocket. Brett chalks his stick, bends down, and studies the angles. A couple in the corner of the sports bar busts out laughing, and the girl's shrill giggling gives me an instant headache.

"Like I said earlier, you need to play it cool. Marching over there all caveman-like would not help your cause." He takes his shot, watching with a shit-eating grin as the ball whizzes into the top right-hand pocket. "I know it's not easy when the douche has a face made for punching. I was seconds away from knocking that smug grin off his face earlier." He pockets another two balls with his next shot.

I may as well just hand Brett victory now. My focus is shot to pieces since catching Lana with Chase. Any euphoria I felt at finally tracking her down dissipated with one look at the douche. "I want to punch his lights out. He better not have laid a hand on her." Chase is a slimy fucker, and he has no place with a sweetheart like Lana. I don't care what it'll take—he is not going to touch her if I have anything to do with it.

"You need to chill and strategize. Chase might be a douche, but he's a calculating douche. If he gets a whiff that you're interested in her, he'll dig his heels in and go after her with everything he's got just to mess with you."

"Lana's smart. She won't fall for his type." At least, the girl I used to know wouldn't fall for a sleazy a-hole like him, but I can't bank on her being the same. I know I'm not. The Lana I knew would never have danced on top of a counter in full view of an entire room.

Just like me, she's changed.

I only hope that the connection we shared hasn't altered irrevocably.

I leave Brett with a couple of his teammates in the bar. Not feeling it tonight. I head back to our dorm room and call Kev the minute I get out of the shower. It takes all my persuasive power, and a hefty dose of groveling, before he agrees to retrieve Lana's schedule and email it to me. I'm perplexed when it finally lands in my inbox. *What the hell? Why is Lana completing a degree in business administration?* For as long as I can remember, Lana has wanted to be a writer. Her ambition was always to study creative writing in college, so I'm flummoxed. I can't imagine what caused her to relinquish her lifelong dream. And it's a damn shame because she's such a natural. For years, I was in awe of her natural storytelling ability. I've read practically everything she's written, and she's too Goddamned talented to push it aside.

I guess it's another piece of the puzzle that is now Lana.

I think she's changed more than I've anticipated.

I'm pensive and melancholy as I crawl into bed. Thoughts of Lana invade my mind, and I drift off to sleep with her beautiful face in my mind's eye.

Loving Kalvin

I have a full schedule the next day, so I'm forced to endure my suffering and wait until later to catch up to Lana.

Seriously, today feels like the longest day of my life.

I duck out of architectural history—my last class—twenty minutes before it ends to make the journey across campus to the Heavener School of Business.

My palms are clammy, and a line of sweat coasts down my spine, gluing my shirt to my back. I tug my ball cap down low to shield myself from prying eyes. I hate how instantly recognizable I am around campus. Although I'm more than used to it—consequence of growing up a Kennedy in the glare of the public spotlight—I had hoped for more anonymity coming here. Turns out, my trial captured the interest of a nation. All it took was a few people to notice me around campus, and then social media started blowing up. The news that the infamous Kalvin Kennedy was attending UF was every-where the next day.

So much for staying in the background.

I wonder if Lana knew I was here and if she's been purposely avoiding me.

Unfortunately, *I* don't have the luxury of changing my name. It wouldn't make any difference. Short of a face lift, there is no disguising who I am. I've never had much of an issue with it in the past, but this last year has been hard. No matter how much Lana sacrificed to ensure my innocence was a matter of public record, people still point the finger at me. Still doubt me.

Hasn't stopped the groupies from forming though. Sometimes, I really can't figure out the female race. Girls should be running screaming in the other direction, but the reaction is usually the oppo-site. It's why I haven't attended many parties. I can't stand the unwanted attention.

The old Kal would've lapped it up, milking it for maximum personal satisfaction, ensuring Chase's current score sheet looked like child's play. Now, even the mere thought of hooking up with random girls curdles my stomach. Apart from that one time with Shelby, I haven't had sex in over a year, and while I miss it, I'm not tempted to go there. I have zero interest. Losing the one girl I always thought would be there for me has changed me. I would give anything for a do over. There are so many things I'd do differently.

Brett thinks I'm insane, but he's more than happy to soften the blow of rejection for the girls I consistently turn away.

At least one of us is happy.

Students start piling out the doors, and I straighten up, focusing laser-sharp eyes on every person emerging from the building. I don't want to miss her in the crowd. I'm frantically searching the large group converging on the sidewalk when all the tiny hairs on the back of my neck lift.

She's close.

I can feel it.

I step nearer to the building and then I spot her. Time seems to stand still. She's skipping down the stairs with a couple of other girls, her head thrown back, laughing. Her entire face comes alive when she smiles. I take a moment to slyly study her. Her usual pale skin is now tanned and glowing, and where once she was boyishly slim, now she's grown into her body. Although she appears thinner than the last time I saw her, curves dip in and out in all the right places. She's all woman, and I can't keep my eyes off her.

She is so beautiful and so completely unaware.

My heart pines for her.

My arms long to hold her.

My cock throbs with possessive need.

I'm striding toward her before I know it, almost running in my haste to get up close and personal. The blonde on her left notices me first, her frown quickly transforming to a gasp of recognition. I'm singular in my focus, and my direction and my eyes haven't wandered from Lana. She is chatting animatedly with her friends, utterly oblivious to my imminent approach.

As her foot lands on the sidewalk, I slam to a halt right in front of her. That delicate floral smell I've always associated with her drifts through the air, tempting and comforting me. At least some things haven't changed. "Lana." My voice comes out barely louder than a whisper. Her entire body goes rigidly stiff, and a tiny whimper escapes her lips. Her head is down and she's studying the sidewalk as if her eyes are physically lasered to the asphalt. Her other friend's eyes expand, and she clamps a hand over her mouth. "Lana," I say again, louder this time. "I've been looking everywhere for you. Can we talk? Please."

"Please leave me alone," she whispers, still not looking at me.

"I can't do that, honeybun." The childish endearment rolls off my tongue without conscious thought. Greta—Lana's mom and our ex-housekeeper—used to make these delicious pastries with honey and nuts when we were kids. It was an old European bun recipe, apparently, handed down over the generations in her family, or so Greta said. They were Lana's favorite treat, and somewhere along the way I started calling her honeybun. The name stuck, even though she hated it. Actually, it was *because* she hated it that I continued to call her it. I resist the urge to chuckle even though I love teasing her. I'm a total dick like that.

"Don't call me that!" she snaps.

"Sorry. It's a difficult habit to break," I murmur, trying to appease her. I don't want to fight with her now. I just really need to speak to her. To find out if she's okay. If there's any possibility she'll give me a second chance.

Slowly, her head lifts, and she gasps when our eyes finally meet. Her familiar, big hazel eyes still contain the same sparkling innocence, the same little amber fleck. My gaze treks around her face, noting how the smattering of freckles dotting her nose and cheeks has deepened. Her glossy hair falls in waves over her forehead, tipping over her shoulders and down her back. Her little nose, so perfect and dainty, rests on the same silky-smooth skin. Her full lips part, and memories of kissing her surge to the forefront of my mind, making breathing difficult. Things are in motion down south, and I have to resist the urge to adjust myself in my shorts. Drawing attention to my growing boner would not help my plight.

Her eyes take in my face with the same intensity. Our eyes lock on, and I could easily drown in her gaze. We stare at one another, a multitude of unspoken sentiments electrifying the space between us. So much emotion is conveyed in her expression, as no doubt there is in mine. She was never able to shield her emotions from me, and now seems no different. My heart thrashes against my ribcage, and my fingers twitch with compulsive need. Not touching her is killing me. Expectation is ripe in the air, and the usual charge in her presence is alive and kicking. I long to close the gap between us and scoop her into my arms. I want to bury myself in her scent, to feel her touch against mine, to worship her lips like they deserve. But I hold back, urging the rampant pounding of my heart to calm the fuck down.

Baby steps, I remind myself. "You look good, Lana," I admit in a choked voice.

"Don't," she croaks. "Please, don't." Her eyes dart wildly around, and then she runs off, racing down the road as her friends stand there with their mouths hanging open.

I take off after her, quickly catching up with my longer strides. Gently, I take her elbow. "Please, stop. I'm begging you, Lana. Please just hear me out."

She tries to shake me off, and I tighten my grip. Her pace slows down, and I ease back until we're at a standstill. I move her over to the wall, out of the way of the passing foot traffic. Her back flattens against the brick as her chest moves up and down. She's chewing on the side of her mouth in an obvious tell. Her head tilts up, and she stares at me. I get lost in her eyes again.

Minutes pass, could be hours, and all we do is stare at one another.

I gulp. She gulps.

Our eyes never stray.

Not till she finally breaks the silence. "Why did you come here, Kal?"

"I came for you." Slowly, I move my hand, brushing a stray lock of hair off her forehead. "I miss you so damn much."

She swallows. "Why?"

I stare at her incredulously. "What do you mean?"

"Why on earth would you miss me?" Her honest expression stings.

"Why on earth wouldn't I?"

"Because I ruined your life?" Now *her* expression is incredulous. "You should hate me, Kal."

"I could never hate you. Never." I plant my hands on the wall, one on each side of her head, leaning in a little, desperately needing to be closer to her. "There is nothing you could do that would make me love you any less." Fuck it. I'm putting it all on the line. "I still love you, Lana, and I want you back. I'll take all of the blame if you want me to, but give me a chance to make it up to you. To prove I can be there for you in the way you've always wanted."

Her eyes turn shiny, and her lower lip wobbles. She opens her mouth to say something but then closes it again. A little sob travels up her throat, crushing me. I want to envelop her in my arms and soothe her pain, but I'm afraid of startling her. Afraid she'll run off on me again, so I fight the craving. Finally, she turns around to look at me again. "I did something unforgiveable. We can never come back from that."

"I forgive you." The words tumble out of my mouth without prompting, and I speak directly from my heart. "I forgave you last November. I meant every word of what I said that day in the courtroom."

A tear slips out of the corner of her eye as she watches me. She opens and closes her mouth again. I can sense how emotional she is. I can relate. I'm an emotional tornado on the inside.

Silence envelops us again.

"You cut your hair," she blurts out randomly. "I like it. It suits you." I send her a cocky grin. Can't help it. If this is how she wants to play it, I'm game. "Shame about the ears, though. There's no hiding them now."

Immediately, my fingers fly to my ear lobes. "What's wrong with my ears?"

Her lips curve into a teasing smile. "Dude, if you don't know what's wrong with your ears, far be it from me to burst your ignorant bubble." She stifles a giggle, and my heart soars. God, I've missed this so much. Missed her.

"Ha! Good one. You almost had me there." I nudge her shoulder, and for a split second, it feels like old times. Like no separation exists. Like we haven't hurt each other so much. "I've never seen your hair so long," I say, deciding to keep it easy-breezy. My fingers toy with the ends of her hair, and she flinches.

"Yeah, well, I haven't had much time to focus on stuff like that." She freezes, and her eyes pop wide, demonstrating the full "deer in the headlights" effect. I arch a brow, curious to understand her reaction. "With school and my volunteer work and extra classes, I'm far too busy," she rushes out.

"You volunteer?"

She nods. "At the local rape support center."

A layer of tension descends, and my throat constricts. "That's ... yeah." Fuck. I don't know how to respond.

More awkward silence flitters between us.

"Why are you studying business admin?" I blurt, desperate to move to safer topics of conversation. "What happened to your dreams of being a writer?"

Her face pales, and she instantly shuts down. Damn me and my big mouth.

"That's none of your business anymore," she snaps, and it hurts. "You may think you still know me, but you don't."

"Give me a chance to get to know you all over again. I know I let you down, but I promise I won't let you down again."

"Those words are too easy for you, Kal."

"I deserve that, but I'll prove I'm serious this time. Please, Lana.

Please forgive me." I'll get down on my knees if that's what it will take.

"It's too late, Kal. Too much has changed."

"I'm not giving up on us, and I'm not going away. I'll be like your perpetual shadow," I joke, trying to alleviate the rapidly building tension.

"Please don't. I don't want that, and I have it on good authority that campus security takes a dim view of stalking." She ducks out from under my arms. "I have someplace I need to be." She starts to walk off but stops. Pivoting around, she straightens her back as she faces me. "You shouldn't have come here, Kal. I asked you not to find me for a reason. Please stop following me. I'm trying to make a new life for myself, and you're not a part of that."

Her words slice a line straight through my heart, and I react instinctively, without engaging my brain. "And Chase is?"

Her eyes narrow to slits, and her hands land on her slim hips. "Excuse me?"

"I saw you, with him, last night," I spit out. "Is he the reason you don't want me here?"

She harrumphs, shaking her head. "This is priceless. You have some nerve showing up here like this and then throwing that out at me. Chase is none of your business. Butt out, Kal. I won't tell you again. Leave me alone."

"Fine, if that's what you want, but promise me you'll stay away from him. He's not a good guy, Lana. He's with a different girl every night of the week. He's an asshole, and he'll only hurt you."

Her nostrils flare, and her cheeks redden. "Are you kidding me right now?" She glares at me. "Have you any idea how hypocritical you sound?"

I wince. There isn't much I can do to defend myself. "I hear how that sounds, but I'm not the same guy you knew. I've changed, Lana. I haven't bee—"

She raises a palm, cutting me stone dead with one cold look. "I don't want to hear it, Kal. I've heard it all before. It was a pack of lies then, and it's a pack of lies now."

Her hurt runs deep, and I have no one to blame but myself. "Please, Lana. We have so much to talk about. Just hear me out. Are you hungry? We could grab something to eat. I—"

"It's not happening, Kal. This"—she gestures between us—"this isn't happening again. It's just like you to turn up here and expect me to fall at your feet." She moves closer to me, jutting her chin out defiantly. "You say you've changed. Maybe you have, but it's too late." She prods a finger in my chest. "I've changed. You can't walk all over me anymore. I'll never be that girl again, and I meant what I said in my letter. A part of me will always love you, Kal, but I don't want to do this. Our relationship is over. Our friendship is over."

My eyes burn painfully. This is like my worst nightmare come to life.

"You need to leave me alone. I have a new life, and it doesn't involve you."

Chapter Seven
Lana

I'm shaking like a leaf when I get back to the dorm. Slamming the door shut, I slump to the ground, pressing a hand to my throbbing chest. Tears pour down my cheeks, and I cry out in frustration. It was so hard to tell him those things. Lies piled upon lies. I know I hit my mark. He was hurting. I could see it in his eyes. But it's for the best. I can't do this again. There is far too much at stake.

It doesn't matter that I still love every fucking gorgeous infuriating inch of Kalvin Kennedy—he can't be mine. And he won't want to be once he finds out.

"Lana!" Olivia yells, rushing to my side. "What's wrong? What is it?"

"He moved here for me, Liv. He doesn't hate me." A hacking sob erupts from deep inside me. From the very core of my soul. "He said he loves me."

"What happened exactly?" She sinks to the floor beside me.

"He was waiting for me outside class."

"How was it?"

"He ... he ... oh, God, Liv, he looked amazing. He's all grown up now, and he's even more gorgeous, and he seemed ... different. He *was* different." I can't deny that. He exuded it like it was something tangible.

"Do you feel differently about him now?" Her earnest eyes bore into mine.

I shake my head. "No. It was all there. I still love him. I still love him so much." Sobs burst free of my throat, and I give into it, burying my head in my hands and crying my eyes out. Liv pulls me into her chest, and I sob all over her shirt. When my crying fest dies out, I lift my head up, piercing her with an apologetic look. "I'm so sorry, Liv. For fighting with you. For ignoring you all week. I'm a crappy friend."

"If you're a crappy friend, then so am I," she protests. "I was ignoring you too, and I had no right to judge you or tell you what to do."

"I've thought of nothing else all week," I admit, sitting upright. "I know I have to tell him. I always knew I would. I just didn't think I'd have to deal with it so soon."

"I think it's the right thing to do."

"How am I going to explain it?" My eyes close momentarily. "I almost destroyed his life once already."

She winces. "It's not the same thing."

"I didn't mean it like that. You know I'd never say such a thing, but I made a call last year, and now I'm going to pay the price. I thought there'd be time. When he has his life together, when it wouldn't derail him, maybe after college ..." I sound like a robot, or a trained monkey, repeating words that have been programmed in my mind.

"There's never a right time to drop a bomb like this."

"I know." I'm quietly contemplative as my mind lingers over my conversation with Kal. "I falsely accused him of rape, and he still doesn't hate me, but he will once he hears this!" I bury my head in my knees. "I've screwed everything up, and I'm so scared, Liv. What if he ..." I can't even finish the thought let alone articulate it.

She wets her lips. "Can I ask you something, Lana?"

I pick my head up. "Sure." I left our last conversation hanging, and I know she must have lots of questions.

"Why did you do it? Why did you accuse him of something he didn't do?"

I massage my temples as I prepare to tell her the rest of my sordid tale. "The day after he took my virginity, he told me we needed to keep our relationship a secret for a little while longer, just until he found the right time to break the news to his mother. He promised he hadn't changed his mind and he was committed to me, but it left a sour taste in my mouth. I thought he was lying. That it was just like the kiss all over again, only this time it was worse. I was wracked with self-doubt. Kal had slept with lots of girls. Who was I to think he'd be interested in little, inexperienced ole me? I clearly wasn't up to the job."

I'm fighting tears again as old emotions return to taunt me. Liv rubs my shoulders, sensing how deeply traumatic this is to relive. "All I could think was that I was an embarrassment to him. That he didn't want to be seen out in public with someone like me. I'm beneath him in so many ways—I've always known that. I was so upset—at him, at myself. We had the most vicious argument, and I told him to get out and leave me the hell alone."

I drop my head on her shoulder. "I thought he'd come back. If not to tell me he'd do the right thing, at least to properly explain, but the rest of the week and the weekend passed without a word from him, and I was growing more and more disconsolate. Then Addison showed up." Fiery pain burns behind my eyes.

"I remember her name from the news reports and that other case that came to trial a couple months back," Liv supplies.

Addison's half-sister was sentenced to life in prison at the start of the summer for the murders of two policemen and the attempted murder of Kal's cousin, Faye. Addison was left paralyzed after her sister shot her when she tried to help Faye escape.

Karma is a bitch.

"Addison was Kyler Kennedy's ex-girlfriend, and I knew she was a total bitch, but she played me perfectly. She told me Kal had come on to her the night before and that she'd had sex with him. At first, I refused to believe her because I knew how much Kal detested that girl. She had cheated on Kyler with his best friend, and he hadn't been the same since. Kal despised her, so I thought it was a lie until she showed me the proof."

"It's true what they reported? She actually recorded it?" Liv looks aghast.

"Yeah. She had a tape of them fucking, which she took great delight in sharing with me." I snort, even though it isn't remotely funny. "I threw up all over her shoes, but she was performing the role of concerned friend, so she had to pretend it didn't matter."

"Lana, that's … fucking awful. I can't even imagine."

"As long as I live, I'll never be able to erase those images from my mind. It doesn't matter that I've since found out she set the whole thing up—got him drunk, came on to him, and recorded them having sex—I will never forget how distraught I was that day. How much it hurt to know he had sex with someone else so soon after promising me he was finished with other girls, so soon after we had slept together. I gave him my virginity, and he did that to me!"

My trip down nostalgia lane is good for me. I can't ever forget who Kal is. *He may believe he's changed, but can a person ever truly change something that's so inherent to their nature?*

I turn to face her. "Can you imagine seeing the boy you love having sex with someone else? The boy who has owned a piece of your heart for as long as you can remember. The boy who only has to look at you and you melt. Our connection was so strong, Liv. I could tell what he was thinking in any given moment just by looking into his eyes. I know his every nuance. I know his deepest darkest secrets, and he knows mine." I sigh, staring up at the ceiling, feeling the pain as if it's the first time I'm experiencing it. "How can two people who are intertwined so completely hurt each other so much?"

Her eyes are damp as she looks at me.

"I don't know how to exist without him," I admit truthfully. "He has always been a part of me, and trying to survive without him is slowly chipping away at my soul, yet the hurt still exists, refusing to go away. It devastated me, Liv, and it turns my stomach every time I think of it, yet the images won't go away. They are as sharp in my mind as if I was an actual fly on the wall. If there was a defining moment, that was definitely it."

I pause, needing to draw a long breath before continuing. "I was beyond livid. More so when I confronted him and he denied it to my face. That's when I knew he'd been lying to me about everything. I was destroyed. Utterly heartbroken. I didn't come out of my bedroom for days. I cried nonstop, and I thought my heart would actually break. I have never experienced such anguish, such physical pain. My parents were extremely worried about me."

My poor parents. I've put them through the wringer this past year. Their marriage has fallen apart because of me, and that's another addition to the list of things I can never forgive myself for. When I think about it, it's a wonder I can haul my ass out of bed each day with the weight of self-revulsion pressing down on me.

"I can't imagine how devastating that must've been," Liv says quietly.

"It was horrendous. Of course, Addison was counting on that, and she manipulated me beautifully. She was there every day with soothing words and apologies. Then she started dropping little hints about how he needed to pay for what he had done. She painted herself as a victim too. Sobbed over how she would never get Kyler back now and how dirty she felt for having slept with his brother. We raged at the Kennedys together. It was a full-on bitch fest, and she fueled my thirst for vengeance. I was hurting so badly, and I wanted him to feel that pain. All the years of rejection, all the years of watching him hook up with other girls, all his false words of love—it took its toll. It replayed in my mind until I felt like I was going crazy. Maybe, I did. Stress can do funny things to a person."

I take a shuddering breath as emotion attempts to overpower me. I still find it so difficult to talk about this. Even though my actions were despicable, and it's a miracle Kal has forgiven me, it's hard to completely forgive him for the part he played when the hurt is indelibly imprinted on my heart. Which is hypocritical, I know. He's as much Addison's victim as I am. We've both made terrible mistakes. Mistakes that have hurt each other deeply.

"When Addison first proposed her suggestion, I was disgusted, and I asked her to leave. There was no way I was accusing him of something he didn't do, no matter how he'd treated me. But the more the thought infiltrated my mind, the more plausible it seemed. I knew it was wrong, but I was in a blind rage, and I veered back and forth for days. Then Addison brought the condom Kal had used the night he was with her, and I saw red. I'm ashamed to admit I lost it. Went berserk. Trashed my room. My brain shut off. I went out and told my parents he raped me, then it all fell into place like Addison said it would."

I start crying again. "I'm a horrible person, Liv. Not just for what I put Kal through but for rape victims everywhere. The thought that my actions might lead a genuine victim not to come forward still haunts me at night."

Liv looks me directly in the eyes. "That's why you volunteer at the center."

"Yes. I need to give something back. To try and atone for my actions."

"Does it help?"

"I honestly don't know. I'd like to think I'm helping them, but I don't know if it's helping me. It's a constant reminder of my mistake. Of how very wrong it was to accuse someone I loved of rape. I told him today there is no coming back from that."

"A part of me understands it now. Why you felt you couldn't tell him, but it's not right that all the responsibility has fallen on you, either."

"It felt like the appropriate decision at the time, but now I'm not so sure."

We are both quiet for a bit.

"I think you were brave to come forward at the trial like you did. That took guts."

"I had to fix things." I look directly into her eyes. "I was less emotional by then, and I knew what I needed to do. I could've retracted my statement before the case went to trial, but Kal's reputation was being slandered in the media, and I know how narrow-minded the local community could be. I was sure they were giving him hell in school, and then my attorney told me he got in more trouble for a fight at a party and he was on house arrest, and I felt awful. He was being punished for something he hadn't done, and if I was going to make amends, then I had to do it publicly. I had to put the record straight in a way that ensured the media would report his innocence. It was the best way I knew to fix things. I didn't even tell my parents. They heard the truth for the first time when I testified."

"That must have been a shock."

"They barely spoke to me for days. I let them down. Let myself down."

"I'm so sorry that happened to you."

I vehemently shake my head. "Don't feel sorry for me. I don't deserve it. I trusted the wrong person, and I'm smarter than that."

"You can't continue to beat yourself up over it. You have to move on."

"I'm trying." I look at her. "Does one mistake define who you are for life?"

"I don't believe so. Everyone deserves a second chance. Kal is here now, Lana, and—"

"Don't go there. Please. I'm hanging by a thread as it is."

"What are you going to do about him then?"

"I don't have a freaking clue."

Chapter Eight
Kalvin

Brett comes bounding into the room, his hair still damp from a post-training shower. Dumping his foul-smelling duffel on the floor, he sends me a curious look. I jump up, stalking toward him, jaw taut and my fists clenched into balls at my side. "Hit me," I demand.

"What?"

"Punch me in the face. As hard as you can."

He stares me out of it. "Dude, are you high?"

I roll my eyes. "No! Hit me! Now!"

His brows nudge up. "Drunk?"

"What the fuck is wrong with you?" I yell. "Just fucking punch me!"

"Hell to the no. I know how this one ends. I hit you and then you'll hit me, and before we know it, we'll be knocking the shit out of one another." He points at himself. "This face is far too pretty to mess up."

"God, you're insufferable," I complain, mentally praying for patience I know I don't have.

"I'm insufferable? Dude, you are one crazy, weird motherfucker."

He shakes his head as he bends over, opening the refrigerator and removing two beers. He tosses one to me. "Calm the fuck down, and tell me what's going on."

"What's a guy to do to get a fist in the face?" I mumble, unwilling to let this go.

"If you're that determined, start an online campaign. There are plenty of dudes who would kill to kick the shit out of the notorious Kalvin Kennedy."

I drop back on my bed, groaning. "Did you have to go there?" It's not like I need any reminders. He smirks, and I sit up, resting on the edge of the bed. Sighing, I drag my hands through my hair, still full of pent-up frustration. "I'm an idiot."

Brett pops the lid on his can. "Well, duh!"

"Now I really want to punch *you*." My throat works overtime as I tip the can into my mouth.

"Dude." Brett leans into my face. "Let the punching thing go, and tell me what has you so riled up. I'm not a betting man, but if I was, I'd bet this was something to do with your girl."

"She's not my girl." The thought cuts me up. "And considering how much I messed up today, I doubt she ever will be."

He leans against the edge of the desk. "What did you do?"

I fill him in quickly. "I think I was holding my own until I brought up that douche, Chase." I pummel my fists into my temples. "Ugh, I'm such a jealous, possessive freak."

"You're right to be wary of him. He's a jerk, and I wouldn't trust his motives."

"Why her?" I plead. "Why does he have to be interested in her! As if this isn't difficult enough. Someone cut me a fucking break here!" I yell at the ceiling, feeling all kinds of sorry for myself.

"We're going out," Brett decides, throwing a shirt at me. "You need to let off some steam."

"Can you find me someone to punch?" I stand up, yanking the shirt over my head.

"No. Punching!" Brett sends me a stern look. "You can find other ways to chill."

We return to the same frat house, and I frantically search the basement for her, but she's a no show this week. I hang with Brett and his football buddies, but I'm not contributing much to the conversation. My limbs start loosening after my third beer, but my head is still an ugly mess.

Lana was different today. There's a cold, apathetic edge to her personality that didn't exist before. Her rejection was blunt and to the point, and it surprised me. One part of me likes that. Likes that she's making me work for it this time. It's no more than she deserves. But that other impatient, lazy part of my personality doesn't want to wait. I have missed that girl more than I ever thought possible.

I need her back in my life.

I don't care what I have to do—I'm going to win her back. Failure is not an option. That word doesn't exist in the Kennedy vocab.

"Your brain is going to implode if you don't stop overanalyzing it." Brett props his butt on the edge of the table beside me.

"I never had to try that hard with Lana before, so I stupidly assumed I could coax her back into my arms. I need a new plan."

"You sure this chick is worth all the effort? Getting emancipated so you can travel halfway across the country, miles from your family and friends, is a lot to do for one girl." My mouth twists into a snarl. He holds up his hands. "All right! I get it. She's worth it." A serious expression washes over his face. "Can I ask you something and you won't get mad?"

I snort. "You know me better than that, and the urge to punch something or someone hasn't gone away."

"You're such an ass sometimes."

I smirk. "You and me both, brother." I tap my bottle against his, and we share a conspiratorial grin. A flutter of catcalls ripples through the crowd, and I glance up. A few girls are dancing on the counter, drawing admiring looks from all corners. Still can't believe she did that. I smile at the memory, wishing I had caught more than a glimpse of my Lana shaking her booty.

"How can you trust her again?" Brett asks, drawing me back to the conversation. "How do you know she won't pull something like that again? Aren't you worried?"

"Honestly? No. Lana only did what she did because I hurt her desperately. I'm never going to hurt her again, and she won't do that to me either." Lana may have changed, but she's still the same person underneath. Good and kind and honest, and my supreme confidence in her trust comes from knowing her on a soul-deep level.

"I'm going to grovel like I've never groveled before," I tell him, with a knowing nod. "I'll do whatever it takes to win her back."

"Nah, dude. No groveling necessary. Woo her." Brett wiggles his brows. "Remind her how much she misses you. You can be devoted without groveling."

Ideas swirl through my mind. "Dude." I slap him on the back. "That's an awesome idea."

He shrugs, tapping his temple. "Plenty more of those up here."

I laugh, and just like that, my melancholy lifts. Showing Lana how much I love her will speak volumes. She said words were too easy, so now I'll prove it with my actions.

Brett nudges my shoulder. "Four o'clock. Is that your girl?"

I whip my head around, and my heart starts doing a victory dance in my chest. Lana is huddled in the corner with the same friend from last week and one of the frat guys I've seen around. I push off the table, knocking back the rest of my beer for Dutch courage. "Wish me luck."

"Blow her mind, Casanova." Brett touches his knuckle to mine.

I navigate through the crowd like a man on a mission. A few girls reach out for me as I pass, but I ignore them. Out of the corner of my eye, I notice Shelby deep in conversation with a couple of her sorority sisters over the other side of the room.

Lana's friend jerks her head in my direction, and Lana's spine stiffens. She turns around, and all the air knocks out of my lungs. Her hair is styled in soft curls, and two sparkly clips hold her bangs off her forehead, showcasing her exquisite features. A light flush radiates her cheeks, and her eyes are smoky behind a layer of thick, black lashes. Her lips are plump and glossy, and they seem to call out "kiss me" to me, and I'd love to oblige, but that'll probably only earn me a slap to the face. Her brows knit as I approach, taking the edge off my enthusiasm.

She's wearing a cute red dress with thin straps and a hem that stops at her knee. Black wedge sandals make her appear taller than her five-foot-three frame. She's an alluring mix of innocence and sexiness, and I'm drawn to her like a moth to a flame. My eyes don't leave hers as I close the final gap between us. Her friends have stopped talking, and everyone is focused on me.

"You look beautiful," I say, stopping directly in front of her. I don't want to crowd her, but I'm also not going to let her run away before I've said my piece. "I owe you an apology. I'm sorry for what I said earlier. I didn't mean it, but the thought of losing you forever is making me desperate." Her friends are listening to every word, but I don't care if the whole room hears. "One hour of your time. That's all I'm asking for. One hour to explain some stuff. What do you say, Lana?" I peer into her captivating eyes.

Conflicting emotions flit across her features. "I ... I can't, Kal. I just can't." She moves to walk around me. *What the hell? She won't even speak to me? How the hell can I woo her if she won't even talk to me?*

I step in front of her, gently taking her arm. "Lana, I'm begging you. I'll do anything. What will it take for you to hear me out?" I drop to my knees in front of her. "Please, honeybun."

"Oh my God!" Her whole face turns puce. "What are you doing?" she hisses, her eyes quickly scanning the room. "Get up!"

"Will you agree to meet me if I do?"

"Yes! Just get up. Please. You're drawing attention."

I scramble to my feet, failing to keep the ginormous grin off my face.

"Kalvin? What are you doing?" a female voice asks from behind me, and my grin vanishes. A tanned arm slides around my waist as Shelby materializes at my side. "I've been looking all over for you." Leaning up, she goes to plant a kiss on my cheek, but I step back as if she's on fire, quickly removing her arm.

"Not now, Shelby. I'm in the middle of a private conversation." I shoot her a furious look.

"You haven't changed at all." Lana harrumphs. "You're unbelievable."

"This is not how it looks. I swear." My eyes are pleading. Then, I turn to face Shelby. "I told you we were finished, and I meant it. Run along now." I refocus on Lana, dismayed to see such a familiar look on her face. I don't care if I was rude. All I care about right now is the disbelieving girl in front of me.

"This is about you and me. No one else. I can explain everything."

"Save your breath." Lana's mouth pulls into a firm line. "I've heard it all before. From you, from Faye. There is nothing left to say. I meant what I said earlier. Leave me alone."

"Lana." Her friend attempts to intervene. "Maybe you shou—"

"Liv. Don't." She flips her gaze up. "I know you mean well, but this is my decision. I'm calling it a night. I'll see you Sunday." She leans in, hugging her friend fleetingly.

"I'll take you home," I offer, desperation creeping into my tone.

"No thank you. I know how to take the bus." She sidesteps me.

"I'll come with," Olivia says.

"Don't be silly," Lana replies. "Stay with Riley. I'm a big girl and well capable of making my own way back to our dorm. I'll text you when I'm there." She waves, before striding toward the exit.

I follow her, shoving people out of my way in my haste to keep close to her. "It's not safe. Hate me all you want, but at least let me escort you home."

She spins around. "I said no! Just leave me alone, Kal. Please, just stop this."

A shadow falls over us. "Lana? Are you okay?"

I bite down hard on my lip, drawing blood. "Fuck off, Chase."

"I wasn't talking to you," he coolly replies.

I notice Brett getting up, heading in this direction, and I subtly shake my head.

"I can give you a ride home, Lana. I only got here, and I haven't had anything to drink," Chase offers.

I put my face in his. "Not happening, douche. I'm taking her home."

"Neither of you are taking me home," Lana argues, her eyes burning with unconcealed anger. "I'm more than capable of looking after myself." She glares at me, and then her gaze softens as she fixes her attention on douche features.

What da fuck?!

"Thanks for the offer, Chase, but I'm good."

He cranks the charm to the max, sending her a blistering smile. "Honestly, it's no problem, and I'd rather ensure you get home safely. I'll only worry, otherwise."

Yeah, I'm sure you will, asshole.

She worries her lower lip between her teeth. "Okay, if you're sure I'm not putting you out."

"What?" I explode. "Lana, what the hell?" I move closer to her. "I know you're still pissed at me, but don't do this. Don't go with him. I'll call an Uber for you, and you can wait with your friends until it arrives."

"I'm not sure what I've done to offend you, Kennedy, but I assure you Lana is completely safe with me." Chase lays it on thick. "The last thing I would do is hurt her." He holds out his arm to Lana. "You ready?"

"Lana. Don't."

She loops her arm in his. "You don't have a say in my life anymore, Kal. Goodnight."

They walk off, leaving me with my mouth hanging open and my heart ripped to shreds. Screw this! I'm not letting her leave with him. I have only taken one step, when Brett moves in front of me, halting my progress. "What happened to not groveling or baiting her about Chase?"

"Not now." I try to push past him, but he's a stubborn prick, and he continues to block my path.

"This isn't the way to win her back. You need to calm down and leave it until tomorrow. She is going with him, and there's nothing you can do to stop it now."

"Dammit!" I claw my hands through my hair as frustration kicks the shit out of my insides. I hate that Brett is right, but he is. There's no point going after her. All it will do is give that dickhead further ammunition. If he was interested in her before, I've just made this an exciting challenge. God, I'm such an idiot.

Well, if he's up to the challenge, then so am I.

Bring. It. On.

Chapter Nine
Lana

"I didn't know you knew Kennedy?" Chase says once we reach his truck, opening the passenger door for me. I slide into the seat, buckling my seatbelt as I stall. I don't want to lie but I don't want to divulge the truth either. I like my anonymity on campus. Chase rounds the front of the truck and gets in his side. Sitting back, he looks at me expectantly.

"I used to know him when I was younger, but I haven't seen him in ages, and I didn't know he was attending UF until recently." There's no word of a lie in that statement.

Chase slowly turns the key, and the noisy engine rumbles to life. "I play football with his roomie, and we constantly butt heads. It appears Kennedy has taken a dislike to me because of it. We don't even know one another, and I'd hate for that to get in the way of our ... friendship." He gives me a cheeky grin as he maneuvers the truck out onto the road.

He must think I'm an idiot if he believes I'll fall for that load of baloney. If there's bad blood between them, there's a good reason. Kal doesn't judge people without due cause. Sitting here now feels so disloyal, and I'm regretting my decision to accept a ride with Chase and wishing I hadn't texted him my number last night. I'd been hesitant for a whole bunch of reasons, and I should have trusted my gut. I know I've hurt Kal again, but it's for the best. I have to get him to see there's no future for us.

Chase seems to be under the illusion I'm looking for more than friendship, even though I've previously attempted to set the record straight. "Look, Chase, you're a nice guy, and I'm grateful for the ride, but I'm not in the market for a boyfriend or a hook-up. I told you this last time. I barely even have time for friends, so it's probably not worth it, especially if it causes issues for you with Kal or his roomie."

"Kal?" His brows nudge up. "Ah, I see."

"It's not like that," I explain. "We were best friends as kids. That's all. Don't go reading anything else into it." All it would take is a quick Google search for Chase to figure out the connection between Kal and me, and then my cover will be well and truly blown. Call me selfish, but I like being able to walk around campus without insults being hurled at me every five seconds. It's another justifiable reason for staying away from Kal. If people see the two of us together, it won't take much to join the dots. I'm still receiving hate mail, even if it's dwindling. Some people have long memories.

"If you say so." He doesn't sound appeased.

"So, this coffee you mentioned." I give him my best smile, hoping to distract him from all thoughts of Kal. "I'm with the fam this weekend, but I have a free thirty minutes after classes end on Monday if you've time to meet up?" I have zero intention of meeting him, but he doesn't need to know that. I just need to steer him off the subject of Kal before he puts things together.

His answering smile is capacious. "Perfect." He pulls up alongside the curb in front of my building. "You sure you have to go home this weekend?"

"Yeah." I open the truck door, hoping he'll get the hint.

"Okay." He says the word in an exaggerated fashion, and I'm praying he lets it drop. Thankfully he does. "I'll text you about Monday."

"Cool." I smile at him as I jump down. "Thanks for the ride. Have a great weekend."

"Take care, pretty lady." He winks, and I keep the forced smile on my face.

Exhausted, I crawl into bed a short while later, nuzzling my pillow. I'm excited at going home tomorrow, like always, but that excitement is tinged in apprehension. I don't know what to do about Kal, and I keep veering back and forth over the right decision, pulled in two different directions.

One part of me says I've made my bed and should stick with the program. It's what my parents want. The other part of me—the one that's never wanted it to be like this—thinks it's time to follow my heart and do what I should have done all along.

No one will ever convince me that Kal is completely over my betrayal. I honestly don't see how he could be. He might think he is, but deep down, it must sting. I nearly had him locked up for flip's sake. That he still wants to speak to me is remarkable, let alone the fact he wants to start over. How I wish it were as simple as that. It is taking every scrap of willpower to resist throwing myself at him, and I'm not sure how much longer I can hold out. If he's serious about not backing down, it's only a matter of time before I cave. I'm enough of a pragmatist to accept that. I'm powerless to resist that boy's charms and know I can't ignore him forever.

How can I make him see I'm doing this for him?

I toss and turn, unable to fall asleep, so when Liv returns a couple of hours later, I'm still wide awake.

"You can turn the light on," I mumble as she stumbles about in the dark room. "I can't sleep."

Her bedside lamp flickers on. "I'm not surprised."

I hear the soft rustle of clothing and then the creak of wood as she climbs into bed. Unspoken words line the space between us, and I don't have to be psychic to know she has stuff she wants to say. "Just say it," I whisper, twisting my head around so I'm facing her. "I know you've got something on your mind."

She angles her body so she's facing me too. "I spoke with him after you left."

"Thought you might."

"I didn't want to, but he can be very persuasive."

"Tell me something I don't know."

"I gave him a hard time, and he took it. He said nothing is going on with that girl, and I believe him."

"Even if that's the truth, it doesn't matter."

"He's not giving up, Lana, and to be honest, I don't want him to."

I sit bolt upright. "What the hell, Liv? Whose side are you on?"

She swings her bare legs out of the bed, leaning her elbows on her knees. "Yours. Always yours. I wasn't there when all that stuff went down before, so I can't comment on how he was back then, but I know what I see now. He means what he says. He misses you like crazy, and he cares about you."

She eyeballs me. "Lana, most guys wouldn't ever speak to you again let alone forgive you. He has. That's huge in my book. I think you should meet him and listen to what he has to say. You two have so much history, isn't it worth at least hearing him out?"

"You don't understand, Liv. It will never just be a meeting. He has this invisible power over me, and if he turns on the charm, I don't trust myself to stay strong."

"Would it be so bad?"

I moan. "Liv, come on. You know why it would. I don't think he can handle this." That makes two of us. "I'll have to drop out." The thought has popped in my head on more than one occasion since Kal showed up.

"Don't go making any rash decisions. It won't come to that."

I rest my head in my hands. "I'm scared, Liv. I'm afraid to meet him. What if I mess up and give the game away?"

"You didn't hear the guy. He's smitten and heartbroken, and I'd chop off my left tit to have a guy talk about me the way he talked about you. I know you're worried, but you don't know how he'll react, and you'll never know if you don't at least listen to what he has to say. If you won't do it for yourself, do it for—"

"Enough. Okay, you win. I'll *think* about meeting him, but that's as much as I'm promising."

"It's a start," she says gleefully, sliding back into bed.

"Please don't tell me you're a new signed-up member of the Kalvin Kennedy fan club," I groan.

She chuckles. "The only fan club I'm a member of is the Lana Williams one."

My mood perks up the instant the bus glides into Earleton. I disembark at the usual stop and make the rest of the journey on foot. The balmy air is still humid despite the early hour, so I remove my denim jacket and stuff it in my back pack. The ground is dry underfoot as I make my way along the narrow road that winds toward the lakefront. The air is slightly cooler under the center of trees, and I turn my face up to the sky, ingesting the sights and sounds as I walk. The lyrical chirping of birds elevates my mood further. Every step takes me closer to Hewson, and there's a definite spring in my step now. I miss him so much when I'm at school, even if everything I'm doing is for him.

Arriving at the high wrought iron gate which leads to my grandparents' vast estate, I punch in the security code on the wall-mounted keypad and step back as the gate opens. I emit a little gasp of surprise when I spot Jerome—my grandparents' butler—waiting in a truck just inside the entrance. "There you are, Ms. Lana," he greets me from the open driver's side window. "Glorious morning."

"It is indeed."

"I was doing some early morning chores, and I thought you might like a ride up to the house."

I already have the passenger door open. "Thanks so much. That was thoughtful of you."

"Anytime, Ms. Lana. You know that."

The silence is comfortable as we maneuver the long driveway. Acres and acres of manicured lawns surround us on both sides as we head toward the house. The property is bordered by a high wall at the front, but at the rear, tall oak trees line the space between the house and the private dock which juts out onto the beautiful lake. Except for my grandparents and their fuddy-duddy beliefs and frosty attitude, this place is like a little slice of heaven on earth.

I can see how Mom grew up so sheltered.

The house comes into view, and the truck eases smoothly onto the redbrick stone path leading to the front entrance. Two massive palm trees reside over a magnificent fountain occupying center stage. My grandparents' house is quite traditional in style. Painted in white, it is a two-story house with six steps leading up to the mahogany-stained double doors. Three mammoth white columns buttress the porch giving a grandiose feel to the place. A massive wraparound terrace extends across the width of the house on both sides. With twelve bedrooms, fourteen bathrooms, six large reception areas, a library, two kitchens, and a fabulous pool and outdoor patio, it is a world away from the bungalow I grew up in. Not that the setting is all too unfamiliar. The Kennedy house in Wellesley was exquisite with every creature comfort known to man. I'm accustomed to being surrounded by wealth and excess.

I'm just not used to living in it.

Not that I'm complaining too much.

My grandparents took me, Mom, and Hewson in despite their misgivings.

I hop out of the truck, bounding up the steps as the front door slowly opens. Mom smiles at me, and the little boy in her arm gurgles happily. Every trace of anxiety lifts off my shoulders as I stare at him. Dropping my bag, I quickly close the distance, sweeping Hewson into my arms. "Hello, sweetheart." I press my lips to his forehead. "Mommy really missed you."

Chapter Ten
Kalvin

I've a mad case of déjà vu. I'm in the same diner as last week, at virtually the same time, with the same girl sitting across from me. I texted Shelby a couple hours ago asking her to meet me here. I'm not sure what last night was about, but I need to make things abundantly clear to her. Other girls are a red flag for Lana, and I'm fucked if I'm going to let Shelby ruin things for me. While I don't intend to confirm who Lana is—I'm guessing she wants to keep her real identity a secret—I need to convey how much she means to me so Shelby understands there's no prospect, whatsoever, of us hooking up or even hanging out ever again. I won't do anything to jeopardize my chances with the girl I love.

Shelby sips from her latte, eyeing me circumspectly over the rim of her cup. She's taken obvious care with her outfit and makeup, but it was a useless endeavor, completely wasted on me. "I knew you'd call." She beams at me. "I knew you would come to your senses."

I can't figure out if she's stupid or delusional or a bit of both.

"Shelby, I asked you here to set the record straight. I thought we were on the same page, but after last night, it seems some clarification is called for. I'm going to sound like a dick, and I don't mean to, but I have no interest in you. None whatsoever. I felt it best to put it out there so you don't waste any more of your time. Like you said, there are tons of guys only too happy to go out with you, so you shouldn't get hung up on me."

Her eyes blaze as a red flush creeps up over her neck. She's seething. "Wow. Your legendary ego is true."

"Shelby, what do you want from me?" I sigh, already tired of this conversation.

"We could be so good together, Kalvin. I know it. You know it."

Delusional it is.

"Everything was cool until that girl appeared on the scene. Who is she?"

"She's my ... best friend, and I came here for her. We lost touch, but I want to reconnect with her. Her friendship is important to me." I was going to admit she's *the* girl, but I don't think Shelby would appreciate that. Lana has had to deal with pettiness from other girls in the past over me, and I'm not subjecting her to it again.

A puzzled look appears on her face. "If she's only your friend, then why would she have any issue with us dating?"

I feel like banging my head against the wall. "I don't know how to put this any more clearly, Shelby. Irrespective of who Lana is or isn't to me, or how she would react, there is no future for us. I'm not interested in you." I stand up. "I'm trying to be a gentleman about it, but if you approach me again when we're out, I won't be nice. I don't want you to come anywhere near me or my friend. It's best if we make a clean break so we can move on."

She flips her middle finger up at me. "Unreal. If this is you trying to be a gentleman, I'd love to see your not-so-nice side," she snarls, slipping out of the booth. She gets all up in my face. "Message delivered. Loud and clear." She casts a derogatory glance over my cargo shorts, U2 shirt, and sneakers combo. "I'm too good for the likes of you anyway."

"Whatever you say, Shelby," I acquiesce, shrugging.

"You stay out of my way, and I'll stay out of yours," she says, as if it was her idea.

"Agreed." I toss some cash on the table, tipping my ball cap at her as I saunter out of the joint.

After spending a couple hours at the track, I head back to the dorm to Skype my brother and Faye. Lana dropped her name in the conversation last night, and I'd like to know why.

"Hey, asshole. What's up?" Faye says, sending me a teasing smirk through the screen.

"Did you know Lana was here?" I get straight to the reason for my call.

Her face contorts. "Eh ..." It's rare to see my cousin at a loss for words. She glances over her shoulder—at my brother, no doubt. Tucking strands of thick, brunette hair behind her ears, she drills me with a serious expression. "Yes. I knew Lana was going to UF."

"Why the fuck didn't you tell me?!" I demand, pacing the room with my cell in my hand. "And why didn't I know you two were in contact?"

"Because she asked me not to tell you."

"I'm your Goddamned cousin! And you knew I was hurting. I can't believe you kept this from me."

"What the hell was I supposed to do, Kal?" She leans into the screen, frustration blatant. "She asked to stay in contact with me on condition I didn't tell you. I thought you'd prefer that at least one of us was still in touch with her."

"What difference did it make when I didn't know?" I yell as all my pent-up frustration rises to the surface.

The screen goes fuzzy, and then I'm looking at my brother's angry face. "Don't you dare take this out on Faye. Lana put her in a very difficult position."

"Did you know, too?" My tone is unrelenting.

"Faye told me on the plane to Ireland," he admits.

"What the actual fuck?" I roar, throwing myself down on my bed. "I can't believe this. You both knew she was coming here, and neither one of you told me! Faye had her fucking number all this time while I've been searching all over campus for her!? I thought she wasn't here! That I'd lost her forever! I've been going insane. This is totally messed up."

Ky glances over his shoulder, speaking in a muffled voice to Faye. Then my cousin appears beside him. "Don't blame, Ky. He's been arguing with me since he found out. He wanted to tell you, but I wouldn't let him."

"Why not?" She opens her mouth to speak, but I interrupt her before she's uttered a word. "If you dare spout any of your usual crap about true love and destiny, I swear I'm going to jump on the next plane and personally wring your neck."

"You are way out of line, brother." Ky glares at me. "Keep this civil or I'm hanging up. This is not Faye's fault."

"Kal, just listen for a minute, will ya?" Faye pleads.

I send daggers at her.

"You never informed either of us of your plans to go to UF until it was a done deal, and you never mentioned this was about Lana. In fact, since the end of last year, you've been noticeably quiet whenever I broached the subject. You haven't been forthcoming either."

"Because it fucking hurt too much to even think about her!"

"I know, Kal, and I'm sorry I kept it from you, but I made a promise to Lana, and I didn't want to break it."

"Bro, Faye was trying to be a friend to Lana and a friend to you, and it was an impossible situation. I'm glad it's all out in the open now."

I snort. "Not that it helps."

"Why?" he asks.

"She doesn't want anything to do with me, and there's this douche sniffing around her. It's pretty hopeless."

"It's not," Faye insists, vehemently shaking her head. "We don't talk about you much. I think it's hard for her too, but she always asks how you are. *Always*. She still loves you, and that means all isn't lost. Besides, she hasn't mentioned any other dude to me."

"She's hardly likely to, though."

She vigorously shakes her head. "No. I only spoke to her last night, and she would've said something. *And* before you go off on another one, I was going to call and tell you. Promise."

"She's telling you the truth," my brother confirms. "We were going to call you tomorrow."

I nod. "It's okay." Some of my anger has faded. "I believe you, and I don't want to fight anymore. It goes against my nature."

Faye rolls her eyes, but some of the tension has left her face.

"Sorry for overreacting," I tell her.

"Nah, it's grand. You've every right to be mad at me. I've told Lana that I won't be keeping important stuff from you again. She understands."

"Cool." I gulp nervously. "So, you're a girl."

"Yep, last time I checked," Faye jokes, looking down at her chest.

My brother slips his hand under her shirt, and she shrieks, slapping his hand away. "She's most definitely a girl," he smirks. Faye elbows him hard in the ribs, and he falls off the side of the couch.

I laugh. "Any ideas on how I should play this? Brett thinks I should woo her. I already tried groveling and that got me nowhere."

She is quietly contemplative.

"Send her a few dick picks," Ky suggests, sitting back up, without a trace of humor on his face.

Faye shoves him again. "Oh my God. How did you ever get any girl to go out with you? That's the worst idea. You grew up with Lana, too. You should know that's not the way to win her over."

He smirks. "I know. Just wanted to wind him up."

"Asshole."

"Payback's great." He grins smugly. "Who's a pansy-ass now, Kal? Hmm?"

I wish I could reach into my phone and smack him. "Hardy, har. You're a great help."

"Knock it off, you two. I'd like to get off this call sometime this century," Faye chastises us.

My brother's expression turns serious. "Kal, are you sure about this? After last year—"

"I'm sure." I pause briefly. I'm not one for mushy sentiments, but neither was my brother until he fell in love. If anyone understands, it's Ky. "If you love someone, really love someone, you stand by them, even when they've screwed up. Especially then. You forgive them for their mistakes."

Ky nods slowly. "Yeah, I hear ya."

"Wow," Faye gushes. "That was pretty profound."

I shrug. "I love her. No one means more to me than Lana."

"Welcome to the pansy-ass club, bro," Ky says with a chuckle, and our grins match.

I look at Faye. "So, how should I go about this? Any ideas?"

"I think Brett is right. You should totally woo her, but be creative. Lana's a sweet girl, and she needs the right approach. You're a great guy, Kal, and you can be very charming and sweet when you aren't being a douche."

Wow, way to stroke a guy's ego.

"You also know Lana, and you have a shared history. Remind her of that." I nod as a slow smile graces my lips. I'm already conjuring up a couple ideas. "And don't forget the most important thing," she adds.

I stare at the screen.

"Don't stop fighting for her. When things are rough, don't give up. Show her she can count on you. That the faith she put in you was not misplaced. Prove to her that you are the guy she always believed you to be."

Lana's roommate Olivia confirmed she wasn't around this weekend; otherwise, I would've engineered some way of bumping into her. Instead, I spend the rest of the afternoon making wooing plans, and I'm in a fantastic mood when Brett returns, readily agreeing to accompany him to a party on the outskirts of the campus. Some guy from his microelectronics class lives there with a couple other guys.

The party's in full swing when we arrive shortly after ten.

I'm taking my time with my beer tonight, sipping it nice and slow as I chat with a few of the guys. It's a nice crowd, and the vibe is chill. Until Chase walks through the door.

Brett catches my attention from across the room, making a slicing gesture with his hand. As much as my fist begs to connect with his face, I stay over on my side of the room, conspicuously avoiding any potential confrontation. The last fight I got involved in ended up with me on house arrest and a fucking monitoring device strapped to my ankle. It's an experience I'm in no rush to repeat.

Every so often, I snatch a quick look at the douche. He sure loves the sound of his own voice. He's in the middle of a group of loud-mouths spouting shit for the benefit of the girls hanging around. My interest is piqued when I spot a tall girl sidling up to him. The blonde has thick pink stripes running through her hair, which reminds me of Faye's half-sister Whitney. She seems to have a similar sense of style too, if her short strapless tank and even shorter skirt are any indication of how she normally dresses. I don't understand girls who think that's attractive. Openly displaying the goodies takes away the allure. I prefer something to be left to the imagination. Memories of Lana in her hot red dress last night spring to mind, and all of my blood rushes to a certain part of my anatomy. Lana's grown into her skin, and it only adds to her appeal.

While I've been fantasizing about Lana, Blondie has wrapped her lips around Chase's, and they are indulging in a gross make-out session in the middle of the room. Tacky has nothing on that pair. Someone shouts "get a room," but they remain lip-locked. I watch in disgust as his hand wanders under her skirt, and he openly gropes her in front of his buddies.

His eyes flit open, and he spies me watching. I fix my gaze on him, keeping a neutral expression on my face. His eyes never waver from mine as he slides a second hand under her skirt, pulling her ass in firmly against his crotch. Bile floods my mouth at the thought of those hands going anywhere near Lana. Then he's lifting the girl up, and she wraps her legs around his waist as he walks them out of the living area and into the corridor leading to the bedrooms.

An hour later, I'm getting ready to call it a night when he resurfaces, shirtless and with the top button of his jeans undone. He swaggers to the refrigerator, snatching a couple of beers. I turn away, motioning to Brett that I'm calling it quits.

I sense him behind me before he opens his mouth. "Hope you got a good look, Kennedy, because the next girl in line for the Chase treatment is that pretty little thing you were salivating over last night."

Blood thunders through my veins, but I keep my voice calm as I turn sideways to face him. "In your dreams, douche. She's way out of your league."

Putting the beers down on the counter, he folds his arms and smirks. "Now, now, Kennedy, don't be a sore loser. Not my fault she prefers my company to yours. Give up while you still have some of your dignity."

"Do you even hear yourself? Grow up, dude, and get real. Lana will toss you to the curb any day now."

"I don't think so."

I'd love to wipe the smug grin off his face. "I know so."

He cocks his head to the side. "You seem very sure of yourself. Why is that, I wonder?"

He's fishing for info, and I'm not going to be the one to give it to him. "Any idiot can take one look at her and one look at you and figure it out for themselves."

His smirk extends as he leans in. "But that's the beauty of it, Kennedy. I'll have sweet, little virginal Lana eating out of my hand in no time."

"Over my fucking dead body," I growl, losing the last shred of my control. I shove my finger in his bare chest. "You will stay the fuck away from her."

He laughs again, as Brett materializes at my side. "Whatever this is, let it go," he urges Chase. "She's not your type and you know it."

"No can do, bro. I want that pussy. She'll be ripping her panties off and begging me to fuck her tight cunt before the week is out," Chase supplies. "You can count on it." He cracks his knuckles, shooting a smug grin my way.

My fists ball at my sides, and I'm seconds away from exploding.

He leans in. "I'm going to screw her senseless, every which way, repeatedly, until she's so fucked she can barely walk."

I lose it, throwing myself at him with my fists up and raised. Before I can punch the bonehead, I'm yanked back and flung aside. Stumbling, I lose my balance and fall to the carpeted floor. "Get out," Brett's friend tells Chase. "I told you the last time this shit isn't cool. Get out and stay out. You're not welcome here again."

Chase shrugs. Another guy tosses his shoes and shirt at him. "Screw you, asshole. Got what I came for anyway."

I'm scrambling to my feet when Chase pushes past. "Let's catch up next week, Kennedy. We can compare notes." He grabs his junk, snorting with laughter as he heads out the door.

"Dude, you have to get your shit together. That was too easy for him," Brett says.

"I don't remember you keeping your shit together at practice," I retort.

He sighs. "Why do you think I'm saying this? That guy has a fucking degree in pissing people off. It's not like I want to argue with him all the time, but he irritates the crap out of me and I blow up. You do realize you've just shown your hand? He's going to make getting Lana under him his life's mission now."

I curse under my breath. Brett's right. I've just set the gauntlet, and he's readily accepted the challenge.

Chapter Eleven
Lana

Sunday morning walks by the lake are one of the things I most look forward to each weekend. We've already attended church, and Hewson is napping in his stroller. Mom is contemplative at my side, her eyes fascinated with the dull sunlight glistening off the calm, clear water as we walk around the lake's perimeter. I fasten the hood over Hewson's head, making sure he's shaded. His thumb is in his mouth, and he's sleeping with his head to the side. His thick, dark hair is growing rapidly, and I may need to take a trip to the salon soon. I can't believe he'll be six months next month. In one way, it feels like only six weeks have passed, and in another, it's as if he's always been here.

"Mom?"

Her head snaps up, and she looks over at me. "Yes, sweetheart?"

"What's going to happen when the Kennedys find out about him?" I haven't told her Kal is at UF yet because I know she'll freak.

"They won't."

"We can't be naïve, Mom. They will find out sooner or later."

"I don't see how." Her eyes darken. "Have you told that girl? Have you told Faye?"

"No, Mom. I haven't." And that's the truth. Besides, Liv, I haven't told a soul about my son. Mom was insistent.

Her breathing returns to normal. "Then I don't think you have anything to worry about. We are well hidden here."

"I'll have to tell him at some point."

She stops walking, placing her hand on my elbow. "No." She shakes her head. "No. You can't tell him Lana. Not ever. We already agreed to this."

She calls it agreement.

I call it emotional blackmail.

And I always planned on coming clean once his life was back on track. Mom was never going to convince me otherwise, even if she thought she already had.

A twisty pain forms in my gut. "Mom, how can you say that? I can't deny him his child forever. It's wrong." I don't want to point the finger of blame at my parents, but they are the reason Kal doesn't know. When I discovered I was pregnant a few weeks after the trial concluded, I planned on telling my parents first and then Kal. However, Mom was adamant that I keep him in the dark. Back then, I didn't know what I know now, but I still can't fathom why she was so hypocritical. Mom said the press would hound me if they discovered I was having his child and they would forever paint me as a lying whore. She said Alexandra would whisk the child away from me, and I'd never see him again. Terrified and hormonal, and already sick to my stomach of the hate mail and death threats, I had agreed when they presented their plan to me. Horrific guilt got added to the maelstrom of emotions after my grandparents laid down terms, but by then it was too late to back out. All that mattered was ensuring I had a roof over Hewson's head and a way to care for him.

However, I've had plenty of time to think about everything since, and there is much to regret. This seems to be a familiar pattern in my life these days.

"Do you want to lose Hewson? Because that's what'll happen if Alexandra Kennedy finds out he is her grandson." There is little love lost between Mom and Kal's mom, although I don't quite understand what's driving it.

"Kal wouldn't let her do that, Mom." I speak with confidence. Kal is many things, but he wouldn't take my son away from me. I'd stake my life on it.

"Kal would have no say, child!" Her grip tightens on my arm. "He is too immature to raise a baby, and he would defer to his mother. Besides, you know what he's like, Lana. A baby would only curtail his lifestyle. He won't want anything to do with him."

I want to defend him. To tell her she's wrong, but I'm too afraid she might be right. I honestly have no idea how Kal would react to the news he's a father. *Would he embrace it or run for the hills?*

"Anyway," she continues, letting go of my arm and taking a step forward, "I thought you agreed it was best to let him live his life. You should never forget how you almost ruined him."

How could I? Self-loathing is my constant companion, my guilty conscience a daily reminder of my many failings. Plus, my grandmother reprimands me often enough.

My grandparents are very religious, and I haven't made a good first impression. They don't think highly of me, at all. Having a child out of wedlock, months shy of my eighteenth birthday, and refusing to reveal the father's identity didn't go down well. We are only living here because my mother made the ultimate sacrifice for me. For Hewson.

All-consuming guilt threatens to suffocate me, and I bite back any further protest, feeling ungrateful for even thinking these thoughts. "You're right. I'm sorry."

"Oh, Lana." She stops walking again, sighing softly. She cups my face. "I know how sensitive you are, and how difficult this is for you, but you've done the right thing. For all of you."

I don't understand how she can say that. Not when she was in almost the same situation as me, yet she made the opposite choice. "Mom? Can I ask you something?"

"Of course, sweetheart."

Hewson stirs in the stroller, and we start walking again. "Do you regret having me?"

"No, darling!" she rushes to reassure me. "Don't ever think that. You are the best thing I've done with my life." She pats my hand. "And your son is a blessing too. If I implied any less, I apologize. He's my grandson, and I love him very much."

Tears prick my eyes. "I know you do, Mom, and I'm so grateful for all you are doing for me, and for him." Mom walked away from my dad so that Hewson and I would have a place to call home. So that I could attend university and get a degree. She is his sole caregiver during the week, while I live on campus, and I wouldn't trust anyone else with him. We have undoubtedly grown closer since I became a mom myself, and I've welcomed that. Right now, she's one of the few I have in my corner. I can't afford to alienate her. It doesn't help me decide what to do about Kal, but, for now, I push that aside, determined to enjoy the last few hours with my son.

Hewson is lying on his back in his playpen, gurgling contentedly while we eat dinner at the table. On Sundays, my grandmother insists we eat in the formal dining room, and we are expected to dress accordingly. I'm wearing a skater-style black silk dress that has a high neck and cap sleeves and reaches just below my knees. Plain black ballet pumps adorn my feet. My hair is fixed in a neat bun, and I'm only wearing lip gloss and mascara.

It's important I toe the line. I can't forget they control the purse strings. One false move. One wrong comment, and they could cut me off. It's why I find it hard to relax whenever I'm here. I'm constantly on guard.

As a child, I couldn't understand why Mom had ceased contact with her parents. One hour in their company, and it all made perfect sense.

Still, I shouldn't complain. They took us in, and they made it possible for me to attend college, and I *am* grateful. They may not be the easiest people to get along with, but they didn't abandon us in our hour of need. Without them, we would have struggled to get by, and I certainly wouldn't be in college. My parents couldn't afford it, and I'd left it too late to apply for a scholarship. Living here may not be ideal, but it's preferable to the alternatives. Some single mothers aren't so lucky, and that's enough to eliminate any uncharitable thoughts.

"How is school, Lana?" my grandfather asks after the maid has cleared away our dessert dishes. Mom's dad is a nice man, but he doesn't have much say in things that go on around here. My grandmother is a control freak, and she has everyone bowing to her every command. She rules this house—and the people in it—with an iron fist. Mom says it's why she was such a successful businesswoman. Most outsiders think it was my grandfather's business brain that took their fledgling retail business from a friendly, local supermarket to a multi-million-dollar national chain of stores and a recognizable household brand, but my grandmother was the driving force in the business as much as she is in their personal lives. There's no denying she's a formidable force and a bully—albeit an impressive one.

"School is good, Grandfather. I've signed up for extra classes, I'm doing some volunteer work, and I've joined a yoga class with some friends."

"That sounds wonderful, my dear." He gives me an affectionate smile.

"I do hope you have the good sense to avoid getting involved with any other young men," my grandmother contributes.

"Of course, Grandmother." I smile through gritted teeth.

She takes a timid sip of her coffee before pinning me with a deadly look. "As much as that beautiful boy is an innocent, no man will want to raise another man's bastard."

"Mother!" Mom is aghast. "Was that really necessary?"

My hand is shaking as I raise the tea cup to my lips. I feel an overwhelming urge to slap her. How dare she!

"Do you dare to question me in my own home?" she replies,

leveling an icy expression at Mom. Her sly barbs are a constant reminder that we are at her mercy. For someone who claims to be pious, she sure has a nasty mean streak.

Mom knots her hands in her lap. "Of course not. I'm sorry, Mother."

"If you had done a better job of raising your own child, she wouldn't have found herself in the same situation as you."

Mom can't disguise the hurt on her face, and I'm indignant on her behalf. "Mom did a great job raising me." I eyeball my grandmother. "And it's unkind of you to imply otherwise. This is the twenty-first century. It's not that uncommon to have a baby as a single mother anymore." Take that and stick it.

"It's a mortal sin!" Her face contorts unpleasantly. "And children should never talk back to their elders."

"I'm not a child." Mom squeezes my hand in warning, but I'm not backing down. "I'm respecting your rules and your conditions, but I won't sit here and listen to you insult Mom when she's done nothing to deserve it."

My grandfather looks out the window, clearly wishing he was anywhere but here. Tension is ripe, and I hate that Hewson is surrounded by an ever-present layer of the stuff. That can't be good for him. At that precise moment, he lets out a rather loud wail that turns into a gutsy cry. It's time for his next bottle. I rise carefully, moving to the playpen and swooping him up into my arms. Cradling him to my chest, I plant a soft kiss on the top of his head. I close my eyes, inhaling his gorgeous baby smell, reminding myself of why I am doing this. I hold him closer to me, this tiny piece of Kal—a permanent reminder of the boy I love.

Tears slide down my cheeks as I press one last kiss to Hewson's cheek, tiptoeing from his room so as not to wake him. Sunday nights are my least favorite part of the weekend. Saying goodbye never gets any easier.

Mom drives me back to the campus, never once commenting on my melancholy mood. I rest my head on the window and close my eyes. Grief and pain battle with guilt and remorse inside me. Leaving Hewson behind every weekend carves a new scar on my heart. I hate that he is parentless all week. Yes, he has my mom, and she's an angel. She loves and cares for him exactly as I would, but it's not the same. I wonder if he'll grow up disconnected from me because I wasn't around for his formative years.

The fact I'm depriving Kal of that too doesn't sit right with me, but what choice do I have?

That's what I tell Liv when I return to the dorm and she asks if I've given any thought to Kal over the weekend.

"Just talk to the guy. You don't have to tell him about Hewson yet," she suggests, noting my glum expression, "but talk to him. Gauge if he's changed. Confirm his motives. Maybe spend a little bit of time with him, and after that, you can decide whether to tell him or not."

"You think I'm a monster for keeping this from him, don't you?"

"I know you had to make tough choices, and I can't imagine being in such a difficult position."

"I regret not telling him when I found out, but I was in such a state back then and my parents convinced me it was for the best. Now, I'm so confused." I pull my knees up under me on the bed. "One part of me thinks it's best to let him go on with his life so he's not missing out on anything, but another part of me says he's missing out on way more by not knowing his son. Then I think of what Mom said and I get scared."

"Courts are generally reluctant to remove a baby from his mother," she says. "And your family has plenty of money to fight the Kennedys if they took this to court."

"It's not my money, and I doubt my grandmother would support that. She won't want her name dragged through the mud. As much as

I want to believe Kal wouldn't do that, I can't emphatically say he wouldn't. I can't ever forget my betrayal, and this could be the final nail in the coffin. What if he thinks I'm the worst person to bring up his son?"

"I honestly doubt he'd think that, but deciding to tell him isn't without risk," she acknowledges.

I slump on my side. "My brain hurts."

"I wish I could offer better advice."

"I'm not sure anyone can advise me, and you're a great friend. Thank you."

She scoffs. "Stop. You'd do the same for me."

"I would."

"I know." She grins, yawning. "Sleep on it. Maybe the right decision will come to you overnight."

I laugh. If only it were that straightforward.

Predictably, I had the worst night's sleep, and I'm struggling to keep my eyes open during classes the next day. My notetaking is abysmal, and it's like everything is going in one ear and out the other. I haul my weary ass to the Reitz at lunchtime with my friends, and we head to our favorite restaurant for lunch. We're sipping on sodas and waiting for our food when the inquisition begins. I've been expecting it since Friday.

"So, you and Kalvin Kennedy, huh?" Maya asks, jiggling her eyebrows.

"I grew up near him, and we used to hang out a bit when we were kids." I hope I sound nonchalant because I need to kill this conversation superfast.

"And?" Brianna pries, straining across the table.

"And, what?" I shrug, feigning indifference. The girls are nice, and I don't think they'd judge me, but I can't risk telling them the truth. The more contained it is the better my chances are of keeping it on the down low.

She rolls her eyes to the ceiling. "I've seen nuns that are more forthcoming than you."

I take a big slurp from my drink.

"What Bree means to say is he's fucking hot and are you screwing him?"

My eyes startle. "You got *that* from Friday?"

"Girl, there was enough electricity between you two to start a fire. So, what's the deal? You fucking him or what?"

"No. I'm not having sex with him, and I have no plans to." A tingle down below makes a liar of me. My body is one hundred percent *not happy* with that statement.

The waitress appears, placing hot plates in front of us.

"Is that so?" Maya slathers a fry in ketchup, popping it in her mouth.

"*Yes.* So can we drop it now?"

"Not likely," Bree says with a toothy grin, and I groan.

I can scarcely keep my eyes open during the last class of the day, and I'm elated when it finally draws to a close. I'm going to skip the library and grab a nap instead before my shift in the center starts. I text Chase telling him I'm not available to meet for coffee now, ignoring his responding call when I see it flickering across my screen. I know if I answer he'll only talk me into it. My bed is calling to me, and it'll wait for no one.

"If you're not having sex with him," Bree says, as we step outside the building, "why is he waiting for you again?" She points across the road, and I jerk my head in that direction.

Kal is leaning against a shiny, silver truck, holding a paper cup and bag in one hand. He straightens up when he sees me, treating me to one of his panty-dropping smiles. He blows me a kiss, before nudging his head to the side in a "come hither" manner. I gulp, rooted to the spot, completely indecisive. Pushing off the truck, he saunters leisurely toward us, his gaze raking over me like a soft caress. My body tingles all over, and raw needs pulses in my core.

No one does intense like Kalvin Kennedy.

I've been on the receiving end of it before, and it's like being trapped in a laser beam.

As his eyes continue to devour me, I sway a little on my feet, a combination of exhaustion and potent longing. This isn't fair. I'd swear he cast a spell over me when I was a kid if I didn't believe that was outside the realm of possibility. He continues to stare at me, like no one else exists, and I'm feeling faint. I lean against Maya's side, clutching her arm to steady me. Kal's eyes twinkle knowingly, and I want to curse my pathetic ass self for being so damn weak.

"Ho. Lee. Shit," Maya exclaims. "He can eye fuck me like that any day. I think I just came in my panties."

As he closes the gap between us, I can't tear my gaze from him though I know I should. His eyes are brimming with naked emotion, and it does something weird to my insides.

"Oh crap," I murmur. "I am so screwed."

Chapter Twelve
Kalvin

Operation Honeybun has officially commenced, and if the look on Lana's face is any indication, I'd say I'm off to a winning start.

"Hey, beautiful," I say, when I'm finally standing in front of her. "These are for you." I hand over my offerings.

She stares at me, all glassy-eyed, and I smother my smug grin. "What ..." her voice is barely louder than a whisper. She clears her throat and blinks her eyes. "What is it?"

"Chamomile tea and a blueberry muffin."

Her startled eyes meet mine. "You remember?"

I momentarily frown. As if I could forget. "Of course." I dazzle her with another expansive smile, taking her hands and wrapping them around the cup and bag. Our fingers meet and fiery tingles shoot up and down my arms. She's always had that effect on me. "I remember everything about you, honeybun. The Imaga could zap my brain with their futuristic memory stick thingy and I'd still remember you. You're in here and no one can erase you." I tap the side of my head as her cheeks flush at the mention of her childhood fictional creation. I wonder if she held onto the drawings I did for that story. I had immense fun imagining warped little green aliens running riot on unsuspecting humans.

The tall good-looking blonde—the same one who was with Lana on Friday—nudges her sharply in the ribs, shooting her a calculating look. My hand thrusts out. "Hi, I'm Kal."

"Maya," she mutters, looking equally as dazed as Lana. Her handshake is firm.

"I'm Bree," the other girl confirms, gulping as her cheeks redden a smidgeon.

"Nice to meet you both. Would you mind if I borrowed Lana for a bit?"

"Oh no," Maya says. "We don't mind at all. You can *borrow* her for as long as you like."

Bree looks a little confused. "Is borrow a code word or something?"

"Oh em gee," Lana says, finding her voice. "Would you two knock it off." She sends an irritated look at her friends, before refocusing on me. "This is really sweet of you, thank you, but I'm heading back to my dorm, so there'll be no, um, *borrowing,* taking place."

A yawn escapes her mouth, and I notice the dark circles rimming her eyes and her wan skin. "You look tired. Are you okay? You're not sick, are you?"

"No," she says, stifling another yawn. "I didn't get much sleep the last couple of nights."

Carefully, I slip my arm over her shoulder, mentally cringing when she stiffens. "Let me give you a ride to your dorm. You look dead on your feet."

She ducks out from under my arm. "It's fine, Kal. I can get the bus." She starts walking away. "But thanks again for this," she calls over her shoulder.

Ignoring her friends, I run after her, planting myself directly in her path so she has no choice but to stop. "Would you please stop running off." It takes considerable effort not to show my frustration.

She looks at her feet, nibbling on her lower lip.

"Lana. Look at me." I fold my arms.

She lifts her head. "Why are you being so nice to me?" she asks softly.

I scratch the side of my head. "Because I care about you, and I want you back in my life. You're my best friend, Lana." My throat catches. "Can't we be friends again?" It's not what I want, but I figure I need to move slow. Ease her into this gently.

"I don't understand why you want to. I don't understand how you can forgive me."

And that, ladies and gentlemen, is the crux of the issue.

My arms drop to my sides. I peer into her eyes. "Look. Please can we go somewhere to talk? I know you're tired, and I won't keep you long, but we can't put this off indefinitely. We've left too much unsaid. Let's just talk about what happened and take it from there?" Indecision is written all over her face. I duck my head down so I'm more on her level, pouting as I give her my best puppy dog eye expression. "Please, honeybun. One coffee. One chat. And if you still want nothing to do with me, then I'll back off. Scout's honor." She knows I was never a scout, so I'm sure my lie is as transparent as the confusion on her face, but desperate times call for desperate measures.

She sighs. "Okay."

I mentally fist-pump the air, sending a shit-eating grin her way. You'd swear I just won the fucking lottery. Very carefully, I take a light hold of her elbow and steer her across the road, conscious of her friends' watchful attention.

She waves them off as I open the door and she climbs in.

I switch the A/C on as I kick the engine into gear. "That little place around the corner from your dorm okay?"

"Sure." Her lips press together, and she looks out the window, giving nothing away.

I scroll through my music, selecting her favorite U2 song. Her lips twitch as Bono's dulcet tones resonate through the cab.

I park in front of the small coffee place, running around the front of my truck to open the door for her. "Thanks." She offers me the barest of smiles. You'd swear I was leading her up the gangplank or something. Not for the first time, I kick myself for all the ways I've unintentionally hurt her.

We place our orders and take a small table at the back, near the window. Lana removes her sweater, placing it over the top of the chair. She clasps her hands together on the table, and I notice she's shaking. I lean forward in my seat. "Don't be nervous. It's only me."

"I still can't believe you're here," she says, as the waitress appears with our lattes.

"Believe it, babe. I'm not going anywhere."

She is pensive as she licks the froth off the top of her cup. "So, um, how are we going to do this?"

"Why don't I go first?" I suggest, putting my coffee down. She nods. "Just hear me out before you interrupt, okay? I've come a long way to say this." She nods again, gulping as she drums her fingers off the table. Fiery reddish undertones glisten in her long hair as she moves her head, and I long to reach over and weave my fingers through the strands.

When we were in elementary school, Greta used to style her hair every morning in the kitchen, and I developed a rather unhealthy fascination with it. I'd go into a trance each morning watching as Greta pulled the comb through her hair, scooping it up at the sides and pulling it back in a ponytail. That's the very first time I remember sporting a semi.

Lana is watching me closely, and her lips are parted in anticipation.

"Sorry. I was just remembering how your mom used to do your hair in our kitchen every morning before school. I used to zone out watching you."

Her eyes widen. "I never knew that."

"There's lots you don't know." Fact, friend.

Her answering smile is sad.

"Faye gave me your letter. I must've read it like a million times." I retrieve the creased envelope from my back pocket, placing it on the table between us. "It made me cry the first time I read it." Man, if any of my brothers were a fly on the wall, I'd never live that admission down. "I never meant to hurt you, Lana. I thought I was protecting you, but I know now that I went about everything all wrong. You have always been the only one for me, but I shouldn't have shut you out and refused to tell you what I was feeling."

A tear trickles out of the corner of her eye, but she swipes it away. "Last year, when I said those things, I meant them. I thought I was ready to commit to you, but I guess I wasn't fully on board with it if I could let Addison get her hooks in me like she did. It doesn't matter that I was drunk and pissed or that our relationship was in limbo. You've been there for me my whole life. You accepted all my shit, without question, and I let you down after you'd given me everything. I will never forgive myself for that."

"Don't. Please don't do that." Anguish is clear in her eyes, and more tears are threatening to breach the surface. "Don't blame your-self because this is so not your fault."

"That's not the way I see it," I answer truthfully. "I hurt you over and over. I knew you had feelings for me, and I deliberately refused to confront them or my own. I continued to play the field, even though I knew it upset you. I was a total ass, and my actions drove you to do it. I placed you in Addison's lair. I'm as guilty as she is."

"Oh my God," she cries, leaning over the table. There's a glint of anger in her gaze. "I can't believe you think that! You are so wrong! It doesn't matter that I was wounded. That didn't give me the right to say what I said, to do what I did. Nothing can excuse that, and if you think telling me you understand makes it all right, then you don't know me. I can't let you take the blame. I won't let you." She shakes her head adamantly.

Fuck it. I reach out and take her soft hands in mine. "We've both made mistakes, baby. Why can't we agree we were both wrong and put it behind us? Move forward instead?"

"It would never work, Kal."

"Why the hell not?" I demand, trying to keep a leash on my temper. Tears slide down her face, and fresh strips rip from my heart. I've always hated to see her cry. "Don't cry, honeybun. Please."

"You may think you've forgiven me, but you can't have. Not really. At some point, you'd start to resent me, and it would destroy us. I would rather hold onto whatever good memories I have than see everything turn to crap."

"I never took you for a coward, Lana." She attempts to snatch her hands back, but I hold on tighter. I'm not ready to let her go.

"I'm a realist, Kal."

"Answer me this. Do I truly own a piece of your heart, Lana? Is it still mine?"

"You already know the answer."

Her voice is cracked, and it chips away at my soul.

Out of the corner of my eye, I spot a couple of girls at another table whispering and looking over at us. One of them eyeballs me, glaring daggers. Ignoring them, I refocus on the fragile creature seated across from me. Lana can be stubborn as all hell when she wants to be, and she's not ready to let go of this yet. I can see I have my work cut out for me. "I need to hear you say it."

"Why torture yourself? Us?"

"Lana," I hiss, straining across the table. "Because I won't give up hope if you still love me. If you tell me you have no feelings for me anymore, then I'll leave you alone. I promise. But if you tell me you still care, then I'm not giving up on us. One of us has to fight." She opens her mouth to speak, but I hold up one finger. "I need the truth, Lana. You owe me that much." I can't make it easy for her to lie. If she honestly tells me she's over me, I *will* walk away. I'm not going to force her to feel something she no longer feels. It will kill me, but I'll do it.

She's full on crying now. A shadow darkens the table, and the girl from the other table looms over us. She plants a cautious hand on Lana's shoulder. "Are you okay?" Her tone is soft, but her expression is furious as she levels it in my direction. "Is he hassling you?"

"What?" Lana looks up at her, furiously swiping at the moisture under her eyes. "No, of course not!"

"Are you sure?" Her eyes penetrate Lana's. "He has history, and you don't have to be afraid."

"Oh my God." Lana yanks her hands from mine, clamping one over her mouth. She looks horrified.

"We are trying to have a private conversation," I say through gritted teeth.

"I'm making sure she's okay," the stranger snaps.

I soften my tone and my look. "And I'm glad there are girls who look out for other girls, but you don't have to worry about me, with her or anyone else."

She stares at me in disbelief.

"Thank you for checking, but I assure you I'm fine. We're ... old friends, and just reminiscing about stuff that makes me sad," Lana says. "Kal wouldn't hurt me or any other girl. I know what you're referring to, and he didn't do it. All charges were dropped because he's innocent."

Now the girl sends daggers at Lana. "That proves nothing," she scoffs. "No one will ever convince me he didn't do it." Her eyes narrow to slits as she glowers at me. Her hostile reaction may as well be a physical punch in the face.

Lana's jaw pulls taut as she stands up. "He didn't do it, and I should know because I'm the one who falsely accused him!"

Fuck! I can't believe she admitted that. There goes her cover on campus.

The girl rocks back on her heels, blinking profusely. "You! It was you!?"

Lana stands her ground, straightening her back and jutting her chin up. "Yes, it was me. I'm not proud of what I did, and I wish I hadn't done it. Kalvin Kennedy is innocent, and he doesn't deserve your hatred. If you want to do good, spread that around. If you need someone to hate, hate me. Now, if you'll excuse us, we *are* trying to have a private conversation."

"Bitch!" the girl snarls at Lana, and I jump out of my seat. Lana pierces me with a look straight from hell, and I quickly sit back down.

A deathly hush has settled over the room, as every single person is riveted on this conversation.

"You are entitled to your opinion, and believe me, I've thought worse things about myself," Lana calmly replies.

Her eyes scan the room, noticing the captive audience. She looks at me with pleading eyes. "Can we get out of here?" I nod, tossing some cash on the table. I take her hand and usher her out the door. All eyes are on us as we depart, and I'm guessing it won't take long before this gossip is shared across campus.

"Why did you do that?" I ask quietly when we are seated in the truck, twisting around so I'm facing her.

Her entire body is shaking, and I long to comfort her. "I cannot believe people still think you did it!" I shrug. It's old news to me. "Does that happen a lot?"

I shrug again. "Reactions vary." I don't want to elaborate. She's shouldering enough guilt as it is.

"That ... that's awful. God, I'm so sorry!" Deep lines furrow her brow. "I confessed publicly so you wouldn't have to endure speculation, but it was pointless, wasn't it? The damage was already done. That is why this can't happen." She gestures between us. "Don't you see?" Her voice cracks on a loud sob. "You are much better off without me. I'm doing this for you! I want what's best for you—and that's not me!" She shakes her head, and more tears spill. I reach out to her, but she jerks back. "Don't, Kal. Don't try and console me. That will only make me feel worse." Her eyes blaze with puissant emotion. "This is what I've been trying to tell you! I don't deserve your sympathy, your comfort, or your forgiveness. I sure as shit don't deserve your love. I have never been worthy of you, even less so now."

"Would you stop saying that!" I roar, losing control of my emotions. "Stop putting words in my mouth and thoughts in my head, and just listen to me." I force myself to draw a calming breath. "I. Forgive. You." I grip her chin, forcing her face to mine. "I love you, and I know you still love me. Fuck the rest of them. Fuck what they say about me. I don't care. All I care about—all I've ever cared about—is you."

She reaches up, cupping my face on one side. I lean into her hand, craving her touch as much as the cold Massachusetts air. "And I care about you," she says softly in between tears. "But you don't own a piece of my heart."

Boulders form in my stomach at her words, and something inherent dies inside me.

"You own the whole damn thing," she quietly admits, and it's amazing how quickly my sorrow transforms to euphoria.

I open my mouth to speak, but she moves her hand, placing the tips of her fingers against my lips. I savor the feel of her skin against my mouth. My tongue darts out, and I snatch a quick taste. She gasps, jerking her hand back. "There is nothing you can say that'll make this right. *I* messed everything up for us. *I* did this. Not you. I can't let you take the blame, and you don't have to do this. I've accepted my fate. I've come to terms with letting you go."

"Aagh!!" I sag over the steering wheel, consumed with pent-up frustration. This is like going around in fucking circles. My brain is starting to pain me. I whip my head around. "How many times do I have to say it? I forgive you! Why isn't that enough?"

Steely determination is etched across her face as she drills me with a serious look. "You have no idea how much I wish it was." She has the door open with one leg out on the sidewalk before I've taken my next breath. "But it isn't."

I throw my hands into the air, beyond exasperated. "Why, Goddammit? Why not?" What the hell is wrong with this picture?

"Because I can never forgive myself."

Chapter Thirteen
Lana

The nap was nonexistent after that encounter. I couldn't find the off switch for my brain, and I spent the hour before my shift in bed staring at the ceiling, attempting to evict all thoughts of Kal from my mind.

It was a fruitless exercise, though.

He claimed permanent residence in my heart and my head a long time ago.

The rape support center is relatively quiet tonight. Mondays are always the same without any scheduled group therapy sessions. I yawn as I type up the reports Brenda gave me an hour ago. Between being up half the night Saturday with Hewson teething and my erratic sleep last night, I haven't managed more than eight hours sleep in the past sixty hours. I'm running on coffee and adrenaline and fueled by a desperate need to occupy my headspace with anything besides the boy who refuses to go away.

Brenda steps into the office, placing her hand on my shoulder.

"Would you mind sitting with the client until Lucinda is ready for her?"

"Flight risk?" I guess, and she nods. Showing up here is a huge step for most of these girls, but some can't follow through, and they bail before they've even spoken to one of the center counselors. I can't contemplate how difficult it must be to deal with something so intimately traumatic.

While my tasks are usually confined to making coffee, typing up letters, reports, and various accounting sheets, sometimes Brenda asks me to sit with one of the girls to provide moral support.

The irony isn't lost on me.

Before I started volunteering here, I came completely clean about who I was and what I had done and why it was so important to me to work here. Since the attack, I haven't been able to get the victims out of my head, and I think I'd go crazy if I wasn't doing something to try to make amends.

"Hi." I smile at the girl cowering on the low couch outside Lucinda's office. "Would you mind if I sat with you?" She looks at me through terrified eyes. "Can I get you some water, tea, or coffee?"

"Water would be good." Her smile is fragile. Nodding, I head to the kitchen and grab her a bottle. When I return, I sit down beside her, handing over the water. We sit in silence. Most times, the girls just need the moral support. Sometimes, we chat about everything and anything *except* the reason for their visit.

"Have you worked here long?" she asks after a little while.

"A couple months. I'm a freshman at UF, and I only moved into the dorms at the end of August."

"I attend FIU in Miami, or at least I did until ..." Her lower lip wobbles, as she brings the bottle to her mouth.

"First time here?" I ask softly, and she nods. Silence surrounds us again.

"No one knows what to say," she blurts a few minutes later. I give her my undivided attention. "My family can't look me in the face, and my boyfriend is afraid to touch me." Her bottom lip trembles. "I thought the worst was over when I got away from … from *him*, but the nightmare was only starting."

Her body is quaking, and my heart aches for her. I take her hand firmly in mine. "I'm sorry it happened to you."

"I don't know if I can do this. I've already relived it a couple of times—when I had to give statements—and it gets harder every time."

"Lucinda is very easy to talk to, and there are no expectations. You can say as much or as little as you want to."

She tightens her grip on my hand. "Does it help?"

"I can't speak from personal experience, but I think so. I see a lot of the same girls show up every week, and they say the support is helping them get through it."

"I think my boyfriend's going to break up with me." Tears pool in her eyes. "We've been together six years, and I know he blames himself, but he can't always be there to protect me, you know?"

"It's hard for the people who love you to see you in pain." That I can attest to personally. Although, my loved ones' empathy was misplaced because I was a filthy little liar. I had no entitlement to their compassion. A new layer of revulsion washes over me, but I force it aside. This isn't about me.

Lucinda's door eases open, and the previous client leaves with her head down not looking at either of us. "Ms. Parker?" Lucinda smiles, beckoning her forward, and we both rise.

I squeeze her arm. "It was nice talking with you. I'll leave you in Lucinda's capable hands."

She clasps my hands tightly. "Thank you."

She is still on my mind, hours later, when I'm lying in bed, over-tired and unable to fall asleep. If she had only known who she was talking to, I doubt she would've been thanking me. Turning over, I bury my head in my pillow, praying for darkness to take me under.

Kal is waiting outside my dorm the next morning. He's lounging against the wall, dressed in figure-hugging dark jeans and a pure white shirt, looking sinfully good. His arms are more defined than I ever remember, his biceps bulging in a sculptured way under the short sleeves of his shirt. His broad shoulders and molded chest are totally drool-worthy and I'm sure my tongue is hanging out in a most unattractive fashion. Running a hand through his dark hair, he pushes off the wall and saunters toward me, whistling under his breath and grinning, as if he didn't have a care in the world.

"Morning, beautiful," he says, yawning, and I can't fight my smile.

"Still not a morning person, I see." I shouldn't tease him, but it's too easy to fall into comfortable patterns.

"Definitely not." He shudders, as if something nasty just crawled up his spine. "But I've had to condition myself. My fault for signing up for too many early morning classes."

"I can always use my tried and tested wake-up method." My lips fight a smirk.

"Oh, hell to the no. An impromptu shower in bed is not my idea of fun."

I nudge him in the ribs. "Aw, come on. You secretly loved it."

"Yeah, I secretly *loved* you jumping all over my bed pouring a pan of ice cold water over my head," he drawls, rolling his eyes.

"It worked though. Like a treat." I titter as the memories flood my mind. "Man, you are such a cranky pants in the morning."

"Hey." He nudges my hip. "Don't be mean. I'm not cranky now." His hand darts out, and he removes my book bag without invitation. "Ride with me?"

"Are you even going my way?" I suddenly realize I have no clue what major he's pursuing.

"Nope," he says, popping the P. "But I have plenty of time to drop you off at class first."

"How long are you going to do this?"

"As long as it takes." His expression is defiant and resolute. "I heard what you said last night, Lana, but I don't agree. It's not going to deter me. I came here for *you*, and I'm not giving up. You're too important to me."

I cross my arms over my chest. "Even if it's not what I want?"

He leans down slowly, pressing his delectable mouth to my ear. The familiar citrusy scent of his cologne swirls around me, and my knees turn weak. "You can protest as loudly as you like, but we both know the truth." His sexy voice, combined with his warm breath and his mesmerizing scent, fry my brain, and I can't even form a response. "You want this too." I sway slightly on my feet, and he chuckles, holding onto my elbow to steady me.

Clearing my throat, I step away, snapping out of it. "What am I going to do with you?" I wail.

He closes the gap between us again, peering into my face. His eyes bore into mine, and I get lost in his gaze. His breath trickles over my skin, ensnaring me in a mystical web of desire. Every part of my body craves his. My eyes flit to his mouth, and I bite my lip, my mouth watering deliciously. His eyes follow the movement, and his tongue darts out, licking his tempting lips. A little whimper escapes me. "I can think of plenty of things." He moves his face closer, until his mouth is only a hairsbreadth from mine. It would take nothing, literally nothing, to breach that tiny gap and kiss him. I'm terrified of how much I want to. I hold my breath and my body rigidly still, afraid to move a muscle. "None of them PG-rated," he whispers.

Oh dear Lord. Everything south of my belly is rejoicing at his insinuation, and a hot flush creeps up my chest and over my cheeks.

A myriad of emotions flitters across his face. His smile falters a little, and he moves back creating some space between us. I'm already mourning the loss, and it's that moment when I acknowledge I'm a lost cause. I've always been powerless to resist his charm, and, once again, he has sucked me in, almost effortlessly. "Please, let me take you to class?" There's a vulnerability in his tone that melts the remaining icicles in my heart, and I figure there isn't much point protesting any further, so I let him lead me around the corner to where his truck is parked.

"Have you declared a major yet?" I ask when we are both seated in the truck, desperate to stick to less-threatening topics.

"Yep. Architecture."

That doesn't surprise me. Kal always had an eye for good design, and he was constantly drawing when we were younger. Where most kids drew people or scenes, Kal sketched buildings. "Good for you." At least one of us is pursuing our ambitions. He shoots me a strange look as the truck glides out into the traffic. "You know I still have the drawing," I say.

"Our house?" he asks, instantly understanding. He'd been twelve when he created the vision of our future home, complete with a stylish library and workspace for me. He let me keep the drawing, and every so often, I take it out and cry. I'd been so sure when he'd designed it that we would be together in that house at some point in the future. Married and with children to fill all the space. It soon became abundantly clear that was a childish dream that would not come to fruition.

I nod, trying to mask my sadness.

"No way." He runs his fingers through his hair, smiling. "I'd like to see it sometime."

"That can be arranged."

An awkward silence settles over us.

He clears his throat a few minutes later. "Did Olivia mention I stopped by last night?"

I shake my head. "She was already asleep when I got back, and I didn't get a chance to talk to her before she left for the track this morning."

"She runs?"

"Yeah. Not seriously or anything, mainly to keep in shape."

"I haven't seen her at the track at all. Like ever."

I twist in my seat, staring at him in shock. "You go to the track?"

Slapping a ball cap down on his head, he chuckles. "You don't have to sound so surprised." I send him a knowing look, and he chuckles again. Kal is one of the laziest people on the planet. His idea of exercise is lifting the remote. He's lucky he's got good genes and a fast metabolism which allows him to eat like a horse and still look like he's stepped off the pages of GQ magazine. "I run a few times a week and do a couple sessions in the gym at the fitness center."

"Ah, that explains all the"— I stop before I embarrass myself—"eh, stuff you've got going on." I gesture flippantly at his body. Heat floods my cheeks. It's a feeble recovery but the best I can come up with in my current sleep-deprived state. My brain cells tend to take a hike when confronted by Kal's uber-hotness anyway.

"Someone's been checking me out." He winks, and his grin turns wolfish.

"Hard not to when you keep turning up everywhere."

"Told you I was going to be your shadow."

"Stalker, more like," I cough, and he laughs.

"See." He reaches out and squeezes my knee. "We can totally do the friends thing."

No, we totally can't.

And just like that, my good mood evaporates.

What am I doing?

A worried expression appears on his face. "Stop overthinking this, and, please, don't shut down on me. Let's just go with the flow and not think about any of the heavy stuff. Can you do that?"

I'm too tired to go over old ground, and I know how pigheaded he can be when he fixates on something. I shouldn't do this. It's risky and most likely headed for a major crash and burn, but I find myself nodding. I've missed him so much, and I'm tired of trying to keep away from him. Since I've discovered he was here, he has consumed my every free moment. Maybe it's time to throw caution to the wind and see how things pan out. I ignore that troubled inner voice whispering negative thoughts in my ear.

I want to spend time with him—I miss his company.

There, I've admitted it.

His answering grin almost blinds me.

Kal pulls up in front of the business school, and I can't believe the whole journey passed by in a blur. He puts the truck in neutral. "Now that wasn't so difficult, was it?" He gives me a saucy wink, and I roll my eyes, my fingers curling around the door handle. "Wait!"

He hands me a cup and paper bag, and my brows lift. "It's that yucky green smoothie you like, the one that looks like edible grass, and a chocolate doughnut."

"Are you trying to fatten me up?"

"Dammit! She's onto my evil plan," he quips. "I'm trying to fatten you up so all the assholes on campus leave you alone."

I roll my eyes again. "You're ridiculous."

"And you're as delusional as ever. You're gorgeous, Lana, and I'm not the only one who's noticed."

"If this is about Chase—"

My explanation is cut short by a primal growl.

"Dude, did you just growl? Like legit growl?"

He scrubs a hand over the light layer of stubble on his chin. "What can I say? That douche brings out the beast in me."

While I don't owe him any explanation, and we are only tentatively trying the whole friends thing I still feel bad for ditching with Chase on Friday. I don't want to intentionally hurt Kal ever again. "Nothing is going on with Chase. We're barely even friends."

"I know you think I've ulterior motives, but that guy is trouble. I know for a fact he has his sights set on you, and not in a good way."

"Now who's the delusional one?" I open the door, climb out, and walk around to his side.

Kal lowers his window, poking his head out. "Trust me on this. I know I've no right to ask anything of you, but just promise you'll be on your guard around him."

I sling my bag over my shoulder, taking a tiny sip of my smoothie. "You are worrying for nothing. I have minimal free time, so even if he wanted to hang out, it wouldn't happen."

He looks somewhat appeased. "Thanks for this," I say, shaking the paper bag under his nose. "I'd better go."

"Lana?" he calls out as I move to turn around.

"Yeah?" I stare into stark, brilliant blue eyes. Eyes that have always drawn me in. Eyes that know me inside and out.

Straining out the window, he twirls a lock of my hair between his thumb and forefinger. "Thank you for jumping to my defense last night."

"It's the least I can do."

He looks like he wants to argue but thinks better of it. "You know what that means?"

I sigh. "Yeah. My ID is blown." I'm not happy about that fact, but I still don't regret what I said. I couldn't stand by and let that girl unfairly berate Kal. "Don't worry about it. I've had to deal with worse."

He visibly stiffens. "What does that mean?"

I groan. *Why did I have to open my big mouth?* "I'll tell you another time."

"If anyone says or does anything, you need to call me." His tone brokers no argument. "You still have my number?" I nod. "Send me a text so I have your new one."

"'Kay." I slant him a wave as I start up the steps.

"Oh, and, Lana," he shouts, and my foot stalls. I spin around. "One more thing. I won't be happy until you forgive yourself, and that's my new goal in life." The truck's engine purrs to life as I gawp at him. "And you, of all people, know how much I love a good challenge." He blows me a kiss and winks. "Have a great day, honeybun." And then the truck is pulling away from the curb, leaving me there with my mouth hanging open.

I was wrong before.

I'm not just screwed.

I'm royally screwed with bells on.

Chapter Fourteen
Kalvin

"Dude," Brett mumbles in a sleep-laden tone early the next morning as I stagger around the room, trying to get dressed without waking him. "Not again!"

"Dude. This whole wooing shit was your idea." I squint in the dimly lit room, scouring the floor for my sneakers. "Fact, friend." I smirk as I toss his words back at him.

"Remind me to keep my mouth shut next time," he says, in between yawns. Brett and I are the perfect combo—both night owls and class-A jokesters—a match made in roommate heaven. I snicker to myself, thankful he doesn't have a direct line to my thoughts. I'm going soft in the head.

"Duly noted." I toe on my sneakers, grab my wash bag, ball cap, and keys, and head for the door. "Catch you later, bro." A loud rumbling sound rips from his mouth, and I quietly chuckle as I tiptoe out of our room.

After a quick trip to the bathroom, I hop in my truck and make it to the coffee place before the crowd descends.

I'm sitting on the low wall across the road from Lana's dorm fifteen minutes later, sipping on an espresso as I wait for her to make an appearance. For the first time in a long time, I feel unburdened. Yes, we've got a shit ton of crap to wade through, but things are heading in the right direction. Nothing or no one could deflate my good mood today.

My heart soars when Lana appears in the doorway. My eyes roam her body, an intense longing grips me on all sides. She's wearing tight skinny jeans that mold to her perfect legs like they were spray painted on. A loose, sheer off-the-shoulder light-pink sweater covers a white tank. Pink and white Converse adorn her feet. Her long hair is still damp from her shower, cascading in soft waves down her back. Without even trying, she is one of the prettiest girls I've ever seen. Her head darts around, and I smile as she clearly looks around for me.

"Yo! Beautiful!" I holler, claiming her attention.

She bounds down the steps and walks toward me, smiling, looking happy and carefree, and I wish I could freeze frame this moment. Capture it for all eternity.

"Hey." She drops down beside me, dumping her bag at her feet. "What you got for me today?" She gestures toward the paper bag resting on the wall beside me.

"Who says it's for you?" I tease, wiggling my brows.

She nudges my shoulder. "I know it's for me, hand it over." She holds her palm out. "I missed dinner last night, and I'm ravenous."

I hand the bag and the cup to her, with a frown. "You need to eat, Lana," I chastise, raking a line over her slim body. "You've lost too much weight as it is." It hasn't escaped my notice.

She takes a massive bite of the muffin, closing her eyes and moaning, and it's like a shot of liquid lust straight to my cock. I squirm a little, discreetly adjusting my jeans so she doesn't notice the boner I'm currently cultivating.

"I stayed late in the library last night, and I was too tired to grab something on my way back," she admits in between mouthfuls. "It's not like I don't eat on purpose. Sometimes, I just forget."

"You should've called me. I would've picked something up for you."

"That's sweet, but you know I wouldn't do that."

"Why not?" I ask, tucking her hair behind her ears.

"Because I'm not your responsibility." She shrugs, finishing off the last of the muffin.

I wish I'd brought her something more substantial. "I'm taking you to lunch today."

"No can do." She stands up, brushing crumbs off her lap. "I already have plans."

If she says with Chase, I'm going to hit something.

"We have a standing girls lunch date every Wednesday. I'd never live it down if I bailed for lunch with a *boy*." She says the word like it's dirty.

I swoop down, grabbing her bag and slinging it over my shoulder. Without thought, I link my hand in hers and urge her forward. Her palm is soft and warm against mine, her touch flooding me with so many feels. Her eyes flit to our conjoined hands, but she makes no comment, allowing me to steer her toward my truck. "That's cool. Once you are eating."

When we reach the truck, I put her bag in the back and wait until we are en route to the business school before I broach my next subject. "You still like bowling, right?"

"Is the Pope Catholic?" she jokes.

I smirk. "Bet I beat your ass now."

"Not a chance," she smugly replies, leaning back in her seat and arching her arms over her head.

The motion causes her tits to strain against her thin sweater, and I can't draw my eyes away. I don't remember them being so voluptuous before. They're fucking magnificent, and visions of sucking on her hard nipples jump into my mind, tempting and distracting me. My cock throbs painfully in my jeans.

"Kal!" Lana screeches, and I swerve, the truck narrowly avoiding eating the sidewalk.

"Eh, sorry." I force my eyes on the road. Fuck!

She clears her throat a minute later. "What were you saying? About bowling?"

"Oh, yeah." I twist my cap around backward on my head, keeping my eyes firmly on the road. "A few of us are heading to the Reitz tonight for a game. I thought you might like to come?"

"That sounds like fun, but I volunteer at the center on Wednesday nights. Sorry."

"What time do you get off?"

"Usually about ten, but it depends. Sometimes it's later."

I park around the corner from her building. "We can still make it work." I twist around so I'm facing her, and it's like a punch to the gut. She's even more beautiful than I remember, and it's becoming so difficult not to touch her. My fingers twitch with intense longing, and my mouth waters at the sight of her lush, slightly parted lips. Memories of our hot make-out sessions in the cabin turn my semi into a full-on raging boner. I hope she doesn't notice. One false move could send her scurrying away. I need to gently coax her into this, but patience has never been one of my strong suits.

She coughs, recapturing my attention. "We can still make this work, how?" she prompts.

God, I'm acting like a total idiot. "I can collect you from work and take you back with me. We'll be there till at least eleven."

"You're sure?"

I frown. "Of course."

She chews on the corner of her nail, pulling her knees up to her chest. "What will your friends think? Do they know who I am?"

I reach out, removing her finger from her mouth. "Brett, my roomie, is the only one who knows, and he's cool." I'm slightly twisting the truth, but I also know Brett would never be hurtful to Lana even if he is slightly wary of her.

"Won't the others figure it out?" Worry lines furrow her brow.

"Overthinking, babe." I smooth her forehead with my thumb.

"And if anyone figures it out, who cares? If anyone dares say anything to you, I'll kick their ass."

"You shouldn't have to defend me."

She hangs her head, and I smother my groan of frustration. *Why can't she just get over this? If I can, why can't she?*

"Honeybun." I tilt her chin up. "We can't do this every time. We are friends, and friends support each other. What happened is in the past. We are moving forward, and you are not going to dwell on it. If other people have an issue with it, let them." I shrug. "All that matters is you and me. You're my best friend, Lana. You've *always* been my best friend. If we don't work to get our friendship back on track, then Addison and Courtney, and all the begrudgers, and people who want to see us fall, have won. They tried to destroy us, but we're stronger than that, right?"

Her eyes glisten with determination. "Yeah, you're right."

"I usually am," I smirk.

She swats my arm. "Good to see you haven't lost your cocky streak."

Well, dammit, she had to go and mention the war. My dick strains against my jeans. "I'm all kinds of cocky for you," I admit without stopping to apply a filter.

"Oh. My. God. You did not just say that." Her cheeks flush, and I throw back my head, laughing.

"Just keeping it real, babe."

Shaking her head, she gets out of the truck. "Thanks for the ride, Kal. I'll text you the center address later."

I love how my name sounds coming out of her mouth.

She rounds the front of the truck as I lower my window. Leaning against my door, she peers up at me. Her mouth opens and closes several times, and I wonder what's so hard to say. "Kal," she finally whispers. "I really have missed you. I felt like I lost a part of myself when I had to leave you behind."

Be still my beating heart. I place my hands over hers. "I know, sweetheart. I know."

Her eyes roam over my face, her chest rises and falls, and so much emotion radiates in her expression, and I *love* it.

I want to kiss the shit out of her right now.

"Are we really going to do this?" she whispers.

I can't help what I do next. Moving fast, I skim my mouth over hers, superfast, just one fleeting caress of our lips, but it's everything.

Everything.

"Yes," I whisper, as she gasps. "Now, get your cute butt in that building before you're late. I'll see you tonight."

I wander around all day with a smug grin on my face, buoyed with renewed hope.

It's the end of the day, and I'm currently parked in front of the business school waiting to drive her home when I see him.

Douchey McDouche.

Lounging against the wall outside, he's eye fucking every female that vacates the building. My fists strain white with the effort involved in not beating his sleazy ass. I want to demand what the fuck he's doing, but I don't trust myself not to lose it.

Lana's eyes startle when she sees Chase approaching. She tightens the grip on her bag, shuffling on her feet as she stares up at him. He smiles seductively at her, and her shy smile gives rise to full-blown laughter as she cracks up at something he says.

I want to rip off my shirt, pummel my fists against my chest, and swing over there with a primal roar, marking my territory, but I can't. I have no claim on her, yet, and I can't afford to jeopardize things by acting all possessive and alpha male. Douche face would only get off on that. When he puts his hand on her hip, I bury my head in my hands, fighting the almost insurmountable urge to get out of my truck, race over there, and thrust my fist in his face. Man, that image is so tempting.

The thought of his hands anywhere on her body—hell, the

thought of *any* guy putting his hands on her—sends me into a murderous rage. I'm a fucking hypocrite, I know, but I can't bear to think of any other guy being with her like that. Although, I'm not naïve. Lana's gorgeous, and she's had her fair share of admirers over the years. We've been apart for over a year. I can't ignore the fact she may have been with others since she was with me. Stabbing pain splinters my heart all over.

I don't want her with any other guy.

She belongs with me.

I love that I was her first—the first boy to kiss her and the first boy to make love to her—but I'm terrified that I won't be her last.

Lana is smiling up at Chase, gesturing animatedly with her hands, and a bitter taste floods my mouth. I start up my engine, gunning it out of there before I do something I regret. Something I can't come back from.

My palms are sweaty as I sit in my truck outside the center waiting for Lana later that night. It's not like me to be nervous, but I get this strange, fluttery sensation in my chest every time I'm around her lately. I bailed in the middle of a game to come get her, much to my teammates' disgust. Comments about being pussy-whipped were bandied about. I may have overused my middle finger a bit.

Lana is wearing the same jeans and sneakers she had on earlier, now combined with a figure-hugging strappy black tank top that is a little too low in the front. Usually, you wouldn't hear me complaining, but it's not the most suitable attire for bowling. If any of the guys even look sideways at her, I'll kill them stone dead. She has teamed the tank with a sparkly black cardigan that is open and flapping gently in the night breeze. Even in the dark, she lights up my world. Spotting my truck, she heads in my direction, pulling herself up into the passenger seat. "Hey."

"Hey yourself." She smiles at me, and I stare at her as if in a daze.

Floral scents waft through the air, tickling my senses. Lana always smells like summer and apple blossom.

"Ready to get your ass whooped?"

I snort. "Now who's being cocky?" I start the engine and ease out onto the road.

"I'm confident. There's a difference." She twists around so she's facing me, tapping a finger off her lip. "Remind me again how many times you've beaten me at bowling?"

I chuckle. "First time for everything, sweetheart. You haven't seen me play in a while."

"Ohh. It's like that I see." Her smile defrosts all the frozen parts of me. She leans toward me, deliberately talking in a low voice. "You're not the only one who enjoys a challenge." I glance quickly at her, and I think I stop breathing. "Eyes on the road, Kal. Let's not have a repeat of this morning."

I try to play it cool. "You caught that, huh?"

"Your tongue was hanging out, and you were panting like a dog in heat. Hard not to."

I snort, loving this more playful side of Lana. It reminds me of how good it was between us. When we were in the cabin, it was as if we were in our own little world. I saw a very different side to Lana then, as she, no doubt, did with me. She's the only girl I've fully let my guard down with, and I want that back. That closeness. That bond. I have to believe we can reclaim it.

"It's not my fault you're irresistible, and, if I didn't know better, I'd say those babies"—I wave my hand in the direction of her chest, carefully keeping my eyes on the road—"have been surgically enhanced."

She slaps my chest, and I jump.

"Shit, sorry," she exclaims when the truck swerves a little. "I won't mess around when you're driving."

"I don't mind."

"Well, I do." She settles back in her seat. "I'm not ready to depart this life yet."

"Is it true?" I ask, wanting to lighten the sudden inexplicable tension. "Did you have a boob job because I know they're bigger."

She fails to smother her giggle. "Yes, they are, and, no, I didn't."

"Well, hot damn." My jeans are straining again. I swear Lana has a unique talent when it comes to turning me on. "Is that like a thing?"

She splutters, laughing hard. "You are so ridiculous. They just grew over a couple of months and ... and they didn't go back down." Her expression turns grave, and I've no idea where her mind has gone.

"Well, me likie. Me likie a lot." I wink, wanting to wipe that serious look off her face. "Do you think you might show me some time?" Her eyes pop wide, and she splutters again. "Purely for scientific research purposes, you understand," I add, grinning wolfishly.

"Don't push it, Stinky."

My smile expands at the use of her nickname. "Oh, I want to push it, Lana. You have no idea how far I want to push it." I smirk, and the look I give her is suggestive in the extreme.

"Mind out of the gutter, dude." She feigns disgust, but I spot the sly curve of her lips as she turns her head.

Lana may want to appear oblivious—she's anything but.

Chapter Fifteen
Lana

"Hey, everyone, this is Lana," Kal says by way of introduction when we reach the end of the bowling alley where a bunch of guys and girls are congregated. All heads turn in my direction, and I offer up a shy group wave. Kal places his arm around my shoulders, steering me to the last lane. "What the fuck, guys?" He scowls at the scoreboard. "I was gone twenty minutes, tops, and you managed to throw the game?" He shakes his head. "Lame."

"Asshole," a good-looking guy with massive shoulders and a smirking face says, thumping Kal in the arm. His gaze flits to mine before returning to Kal. "Aren't you going to introduce me?"

"Lana, this is my roomie, Brett. Brett, Lana."

"A pleasure." Brett says, taking my hand and planting a soft kiss on the back of it.

"Likewise."

"Happy now?" Kal asks.

"Fact, friend," Brett says.

"It just so happens," Kal says, his gaze skipping around his friends before fixating on me, "that I've brought a secret weapon."

"Kal!" I hiss, digging him in the ribs, attempting to hide my embarrassment.

He ignores me.

Of course.

"Lana is an *epic* bowler. Made it to the Junior Gold Championships two years running."

"I came home empty-handed," I remind him.

He takes my wrist, rubbing his thumb against my sensitive flesh. "You were so close that last time."

I can still remember the buzz in the arena, and the adrenaline shooting through my veins. All Kal's brothers had traveled with us, and I remember how desperately I wanted to win, but it wasn't meant to be. "I know, it sucked."

"You're still the best bowler I know, babe." He smacks a loud kiss off my cheek before turning to his teammates. "We are going to whoop those pansy-asses!" he yells, and the group hoots and hollers in approval.

He shunts me forward so I can choose a ball. "You know I hate when you do that," I murmur in a low tone so no one else can hear us.

"Babe." He spins me around so I'm facing him. "And I'll tell you what I've told you a million times. You are unbelievably talented, and you shouldn't be shy about that. Put a bowling ball in your hands and you're on fire. Own it!"

I roll my eyes. "Great speech. Unoriginal, but great." I've heard it a thousand times, but no matter how many times Kal says it, I will never be *that* person—the one who brags, who shows off, who claims center stage. I like bowling. It's fun, but I'm fairly certain I'd feel that way even if I were shit at it.

Blocking everyone out, I position myself in front of the lane and align my shot, stepping forward a few paces and thrusting my arm out in a precise, skillful move. Our team cheers when I hit a strike.

I'm showered with compliments after my fourth strike in a row, and I'm starting to relax and enjoy myself. Most of the guys are on the football team, along with Brett. The girls with them are friendly, and we chat casually in between bowling. Kal hovers near me the whole time, and he hasn't stopped touching me. Either his fingers are linked with mine or his hand is on my lower back or he has me tucked into his side, but he finds some way of touching me, and I'm lapping it up.

I know he's spouting the friendship line, but this feels like more than that. I don't want to overanalyze it, and I'm trying to do as he suggests and not overthink things, but I can't help speculating. Over the years, I've spent plenty of time imagining what it would be like to date Kal, to feel the weight of his undivided attention, to be on the receiving end of his love. Now, I'm experiencing a teensy part of what that'd be like, and it's more than I ever imagined. I both hate and love the little burst of hope building inside me.

If this ends badly, it has the power to utterly destroy me.

Destroy us both.

And it's not just the two of us anymore.

Am I being selfish again?

I don't know.

Is it wrong to want this?

Because, oh, God, I do want this. I want him. I want him so badly.

"You're up, honeybun," Kal says, planting his hands on my shoulders and nudging me forward.

Brett's head whips around fast. "Back up there, dude. Did you just call her honeybun?"

Oh cripes. I mentally cringe.

Kal shrugs, unconcerned, and there's a twinkle in his eyes. "I did. You know we have history."

"And cheesy pet names, it seems," Brett drolls with a teasing smirk. "What do you call him?" His eyes brighten with interest.

I have my mouth open to respond when two things happen at once. Kal turns pleading eyes on me at the same time a female voice gasps, crying out, "Oh my God, you're *her!* You're the girl who accused him!"

It's as if all the air has been sucked out of the room and my lungs.

I knew this was coming, yet I'm totally unprepared.

A quiet hush descends over our group, and I'm conscious of the attention of every person. Kal pulls me back into his chest, his arms snaking around my waist. My heart is hammering, beating way too fast, looking for a way out, but I can't shy away from this. Before Kal can rush to my rescue, I clear my throat. "Yes. I'm that girl." I hold my head up and meet every pair of curious eyes. "I made a terrible mistake," I add, gulping over the lump in my throat. "One I will have to live with for the rest of my life."

The girl that made the comment steps directly in front of me, a look of utter contempt across her face. "You think that makes it okay?!" she yells.

"No. Of course, I don't."

Her lips curl into a snarl. "I despise girls like you."

"Hayley," Kal cuts in. "That's enough." The warning in his tone is clear.

"How the fuck can you stand there holding her? You're as bad as she is."

"This is none of your business." Kal grits the words out, and his body is tense behind me. I attempt to shuck out of his embrace, but his arms tighten around me.

"The hell it isn't!" She's shouting now, and a larger crowd has gathered around us. I want the ground to open up and swallow me. She jabs her finger in my chest. "What she did affected every rape victim!"

"That's a bit of a sweeping generalization, don't you think?" Kal's tone is laced with anger.

I curl my hand around his arm, urging him to shush. This is my battle, not his. "You think I don't know that?" I ask quietly. "I think about that every minute of every day. If I could take it all back, I would."

She harrumphs, planting her hands on her hips. "You seriously expect me to believe that?"

"It's the truth."

"As if anyone can believe a word that comes out of your mouth. Lying whore!"

I recoil at the familiar words, and festering wounds crack wide open inside me. My heart is galloping, slamming painfully against my ribcage. Every word out of her mouth is like a physical blow, each one more potent and hurtful than the last. My eyes graze the crowd. Some are as furious as this girl, glaring at me with hateful expressions. Others look away, refusing to meet my eyes. Brett and some of his teammates look apologetic.

Kal starts to turn me in his arms. "You don't have to listen to this. We're leaving."

The girl darts forward, and the next thing that registers is a stinging pain across my left cheek. Tears prick my eyes. "That's for my friend. She was raped and she was afraid to report it after what you did."

Kal is trembling as he pulls me around, inspecting my face with tenderness. It's completely at odds with the thunderous expression on his face. I swat his hands away. "Don't."

"You have no right to pin that on her!" he says to the girl. "Your friend is responsible for her own actions, not Lana, and if you ever touch her or speak to her like that again, I will lodge a formal complaint of assault with campus security."

"Kal." Brett steps forward.

"Don't, dude." He looks around at his friends. "What you think you know isn't the truth. I shouldn't have to explain myself but ..."

I don't stick around to listen to the rest of it. The urge to put as much distance between myself and this place is overwhelming. I turn around and run. As fast as my legs will carry me.

He calls after me, but I keep running, tears streaming down my face.

Chapter Sixteen
Kalvin

I've been driving around for hours, frantically searching for her. It's after one a.m., and I'm going out of my freaking mind. She hasn't returned to her dorm, and Olivia hasn't heard from her either. She isn't answering any of my calls or texts, and I'm sick with worry. Realizing it's pointless driving around aimlessly, I park in front of her building, hoping she'll return home at some stage. I'm giving it one hour, max, before I call campus security.

Minutes before two a.m., a lone figure rounds the bend, and I release the breath I'd been holding. I'm out of the truck, racing across the road, before I've even had time to register the action. "Lana!" I pull her into my arms, hugging the shit out of her. She's like a statue against me, and she's unnaturally quiet. Slowly, I ease back a little, tilting her head up so I can check she's okay. Under the dim glow from the lamppost, I detect red-rimmed swollen eyes and blotchy skin. She's been crying, and I hate that. "You scared me. I've been driving around for hours trying to find you."

"Sorry," she mumbles, looking at me as if she's looking through me.

"Don't cry, baby. I'm here now, and I've got you. You don't have to face this alone." I crush her against me, pressing a fierce kiss to the top of her head. My protective instincts are cranked to the max. This, right here, is exactly why it was worth taking a risk in coming to UF.

She shivers, and I tuck her against the side of my body, heralding her inside. She stalls just outside the elevator, twisting around to face me. "Kal? How do you deal with it? How do you remain so unaffected by the looks, the slurs, and the whispers?"

Gently, I cup her face. "It hasn't been that bad for me."

She looks down at her feet, and her shoulders hunch over in a defeated manner.

I don't hesitate to encase her in my arms. She rests her head on my chest and her arms grip my waist. I smooth one hand up and down her back, pressing a kiss to the top of her head. "Some people still think I'm guilty, but I don't care what random strangers think. I know the truth, and those close to me know the truth. That's all that matters to me."

"I wish I could see it like that."

"Hey." I press a kiss to her forehead. I can't stop touching her. "I grew up with all kinds of crap being spouted about my family in the press. I've had more experience dealing with the media, and I've learned to block it all out. Don't be too hard on yourself. Most people would struggle with the attention in your position."

"Can we ... could we talk? I mean, I know, it's late and—"

"Of course. Whatever you need."

She leads me by the hand to a communal living room in the basement. She flicks the switch by the door, and the room floods with light. A bunch of soft couches are arranged in a rectangular space in the room, and we gravitate toward one. Lana toes off her sneakers and curls onto the couch, pulling her knees in to her chest.

I sit alongside her, not crowding her but making it clear I'm not going anywhere.

"I'm sorry you had to endure that tonight," I admit. "I ... I didn't think it through." Winning Lana back was always going to be tough, but I never realized quite how many external obstacles stand in our way.

"It's not your fault. I was hopeful that people wouldn't find out about me here, but it was wishful thinking. I can't outrun my past. Even if I hadn't admitted who I was the other day in the café, people would've figured it out once they saw us together. I just wasn't prepared for it to happen tonight, and in such a public way." She lifts her head up. "I'm sorry if I embarrassed you in front of your friends."

"You know I don't give a monkey's ass about that! I came here for you, not them, and I'm the one who should be apologizing for putting you in that situation."

"Oh, God, don't, Kal." A tear trickles down her cheek. "I can't bear it when you do that."

Familiar frustration bubbles inside me. "I'm sick of this blame game, Lana, and I want it to stop. We've both done things we wish we could undo. I hurt you, you hurt me. It happened. Accept it, and move on. Please. For the love of God, please." My voice raises a notch, and I try to keep my temper under control, but it's fucking hard because I'm getting sick of this broken record.

"You cannot explain it away like that! This is not a tit for tat situation. What you did pales in comparison to my actions, and you know it!"

"This isn't a competition over who inflicted the worst pain! We both made mistakes, and if we want to move on, we have to accept that and agree to leave it in the past."

"I want to!" Tears are streaming down her face now. "I want to so much! But how can I leave it in the past when people won't let me?! When virtual strangers accost me, slinging obscenities and attacking me! Tell me, Kal, how can I ever move on or forgive myself when my failings are shoved in my face every day?"

A bitter taste fills my mouth. "That happens to you a lot?" She nods, and a sharp pain stabs me in the gut. "Tell me, please."

She takes a shuddering breath, resting her cheek on her knees as she talks in a hushed tone. "I was expecting a backlash after the trial, but I thought it would die off. The media made up whatever they wanted, reporting all kinds of crap about me."

I remember. After the first week, I stopped reading the garbage they published. Dad noticed how upset I was, and he dealt with it. I'm not sure what Dan—our family attorney— did, but he made it go away.

"Then my grandparents gave us shelter," she continues, "and it stopped once they couldn't get to me."

Or most likely because of whatever injunction Dan took out, but Lana doesn't need to know that.

She sits upright, leaning her back against the arm of the couch. "I was so stupid. I thought that'd be the end of it. I'd moved far away, and I naïvely thought no one would know who I was, but I underestimated how much the story gripped the nation. People recognized me. Called me a lying whore and other similar sentiments. Spat in my face in the street. This one lady even verbally abused Mom one day we were out shopping. Said it was her fault for not raising me with the right moral standards."

I shake my head sadly, disgusted and heartbroken that she's had to deal with such venom. "You said attacked, Lana. What did you mean by that?"

She wets her dry lips. "It was a couple weeks before Christmas. I was out by myself, picking up some gifts, when this girl confronted me in Wal-Mart." Her chest heaves up and down. "She grabbed my arm, explaining how the case she'd taken against her rapist had been thrown out of court two weeks after your case went to trial. They accused her of lying and destroyed her character to the point where the jury didn't believe she was legitimate. She said it was all my fault and now her rapist was free to torture other girls. When I said I was sorry, she slapped me, really hard." Her voice trembles. "Then she slapped me again, and she wouldn't stop, slapping me harder and harder each time. I tried to fight her off, but she was stronger than me, and she had a tight hold on my wrist. It only ended when the store security guard hauled her off me."

I take her hands, rubbing soothing circles on the back of her skin. "Fuck, Lana. That is awful. Please tell me you pressed charges against her?"

She looks at me like I'm stupid. "Of course, I didn't. No one would've taken it seriously. She was the victim, not me."

This girl is ripping my insides apart. My heart bleeds for her. No one is on her side, and I'm so unbelievably grateful that I followed my heart and came here. She may not be willing to accept it yet, but she needs me. And I'm not leaving her to deal with this shit on her own anymore. "I hate that you've had to deal with such prejudice." She opens her mouth to speak, but I stop her with a stern look. "Do not say what I think you're about to say. If you breathe one word about how you deserve it or it's a punishment, I will fucking lose it. Everyone makes mistakes, Lana, it's part of being human. How you deal with it is what matters. You owned up in front of the world, and that took courage. I know you did that for me."

I bring her hands to my mouth and press my lips to her skin. "All those people who cast stones have made mistakes. The only difference is theirs didn't play out in front of the media. Their mistakes didn't involve someone who was a public figure. If I was any other boy, the case wouldn't have gotten any publicity, and you would've been able to quietly retract your statement and deal with the consequences in private. Neither of us were afforded the luxury of privacy, and I hate that, but I'm not going to let it ruin you or me."

She sniffles, and I move fast, scooping her up and hauling her onto my lap. My arms go around her as she rests her head on my shoulder. "That woman had no right to lay that on you, and she certainly had no right to hit you. That shit is never acceptable, and you need to believe that because no one has the right to physically attack you. Never. No matter what."

"Will it ever get any easier? Do you think they'll ever forget?" Her warm breath lingers on my skin, heating me on contact.

I run my fingers through her hair. "They will. It will go away, and until then, we'll be strong enough to deal with it. You don't have to handle this on your own anymore. You have me."

She's so quiet I think she's fallen asleep. Then, she shifts, sighing deeply. "I wanted to die," she admits, lobbing a new chunk out of my heart. "I hated myself, and I was missing you so much, and some days I thought I couldn't go on living with the thought of never seeing you again. I was a mess. I know now I was depressed, but at the time, it seemed like I was stuck in a hell of my own making and that I had to accept my punishment. There were days I couldn't even get up out of bed. Days where I refused to eat. Where I locked myself away in my room and refused to talk to anyone. Only for ..."

She trails off, her body tensing underneath me.

"Only for what, baby?" I whisper, pressing a kiss to her temple. Silence engulfs us again, and I bite back my impatience. This can't be rushed. She needs to get stuff off her chest in her own time.

Sitting up straighter, she palms my face. "Kal." She gulps, and her entire body is shaking.

I run my hands up and down her arms. "Whatever it is, you can tell me. I'm here for you, and I'm not going anywhere."

"Promise?"

I press a kiss to her forehead. "I promise. I will never give you cause to doubt me ever again. I will never let you down. You're my person, Lana."

"I am?"

"You always have been."

She leans in and kisses my cheek. "You've always been my person, too, Kal."

I want to kiss the shit out of her right now, but I manage to restrain myself. The first time we kiss again is going to be special. This time, I'm going to do everything right by her, and I'm not going to fuck things up.

Her lower lip wobbles as she gazes into my eyes. Conflict is waging a visible battle across her features.

"I ... I ..." she says, and I suck in my breath in anticipation.

Chapter Seventeen
Lana

"**I** am such a coward," I wail, mid-yawn, to Olivia the following morning. "It was on the tip of my tongue. I was going to tell him about Hewson but I flaked." I bury my head in the pillow.

"The longer you leave it, the worse it'll be."

I sit up in the bed. "I know, but I'm terrified. We're reconnecting, and it feels so good. I'm scared that when I tell him this I'll lose him forever."

"You'll lose him if you don't tell him soon, and you've got to trust him. If he can forgive you for the rape accusation, he can forgive you for this. Explain it to him like you explained it to me, and once he's had time to process it, he'll understand."

"What if he doesn't?" I sit cross-legged, chewing on the ends of my hair. It's a disgusting habit from childhood.

"Then you'll adjust. You are stronger than you give yourself credit for."

"I think you're pursuing the wrong major," I tell her in all sincerity. "You should switch to psychology. You'd make an awesome psychologist. You always know the right things to say."

She snorts, and a bubble of laughter flies out of her mouth. "I don't know about that." Her expression turns serious. "I care about you, and I hate to see you worried is all."

"I am going to tell him," I say, with more confidence. "I just need to grow a pair and man up to it." I swing my legs out of bed, yawning again.

"I'll be here for you when you do." She gives me a quick hug before leaving. I'm glad I don't have an early morning class today. It was after three before I crawled into bed, and I'm exhausted.

Kal is waiting outside for me again. I shake my head, smiling as I cross the road to his truck. I climb inside and turn to face him as something occurs to me. "How do you know my schedule? And what about your own classes?"

"Good morning to you too, babe." Ignoring me, he leans in to kiss my cheek. A flurry of feather-soft tingles dance over my skin. My eyes flit to his scrumptious lips, and my mouth waters. My heart starts accelerating, and the urge to kiss him is almost too much to resist. The more I'm around him, the more he touches me, the more I want to move us out of the friend zone.

But I can't do that.

Not until he knows about his son.

The thought is sobering, and I scoot back in my seat, averting my eyes.

"Is everything okay?" he asks softly.

"Sure." I give him my best effort of a smile. "Good morning. Did you sleep well?"

"You know me." He shrugs as the truck kicks into gear. "I'm asleep the instant my head hits the pillow."

I've always envied him his ability to sleep at the drop of a hat. As someone prone to bouts of insomnia, I wish I could sleep anywhere, at any time, like him. "You didn't answer my question," I remind him.

"I *might* have acquired a copy of your schedule."

I groan, leaning my head back against the headrest as it all slots into place. "You got Keven to hack into the college server, didn't you?"

"Busted." He grins proudly, reaching over and lacing his fingers in mine. "Don't worry. He left no trace."

"Your brother is going to get himself into deep shit one of these days," I mutter, shaking my head.

"Nah, he's way too smart for that."

I stare idly out the window as an idea comes to me. "Do you have any plans tonight?"

"Nope. I'm all yours." He sends me a cheeky wink.

"Can you meet me at Lake Alice at five? Don't eat. I'll bring food."

"Is this a date?" He brings the truck to a standstill.

I lace my hands in my lap as I look up at him. His cerulean eyes glisten mischievously. "Do you want it to be?" My heart is thumping inside my chest.

His other hand threads in mine, and he tugs me forward until there is hardly any space between us. He stares at me through hooded lashes, and strands of his hair fall forward over his forehead. Electricity crackles in the air. My heart skips a beat when his gaze lands on my mouth. He leans in, and fireworks detonate inside my chest. My mouth feels dry as sandpaper. "More than anything," he whispers. I close my eyes as his seductive breath fans over my face. "Lana," he whispers again, and my eyes flit open.

His eyes have darkened, and the look he's giving me would melt panties and hearts the world over. "I want to kiss you so badly right now."

My gaze zones in on his tempting mouth, and I want to meld my lips and my body to his and only stop when I need to come up for air, but I can't let this happen. Not yet. Not until after I tell him tonight.

"I want that too, Kal," I whisper. He moves in for the kill, and I jerk back in the nick of time. "But we can't. Not until we talk some more. There is other stuff that needs to be said."

He groans, clawing his hands through his hair. "Just so you know, you're killing me. I'm, like, dying right now." His flair for the dramatic is showing. "You have no idea the things you do to me." His lustful gaze fixates on me again. "No idea the things I want to do to you."

I gulp, and he chuckles. His hand cups my cheek, and I lean into his touch. "Can I ask you something personal?" I cautiously nod. "You don't have to answer, and you can call me out for being a dick, but it's something that's driving me insane. I need to know."

"Shoot."

"Have you slept with anyone since me?"

"I haven't even kissed anyone since you."

He looks shell-shocked and happy. Then he's lifting me over the center console, and I'm in his lap. I spot several curious gazes as people walk past the truck. "That makes me unbelievably happy."

"Have you?" I whisper. I'm not sure I want to know. His answering scowl tells me everything. I look away.

"Baby." He tilts my chin up with his finger. "I hadn't kissed anyone in over a year until I got here. I didn't even look at another girl. None of them were you." That goes some way toward appeasing me. I urge him to continue with my eyes. "The first few weeks I was here, I scoured the campus looking for you. I had Kev search the student database for you, and when he told me you weren't registered, I got depressed. Brett took me out that night, and when this girl came on to me, I let her comfort me, because I felt so empty inside, and I just needed to feel *something*, anything. I slept with her, but it was only that one time, and I regretted it straightaway. She was a bit clingy after that, and we kissed a couple times, but that was it. I swear. I wasn't into it, and I would've ended it even if you hadn't been at the frat that night."

"You're talking about that blonde girl?"

"Yeah. Shelby, but you don't have to worry about her. I set her straight."

"And she's the only one you slept with all year?" I'm skeptical because that's not Kal's usual modus operandi.

"I swear it. After everything, after I lost you, I changed." He pauses, and I sense he wants to say more. "Look, let's talk more tonight." He glances out the window. "You need to get to class." He opens the door and slides out, holding me in his arms. Very gently, he places my feet on the ground and reaches in to retrieve my book bag. After depositing it on my shoulder, he hands me my takeout bag, and I smile. He pulls me into his arms, holding me tight, and I sigh, more content than I've felt in a long time. He kisses my cheek. "Have a good day, honeybun. I've got a late class today, so I can't give you a ride home, but I'll pick you up for our date. We'll travel to the lake together."

"Okay."

He pulls my free hand to his mouth, kissing it. "I miss you already."

His blue eyes twinkle with sincerity, and I practically melt into a puddle of goo by his feet. "I'll miss you too." I lean up, pecking his lips briefly, pulling back before he can latch on. "See you tonight."

Bree and Maya are waiting at the top of the steps for me, and they grill me relentlessly the whole way to the auditorium, only letting up when the professor calls the class to order. At lunch, I try my best to answer their myriad of questions, but it's difficult to define the status of my relationship with Kal. A horde of butterflies takes up residence in my chest, and I veer from heart-stopping excitement to stomach-churning anxiety as the day progresses. Tonight is all-important and never far from my mind.

I'm dismayed to find Chase waiting for me outside my last class of the day. I'd thought he would have read between the lines by now. I've consistently knocked him back, but he's either too stupid or too stubborn to grasp my lack of interest. He seems like a nice guy, but there are obvious issues between him and Kal, and while I don't want to string him along, I also don't want to do anything to upset Kal. I know where my priorities lie, so it's time to fix this.

"Hey, pretty lady," he greets me. "Can I give you a ride home?"

"No thank you, Chase." I peer earnestly into his face. "Can we talk for a minute?"

He crosses his arms over his chest. "You're blowing me off?"

"I can't hang out with you. It's nothing personal, but I'd like it if you could stop texting me and stop turning up like this."

His features harden. "This is because of Kennedy, isn't it?"

"Yes, and no," I truthfully reply.

He leans into my face, all serious like. "Do you know what he did? There's a reason plenty of girls on this campus are wary of him."

"What?" Crap like that makes me so mad.

"You don't know?"

Okay, he doesn't seem to know my true identity, and I'm not going to tell him, but I want to set the record straight. His animosity toward Kal makes sense now. "He didn't do anything, Chase. He was wrongly accused and released without charge."

"You can't be that naïve," he scoffs.

Now I'm getting irritated. "Don't be an ass. Kal is innocent, and you shouldn't be spreading malicious gossip about him—it's not right."

He barks out a laugh, and his face contorts unpleasantly. Tiny hairs lift on my arms, and, instinctively, I take a step back. "Or is it his money? Huh? He can do anything once he splashes the cash?" Anger ripples across his face.

"I don't have to explain myself to you. Please, leave me alone, Chase. I don't want to see you anymore."

He schools his features into an impressive neutral line, stepping back. "Your loss, Lana. See you around."

Yeah, not if I can help it.

He takes off and I release the breath I'd been holding.

Chapter Eighteen
Kalvin

I rap on Lana's door, shuffling anxiously on my feet. Wiping my hands down the front of my jeans, I give myself a mental pep talk. Even with my limited dating experience, I've never been this nervous. All day, I've been on a countdown for tonight.

The door swings open, and Lana stands before me looking like a freaking angel. She's wearing a pretty white sundress that stops just above the knees. A light blue cardigan covers her arms. Her hair is loose, tumbling down her back and her skin is radiant and glowing. Her welcoming smile is timid. "You look beautiful," I tell her, stepping into the room, and she blushes.

"So do you." A cocky retort hovers on my tongue, but I hold back. I'm determined to be a complete gent tonight.

"Hey, Kal." Olivia pops her head around Lana. "Nice to see you again."

"You too." I can't tear my eyes from Lana. I extend my hand. "Ready?"

"One sec." She moves to the bed, hefting a wicker basket up.

"Give that here." I take it from her before she can protest, lifting the lid and peeking in. My grin expands. "A picnic?"

"Yep. Just like old times." She smiles and this time it meets her eyes. "Let's get going before it turns dark."

"Have a good time, kids," Olivia drawls, her tone laden with sarcasm. "And don't miss curfew!"

"Funny," Lana says drolly, sticking her tongue out at her friend.

I keep a firm grip on her hand the whole way to my truck. Stowing the picnic basket in the back, I open her door, helping her into the passenger seat. She sits rather stiffly in her seat, with her hands knotted in her lap. "You nervous?" I ask, sliding into the driver side.

She nibbles on her lip. "A little."

"Me too." Her brows nudge up. "I haven't been on many dates."

"You haven't?" I hear the skepticism in her tone, and I fully understand where it's coming from.

The engine purrs to life, and I ease out onto the road. "Nope. I hooked up with girls at parties, but I rarely asked anyone out on a date. Most times it was only a one-time thing."

She is quietly mulling that over, and I let her. "How come?" she asks a few minutes later.

"Let's get to the lake and then I'll tell you." I have plenty of things I need to tell her tonight, and I won't rush it.

We arrive about twenty minutes later, quickly securing a secluded spot away from the edge of the lake. Alligators have been known to inhabit these waters, and I'm not taking any chances. I spread a blanket out on the ground, under the shade of a large tree. Lana starts unpacking the picnic basket while I kick off my sneakers and drop down beside her. Although the temps are definitely cooler at night, it's still warm enough to sit outside without the need for a jacket.

"No way!" I exclaim when I spot the honeybuns. "Where did you get those?"

"I found a bakery in Gainesville that makes them from scratch. They aren't quite as nice as Mom's, but they'll do."

I watch in awe as she unloads all our favorite picnic foods, and

I'm almost choking on the wedge of nostalgia in my throat. Memories surge to the forefront of my mind. "Remember that last summer in Nantucket, that time your mom packed a picnic for us for Surfside Beach?" The private strip of beach in front of my parent's vacation property is decent, but my brothers and I enjoyed cycling to Surfside Beach to mingle with the crowds. That day, Lana and I had managed to sneak out by ourselves and Greta had surprised us with a basket packed full of yummy goodness.

"I do." She smiles up at me. "That was the day my face got sunburned, and Mom threw a hissy fit when we got back."

I remember that day for an entirely different reason. "You got a flat and I had to put you on my handlebars, and we rode home the rest of the way like that."

"I remember. Fun times." Her smile is whimsical.

"I think we almost crashed a few times because I was too busy staring at your ass to concentrate."

Her eyes almost bug out of her head. "You were only thirteen!"

"Thirteen-year-olds still have eyes in their head, Lana. And I was horny as shit that summer," I freely admit. I smirk as her mouth hangs open. She looks incredulous. *Doesn't she understand my feelings for her at all?* "You were all I thought about that summer, Lana," I add quietly. "All I dreamed about."

She gulps, and there's a bit of an awkward pause. "I loved those summers," she admits a minute later, clearly avoiding acknowledging my declaration. Fine, we'll do this her way. "I was devastated when I was no longer invited."

"That was my fault." I take a sip of the sweet pink lemonade.

Her head tips up. "I always wondered. I assumed it was because your mom saw us kissing and she didn't like it." She takes a small bite of her salad.

Twisting around on my side, I lean on one elbow, supporting my head with my hand. She mirrors my position, placing her salad aside. "I know I should've explained, but I didn't know how to do that without hurting you."

"I was so confused. I thought I must've been a terrible kisser for you to kiss me like that and then never mention it again."

I gasp, genuinely horrified. "That's what you thought?" She nods. Reaching out with my free hand, I rub my thumb across her lush mouth. "Lana, that kiss was the most memorable kiss of my life." The look on her face tells me she doesn't believe me. "You remember how weird I was that trip?" She nods again. "That's because I was dying to kiss you the whole time, and I'd been trying to work up the courage to do it. To tell you I had all these feelings for you. I was a bit confused myself, but not about wanting to kiss you. I wanted to kiss you so much, but I was scared you didn't feel the same way. I didn't want to ruin our friendship."

"Really?"

I cup her face. "Yes, really. That last day, I kinda panicked, because we were going home and I still hadn't done it, so, before I lost my nerve, I just pushed my way into your room and kissed you. Man, I can still remember how amazing it was."

Her eyes turn dreamy, and she brings her fingers to her lips. "Me too," she whispers.

"I thought I was going to explode in my pants." Her face scrunches up in gentle laughter. "Oh, she laughs at my suffering," I tease. "I had the worst case of blue balls that entire vacation." She blushes again, and it's unbelievably cute. "I love that you were my first kiss."

Her jaw slackens. "I didn't know that."

"Well, you were, and it was the best first kiss ever. That's when I knew you were the girl for me."

"What?" she splutters, her eyelashes fluttering incessantly.

I lean in, grazing her cheek with mine, needing to have her close. "Mom knew it too, and she wasn't happy. She warned me to stay away from you. Told me she couldn't invite you to come away with us anymore."

"I figured as much," Lana says in a breathy tone.

I move my face back, peering directly into her eyes. "I was furious with her, but there wasn't anything I could say to change her mind. Besides, I was kinda freaked out by it. My feelings for you scared me. I was way too immature to deal with it, so I took the coward's way out. I didn't know how to tell you, and I didn't want to hurt you, but I see now that my silence was worse."

"I knew she didn't want you to be with me. I understood that perfectly well."

"Mom's a snob, you know that, but it was never anything personal. She likes you."

Lana's smile is sad. "In her eyes, I'm just not good enough for you. I can't say I disagree. All those years, I loved you, hoping you would love me back, but you were always out of my league. You were never going to love someone like me."

I roll my eyes. "Lana, how have you stayed so clueless all this time?" Her smile falters a little, and I inwardly curse myself for my insensitivity. It doesn't take a genius to work it out. "I'm sorry, I take that back. You see, I always thought you knew how I felt, that you understood my feelings for you." I sit up, crossing my legs, pulling her up with me until we're facing one another with our knees touching. My eyes eat her up. "Lana, it was always *you*. You were always the only one for me. All that other stuff I did was stuff I needed to get out of my system, or at least that's what I thought at the time. None of those girls ever mattered. Why do you think I never had a girlfriend? Barely dated? I had no interest because I was saving all that for you. I didn't want to declare myself until I knew I could commit to you exclusively. I thought you knew that, but I made a total mess of every-thing because I never leveled with you, and you deserved better. I toyed with your feelings, hurt you time and time again, and I'll always hate myself for that."

"I tried everything to get you to notice me, but you didn't seem interested. And I thought you were ashamed of me. That's why we always met in private. Why you never wanted me to come to any of the parties."

"Fucking hell." I want to punch and kick myself until I bleed.

"Nothing could be further from the truth. Firstly, I loved spending that time with you alone. When it was just you and me, I could be myself. You know stuff about me no one else knows. You were always so easy to talk to. I didn't want to share that with anyone else—I was selfish, and I wanted to keep you to myself, but I'll admit I also wanted to hide it from Mom. She must have suspected where I went every day, but she never mentioned it."

My fingers weave in and out of her hair as I talk, and her eyes open and close. "As for the parties, there were two reasons I didn't want you there." I hate to admit this, but there's been enough lies and untruths between us. If we have any shot of a future, we need to be brutally honest with one another. "I didn't want you to see me with other girls." I wince, hating myself when I see the same familiar hurt and disappointment flaring in her eyes. "And I didn't want other girls bullying you. I knew what they said about you behind your back. I knew how some of them used you to try and get to me, and I wanted to protect you from that."

"You couldn't protect me." She shakes her head sadly. "It never went away."

"What?" Every bone in my body locks up.

"Other girls took great enjoyment in telling me how they'd hooked up with you. Everyone knew I lived on the Kennedy estate, and it was obvious I cared about you. Some of the other girls were so cruel."

"Shit, Lana. I'm so sorry. I was a total ass, but those days are behind me. I promise. I'm going to prove that you're the one I love. That you're the only one I want. If you'll just give me another chance."

Her eyes are wet, and she's staring at me as if I've just told her I have proof that Tupac is alive and well and living in some Godforsaken town in Wyoming. "You love me?" Her voice wavers.

"I've always loved you, even if I didn't show it. I was an immature punk who couldn't keep it in his pants, but my heart always belonged to you."

"And now?" she whispers.

I pull her over into my lap. My arms lock tightly around her waist, and I get lost swimming in the depths of her intoxicating hazel eyes. That little amber fleck sparkles expectantly. Her entire body shakes against mine. "My heart still belongs to you. *I* belong to you. I love you, Lana, and I'm ready to give you the world if you still want that and me."

Chapter Nineteen
Lana

I have dreamed of this moment for years, and I'm choked with emotion at his heartfelt words and fearful of what I need to say next. Before I tell him about Hewson, I need to ensure he knows the totality of what's in my heart.

"Kal, I love you so much. There has never been anyone else for me. Whenever I imagined my future, it always revolved around you. I don't want or need the world. All I've ever wanted, ever needed, is you."

I palm his face, my heart brimming with love. "I can still remember the moment I knew I loved you. I was so young, but it didn't matter. I still knew." The images rebound in my mind, and I'm experiencing it as if it's the first time. "It was that same day—the day we went to Surfside by ourselves. We were in the water, racing to shore."

"I remember." He grins. "I kicked your ass."

He had won, not surprisingly. Even back then, his legs were twice the length of mine, and my determination was no match for his long, fluid strokes. I can still visualize him standing before me as I came out of the water, breathless and panting. It was a glorious day, the sun hot and heavy and the sand scorching underneath our feet. At the precise moment I looked up and locked eyes with Kal, the sun bathed him in a golden glow—illuminating his form like a full body halo, his skin glistening with beads of water, wet hair falling over his forehead, eyes shining and twinkling with amusement, and his grin wide.

I had stood there staring at him, rooted to the spot, unable to tear my eyes away. My heart pounded. Blood rushed through my veins. A surge of emotion so strong washed over me like a tsunami wiping everything in its path. Everything I knew before was gone in an instant. And I knew the truth.

I knew I loved him dangerously.

"Brave effort, but you'll never beat the champ, honeybun," he'd said, winking proudly.

"I stuck my tongue out," I tell him, returning to the present. "And you chased me, caught me quickly, scooping me up in your arms." My eyes skim his face, my fingers tracing soft lines across his cheeks, his strong jawline, his face the same yet not the same. "You held me so tight," I whisper, "and I never wanted you to let go." The feel of his damp skin underneath my hands and the brush of his body against mine is as vivid as if it was yesterday.

"I wanted to kiss you then," he whispers back, his fingers winding around my neck.

"Do you remember how we looked at each other?" He nods. "It was like time stood still. Like no one else existed in the world but us." Something passed between us in that moment, some unspoken, inexplicable connection, and I knew I'd never love any boy like I loved him. "I knew then that I loved you. That I'd never love anyone else but you."

"Lana." His voice is breathy, needy, as his hand fists in my hair and he draws me closer. His eyes darken with lust and pure unadulterated emotion, and he moves in for the kill.

"Wait!" I plant my hand on his chest. "There's something I need to tell you first."

"Don't say it," he whispers, pressing a soft kiss to one corner of my mouth. "Nothing else needs to be said. I love you. You love me. I don't want anything to take away from this moment." He presses a kiss to the other corner of my mouth, and my brain goes blank. He trails a line of hot, sweet kisses up and down my jaw, nibbling on my earlobe and licking the throbbing pulse at my neck.

My head falls back, and I'm losing control and all sense of right and wrong.

His hand slides from my waist to my hip, and he grips me firmly, his arousal pushing against my ass. A whimper flies out of my mouth as I rock against him, my own need throbbing almost painfully. His mouth brushes against mine, and that one touch unravels me. Seizing the back of my head, he closes the remaining distance between us, fusing our mouths. His kiss is surprisingly soft and tender, and his lips caress mine with infinite adoration. The kiss deepens, his mouth moving more demandingly against mine. He tugs my lower lip between his teeth, and I gasp into his mouth. His hand moves down my back, gripping my ass, hoisting me even closer as my legs straddle either side of him. His erection is thick and hard against my stomach, and my panties are soaked with need.

His tongue runs along the seam of my lips, requesting entry, and I open for him. He explores my mouth with growing intensity, and our tongues tangle wildly. His kisses brand my lips, leaving scorching-hot imprint marks. My skin is on fire, and I writhe against him as a surge of pent-up desire breaches the surface.

He breaks away, and we both pant, gasping for air. His eyes are heavy with desire, his lips swollen. "We have to stop," he pants. "Or I'll end up taking you right here." There isn't a single part of me that objects to that plan. He pecks my lips quickly. "I love kissing you so much."

"Ditto." I chuckle at my breathy voice.

He intertwines our hands as we attempt to get our breathing under control. "Spend the day with me tomorrow."

The corners shave off my happiness. "I can't. I have to go home."

"Again?"

All the warmth leaves my body at once as reality comes a calling. "I go home every weekend. I ..." My mouth turns dry, and I'm like a solid brick of ice in his embrace. I shudder all over.

Say it, Lana! Get this over and done with.

But I can't force the words out. I don't want anything to ruin this moment.

Kal wraps his arms around me more snugly. "It's okay. You don't need to explain, but can I book a date for the following Saturday, please?"

"Why?" I croak, struggling to breathe over my mounting panic.

"I hate that I missed your eighteenth birthday, so we're having a do over. I want an eighteenth birthday date."

My heart spikes in a new burst of happiness. "You don't have to do that. It wasn't a big deal." I didn't want any fuss. Mom took me out for dinner while my grandparents babysat Hewson. Dad sent me a gift voucher for my e-reader.

"Well, I happen to think it is. I was really depressed when the day rolled around because I wasn't with you." He tweaks my nose playfully. "I want to give you a day to remember, so, what do you say, are you in?"

I know Mom won't mind if I tell her I have to work an additional shift or I have an assignment to do. I shouldn't lie, but I want to spend the day with Kal.

I'm a selfish bitch. I know that, but it doesn't stop me from agreeing. "Okay, I'm in."

We finish the rest of our picnic reminiscing and chatting about more casual stuff. I'm on cloud nine when he drops me home, kissing me for an eternity outside my dorm. Ignoring the inner voice berating me for my cowardice, I fall asleep dreaming of Kal's lips, his beautiful words, and the way it felt being held by him.

Kal wants to drive me home on Saturday, but I manage to win that argument, thanks to the ungodly hour I need to leave. Still, I know I won't be able to deflect questions about my weekends, and why I need to go home, for very long.

I'll tell him after the date to celebrate my eighteenth, I promise myself.

Mom greets me at the door—like she always does—with Hewson snuggled against her chest. I rush to his side, holding my arms out for him, but he clings to Mom, refusing to even look up at me.

This has never happened before. Someone may as well have made mincemeat of my heart. Tears glide down my cheeks as I follow my mother into the house. She places Hewson in his playpen and turns around, enveloping me in her arms. "Don't cry, sweetheart. He's just going through a phase. It's his way of punishing you for not being here. Give him some time, and he'll come to you." She pats my arm, wiping away my tears. "It'll be fine."

Mom was right, and after a little bit, Hewson lets me pick him up. I spoil him rotten all day, and he's barely out of my arms.

That evening, I take my time getting him ready for bed. I fill the tub with the rubber ducks he loves and get in with him. We have great fun splashing about, and we only get out when the water starts to turn cold. After we're dressed in our pajamas, I hold him close to my heart while he drinks his bottle. I regale him with stories in a hushed voice while U2 plays quietly in the background. I tell him about Kal, and he falls asleep with my whispered words of his father in his ear.

On Sunday, I take him to the local playground, pushing him on the baby swing and holding him as he slides down the slide. In the afternoon, we take a dip in my grandparents' heated pool while Mom reads on a lounge chair, sneaking sly looks when she thinks I'm not watching. Her loving smile and my son's playful chuckles fill my heart with so much joy.

I stand by his crib for longer than usual Sunday night, staring at my beautiful baby boy, awash with conflicting emotions. His chest rises and falls as he sleeps with a contented smile on his face. His hair is growing longer and darker by the day, an exact match to his father's. I skim over his face, noting the strong jawline, broad nose, and golden skin. I imagine if I asked Alexandra for pictures of Kal as a baby that it would be like looking into a mirror. Apart from the little dimple in one cheek, all his features are a carbon copy of Kal's.

What is he going to think when he finds out?

It's not like he purposely chose to be a father at seventeen, so it's a lot to take on board. Then again, I've adjusted, and I can't imagine my life without Hewson. Even though I've sacrificed my dream of being a writer, and some days I'm dog tired and teary and ready to give in, I don't have any regrets. The love I feel in my heart for this little boy is indescribable. I would move heaven and earth to give him everything he needs. I want him to grow up happy and well cared for and to know he is loved so much. I may not have planned this, but there can be no greater gift than creating such a beautiful new life with the boy I love. I hope Hewson grows up to be the very best parts of both of us.

No, as I look at my precious miracle, sleeping soundly in his crib, I don't regret bringing him into this world—only shutting his dad out. Kal has already missed so much, and I won't blame him if he can't ever forgive me for that. Even if he hates me, even if he refuses to have anything more to do with me, I will always have this little piece of him by my side. Very softly, I trail my fingers across Hewson's little face. He stirs, and his lips curl into a smile. My heart swells with love. No child will ever be more loved by a mother.

I pray Kal feels the same way. Despite how he might feel about me once he hears the news, I hope he'll want to form a relationship with his son.

I want that for Hewson.

I want that for Kal.

Chapter Twenty
Lana

Leaving Hewson this time is the hardest of all, because I know I'm not going to see him until next Sunday. Guilt is chipping away at my defenses, and I'm tempted to text Kal and call the whole eighteenth makeover birthday date off; however, the instant I see him—waiting across the road from the bus stop for me, looking hotter than any mortal has a right to—all honorable intentions fly out the window.

I run to him, and he picks me up, swinging me around in his arms. His mouth crashes to mine with urgent need, and we devour one another, kissing each other frantically as if it's been two years instead of two days since we last kissed. "Baby, I missed you so much," he says when our lip lock ends, hugging me close to his chest. "Please stay the night with me? Brett is away at a game, and we have the place to ourselves. I just want to hold you and kiss you. I have no other expectation. I just can't be without you tonight."

"Okay." I send Olivia a quick text as Kal drives us to his dorm.

"I love what you've done with the place," I quip as we enter the messy space. A large U2 poster is hanging on the wall by his bed. Clothes litter the floor, and empty pizza boxes and cans are scattered across the table. Both beds are unmade. I shake my head. "Still a slob."

"I was going to clean up before you came, but then I figured there's no point. You already know all my bad habits, and you still love me." He grins smugly, flashing his perfectly straight perfectly white teeth. Flopping down on the bed, he pats the space beside him.

"No chance. I'm not getting into that bed until I've changed the sheets."

He rolls his eyes before burying his nose in the comforter. His nose wrinkles. "It doesn't smell that bad."

"And that's all the answer I need." I plant my hands on my hips. "Sheets, please?"

I change the bed, while Kal clears away the dirty clothes and the empty boxes. Then we get changed—sleep shorts and a tank for me and track shorts for Kal—and snuggle up in bed, watching a movie on his laptop. My head is resting on his bare chest, testing my willpower to the limit. Kal is all sharp angles, and defined muscles, and my hands start wandering without permission.

"Are you feeling me up?" I can hear the amusement in his voice.

No point denying it. Not when my fingers are currently exploring every dip and curve of his abs. "Yeah. Got a problem with it?"

He laughs lightly. "Hell no. Don't stop." His arm is firm around my waist, and, with his other hand, he plays with my hair. "Lana," he whispers.

"Yeah," I whisper back, looking up at him.

"I love you."

Tears well in my eyes. "I love you too."

I want this to be real. So, so much. I wish there was no other secret between us. No risk of this all falling apart. Not when it feels so exquisite. So perfect. So right. We're on borrowed time and I'm clinging to it like a drowning woman clinging to a life preserver.

"I hate that I'm still making you cry." He dabs at the moisture on my cheeks.

I reposition myself, running my hands up his impressive chest. "These are happy tears." In part. "I never thought you'd ever say those words to me."

He pulls my head to his. "Get used to it. I'm going to repeat them so much you'll be begging me to take them back." His smile is teasing before he pecks my lips.

"Never," I whisper against his mouth. "I will never tire of hearing you say that."

I lean in and kiss him, covering his mouth in short, teasing strokes. His hand grips the back of my head, and he pulls me on top of him, our bodies flush against one another. Angling my head, he kisses me passionately, his tongue dipping in and out of my mouth. My arms snake around his neck, and he maneuvers us so we're on our sides, our bodies pressed against one another. My leg curves up, wrapping around his thigh. He groans, grinding against me, and as his hard-on pushes against my core, I whimper, gripping his thigh more tightly. My hands move down, exploring his ripped chest and abs, and I revel in the way he flinches and quivers at my touch. His hands slide under my tank top, inching higher and higher until his fingers reach the edge of my bra. "Can I take this off?" he asks in a sultry voice.

I sit up, lifting my tank over my head and tossing it on the floor. I unclip my bra and fling it aside, never taking my eyes from his. He moans, licking his lips as he watches me. "Fuck!" He reaches out, and his fingers caress the tip of one nipple before he grabs my full breast in his hand, squeezing softly. "These are fucking magnificent." His other hand grips my other breast in the same manner. "Didn't want this one to feel left out," he jokes with a smirk. "Lie on your back." I oblige, and he crawls over me, peppering my face and neck with kisses before moving slowly down my body. He presses the softest kiss in the gap between my breasts, and the most embarrassing moan leaves my mouth. He chuckles as his tongue flicks out, tasting one nipple. My back arches off the bed as I make another embarrassing sound. "You are so responsive. I love it." His lips suction over my nipple, and he draws it deep into his mouth, sucking and grazing the tip, and the pulsing in my core is going haywire. He moves to my other breast, lavishing it with the same attention, as his lower body presses down gently against me.

I raise my hips, rocking against the bulge in his pants, squirming with need. He lifts his head from my chest, piercing me with a heady lust-filled gaze. "Can I make you come?"

"Please," I beg, squirming underneath him.

Bracing himself on his hands, he leans down and kisses me deeply. I wrap my legs around his waist, tugging him down on top of me, and he chuckles into my mouth. He takes his time moving down my body, kissing, nipping, and sucking as he goes. "Kal, please." I'm frantic with need.

His fingers reach the band of my shorts, and he slips his hand under, rubbing along my belly. Then he eases my shorts and panties down my body, pulling them off until I'm completely bare in front of him. Liquid lust radiates in his gaze as his eyes roam up and down my naked body. "Spread your legs," he commands, nudging my thighs apart.

His breath tickles my core as he kneels between my legs. I buck up when he slides one finger inside me. "Fuck, you're so wet." My core is aching, and I'm moving with the rhythm of his finger, needing urgent release. Then he adds a second finger, and I scream as he starts pumping more frantically before withdrawing and replacing his fingers with his mouth. I last about twenty seconds before an explosion detonates in my body, sending shards of blissful tremors ricocheting throughout every part of me. He stays with me, milking every last delicious tremor until my body stills.

My hair is a tangled mess across my face as he moves up beside me. His lips are swollen and glossy from me, but I don't care, yanking his mouth to mine and kissing him as if my life depends on it. "Oh my God, I needed that."

"I love making you come." He kisses my nose. "I intend to make it my life's mission to make you come every day."

"Oh, God," I moan, running my hands up and down his back.

"You can't say things like that to me." I push him down until he's flat on his back. "Stay." Kneeling before him, I grip the hem of his shorts and start tugging, but he takes hold of my wrists, stopping me.

"You don't have to do that."

I pierce him with a furious look. "Fuck off, Stinky. You just rocked my world, and I'm going to return the favor."

He locks his hands behind his head, smirking. "If you insist, honeybun."

I flip him the bird before whipping his shorts off. His erection springs up, and I lick my lips in anticipation. Wrapping my hand around his impressive length, I start stroking him slowly on purpose. His eyes roll back in his head as his body jerks underneath me. I tighten my grip, quickening my pace, and he moans out loud. Without warning, I lower my mouth onto him, taking him deep as I continue to grip him at the base. I graze my teeth along his length, and he shouts out. Sucking harder and faster, I bring him to release, suctioning on when he tries to free himself, swallowing every last drop.

I crawl up beside him, snuggling into his side. "Ho. Lee. Crap. Lana. I have no words."

"Ha!" I laugh. "I brought the mighty Kalvin Kennedy to his knees." Literally. I snicker.

"I've just amended my life's mission." He tips my chin up so our eyes meet. "It's my mission to make you come every day and for you to reciprocate."

"I think that can be arranged," I tease, deliberately ignoring that chanting, negative voice in my head.

After cleaning up and redressing, we turn off the lights and cuddle. "Night, babe," Kal whispers, ghosting a kiss across my cheek. "Love you."

"Love you, too. Goodnight, Stinky."

He is out for the count within seconds, snoring softly as he holds me secure in his arms. And even though my mood swings are veering between dangerous highs and abysmal lows, and my brain is churning with apprehension, I follow him a little while later.

The alarm on my cell phone wakes us both the next morning. We've changed positions during the night, and when I wake, Kal has his arms wrapped around me from behind and our legs are tangled together. "Ugh," Kal mumbles, "turn that noise off." He buries his head in my shoulder, and delicious tingles caress my body. "Go back to sleep," he murmurs.

"I can't." I run my hands up and down his strong arms. "I need to drop my bag at my dorm and pick up my stuff for today."

He tightens his arms around me like a vise-grip. "Not letting you go. Let's ditch and stay in bed all day."

Warmth suffuses me, and I lean into the outline of his erection against my lower back. My core starts a happy dance, and it takes enormous self-control to wrestle out of his hold. "I can't, Kal. I can't miss any classes."

He sighs, rolling onto his back and yawning, as he rubs the sleep from his eyes. He peers up at me. "Okay. I'll drive you."

I push him back down. "Don't be silly. I can make my own way there." I bend down and kiss him quickly. "I'll catch you later."

His hand darts out, grabbing hold of my elbow before I can get up. "Nuh-uh. I'm not letting my girl walk around campus this early by herself. I'm driving. No argument."

And my heart melts all over again.

After we stop off at my place and I change bags, I go with him to pick up coffee and doughnuts, and we eat them in his truck parked around the corner from the business school. "I've decided I'm going to tell my other friends who I am," I tell him in between bites of my chocolate doughnut.

"You sure?" He's leaning back against the door, with one knee crossed over the other.

I nod. "I don't want to risk them finding out from someone else. It's only a matter of time before everyone knows. I'd rather take control of it. I'm not going to let it derail me."

Leaning over the center console, he kisses me. "I won't let it either."

I lace my fingers in his. "I'm really glad you're here, Kal. Thank you for coming after me."

"I would go to the ends of the earth for you." He sweetly kisses the tips of my fingers.

We part ways then, agreeing to meet up at the end of the day. I practically float into the building and skip through my morning classes with a dreamy grin on my face.

At lunchtime, we head to one of the open areas around the back of our school to enjoy an al fresco lunch, stopping to pick up sandwiches and soda on the way. "I'm so glad I decided to come here," Bree says, tilting her face up and allowing the balmy air to coast over her skin. "I love the climate and the campus."

"You coming to the game Friday night?" Maya asks, balling up her sandwich paper and throwing it skillfully into the adjoining trash can.

"All hail the Gator Nation," Liv jokes, pumping her fist in the air.

I shrug noncommittally. I'm not a big sports fan, although you're almost a pariah around here if you don't support the Gators. "I'll check with Kal."

Maya nudges me in the ribs. "So, things are heating up between you and the stud?"

I wipe my clammy hands over the front of my jeans. It's now or never. "I guess so." I gulp as Liv shoots me a subtle, reassuring nod. I told her I planned to talk to them, and she agreed it was a good idea. "Actually, there's something I need to tell you both." My eyes flit between her and Brianna. They give me their undivided attention, and, before I lose my nerve, I launch into my story, explaining who I am and why I enrolled under a different name. I don't go into all the details, giving them enough so they have a good picture. I don't breathe a word about Hewson, for obvious reasons. As I speak, I watch their expressions alter. Neither of them interrupts me, giving me the full floor.

"And that's pretty much it," I finish up, feeling a little lighter.

"You knew?" Maya asks Liv in a clipped tone.

"I only found out recently."

"I understand why you did it." Bree reaches across the wooden picnic table, touching my arm. "And I can tell you're genuinely remorseful. Everyone makes mistakes. Everyone deserves a second chance."

I squeeze her hands. "Thanks, Bree. That means so much to me."

Maya snorts, a look of naked disgust on her face. "I call bullshit. You honestly expect us to believe you were manipulated by some bitch into accusing the guy you loved of rape, all because he hurt you?" Her voice raises a notch, and I hope no one else is tuning in to this conversation.

"That's what happened. It's pathetic, I know, but it's what went down."

"It's beyond pathetic," she snarls. "It's disgusting! It's immoral! It's wrong on so many levels! How can he forgive you for that? I would never speak to you again. In fact"—she rustles up the remnants of her lunch, shoving it in her bag and standing up—"I don't want to speak to you again." She glares at me. "You are not the sort of person I want to call a friend. Stay the hell away from me."

She storms off, leaving the three of us speechless.

Chapter Twenty-One
Kalvin

"What's wrong?" I ask the minute Lana appears in front of me. It's the end of the day, and I've been hanging out here the last fifteen minutes waiting for her to show.

"I'll tell you in the truck." The glum expression on her face concerns me. I attempt to tuck her into my side, but she shucks out of my reach.

"What's happened, babe?" I ask again once we are seated in my truck.

She glances out the window, her frown deepening. I follow the direction of her gaze, spotting her friend Maya glowering at her from across the street.

Oh shit. That conversation clearly didn't go well.

"Can you just get out of here, please," she beseeches, and I hate how her voice trembles.

My jaw clenches, but I say nothing, putting the truck into first and driving off.

I come to a complete stop outside the park, twisting around in my seat and taking her small hands in mine. "I gather your conversation didn't go too well?" I scrutinize her face.

"Bree was okay with it. She understood, but Maya ... Maya kinda flipped." She chews on the corner of her lip, averting her gaze.

"Screw her." I gently grip her chin, turning her face to mine. "She's not a real friend if she can turn on you so quickly. She has no right to judge you."

Her beautiful eyes are vulnerable, and she looks so upset. I want to rage at the world for dealing her such a shitty break. *Can't they see how sorry she is? How she's trying to make amends? Hasn't she paid enough of a price?* A searing need to run away with her, to protect her and keep her safe, is riding me hard.

I open my mouth to speak, but she cuts me off with a look. "I know you mean well, but I don't want to talk about it anymore. I need to get ready for my shift." She pulls her hands away from me, and it feels like we've just taken ten steps back.

"Lana, please. Don't let her do this to you."

"Take me home, Kal. Please."

She's retreated into her shell, and I know if I continue to plead she'll only dig her heels in further. It's like that time she discovered I kissed Jan Matthews at a party. Lana asked me about it on the Monday after the party, and I told her it was meaningless, but she went all kinds of quiet. When I pressed her for details, she clammed up, ignored me for a solid *two weeks*, and wouldn't tell me jack shit about what was going on. When I discovered that Jan was one of a group of girls bullying Lana at school, I was sick to my stomach.

Even thinking about it now turns my insides. I hate that I did that to Lana. I am never going to stop trying to make up for it.

I got my revenge on Jan at the next party—rejecting her very vocally and publicly—before pulling her aside and telling her if she ever threatened Lana again I would ask my buddy, Cole, to share the naked photos she'd texted him all over school. She never came near me or Lana again.

But it took Lana ages to thaw out, to forget what I'd done.

I hate the thought we might be back in that space.

Sighing, I power up the engine and drive to her dorm.

The rest of the week follows a similar pattern. Lana is subdued and closed off, and I'm at a loss what to do. I continue to show up, driving her to and from her dorm each day, picking her up from the center, and she spends time with me on her free nights, but she may as well be a ghost.

We kiss.

We cuddle.

A lot.

And it seems like the only time she's able to let go of whatever's troubling her.

Friday night, I convince her to come to the Swamp to watch the Gators game with Riley and Olivia and a couple of the guys as a show of support for Brett. While he doesn't start, and I'm not that big of a football fan, I like to attend some of the games so he knows I'm here for him.

After, we hit a party outside campus with the football team. Lana is a little more animated, and I'm hoping she'll be in better form for our birthday date. "So, where are you taking me tomorrow?" she asks, sipping on the same beer she's had since we arrived.

I plant my mouth against hers in one brief, sweeping gesture. "That's classified. If I told you, I'd have to kill you."

She rolls her eyes. "Could you be any more cliché?

"Says the writer," I tease.

"Not anymore."

"You're not writing?" As long as I've known Lana, she's always writing some story. It's as natural to her as breathing.

She casually shrugs. "Well, I do have one project, but I hardly ever get to work on it."

"What's it about?" I swig from my bottle.

She ponders this a minute, and I wonder if she's going to shut down again. Lana has never had any trouble confiding in me about her ideas. Hell, we discussed plot lines and character development so much in the past I could demand co-writing credit, and she'd be hard pushed to deny me. She knows I love discussing her work.

"It's kinda semi-autobiographical," she admits a minute later.

"What's the title?" I know there is one because it's always the first thing she considers when an idea has popped into her head. She has an uncanny ability to nail it even before she's started writing the damn thing.

She hesitates again before responding in that soft-spoken tone of hers. *"The Story of Us."*

I almost choke on my beer. Brett approaches, slapping me on the back. "They have words for dudes who can't handle their beer." He pretends to whisper. "Pussy!"

"Takes one to know one, asshole."

"How's my girl?" Brett asks, sliding an arm around Lana's shoulders, surprising her and me.

"I'm good." She smiles up at him, but only I can tell she's lying. She's wound as tight as a ball of yarn.

"Hi, Kalvin." The voice comes from behind me, but I'd know Shelby's faux sultry tone anywhere. I inwardly groan. After our last convo, most girls would run a mile before accosting me. That girl has skin as thick as a rhino's hide.

Lana's smile fades, and her body goes rigidly still. Pulling her out from under Brett's arm, I tuck her possessively into my side and turn us around to face my most recent mistake. "Hi, Shelby. Have you met my girlfriend, Lana?"

Brett grunts out a laugh. Lana is like a frigging statue in my arms. I smooth my hand up and down her back, urging her to chill the fuck out.

"No." Shelby fakes a smile. "Nice to meet you." Her endearment is as fake as her smile. Her lips purse into a thin line as her gaze rakes over Lana in a transparent disbelieving manner.

I don't like it one fucking bit.

"Was there something you wanted because we're having a private conversation here." I'm being deliberately rude, and I couldn't give a flying fuck. Her blatant disregard for Lana has me irritated and grouchy.

Brett snorts, spraying beer out his nostrils.

"Actually, I was hoping we could chat in private." She bats her eyelashes at me, and Lana squirms in my grip. I clamp my hand firmly around her waist. She's going nowhere.

"Anything you have to say can be said in front of Lana and Brett."

She scowls, and it's remarkable how much it transforms her pretty face. It's like taking a sneak peek into the ugliness of her soul. "Fine!" she hisses. "Have it your way." She pulls a garment out of her purse, throwing it at my face. "I just wanted to return these. You left them at my place." I fist my hand in a pair of my boxers, cringing as Lana stiffens again. Shelby's eyes glisten maliciously as she eyeballs Lana. "After we fucked."

I've never wanted to hit a woman before, but I do now.

She cocks her head to the side. "You remember?" Running the tip of her finger up my chest before I can stop her, she leans in. "I'm still sore all over."

What a fucking bitch.

I'm done trying to be nice.

I've stood by and watched other girls trample Lana's feelings in the past, and I'm not going to make the same mistake again.

I shove her hand away from me. "Fuck off, Shelby, and to answer your question, no, I don't remember that one time *over a month* ago because it wasn't memorable in any way." A muscle ticks in my jaw. "I'm with Lana, now. And if I wasn't, I still wouldn't touch you even if you were the last vagina on the planet. I'd rather suck my own dick than go there again."

Brett is doubled over, clutching his stomach, trying to withhold his laughter.

"You're a fucking asshole," she rages, her face as red as a tomato.

"You're welcome to the douche. I don't want him anymore," she flings that parting comment at Lana before stomping off.

"Dude," Brett says, slapping my shoulder as he struggles to breathe. "I'd rather suck my own dick. Fucking-A!" He convulses with laughter.

"Don't knock it, bro. I heard you can get a couple ribs surgically removed and then you're all systems go." I give him a knowing wink, and he doubles up laughing again.

"Dude, seriously, is that a thing?"

"Fact, friend. Google it."

"Can you take me home, please," Lana says, not meeting my eyes.

That sobers me up. "Of course, if that's what you want."

"It is."

Brett sobers up real quick too. He raises his brows, and I subtly shake my head. Old wounds are the hardest to heal, and all it takes is one confrontation, one whisper of suspicion, for the wound to rip open, festering and aggravating sore feelings all over again. Lana's hurting, and I'll do whatever it takes to make it go away.

"I'm sorry about Shelby," I tell her once we're comfortably seated in the back seat of the Uber.

"Forget it." She looks out the window, staring into the bleak darkness, as we turn onto the campus. "It's not like it's anything new."

I bite back my groan of frustration. This time last week everything was fucking perfect, and now it's all in the toilet. Guess it wouldn't be worth fighting for if it was drama-free.

The Uber stops in front of Lana's dorm, and I move to pay the driver, but Lana stalls me with one look. "I'd like to be by myself tonight, Kal."

"If that's what you prefer." I grit the words out, failing to disguise how pissed I am. I know Olivia agreed to stay with Riley to give Lana and me some time alone.

"It is."

"I'll collect you at eight in the morning. We need to get on the road early."

"I—"

"No, you don't," I cut her off. There's no way in hell she's backing out of tomorrow. I do the only thing I can to ensure she follows through. I guilt her into it. "I've gone to tons of fucking trouble organizing everything for you to pull out at the last minute."

I watch the silent battle waging war inside her. "Okay. I'll see you then."

I'm at her door at eight a.m. sharp the next morning, determined to put things back on an even footing. The door opens slowly, and I hold the large bouquet of red, white, and pink roses out in front of me. "Good morning, birthday girl. I hope you slept well."

She looks exhausted, and I can tell she didn't have a good night. I wish I knew what the hell was occupying her mind.

She buries her nose in the roses, inhaling deeply, and a genuine smile graces her lips for the first time this week. Thank fuck. "They're beautiful, thank you."

After she arranges them in a vase, she grabs her purse, and we set out on the two-hour trip to Orlando. She's jittery the whole ride, and we don't talk much. I'm not at my best first thing in the morning, and she's still playing the virtual mute role. We listen to some U2, and I hide my smile when she hums along with the songs, afraid she'll shut down if she notices my observation.

I pull into one of those all-you-can eat buffet places a few miles outside of Orlando, and we fill our bellies.

When I pull into the entrance for Universal Studios, her beautiful face lights up, and she turns to me with blatant excitement on her face. It's contagious, and soon I'm sporting a matching smile. I pay and pull the car into the express parking zone, slotting into a vacant space. The crowds are starting to form, but we don't need to worry about that. Dad's guy is already waiting off to the side with a sign bearing my name.

I take her hands in mine. "I wanted to pack as much into today as I could so we're only here until lunchtime, but we have an official VIP guide who will get us right to the top of the express line so we should still get to go on tons of rides." Having money and contacts definitely comes in handy sometimes.

She's practically bouncing in her seat now. I laugh as relief washes over me. Helping her out of the car, I enjoy the opportunity to put my hands on her. I introduce myself to the guide, and he escorts us down to the park. Lana points out several things on the long walk, and I don't miss how her eyes go out on stalks when she spots Bubba Gump. She was with us one time when we visited their restaurant in New York, and I know how much she loved it. That's why I've reserved a table for lunch there.

But that look in her eyes is nothing compared to the look of wonder on her face when we reach The Wizarding World of Harry Potter. Her eyes are glassy and awestruck as we stroll through Diagon Alley, and I pull her into my side, hugging the shit out of her. We go on the Gringotts ride and take the Hogwarts Express to Universal's Islands of Adventure where we almost make ourselves sick as we rush to go on every ride. Lana's as much of a thrill seeker as I am, and she doesn't back down from any challenge, even if she screams her lungs out on a few of the scarier rides.

Our last stop is the Jurassic Park ride, and we disembark soaking wet and laughing our asses off.

After we've dried off, I escort her to Bubba Gump for lunch. As requested, the restaurant has booked us a table in a private corner, and they have decorated the table with balloons which is a nice extra touch. The smile hasn't left Lana's face all morning, and that makes me unbelievably happy. She leans into me after the waitress leaves with our orders. "I can't believe you organized all this, Kal. I'm having the best time ever."

"You deserve it, babe. And we've still got lots more to do."

She takes my hand in hers, grinning. "I know what you're doing."

I pop a piece of bread in my mouth, not giving anything away.

"You remembered." She squeezes my hand.

"I told you I remember everything about you, Lana. Every memory is permanently stored here." I touch my chest in the place where my heart beats for her.

She pecks my lips, and I seize the opportunity, hauling her against me and kissing her deeply and slowly. The clearing of a throat has us breaking apart. The waitress sets our appetizers down with a knowing smirk.

Lana's cheeks are bright red, and I bust out laughing. "Your face is hilarious!"

She swats my arm, lifting up her fork and waving it in my face. "That's your fault."

"If you think I'm ever apologizing for kissing the shit out of you, you can think again."

"It's impossible to stay mad at you."

I kiss her cheek. "I'm glad you've finally admitted I'm irresistible."

Her fork clangs on the table. "I said no such thing!"

"Aw, come on, baby." I graze my nose up the column of her neck and she shivers. "Admit it. You know it's the truth."

She cups my face lovingly. "I can't deny something that's fundamentally true. You've always been irresistible, Kal." She kisses me sweetly. Just once. "Why the hell do you think I've been in love with you my entire life?"

Chapter Twenty-Two
Lana

Kal demolishes his lunch and the remainder of mine after I push my half-eaten plate away. "I don't understand how you look like you do when you eat like such a pig," I remark.

"Genetics," he jokes.

I sigh. "Can't deny that. The Kennedy gene pool is something else." My son is a part of that now.

The waitress clears the table and takes our coffee orders.

"You ready for the next part of our date?" He stretches back in the seat, snaking his arm around my shoulders. I love how touchy-feely he is with me. It'll never grow old.

"Yep. Are we going alligator watching or to the Kennedy Space Station?"

"You've figured it out, huh?"

I nudge him in the ribs. "What kind of a dummy do you take me for? When we arrived here, I knew straightaway."

That last summer in Nantucket, Kal and I had talked about our plans for the future. It's where I first mentioned I wanted to go to college in Florida to be near my grandparents. Kal said he would come too, and we planned tons of cool things we were going to do. We each had a top five list of places to visit, and I know he's trying to make that dream come true. Even if we were only kids on the cusp of our teenage years, he still understood how important it was to me.

"Is the reality stacking up?"

"Today it is." I squeeze his knee as I smile up at him.

"But not the rest?" He sits up straighter in his chair, just as the waitress arrives with our coffees and the check. He hands her a snazzy black credit card, and her eyes almost bug out of her head.

"When we were kids, everything seemed so black and white," I start to explain. "But reality is so many different shades of complexity."

"Tell me about it." He dumps four sugars into his coffee.

"That's disgusting, and really unhealthy."

"Sorry, Mom." He winks, licking the froth off the top of his cup as I shake my head.

"I understand now why Mom had severed all contact with her parents. They're not very warm people, and they haven't treated her right."

"In what way?"

I take a small sip of my coffee before speaking. "Mom got pregnant with me when she was eighteen, a few months shy of getting her high school diploma." That had been a shock. Mom has always seemed so prim and proper and very strict when it came to dating and boys. Although, thinking about it now, it kind of makes sense.

Kal is waiting for me to continue. "My grandmother is deeply religious, so you can imagine how that went down. Even worse was the fact that my father was the butler's son and older by four years. They were disgusted. Abortion was out of the question, even though I know my mom would never have considered that, and they were opposed to her marrying my dad, even though he assured them he loved her and would stand by her. They doubted his ability to provide for her. Marriage to the help's son was not what they had in mind when they'd enrolled her in an exclusive private school."

"Your grandparents have money?" Surprise is evident in his tone.

"My grandparents are wealthy. Not in the same league as your family, but they built a very successful retail business from the ground up. They sold it ten years ago and made a fortune—apparently—not that Mom benefitted."

"What happened after they found out she was pregnant?"

An anxious fluttering feeling takes up residence in my chest. I wish I hadn't opened this particular line of conversation now. It's far too close to the bone, and my nerves are stretched thin. "They told her they'd support her if she had the baby and gave it up for adoption. That was the only option they were comfortable with."

"Obvs, your mom told them to stick it."

My lips curve up involuntarily. "Nicely put," I tease. "Yes, she told them she was marrying my dad and keeping the baby, so they threw her out and cut her off."

"Harsh."

"I don't know how anyone can do that to their own flesh and blood. Even now, grandmother only let us move in upon certain conditions." I shake my head sadly. "She acts as though she's come from old money, and she's obsessed with how the outside world perceives her and her family. She seems to have forgotten that she was dragged up, pitifully poor, and fought her way out of it. It's as if she's erased her past."

"And you only found all this out after you moved in with them?" he asks. I nod, unwilling to elaborate on how exactly that came to be.

Rampant guilt runs riot inside me.

I'm telling him tomorrow.

I've been dead set on it all week.

I'm not chickening out this time.

Kal is going to know in the morning that he has a son.

It takes about thirty minutes to get to the airboat rides place. We wait in line behind a young couple with two small children. A boy and a girl. Twins, if I had to guess. They look to be about five. "I'm very sorry, ma'am, but we're fully booked," the man behind the counter says. "You'll have to wait until the next run in an hour. Though, the forecast isn't good, and I can't guarantee it'll run to schedule." The woman's smile disappears as the little boy starts to cry. They move away from the counter, and Kal steps up.

We head outside where a private airboat waits for us. "How many can this boat accommodate," I ask the driver.

"Up to six, ma'am."

Kal's smile is knowing as I pose my question. "Would it be okay if that family came with us?"

Hauling me into his arms, he kisses the top of my head. "Of course, babe. I was going to suggest it inside, but this is your day, and I had planned on going out alone."

Glancing behind him, I see the little boy seated on a bench outside, crying his eyes out. His mother is crouched in front of him, offering soothing words. "I'll go tell them if you fix things with the office."

Ten minutes later and we are off. The little boy and girl, Cade and Camilla, are tucked between their parents, shrieking with glee as we take off through the murky waters. Water sprays us on both sides as we speed off.

After about ten minutes, the boat slows down, and the driver–slash–guide points out several interesting things in the swamp as we all keep beady eyes open for any sign of alligators. Our patience is rewarded, and a few minutes later, we happen across a female alligator and her two babies. Instinctively, I move closer to Kal, and his arm tightens around my waist with a low chuckle.

Momma alligator turns her stare directly on us as she slinks forward, edging unbelievably close to the boat. The driver assures us we are safe, but adrenaline is still pumping through my veins. We both take copious pictures with our cell phones. At this proximity, the magnificence of the animal can't be mistaken. Its bulbous brown eyes observe us with a sharp intensity that sends shivers up my spine. Its maternal instincts are strong, the guide informs us as the first plop of rain lands on my forehead.

The driver reacts fast, turning the boat around and speeding away. More rain falls, coming down in heavy sheets, pelting my skin so hard it feels like a shower of stones bouncing off my arms. I bury my head in Kal's shoulder as the heavens open up.

By the time we get back to the office, we are all completely soaked through. My hair is plastered across my face, and my clothes are stuck to my skin. Our feet squelch as we walk back to the car, laughing despite the unscheduled bath from Mother Nature.

"It's crazy how humid it is even though the sky just emptied its guts," Kal says from the dry, hot cabin of the truck.

"It's always humid around here. Takes some getting used to."

"I'm with ya, babe." He tosses a pair of his sweats and a plain white shirt to me. "That's all I've got, but at least they're dry."

"Getting drenched twice in one day has got to be some kind of record," I quip, squeezing water out of my hair.

We have to peel the clothes from each other's bodies, which is fun. Of course, Kal can't resist cracking a few smutty jokes, and when his hand makes a grab for my bare boob, I slap him away. Thank God for tinted windows. "Behave. We're still in a public place."

"No one can see," he replies, making another grab for me.

"Kal." I pin him with a serious look, and he returns it with a faux innocent one.

"What?" He raises his palms. "You can't expect me to watch you stripping naked in my truck and not get turned on. You make me hard, baby."

My eyes flit to the loose gym shorts he has on, noticing the discernible bulge. Heat swarms my body, and all my lady parts react enthusiastically. I lick my lips, and he growls. "Unless you intend on following through, you can't look at me like that."

"Like what?" I smile sweetly, as if I'm completely oblivious.

"Like you want to feast on my dick."

I splutter. "Oh my God. You are such a guy."

"Last time I checked." He smirks, adjusting himself.

"Drive, Kal," I command. "You are not defiling me in *a truck*."

"Can I defile you in a bed?" he retorts with a naughty glint in his eye. The engine hums as he thrusts the stick in gear.

"That depends."

"On what?"

"On how well the rest of our date goes."

"Oh, yeah, baby. We are *so* getting it on."

Because we stayed longer than planned in the theme park, we've had to forgo the trip to the Kennedy Space Station, but Kal promises he'll take me back. The stupid, idealistic, romantic side of my brain kicks in, visualizing a family trip with Hewson. My heart swoons at the thought, but I can't afford to indulge such thoughts. He may wash his hands of me for good after I confess.

I can't afford to dream.

Because it may just be another one shattered.

Kal has checked us into a luxurious suite in a hotel in Gainesville for the night. I find a stunning strapless red dress with matching heels waiting for me in the room. Apparently, he's got one more surprise up his sleeve.

After taking a long soak in the tub, and beautifying myself while he's disappeared to God knows where, I get dressed and leave the room to find him.

I meet him down in the lobby, and he whistles low under his breath as I twirl for him. I'm not sure what the dress is made of, but the material is silky smooth against my skin, swishing gently around my thighs as I spin around.

"I knew that would suit you the minute I spotted it." His lips graze my bare collarbone. He's wearing a tux, and I've never seen him look so hot. His eyes are attentive and hypnotic as he slides a corsage on my wrist.

"What's this?" I give him a puzzled look.

"You missed prom." He cups my face, leaning in for a soft kiss. "So, I figured we'd do a prom makeover tonight."

We step outside and I gasp at the stretch limo waiting for us. Once we are situated in the back, Kal pours me a glass of champagne, wrapping his arm around me as we toast. "Happy birthday–slash–prom, honeybun," he purrs, clinking my glass.

"Thank you so much for today, Kal. I've had an amazing time."

"You're welcome. I'm glad I got to do this with you."

"Did you go to prom?"

He shakes his head. "Nope. Faye and Ky begged me to go with them, but I knew I wouldn't enjoy it without you. Besides, we had sworn a vow."

We had.

We'd agreed years previously that we would be each other's prom date, although, I never expected him to follow through. Not once he started chasing after any female with a pulse. I assumed he'd ditch me for some sexy hottie who'd happily spread her legs for him. I'm flabbergasted that he didn't attend. Kalvin Kennedy is one of Wellesley's most notorious party boys.

He chuckles. "I fucking love that you're surprised."

"I am," I readily admit, sipping the sweet, dry amber-colored liquid. "It's not like you to miss a party."

He stretches out his legs. "That was the old me. That person no longer exists."

I know why, but I want to hear the words from his mouth.

"Tell me what happened after I left."

Chapter Twenty-Three
Lana

He waits until we're seated at our table in the restaurant, having ordered, before telling me. Some of this I've heard third-hand from my attorney, but I need to hear this from him, even if I know it's going to launch my guilt-o-meter into outer space.

"People believe what they want to believe, and I've made my fair share of enemies back home, so it's not surprising that some people believed I was guilty."

"I heard you were placed on house arrest."

His Adam's apple bobs in his throat. "Yep. You know Ben Roberts? He called me a rapist in front of a bunch of people at a party and I lost it. Rearranged his face a bit. A few others jumped into the fray, and it turned into a massive fight. Myself, Faye, Ky, Brad, and Keaton all got arrested."

"Crap." I sink a little in my seat. Indirectly, this was my fault. "I can't believe Faye was arrested. Surely, she wasn't involved in the fight?"

"No, but there was other stuff going on with her that night. Dad showed up with Dan, and no charges were brought against any of us, but the D.A. insisted I was put on house arrest, and I had to wear one of those fucking anklet things." His face contorts. "Not the happiest few weeks of my life."

"I'm sor—"

"Babe," he interjects, reaching across the table to take my hand. "It's not your fault, and we're not discussing it any more. Not if it's adding to your guilt. It's over and done with, and I survived to tell the tale."

I flick my lip between my teeth.

"Honestly, babe, it ended up being a good thing. Dad hired a private tutor. She was a fucking ball buster, but I earned enough credits to skip senior year and graduate with my brother and cousin. If that hadn't happened, I wouldn't be here with you now." He massages my hands with his thumbs. "Sometimes, things happen for a reason."

That makes me feel a teeny bit better. "You have such a good heart, Stinky."

"You should know." His adoring eyes pierce straight through to my soul. "You own it."

"I didn't know you had such a romantic side," I admit, swooning under the glare of his adoring expression.

"Babe, I've been nurturing it for years, just for you." He gives me a cheeky wink, and I laugh, all traces of my recent stress subsiding.

"I'm a lucky girl."

His face turns more serious. "We're both lucky. Lucky to have found each other so young, and lucky that the mistakes we've made in the past haven't risked our future."

A bucket load of new stress dumps all over me.

"So." He draws the word out. "*The Story of Us*, huh?"

"I'd hoped you'd forgotten about that."

"Not a chance in hell. Am I in it?"

I slant a knowing look at him. "What do you think?"

His grin turns smug. "Can I read it?"

"It's chicken poop."

He laughs. "You say that about every draft."

"This time I mean it. I told you I haven't had much time to work on it. When, or *if*, I get it finished, and it's in reasonable shape, I *might* consider showing it to you."

"Might?" I blush, and he strains forward. "What?"

"There's some stuff in it that you don't know. Stuff you might get mad about."

"Like what?"

I bite my lip. *Why did I have to go there?*

"Come on, babe. No secrets. Total honesty is how we roll now. You tell me something I don't know, and I'll tell you a secret too."

I suck in a brave breath. "I kissed Kent."

He blinks at me as if in a daze. "What?" he explodes a minute later, and a few disapproving heads turn in our direction.

"Shh," I hiss. "I knew I shouldn't have said anything."

"You can't tell me you kissed my brother and leave it at that." His eyes burn.

"Technically, I've kissed all your brothers."

"Kiss chasing as kids doesn't count," he snaps, "and, unless I've picked this up wrong, whatever happened with Kent is different."

"I'm not telling you if you're going to get grumpy." I slouch in my seat, my happy mood flittering away. "It's not like it meant anything." It's my own fault for raising such a stupid subject. I half-expected him to laugh.

He massages his temples. "You didn't—"

"No, I didn't sleep with him." I fling my napkin down. "You know there's only been you." That seems to calm him down.

"Tell me."

I sigh. He's not going to let this drop. "It was a few months before you and I made our agreement. It was the night I saw you groping Luce Parker out on the deck of the cabin during one of your parties." A bitter taste fills my mouth as another horrible memory returns.

His face pales. "I didn't know you were there."

Tension ties my shoulders into knots. "You had those parties most weeks, Kal. You think I didn't sneak out and watch? I wish I hadn't. I wish I could erase all the images of you with other girls from my mind."

I look down at the table, tears pricking my eyes. He takes my hand. "I wish I could take it all back."

Slowly, I lift my head. "Yeah, I can relate." But resurrecting the stuff that filled my nightmares for years isn't going to do either of us any good. I'm an idiot for steering the conversation in this direction.

"And what? Kent saw and he comforted you?" Kal guesses.

I nod. "He was only arriving to the party. I had fled in tears after I saw you with her, and I crashed straight into him. He saw I was upset, and he wanted to know why. I couldn't tell him. I couldn't admit how much I felt for you. I was so mad and so upset, and I didn't know what I was doing. All I knew was that I needed a distraction. Needed to kiss someone else. To try and erase you from my heart. So, I kissed him. *I* did it, not him."

"But let me guess," he snarls. "The horndog didn't exactly push you away."

"Actually, he did." He quirks a brow. "He said he didn't want to get in the middle of whatever was going on between us. Seems I didn't need to say anything for him to understand. I told him it was pointless because every slut in town had already come between us."

Kal winces.

"I told him if he didn't want to kiss me I'd find someone else who would. He didn't need much persuasion after that." His Adam's apple jumps in his throat, and by the look on his face, I can tell he's very unhappy about this. "Does it help that I imagined he was you the whole time?"

"That only makes it worse." His lips pull into a thin line. "I'm going to kill him when I get my hands on him." His fists clench on top of the table.

"No, you're not. It meant nothing to either of us. He was there for me when I needed him, but that was it. We made out for a while, and then I went home, and he went to the party. End of story." And it's not like Kal's in any position to judge. "Now it's your turn." I lean back, folding my arms. He clears his throat, opening and closing his mouth successively. Alarm bells blare in my head. I lean forward. "Say it."

His eyes penetrate mine. "Zoe kissed me."

"What?!" I shriek, jumping up in my seat. The waiter approaches, and I hastily sit back down. Kal assures him we're fine, and he eyes us both suspiciously before stepping away. "Zoe? Really? You just had to make a move on my best friend?"

Screw this shit.

Reaching across the table, he grabs my hands before I can pull away. "I did not make a move on her. She. Kissed. Me."

"I'm going to fucking kill her!" I think back to all the times she criticized me over Kal. All the times she told me I was stupid and a fool. Called me crazy, obsessed. *Was that all some scheme to get me away from him so she could have him for herself?* "You think you know someone." I shake my head. "I thought she was my friend."

"To be fair, she was drunk, and I'm not entirely convinced she knew what she was doing."

"Don't defend her! She made a move on you, and that's not cool. She knew exactly how I felt about you. It's why you two were always snarking at each other, right?"

"I can't speak for her, but I think she was embarrassed. I didn't kiss her back, Lana. She pressed her mouth to mine, and once I got over the shock, I pulled away. I accused her of being a shitty friend to you, and, of course, she threw that right back at me."

"I can't believe it," I murmur, hurt over my friend's betrayal. "Why the hell did I even start this conversation?"

"Hey." He rubs his thumb on the back of my hand in soothing circles. "We promised each other honesty, and it's good that we both know. Now we can forget it."

It's not as easy as that, but I let it go, wanting to get this night back on track. Too many girls have ruined things between us, and I'm not going to let old history drive a wedge between us tonight. Not when this might be the last time I'm with him like this. "Fine. No more talk of the past."

"I'm still going to kick Kent's ass," he murmurs, and I give him the evil eye.

He raises his palms. "Fine. Fine. Let's move on." He examines me for a second. "There is something I'm curious about. Why are you studying business, Lana? Why have you given up on your dream?"

Wow. What an awesome subject change. Barely less painful than the last topic. "It's classified. If I tell you, I'd have to kill you," I reply, hoping to deflect by throwing the same words back at him.

He leans back in his chair as our entrees are placed in front of us. "Why, Lana? I want to know why."

I say the first thing that pops into my mind. To be fair, I'm pretty sure this is exactly how it would've gone down if I'd asked to study creative writing. "My grandparents are paying my college fees, and they didn't support my dream. They wanted me to study something more practical, something that would help me find a job." I shrug, attempting to downplay it so he'll drop the subject before I tie myself up in more lies.

"That sucks butt," he exclaims a little too loudly. A few older couples at the adjoining tables look over at us again, disdain etched across their faces. This place is as hoity-toity as you'll find around these parts, and we're obviously not acting appropriately.

"It's not the end of the world. I can always pursue it later."

He looks quietly contemplative, and we eat our entrees in silence.

After the waitress has removed our empty plates, he pins me with a grave look. "There's still time to switch majors. If you want to follow your dream, I'll pay your fees."

My insides turn to mush, and I'm fighting tears. "You would do that for me?"

"Of course, I would. I love you, and I want you to be happy. I hate that you still doubt me so much. I'm determined to prove I'm serious. There's nothing I won't do for you. Nothing."

"Kal." I turn my head around so he can't see the tears forming.

"Just promise me you'll think about it?"

"Okay," I whisper.

Cozied up in front of the TV, snuggled into Kal, is one of my favorite pastimes. I've a multitude of memories of nights like this from our childhood. "Remember when I fell out of the tree house and broke my leg?" Kal asks, barreling through my reverie.

"Yeah. You were eleven."

"I prayed to God every night to keep my leg broken," he admits. I sit up, staring at him like he's just grown an extra head. "You spent every second of every day with me and I loved it. We read and watched movies and talked, and you took such good care of me. I didn't want it to end."

"Oh. My. God. That's why you threw yourself off the tree the week after the cast came off? You were trying to break your leg again?"

He laughs. "Yep. I was an idiot. Lucky Dad was there to catch me or I would have ended up back in the ER."

I slap him hard across the chest.

"Ow. What was that for?"

"Your dad dismantled the tree house the next day. I loved that place. All that time, I thought your dad was so mean, but it was all your fault! Jerk!"

He laughs again. "You can't help a guy for trying."

I snuggle back into his chest, curling my legs up under me. I wonder how many of my other memories tell a different side to the story. I never imagined Kal shared the same feelings I did, and it makes me giddy with happiness. I sigh contentedly as I close my eyes, allowing his body heat to warm me. Even though I've had an amazing time on our date, this is the highlight of my day. I've always been more of a simple pleasures kind of girl. Which isn't me saying I'm ungrateful for everything he did today. Today was magical, and I will remember it for the rest of my life, but I don't need grand gestures from Kal.

I just need him.

"Are you ready for your present?" he whispers, pressing his delectable mouth to my forehead.

"No way, Kal. You've already given me so much!"

He gets up, returning with a large gift-wrapped box. "I haven't given you nearly enough, but that's a work in progress."

"You are spoiling me."

"You deserve it."

I don't. That's not even debatable.

I set about opening my present, and it's almost a shame to tear through the pretty wrapping like I do. When I pop off the lid, I gasp, then shriek, and then gasp some more. He laughs. "Take them out, read the inscription."

My hands shake as I remove the entire Harry Potter collection with the original hardback first edition covers. There were only a limited number of these printed, and I know they must have cost a fortune.

I open the cover of the first book, and I almost faint on the spot. "Oh. My. God." I stare up at him, awestruck. "Kal!" I whisper. "How did you ..." I'm speechless as I reread the personal inscription J.K. Rowling has written to me. *Me.*

He shrugs, like it's commonplace to give your girlfriend a rare collection of her favorite books that have been personally signed by one of the most famous authors on the planet. "Kennedy Apparel dressed her for a few prestigious events, and Mom had her contact on speed dial. Keaton snagged the number for me, and I gave her a call. I told her about you and what I was hoping to do, and she was only too happy to help."

I fist my hand in his shirt, pulling him to me. Surprised, he stumbles a little. I grip his face, smashing my lips against his with urgent need. I plunder his mouth, using my lips and my tongue to feast on him. My heart is swollen with so much love. He is everything I'd hoped he would be, and more.

I can't lose him. I just can't.

He grips my hips, pulling me down on top of him. My thighs spread and I straddle him, grinding against the bulge in his pants.

He moans, and his lips leave mine, his hot mouth trailing a path up and down my neck.

I'm panting and writhing on top of him, awash with so many conflicting emotions.

All that I feel for him is breaking me apart.

Everything he has done for me has proven his love.

There is only one more thing he can do to prove he means it forever.

The irony of the timing isn't lost on me.

"Have we arrived at the defiling part yet?" His mouth latches on to the throbbing pulse in my neck, sucking hard, and I whimper in ecstasy.

I want to rip our clothes off and lower myself on top of him. I want to feel him moving inside me. Feel his lips as they worship my body. Feel every thrust, every sensation, every part of him.

But I can't be that selfish.

There can be no barriers between us when we breach that final step—corporal, invisible, or other.

So, I pour everything into my kiss, deliberately not answering him. Every hungry caress of my mouth is telling him how I feel. The unquenchable, infinite love beating in my heart for him. The gut-wrenching regret twisting my stomach into knots. The splintering guilt threatening to destroy me. Fear and hope battle against one another as I think of what my revelation is going to do to him.

All these emotions infuse every kiss, every caress, and I need him to feel it. To feel me. Right down to the very essence of who I am.

To understand how much of myself I've already given to him.

How much more I want to give.

To know how much I cherish the part of him I've already claimed.

To feel my undying, painful need for him.

A sharp pain jackknifes my insides, and I can't stop the sob that rips from my mouth, so primitive and raw it could have come straight from my soul.

Loving him the way I do, it physically hurts.

And I can't wait a minute more.

I have to tell him now.

"Baby?" Kal's concerned tone only makes things worse. "What's wrong?" Moving stealthily, he repositions us so I'm sitting on his lap on the couch. I can't stop crying. "Did I hurt you?"

I hate that that's his first instinct.

"No," I sob. "I'm the one who's hurt you."

My sobs become uncontrollable, and my entire body shakes as I cling to him, knowing this could be the last time.

"I love you, Kal. I love you so Goddamned much. Never forget. Never."

He palms my face, and worried eyes meet my tear-stained ones. "Lana. You're scaring me. Tell me what's wrong."

"I have somethi—"

I'm interrupted by the loud ringing of my cell phone. The shrill tone breaks through the emotional tornado surrounding me. I glance up at the clock. It's after one a.m. Very few people have cause to call me, and a call at this time of night raises all the tiny hairs on the back of my neck. My sixth sense is blaring all kinds of alarms. "I need to get that." I jump up, grabbing my cell and staring through blurry eyes at the screen. My internal warning system is on high alert, and a trickle of sweat glides down the gap between my breasts. "It's my mom. I'll, uh, just talk to her out here." I race from the living area out into the bedroom and beyond to the en suite bath as I press the accept button. "What's wrong?"

"Lana, you need to come quick!"

"Is Hewson all right?"

"I don't want to worry you unnecessarily, but he's not well. Not well at all. The doctor is en route. He has an extremely high temperature and a strange rash. I'm scared it's meningitis."

"Oh my God," I shriek. My breathing is erratic, and my heart is pumping way too fast.

"I'm leaving now. I'll be there as soon as I can." I burst into tears the minute I hang up.

Kal is beside me in a heartbeat. "What's happened, Lana?"

Our son is sick. He could have meningitis. We need to go to him.

I want to be able to say those words, but how the hell can I? I can't break the news to him like this!

"It's my grandmother," I lie. "She's really sick. Mom has called the doctor, but she wants me to come home right now."

I want to throat punch myself.

Either that or repeatedly bang my forehead against the wall.

I'm a disgusting excuse for a human being.

My son should have his father with him, and the reason he doesn't is all because of me.

"Come on, I'll drive you." Kal ushers me out of the bathroom.

"I'll take an Uber."

"Don't be fucking ridiculous, Lana! I'm driving you and that's that. I won't come near the house if that's what you're worried about."

I reluctantly nod. I don't have time to argue with him. I change into jeans and a shirt, snatching my purse and my cell, leaving the rest of my stuff behind as we race out of the room.

Kal floors it and we make good time on the quiet, nighttime roads.

When we enter Earleton, my heart rate accelerates and blood pounds in my ears. My palms are clammy. Kal has kept a reassuring hand on my knee while he drives, but we haven't spoken. He knows I'm upset and scared but he's respecting my need for privacy. "Stop here." I point at the end of the narrow, winding road that leads to the lake and my grandparents' house. I can't let him get any closer. I've promised myself that if the situation is grave, I will call him back, but, until I know what I'm dealing with, I'm not taking any chances.

I don't want him to find out like this.

It'll destroy him.

"I'll drive you to the entrance."

I vehemently shake my head. "You can't. The road isn't suitable for vehicles. I'll make it on foot from here," I lie.

He kills the engine and puts the truck in neutral. "I'll walk with you."

"No!" I yell, and he jumps a little.

"I'm not letting you walk out there on your own in the dark. It looks creepy as fucking hell," he adds, his eyes narrowing as he surveys the woodland bordering the area.

I can scarcely breathe or think over the thrumming of blood in my ears. This can't happen. "He has a shotgun!" I exclaim, facing him with panicked eyes. "My grandfather. He has a shotgun, and, he, ah, likes to hunt."

"Okay?" Kal looks confused.

"He'll shoot you!" I grip his arm. "I'm not allowed to date. Not even allowed to look at a boy," I babble, desperately grasping at straws. "My grandmother is even stricter than Mom. If they see me approaching with you, they'll freak. He'll shoot you," I repeat, curling my hand around the door handle. I lean over and kiss him quick. "Thanks for the ride, but I need to go! I'll text you later."

I don't give him time to raise other objections, jumping from the truck and sprinting away. Tears are cascading down my face. I reckon I've cried enough tears these last few weeks to fill my own damned lake. Pushing thoughts of Kal aside, I focus on my son, allowing my fear to propel my legs faster. When I reach the end of the road, rounding the bend toward our property, I skid to a halt. Mom's car is emerging from the gate, the lights illuminating my form. She lowers the window. "We need to get to the hospital. Get in." I open the back door, gasping at the sight of Hewson.

His hair is stuck to his forehead, and a heavy layer of sweat coats his entire face. His cheeks are flushed bright red, and he's exercising his lungs like I've never heard before. Each high-pitched wail is like a dagger straight through the heart. I place my palm on his forehead, whimpering at how hot he is. "Shh, baby." I caress his hot cheek. "It's okay. I'm here. Mommy's here now," I say, climbing in the back seat alongside him.

Chapter Twenty-Four
Kalvin

Something is seriously up with Lana. I've never seen such blatant panic on her face. Before I could protest, she high-tailed it out of the truck. My concern for her safety overrode any wrath I might incur which is why I gave chase.

Why I'm standing now under the shadow of a large oak tree reeling at what I've just seen. What I just heard.

"Shh, baby. It's okay. I'm here. Mommy's here now."

I stumble backward, lose my footing, and crash to the ground. My head spins, and I'm shivering all over. My legs feel like Jell-O.

Lana has a baby.

A freaking real-live baby.

I didn't see it, but I heard its pitiful cries.

Lana has a baby.

Baby.

Baby.

Baby.

I think that baby could be mine.

My stomach churns, and I lean over, hurling up the remnants of our expensive dinner. I puke repeatedly, until there's nothing left to expel. Wiping my mouth with the sleeve of my shirt, I scramble to my feet. My legs are shaky as I stagger back along the uneven road in the dark. My mind is whirling at ninety miles an hour.

Is that my baby?

I keep asking myself different variations of the same question.

Is that baby mine?

A light bulb goes off in my head, and I slam to a halt, leaning against the nearest tree.

I know someone who knows.

Fissures of rage start building in my gut, tangling with the confusion and the shock as I pull myself up into the truck. Thrusting the truck in gear, I whirl around, wheels spinning, smoky dust clouds billowing, and head for the airport.

The plane touches down in Logan International Airport shortly after 9 a.m. Sunday morning. I didn't sleep a wink on the flight. My mind is contemplating all kinds of thoughts. But it all comes down to one thing: Lana has a baby and she never told me.

Why?

Because it's mine and she wants to hide it from me? Or she was too afraid to tell me because she knows keeping something like this a secret is unforgivable? There's another alternative, but it's too upsetting to even consider—that she lied about not sleeping with anyone else and the baby is some other dude's.

Certain things click into place now—how she spends every weekend at home and the regular, nightly calls to her mother—it's because of the baby.

If I'm right, and the baby is mine, it goes some way toward explaining her reticence this past week and her mini breakdown in my arms last night.

I think she was on the verge of telling me.

At least I hope she was.

Loving Kalvin

I drag my weary ass off the plane and head outside to catch a cab. I bought new clothes in Orlando International Airport, ditching my rain-sodden puke-stained previous ones. I rinsed out my mouth and cleaned my teeth. Had a couple of stiff whiskeys in the VIP lounge, but even that hasn't stopped the constant shaking of my hands. I think my body's in as much shock as my mind.

Anger flows through my veins the nearer the cab gets to Harvard. Faye and Ky don't share a living space—he shares an apartment with his friend Brad, and she's in one of the campus dorms—so I send a text to Kyler asking where he is. Most college students are still snoring in bed, but my brother is a creature of habit, and he's fanatic about his early morning workouts, so, I'm not surprised to receive an immediate reply.

Ky: My place.
Me: Is Faye with u
Ky: Seriously, asshole?
Me: Don't go anywhere
Ky: ??????
Ky: Kal?

My cell rings but I terminate Ky's call. What I've come to say needs to be said face to face.

My fist pounds on his apartment door fifteen minutes later. It swings open and my brother stares at me for a second, silently stepping aside to let me in. He's wearing jeans that are unbuttoned at the top, hanging slightly off his hips. His chest and feet are bare, his hair damp from a shower.

"You look like shit," he says.

"Where's Faye?" My eyes dart around the room.

"I'm here." She yawns as she steps into the living room, rubbing sleepy eyes. Her hair is all messed up, and she's still in her pajamas. Her nipples are poking out through the thin fabric of her top. "Kal!" My cousin's face lights up at the sight of me.

"Babe," Ky says, groaning unhappily. "Please put some clothes on." She rolls her eyes, taking a step back.

"No!" I stalk toward her, gripping her elbow as I eyeball her. "Did you know? Have you known all this time and you've kept it from me? Is that really why you didn't tell me about her?" My voice is getting louder and louder as anger ignites a flame inside me.

"I don't understand, Kal. What do you mean? What's going on?" Her expression is a mixture of confusion and anxiety.

My grip tightens involuntarily, and I narrow my eyes at her. "Don't treat me like I'm a fucking idiot!" I roar as explosive emotion emits in a dangerous volley. "I didn't come all this way so you could continue to fuck with me! I can't believe you kept something like this from me! Just tell me, Goddammit. I have a right to know!"

I'm ripped off her with force, stumbling as I'm pushed aside. "Get your fucking hands off her, and stop shouting." Ky glares at me as he steps in front of his girlfriend, shielding her with his body. "What the hell, bro? You need to calm the fuck down."

I lean forward, placing my palms on my knees. My heart beats furiously in my chest. I'm panting as my breath hitches painfully in my throat. A mad fluttery sensation has invaded my chest, and a heavy pressure weighs me down, like invisible hands are pushing and constricting my chest cavity. I suck air in and out in fast, exaggerated spurts, and it feels like I'm having a coronary. Or what I imagine one feels like. Black spots distort my vision, and I sway a little, reaching an arm out to balance myself. "Fuck."

Faye darts out from behind her protector, planting herself in front of me. "This is something to do with Lana?" she guesses. Tentatively, she takes my hands in hers, helping me straighten up. "Breathe, Kal. In and out. Nice and slow."

I do as she says, drawing in big gulps of air and willing my heart rate to slow the fuck down.

She rubs my back. "That's it. Take your time." Her head whips up, and she shares a concerned look with my older brother. "Can you fix him something to drink?" she asks, and he steps away.

She steers me over to the couch, gently pushing me down. Then she flops down beside me, wrapping her arms around my waist. It feels like her arms are the only things holding me together. I'm shaking all over.

Ky returns, resting his butt on the edge of the coffee table. He hands me a steaming hot mug. I wrap my hands around it as if on autopilot, but it does nothing to ward off the chills or the shaking that is racking my body from head to toe. I can't stop trembling.

They exchange another worried expression.

Liquid spills out of the cup onto the hardwood floor as it rattles in my hand. Ky takes it from me, placing it on the table beside him. "Kal, you're scaring the shit out of me. Please tell us what's happened. Is Lana okay?"

"She ... she ..." My mouth tastes like sandpaper, and that nauseating feeling is back. I rest my head in my hands. *Get a fucking grip, man!*

Faye presses a kiss to my cheek. "We've got you. We're here for you," she says quietly. "Let us help."

Drawing a deep breath, I lift my head and stare at my brother. "Lana has a baby." His eyes startle, and Faye gasps.

"What?" The note of shock in her high-pitched tone tells me this is the first time she's hearing this.

"You didn't know."

"No! She never mentioned a baby. She ..." She clamps a hand over her mouth as she figures it out. Her eyes are out on stalks.

"It's yours?" Ky asks, his shell-shocked expression meeting my hazy gaze. "Lana had your baby?"

"I don't know. I think so but ... I don't know."

Understanding dawns. "She doesn't know you know," he surmises.

I nod and then proceed to tell them everything that went down. Faye never leaves my side, rubbing my back in soothing gestures as I speak. Ky has a mask of indifference on his face as he listens intently to every word, but I know better than to believe it. My brother is an expert in disguising his true emotions, and he has always put others before himself.

We are all mute for a few minutes after I finish up, digesting everything.

"It's got to be yours," Faye says, cleaving a line through the invisible tension in the air. "I know it's been almost a year since you've seen her but that stacks up," she muses out loud.

I think back to that time we slept together, doing some calculations of my own. "Then she would've been pregnant during the trial, and she wasn't." I gulp. "It isn't mine." A strange emotion washes over me—one I can't decipher.

"She must've gotten pregnant soon after the trial ended," Ky deduces, his shoulders visibly relaxing.

"I hate to say this," Faye interjects in a strong Irish accent. Her lyrical Irish brogue is most pronounced during times of high stress. "But it needs to be said. If Lana has a baby, I'm one hundred percent certain it's yours," she tells me. "Lana loves you, Kal, and she hated herself for what she did. There's no way she went out after that trial, met some random bloke, and got herself knocked up. No fucking way." She turns my face to hers. "When did you sleep with her?"

I reply automatically. I haven't forgotten one detail about that night. "August sixteenth."

We're all quietly computing in our heads.

"You didn't actually see the baby, you only heard it, right?" she asks.

"Yeah," I croak, trying to speak over the block of raw emotion in my throat. I'm no expert, but the baby didn't sound right, and Lana was frantic, and although I'm screwed up over this entire situation, I'm also worried that the baby is sick. If it's mine and he or she is sick...

Faye nods her head repeatedly, and I try to refocus on the conversation. "Think back to the trial, Kal. Remember how she looked. She was pale, and she looked unwell. She was wearing an ill-fitting, loose skirt suit. She *was* pregnant. I'd bet money on it."

We let that statement hover in the air. My eyes jump between my brother and my cousin.

"We can sit here speculating all day," Ky says, "or you can get your ass back on that plane and go and talk to her."

I stare off into space. My head is cluttered, and I can't think straight. "What if it's mine?"

Ky and Faye share some wordless communication. She subtly shakes her head at him. Leaning forward, he places his hands on my knees. "If it's yours, Lana has a lot of explaining to do."

I crash for a few hours, managing to get a bit of shut-eye. When I saunter into the kitchen, the most delicious smells infuse the air, and my stomach growls. I haven't eaten a thing all day, and now I'm ravenous. At least this fucked-up situation isn't messing with my appetite.

Faye turns around, approaching me with her arms out. I'm pulled into her hug whether I like it or not. "Did you manage to sleep?" She holds me at arm's length, scrutinizing my face.

"Yeah. I conked the minute my head hit the pillow."

She chuckles, releasing me to return to the stove. "Some things never change." She removes a dish from the oven.

"I didn't sleep at all last night," I admit, leaning over to inhale the delicious smells of lasagna. My mouth waters in anticipation. "You made my favorite."

"Yes. And I've garlic bread and tiramisu too."

I rest my chin on her shoulder. "You're spoiling me."

She spins around, and there's a heartfelt expression on her face. "I'm caring for you the best way I know how."

"Thank you." I'm embarrassed when my eyes grow moist. God, I'm a complete mess.

She takes my hand. "It's going to be okay. No matter what, things will work out."

"I'm not sure I share your optimism."

"You need to give her a chance to explain."

Further conversation is interrupted at the sound of voices in the hallway. Then Brad strolls into the kitchen, wearing a couple of days' worth of stubble on his chin. His clothes are disheveled, his hair is sticking up in all directions, and he smells like a brewery. His cautious expression transforms into a smile when he sees me. He slaps me on the back. "Bro. I didn't know you were visiting."

"It was a spur of the moment thing." I shove my hands in my jeans.

"Kal just discovered Lana has a baby," Ky says from behind him. I'm not mad he's admitted that. Brad has spent so much time in our house, I consider him my pseudo brother. "We think it's his."

"Da fuck?" Brad glances over his shoulder at Ky. "Are you fucking with me?"

Ky slides his arm around Faye's waist from behind. "Nope." He presses a kiss to the top of her head. "We're trying to decide what to do." Faye reaches an arm around, clasping the back of his neck as she angles her head to kiss him.

A pang of jealousy slaps me in the face, and Brad looks like someone just throat punched him. Guess I'm not the only envious one, except the emotion is coming from different places. "I don't know what to say," he tells me.

I shrug. "That makes two of us. I can't wrap my head around this."

"What are you going to do?"

"Fucked if I know."

I have a full belly when I say my goodbyes to my cousin and Brad a couple hours later. Brad has football practice, and Faye has to finish an assignment that's due in the morning, so Ky is driving me to the airport on his own.

"How are the living arrangements working out?" I ask.

He sighs. "It's up and down, man." He glances quickly at me.

"When it's just him and me, things are okay, but when Faye is over, it's another matter entirely. Brad either disappears or goes all moody."

"He looked rough."

Ky sighs again, switching lanes to take the next exit. "No one can accuse Brad of not throwing himself into the college lifestyle. It's like he's on a mission to win the title of 'most laid' on campus. He's going through pussy like no one's business. At least three times a week, I find some half-naked chick sneaking out of his room."

"He's trying to bang Faye out of his system," I suggest.

Ky curses, and the SUV swerves. "Do you have to be so fucking insensitive?!"

I rub the back of my neck. "Sorry, just being honest. As someone who once screwed around in an effort to forget the only girl who mattered, I think I know where he's coming from."

"This is different," Ky snaps, and I'm instantly guilty.

"I know it is. I'm sorry. I still think you and Faye should've moved in together. I can't see how this is going to work out."

He turns off for the airport. "I agree, but she wanted the full college experience. She wanted to live in the dorms and have a roommate, and I didn't want her missing out on that. I also know how much guilt she's harboring over coming between me and Brad, and I think she thought this'd be good for us."

"But it's not."

He shakes his head. "It's not. The tension is growing by the day, and shit's going to hit the fan any day now."

"Maybe it needs to happen for all of you to move on."

"Perhaps."

Ky parks the car and gets out, coming with me to the departures area.

They call my flight, and I get up. Ky stands, pulling me into a hug. "Call me after you talk to her."

"I will," I promise, shucking out of his embrace.

Ky plants his hands on my shoulders. "I mean it, bro. You're not on your own with this. Faye and I will support you, no matter what."

"I appreciate that. A lot."

"We'll hop on a plane anytime you need us. Just say the word."

"Thanks, man. And you promise you won't say anything to the others. Not yet. Not until I know for sure."

"Of course not. We'll figure this out together."

I get back on the plane, feeling slightly less alone than I did on the outbound journey.

Chapter Twenty-Five
Lana

It's Sunday night, and I've decided to skip classes on Monday so I can stay home with Hewson for a little while longer. Thankfully, it wasn't meningitis—just a very bad throat infection. But I'll never forget the horrific terror I felt as we drove toward the hospital with my son burning up beside me, crying his little heart out. If anything had happened to him, I would've lost my mind.

The hospital admitted him for a few hours to run tests, and I'd been frantic with worry. I actually burst out crying when they told me he was going to be fine. The sheer relief I felt almost took the legs out from under me. They gave him an intravenous injection of antibiotics and sent us home with instructions to give him plenty of fluids and pain medication. I moved my bed into his room, and I haven't left his side since.

Huge guilt chips away at me. I should've been here with him. Instead, I was out having fun while my baby was gravely ill. Not only that, if it had been something serious, his father wouldn't have even known, and that's not something I can live with anymore.

I told Mom this morning that I'm telling Kal the truth. She was furious I've concealed the fact he's at UF, and we had the mother of all fights. Now, she's refusing to speak to me.

Hewson is sleeping soundly, and I press a soft kiss to his forehead before stepping out onto the adjoining veranda. I sit down on the loveseat, staring out into the dark, still night air. I check my phone again. I'd texted Kal this morning to let him know everything was okay, but I haven't heard a peep from him all day. He must be mad that I ran off on him like that. I send him another quick text, letting him know I won't be returning until tomorrow night. I don't want him hanging around outside my dorm waiting for me unnecessarily.

I kick off my shoes and pull my feet up under me, tugging the blanket over my lower body. It's starting to get a lot colder at night. I lean back and call my dad. He answers on the third ring.

"Hi, honey. It's good to hear from you."

"You too, Dad." And it is. His strong, calm, self-assured voice has always had the power to soothe me. I can't ever remember a time when he's raised his voice at me or my mother. He reminds me of a gentle giant. Tall, strong, and protective with the heart of a big cuddly bear.

My mother chose well.

"What's wrong?"

"How do you know something's wrong?"

"I know every inflection of your voice, Lana. I know when something is bothering you. Is Hewson okay because your mother said it wasn't meningitis."

I sit bolt upright. "You talked to Mom?"

He exhales deeply. "Sweetheart, your mother and I are still very much together. We talk every day."

I swing my legs around, planting them flat on the hardwood floor. "What the what?"

My grandmother agreed to take us in on a few conditions. One of which was that my mother walked away from her marriage. It seems the years haven't endeared her to my father. I've been crippled with remorse and guilt at the thought I'd been indirectly responsible for breaking my parents up.

It seems that emotion was misplaced.

"Don't be mad, honey. We didn't tell you because we didn't want you to have to lie to your grandparents. You didn't need the additional burden."

"Let me get this straight. You and Mom haven't split up?"

"No. We did what we needed to do for you. So you and Hewson would be well cared for, and you could plan your future."

I'm speechless. My parents never cease to amaze me. A few months ago, I would've told you I couldn't imagine how they could continue to put my needs before their own, especially after I disappointed them. However, now I'm a mom myself, I understand it. There isn't anything I wouldn't sacrifice for Hewson. "I don't know what to say."

"You don't need to say anything, honey. I hate being away from your mother, from you, but this is only temporary until you graduate and get a job. Then we can be together again."

"I've felt so guilty," I admit. "I thought I'd split you up."

"I'm sorry, Lana. Perhaps we made the wrong decision not telling you. I didn't consider you might feel like that."

"I love you, Dad, and I miss you so much."

"Me too, sweetheart."

Now, I feel terrible for arguing with Mom earlier. "Dad? Can I ask you something?"

"You can ask me anything, pumpkin."

I tell him about Kal turning up in UF in the hopes of finding me and how I've struggled with the secret I'm keeping from him. He doesn't say a word. Just listens as I explain everything. "I want to tell him, Dad. He has a right to know he has a son. I was wrong to keep this from him."

"No, Lana. *We* were wrong. You've always wanted to tell him, and we should've respected your wishes, but we were worried."

"That his mom would take the baby, I know."

"Not about that. At least, not on my side. This is the one thing your mother and I disagree on. Alexandra Kennedy is a lot of things, but she would never deprive a mother of her son. You don't remember this because you were too young, but that lady sacrificed a lot so she could build her fashion business and provide a comfortable life for her family. I remember her tears every Sunday night when she left on a business trip. It broke her heart to be away from those boys. That's why I'm sure she'd never do that to you."

I'm quiet as I mull over what he's said. "Why then, Dad? Why strong arm me into keeping this a secret from him?"

"I can only speak for myself. You'll need to ask your mother, but I was trying to protect you. From him. You think I didn't know how much my little girl was in love with that boy? I've stood by for years and watched you pine after him. Watched him struggle with his emotions, hurting you in the process. I can't bear to watch it again. I'm worried Kalvin isn't mature enough to deal with this, Lana, and I fear you're going to get hurt again. I wanted to spare you that."

A slicing pain stabs me clear through the heart. *Is he right? Will Kal crumble when he finds out?* "Irrespective of how he reacts, he still needs to know."

"I agree," Dad says.

"You do?" After his last statement, I'm surprised.

"Yes. And I also believe you're strong enough to handle this. I'm hoping he proves me wrong. I know he has feelings for you, Lana. I just don't know if they're strong enough to be who you need him to be."

"He came after me, Dad, and he's different. He's changed. He's grown up."

"I'm glad to hear that, Lana, and I'm hoping it works out for you, but you've got to be realistic. Don't set yourself up for a fall. That little baby needs you. If Kalvin can't man up and support you and his son, then you are better off without him anyway."

I check in on Hewson again before hunting Mom down. He's still fast asleep with the covers kicked off.

Mom is sitting on the balcony outside her bedroom, drinking a glass of wine. "Mom? Can we talk?"

"Of course, sweetheart." She pats the space beside her. "Come join me." I sit down on the wicker couch alongside her. "Would you like a glass of wine?"

I almost fall onto the floor. "What?" I splutter.

A small smile plays over her lips. "I think we might need it for this conversation. If you're old enough to be a mother, you're old enough to have a glass of wine."

"Okay."

She pours the wine, handing the glass to me. "I'm sorry for what I said this morning," she admits, speaking first. "All my life I've tried to do the right thing by you, but you're an adult now. A mother. I've got to let you make your own decisions."

"Dad told me. About you two." I take her hand in my free one. "I'm so glad. I hated the thought that I'd split you up."

She squeezes my hand. "I love your father too much to give him up just because my tyrant of a mother demanded it."

"Why, Mom? Why did we do this? Why did we come here?" I mean, I know why, but all the reasons that seemed logical last Christmas aren't so plausible now. "I could have waited another year and then applied for a scholarship. We could be with Dad now."

"Trying to raise a baby on a scholarship is a hardship I didn't want for you, Lana. It's difficult enough as it is. And I know how much it's hurting you to be away from Hewson during the week, but I also know how smart, hardworking, and talented you are, and I know you'll get that degree in next to no time. I want you to have options, honey. Options I didn't have."

"Do you regret it? The choices you made."

She puts her glass down, before doing the same with mine. She clasps both my hands in hers. "Never. I don't ever regret having you or loving your father. Your father has been my whole life, and I will be by his side until I no longer exist. I've been blessed with the love of a good man. Blessed with an amazing daughter."

"But?" I ask, because I sense one coming.

"But I regret that I left myself with limited options. Do you think I wanted to wait hand and foot on the Kennedys? I'm better than that, but I never got to go to college, so I had to take whatever opportunities I could. And, to be fair, we were lucky they took a chance on us and gave us somewhere nice to live. It wasn't all bad, but I regret not doing more with my life."

"I can't believe your parents have all this money and they denounced you in such a horrible manner."

"You've seen for yourself what my parents are like. Daddy, God bless him, isn't a bad man. He has a good heart, but she bullies him. He has lost control of his own mind. He has no opinion. No say. No power. My mother was always a cold, calculating woman. I often wonder if I was a mistake, if my mother hadn't intended on having children at all. Growing up, she threw herself into the business. I was raised by a succession of nannies and household staff. Mother paraded me about when it suited her. She sent me to the best school, and I would've gone to an Ivy League college if I hadn't gotten pregnant. She wanted me to mix in the right circles. To marry into old money. She was disgusted when I fell for the butler's son. I will never forget the look on her face when I told her I was pregnant with his baby."

A tear slides down her cheek. "She slapped me. Imagine if I'd slapped you when you told me you were pregnant."

I lean over and hug her. While my parents were shocked and upset when I told them I was pregnant, and we had a difference of opinion on how to deal with it, they have never been cruel or unkind. Instead, they have been supportive and self-sacrificing. I'm only just beginning to understand how very difficult it was for my mother to come back here.

"Mom, do you genuinely believe Kal's mom would take Hewson?"

She shrugs. "I don't honestly know. I hope not, but she likes to be in control too."

"Don't take this the wrong way, Mom," I say softly, "but it's possible you're projecting feelings of your own mother onto her. Alexandra isn't Grandmother. Yes, they are both snobs and workaholics, but the key difference is that Alex would do anything for her children. She wouldn't abandon them like your mother did you."

She says nothing, but I see the enhanced rise and fall of her chest, and I know I've struck a chord. I don't want to upset her, but, the more I think about it, the more my father's point of view makes sense. Not that I'm letting that cloud my judgment either way. I'm telling Kal even if his mother tries to gain custody. That's a battle for another day.

"I don't want to stay here any longer." She opens her mouth, but I shake my head, stalling her objections. "I'm telling Kal because he deserves to know. I'm not sure how he's going to react. I think he'll probably hate me, but I can live with that once he does right by his son." I've given a lot of thought to this in the last few hours. "Hewson is the only priority in all this. At the very least, he will provide for him financially. I know what you think of Kal, Mom, and I'm not going to deny that some of that is true, but it's only part of who he is. He cares for me, and he has a good heart. He'll do the right thing."

A throat clears behind us. "Excuse me, ma'am. Miss." The butler bows at both of us. It's ridiculous and archaic and it makes me hugely uncomfortable but the tyrant insists. "I apologize for interrupting, but there is a young man at the front gate asking to be let in. He refuses to leave until he speaks to Miss Lana."

My stomach plummets to my toes, and I think I'm going to be sick.

"Is his name Kalvin Kennedy?" I ask, although I already know the answer.

"It is, Miss Lana."

I stand up, holding my spine straight. "Please let him in, Jerome. I'll talk to him."

Chapter Twenty-Six
Kalvin

I came straight to Lana's grandparents' house from the airport, having already showered and changed clothes before I left Harvard. As I stand outside the vast, ornate mahogany doors, my nerves are stretched to breaking point. My heart is racing like it's doing a few laps around a Formula One track. I wipe sweaty palms down the front of my jeans as the door creaks open.

Lana stands before me, dressed in a pair of cut-off denim shorts and a long-sleeved tight-fitting top with a pink-and-purple-butterfly pattern. Her legs and feet are bare, and her hair is pulled back in a ponytail. There isn't a lick of makeup on her face. She looks so young, so beautiful. Exactly how I always picture her in my memories.

Silently, she steps aside to let me in, but I'm rooted to the spot. Unable to move. I stare at her, noting the steely determination in her expression. Various emotions are etched across her face. She's not hiding. Not anymore. My heart is thrashing against my ribcage as we continue looking at one another. Her gaze coasts over my face with concern. My eyes penetrate hers, seeking the answer I already know.

"Is the baby mine?"

"Yes." Her voice is firm, confident. "We have a son, Kal."

My heart careers around my chest cavity, screaming, rejoicing, panicking. I stumble, reaching out and gripping the edge of the doorframe to steady myself.

Oh fuck. Fuck. It's true.

I have a son.

I'm a dad.

I cling to the doorframe, digging my fingers in. My heart rate is elevated, my breathing exaggerated. I'm struggling to keep myself upright.

The acknowledgment hits me harder than I imagined. I'm feeling so much.

Too much.

A strangled sound flies out of my mouth.

She moves toward me, but I raise my hand, holding her back. "Is he ... is he okay?" I haven't forgotten the frantic cries I heard last night or Lana's blatant fear. "Is he sick?"

She nods, not looking too surprised, and it's obvious she realizes how I've figured this out. My anxiety elevates a few notches. "Not seriously," she rushes to add. "Mom thought it might've been meningitis, so we brought Hewson to the hospital, but he's fine. He has a bad throat infection, and he's been really sick, but he's doing better the last couple hours."

"That's ... that's good." I barely recognize my own voice.

"Would you like to see him? He's sleeping but you can peek in." Expectant eyes meet mine, and I swear she's holding her breath for my response.

My heart rate accelerates again. "I ... yes. I'd like to see him." Oh fuck.

"Come in." She gestures with a swish of her hand, and I step into the marble-tiled entranceway. A sweeping mahogany balustrade frames a long staircase on our left. Broad corridors extend in three different directions off the main lobby. A massive old-fashioned crystal chandelier hangs overhead. "Hewson's room is this way." She points at the stairs. "Follow me."

Loving Kalvin

I walk after her like a zombie whose every move is instinctual rather than contrived. "Hewson?" I ask when we're halfway up the stairs, as the name registers in my foggy brain. "You called him Hewson after Bono?" Bono's real name is Paul Hewson, a fact Lana is well aware of having listened to me obsess nonstop over my favorite band for years.

"Yes." She stops at the top of the stairs, turning to offer me a shy smile. "I wanted him to have something of his father, so I named him Hewson Kalvin."

I can't believe we're having an almost normal conversation. I'll add it to the list of surreal moments over the last twenty-four hours.

"What's his last name?"

Her smile fades. "Williams," she whispers, and I wonder if that was one of her grandmother's conditions.

I don't like it. Don't like it one bit, but I say nothing, locking it away in a mental cubbyhole along with a million other things we need to discuss.

I trail after her, looking around anxiously. The hallway is dimly lit and painted in a drab green color. I'm half-expecting her grandfather to jump out with a loaded shotgun. "Eh, Lana?" I whisper, scrubbing a hand over my prickly jaw. "Your grandfather doesn't really have a shotgun, does he?"

She attempts to stifle a giggle.

Surreal moment number 497.

"No. I made that up," she admits sheepishly, "and they aren't here, anyway. My grandparents have gone to their cabin in Aspen until Tuesday." She nibbles on her lower lip. "I'm sorry, Kal. More than you can realize," she whispers. Her words bounce off me, falling meaninglessly to the floor.

Sorry is far too easy a word for her to say. Sorry cannot even begin to compensate for how she's treated me this time.

My eyes narrow at her, as anger competes with trepidation for prime position. Her hand stalls on the door handle. "This is his room.

You need to be super quiet so you don't wake him. He had a difficult time last night, and he needs to catch up on his sleep."

I nod curtly. *Does she think I'm an imbecile?*

Her hand goes to my elbow, and I jerk away without conscious thought. Hurt flares in her eyes. "We have a lot to talk about. Can you stick around for a while so I can explain? Please."

I jerk my head in agreement. As if I have any intention of leaving without some answers.

As she opens the door slowly and carefully, time seems to stand still. Blood rushes to my head, making me lightheaded. I quietly crack my knuckles as I step into the room. The room is large with a vaulted ceiling and two wide windows, curtained with heavy ornate drapes. A small glow emits from the tableside lamp in the corner of the room. My eyes hone in on the wooden crib in the middle of the room. I stop breathing as I detect the little bundle atop the mattress. A single cot, with an unmade comforter, is pulled alongside the crib. Lana must have been sleeping in here beside him. I watch her for a moment, bent over the crib, staring at our son with a look of joy and adoration on her face. My spout of anger splutters and dies as I watch her watching the baby with unbridled love and pride, not even realizing I've stopped moving. I'm rooted to the spot again, drenched in emotion. My heart does a funny jump.

She lifts her head, smiling expansively, waving me forward.

My sneakers don't make a sound on the plush carpet as I take another step. Then another. With every inch I move, my heart swells in my chest. My breath is oozing out in exaggerated, heavy spurts. She meets me halfway, taking my hand confidently in hers and urging me forward. I cling to her arm, more terrified and elated than I've ever been in my life.

And then I see him.

This small, perfectly formed little human.

This little part of me and Lana.

He's lying on his side, with his thumb in his mouth. I clamp a hand over my mouth as the most powerful burst of emotion hits me full on. My hand shakes as I look over my son for the first time. A light sheen of sweat dots his brow. His hair is thick and dark like mine. Tiny curls adhere to his sticky brow. His little chest rises and falls, his feet tangled in a white blanket. A serene sort of reverence washes over me as I stare at him in amazement.

Naked emotion brims in my chest, and I can't stop the tears from flowing. I'm clinging to Lana's side like I'll fall over without her. I feel her eyes on me, but I can't tear my gaze from our son.

I don't know how long we stand there, holding each other and staring at our baby boy. Silent tears continue to glide down my face, and when I glance at Lana, I notice she's crying too. There is a lot still to be said. A crap ton of explanation necessary, and I'm not entirely sure how I feel about Lana now, but, in this moment, all I want is to hug the shit out of her.

So, I do.

I reel her into my arms, hugging her tightly as I continue to gaze, awestruck, at my son asleep in his crib. "He's perfect," I whisper.

She nods, smiling through her tears. "He is, Kal. He really is."

After a while, she eases back, looking up at me with sad determination. "We should talk," she mouths.

I nod, watching as she bends over the crib, planting a delicate kiss on his brow. She looks inquisitively at me, and I step beside her, blood thrumming wildly through my veins. I lean in slowly, memorizing every second. My lips press gently against his brow, and his skin is warm but so soft under my touch. His breath trickles out of his mouth, and a delicate, fresh, clean fragrance lingers over him. I hover over his face for a minute, enchanted by the smell and feel of him.

Lana curls her fingers around my arm, and we tiptoe out of the room like thieves in the night. I startle in the corridor when I spy Greta waiting for us. She nods before walking away.

We follow her into a large, formal living space. Greta sits down on a stiff-looking couch in front of an open marble fireplace. I sit down on the couch across from her, and Lana perches on the edge beside me. "Hello, Kalvin."

"Hello, Mrs. Taylor." When she worked for my parents, we used to call her Greta, but things are different now.

"I only have a few things to say, and then I'll leave you and Lana to talk in private." She folds her hands primly on her lap. "You should know Lana wanted to tell you when she first found out she was pregnant. John and I are responsible for the fact she didn't. We see now that it was wrong, but we thought it was the best way of protecting her after everything that'd happened."

My jaw locks tight, but I borrow from my brother's repertoire, schooling my features into a neutral line. "I can't pretend to imagine what you must be feeling, and I'm sure this has come as a huge shock, but all I ask is that you treat my daughter with the respect she deserves. She has done a wonderful job with that little boy, but there is no need for her to do that alone anymore. Whether you two are together or not isn't a factor. You are both his parents, and, as such, the responsibility should be shared. All we ask is that you do right by Lana and Hewson."

I nod in agreement, because I don't trust myself to speak. She can't expect me to have any clue what to do when I've just been hit with this news, but I don't want to waste time arguing with Greta.

I need answers from Lana.

"Okay." She rises, moving over to Lana and pulling her into a gentle hug. "I'm going to bed, but wake me up if you need anything."

"It's okay, Mom. You get some sleep." She points to a small white unit on the coffee table. "I have the baby monitor, and I'll watch Hewson. I want to feed him his bottle tonight." She kisses her on the cheek.

"Goodnight, Kalvin." She gives me a small smile before exiting the room.

Lana moves to the couch her mom just vacated, sitting down across from me. She clears her throat. "I'm sorry you found out like this, but, I swear I was going to tell you. I tried a few times, but I kept chickening out."

"You should've told me the minute we met on campus." I lean

forward, placing my palms on my knees. "That's why you ran, isn't it?" She nods. "If I hadn't shown up here, were you ever going to tell me?"

"Yes." She holds my eyes, and I see the stark truth in her gaze. "What Mom said is true. I wanted to tell you when I discovered I was pregnant, but they convinced me not to. I thought it was better to let you get on with rebuilding your life, and, in a few years, after you'd gotten things back on track, I would tell you."

I snort out a laugh. "That is fucking priceless! How could you ever think that was fair?"

"I wasn't in a good place, Kal." She's gone very quiet. "I'm not offering excuses because I know it's unforgivable, but I was very depressed after the trial. I couldn't eat or sleep, and I was existing in a haze. Like I was surrounded by constant fog, and I couldn't see straight, couldn't think clearly. I'm not proud I allowed myself to be convinced of something I knew was wrong for a second time, but I wasn't myself. Plus, I was feeling sick all the time. I didn't realize it was because I was pregnant until a few weeks before Christmas."

There's an uncanny sense of déjà vu in her sentiment.

Secrets and lies. That's the sum of what we've become.

"You expect me to believe you were pregnant during the trial but you didn't know it?" *How can you not know you're pregnant?* It sounds a bit fishy to me.

"I know what you're thinking, and I don't blame you, but I'm not lying. I hadn't had periods for a couple of months, but I was distraught and stressed, and I presumed that was the reason. It never even crossed my mind that I could be pregnant until I was in a pharmacy picking up some meds for Mom and I happened across a pregnancy test. Something just snapped into place, and I knew. Knew I was pregnant. I bought two tests and went to the bathroom at the back of the store and confirmed it."

The magnitude of that moment hits me, and, although I'm still all kinds of messed up, I can't help feeling sorry for Lana. I hate that I was denied that experience with her. "I should've been there with you."

Her foot taps restlessly off the carpeted floor, and she worries her lip between her teeth. "What would you have done if I'd told you back then?"

I lean back, sighing as I stare at the ceiling. "I'm not sure," I admit truthfully, "but I wouldn't have left you to deal with it alone."

"I wasn't alone. Mom and Dad were great."

"I should have been the one supporting you," I snap. "Supporting our baby." My voice cracks, and I'm starting to lose control of my emotions. I'm all over the place. Feeling hurt and angry one minute, happy and awed the next, sad and aggrieved after that. My head hurts, and I don't know how to fully express all that I'm feeling, or if I even should. "I hate that you went through that alone, but you didn't even give me a say. I know things were broken between us, but how could you do that to me, Lana? How could you deny me that knowledge?"

"I wish I could take it all back. I do."

"But you can't, and I'm the one who's missed out on ..." My head whips up. "How old is he?"

She gulps. "He'll be six months in a few weeks."

Air whooshes out of my mouth, and I rest my head in my hands.

I can't. I just can't.

I lift my head, and tears sting my eyes. "I will never get that time back. How could you do that, Lana? The girl I knew would never have done that to me."

Her lower lip wobbles, and tears pool in her eyes, but she doesn't cry. She keeps it together. "I know," she whispers, and her face falls. "I'm not the same girl."

My eyes skim over her face, seeing so much of the Lana I knew, but she's right. She's changed. So have I. "And I'm not the same guy you knew." Truth.

"Where do we go from here?" Her tongue darts out, wetting her lips, and she fidgets with her hands in her lap. "I mean, what about us?"

I just stare at her, numb, as if in a daze. A heavy tension settles in the room. "I don't know how or what I'm feeling now," I admit. "All I wanted was honesty, Lana. Was that too much to ask for?"

A high-pitched cry erupts from the digital monitor on the table. The video screen is a little blurry, but the baby is clearly awake, his lungs in full working order, as the crying intensifies. Lana jumps up, glancing at her watch. "His routine is shot to pieces, so he's probably looking for a bottle now." Her pace is brisk as she strides toward the door. She casts a look over her shoulder. "You could give him his bottle, if you like?"

My Adam's apple bobs in my throat, and my mouth turns dry. I nod slowly, without conscious thought. Her answering smile is luminous as she hurries out the door. I'm in a kind of daze as I watch her arrive in the room through the monitor. She lifts the baby up, cradling him to her chest and murmuring soothing words as she gently rocks him in her arms. "It's okay, sweetheart. I've got you."

A massive lump clogs my throat, constricting my airways. A layer of sweat breaks across my brow.

"Daddy's here, and he's going to give you your bottle," she coos.

An icy-cold shiver creeps up my spine and bile fills my mouth.

I start frantically pacing the floor.

I don't know what I'm doing.

I can't do this.

How can I take care of a baby when I can barely take care of myself?

This was a mistake.

I shouldn't have come here yet.

I'm not equipped to deal with this.

Lana thinks I can slot into some role, a role she denied me for six months, and that everything will be sunshine and rainbows.

Well, it's not.

It's completely messed up.

Panic is doing a number on me, and I can't think straight. My heart is beating so fast in my chest, and my shirt is stuck to my back.

I need to get out of here.

I race out of the room, run down the stairs, and fly out the front door.

I clamber into my truck, quickly putting it in gear. Without looking back, I take off, desperate to put as much space between me and this house as possible.

Chapter Twenty-Seven
Lana

My heart sinks when I return to the room and there's no sign of Kal. Without checking, I know he's left. I position Hewson in my arms and give him his bottle with tears rolling down my face.

I knew it had been going too well.

Maybe, I pushed too hard.

It's an awful lot to take in. I had months to get used to the idea; he's had less than one day. My tears dry up. He just needs some time to get used to the idea. To process all his feelings.

I trust him to do the right thing.

I can be patient.

We can be patient.

I don't tell Mom how Kal disappeared last night because I don't want her scowling at me in an "I told you so way." I tell her we have lots to work through but so far so good.

What's one more lie in a sea of lies, right?

Hewson is vastly improved on Monday. He isn't back to his usual self, but he's catching up on his sleep, and his temp has come down plus he's taken all his bottles today. I hate the thought of leaving him, and although I don't like skipping my shift in the center, my son is my priority, so I decide to stay another night. I'll catch the first bus to UF in the morning so I don't miss classes again.

I press a soft kiss to his brow as I tiptoe out of the room at the butt crack of dawn on Tuesday morning. I'm crying again. It feels like I'm always crying these days, but I vow that's going to be a thing of the past.

I need to be strong.

For Hewson.

For Kal.

For me.

I fill Liv in on everything after classes on Tuesday, and she listens intently, never once interrupting or telling me she knew this would happen. "What are you planning to do?"

"Give him some space. Let him work through it in his own time." Even though it kills me, because now he's become a fixture in my life again, I'm missing him terribly. But I can't be selfish. And I can't rush him. "I trust Kal," I tell her truthfully. "He'll make the right decision."

The week and weekend comes and goes without a peep from Kal, and I'm beginning to doubt myself. I thought he would at least have checked in on Hewson by now, but I haven't heard from him or seen him around. The early morning coffees and end of day rides are a thing of the past. With every passing day, my hopes dwindle and my fears grow.

I head to the center on Monday night with a heavy heart. Brenda puts me straight to work, and I'm grateful for the preoccupation. A couple of hours into my shift, she asks me to sit with a new client while she waits for her first appointment.

The girl waiting on the couch looks deeply troubled. Turning haunted blue eyes on me, she frowns a little. Her stringy red hair has pronounced bangs that have been bluntly cut, and they don't do much for her. She's wearing a loose-fitting dirty gray shirt and black pants. A pang of sorrow assaults me. *What was done to this girl, and is it something she can come back from?*

"Hi. I'm Lana. Can I get you something? Water? Coffee?"

She looks up at me, and her expression turns to one of confusion. "Do I know you?"

Prickles of alarm wash over me. "I don't think we've met before."

She brushes it aside, shaking her head, and my shoulders relax. "A black coffee would be great."

"Coming right up." I smile and leave to fix her drink.

When I return, she is sitting stiffly on the couch, her eyes boring into mine as I approach. My smile falters as I hand her the steaming hot coffee. "Is everything okay?"

"You're her, aren't you?" she says, standing up. "You're that Lana bitch from the Kennedy trial."

I'm not hiding anymore. Keeping secrets and telling lies has brought me nothing but pain. I stand tall. "Yes, I'm that Lana."

Her eyes narrow. "Why are you here? You shouldn't be here!"

"I volunteer here because I want to help."

"Don't you think you've *helped* enough?!" she spits, her tone turning nastier by the second.

"I'm sorry. I don't wish to offend you or cause you any further pain." I take a step back. "I'll leave. I'll get Brenda to come and sit with you."

"Yeah, just run away," she sneers. "Run away and leave a mess in your wake. You're good at that."

I take the hit directly to my heart. Her aim couldn't have been better. "I'm sorry." I'm beginning to hate those two words, and I'm sick of hearing them come out of my mouth. I hate that my actions have necessitated their frequency. The girl is glaring at me like I'm the most evil person on the planet. What she fails to comprehend is that she couldn't hate me as much as I hate myself.

I'm turning around to leave when she flings her coffee at me. Scorching-hot liquid soaks my shirt, splashing the exposed skin at my neck. A few drops land on my face, and it feels like someone is peeling the skin off with a carving knife. Wild screams rip from my throat as unbearable pain slices across my upper body. I grab my shirt and whip it off, using the dry side to mop up the liquid currently burning my chest, neck, and face. I'm on my knees, screams intermingling with tears, when Brenda and two of the therapists rush into the corridor to see what the commotion is about.

Lucinda swings into action. The girl is taken into one of the rooms, and I'm brought to Brenda's office. Lucinda removes the first aid kit from the wall while Brenda helps me into a chair, softly extracting my hands from my neck. She winces. "She needs to go to the ER."

Lucinda crouches in front of me. "How badly does it hurt?"

"A lot."

She applies some salve before removing her sweater and handing it to me. "Put this on. Brenda will take you to the hospital. Do you want me to call anyone for you?"

Kal's face swims before me. "Could you call my roommate for me?" I send Liv's number to her phone and let Brenda escort me to hospital.

In the car, she asks me what happened, and I tell her everything that went down. She pats my hand but says nothing.

Liv arrives about an hour later. We're still waiting to be seen. Brenda refuses to leave, so the three of us wait together. Eventually, I'm seen by a doctor who confirms I have superficial burns to my face and second-degree burns to my right side, neck, and chest area. Blisters are already forming in a little row of bubbles over my right breast. It's just as well I'm finished breastfeeding. He dresses the wounds on my neck and chest and applies a cooling balm to the marks on my face. Giving me a script for pain medication, he sends me on my way.

Back in the dorm, I crawl into bed, lying carefully on my uninjured side. Liv hands me a bottle of water, and I pop a couple of pills. "Do you want me to call him?" she asks quietly.

"No. He doesn't want to speak to me."

She nods sadly. "Okay. Let me know if you need anything else."

"I will. Thanks for coming tonight."

"No problem. Try to get some sleep."

Surprisingly, I actually manage to sleep quite well, but when I wake the next morning, I'm in excruciating pain. I'm afraid to look in the mirror for fear of what I'll see. I have no choice but to stay at home, and I inwardly curse, hating to miss more classes.

After a couple of days, the pain isn't as bad and the redness on my face has reduced enough that I can venture out in public.

Thursday is my first day back since the incident, and it turns out to be eventful for a number of reasons. "What the hell happened to you?" Maya asks, dropping into the seat beside me before our financial accounting class starts.

I startle, surprised to see her talking to me. She's avoided me like the plague since my confession. "A girl threw coffee at me at the center Monday night."

She looks horrified.

I shrug. "It's not the first time I've been attacked."

A shameful expression crosses her face. "That's terrible, Lana. Are you in much pain?" She gestures toward my neck which is still bandaged. The marks on my face have faded so they're only barely visible.

"Not much. I'm taking some pills, and I change the dressing every day. The blisters on my chest and side are the sorest, but they appear to be healing." Thankfully. The doctor had suggested they might have to be drained otherwise, and I can only imagine how painful that would be.

She goes quiet. The professor steps into the room, setting up the session. "I owe you an apology."

"No, you don't. It's fine."

"I do." She turns in her seat, facing me. "I was horribly judgmental when I should've been more understanding. You're my friend, and I didn't even let you properly explain."

"Honestly, Maya. It's fine. I'm used to it."

"That doesn't make it right. And no one has the right to hurt you. That's just so wrong."

"It is what it is. I'm beginning to think this is going to follow me my whole life."

"I hope not, because that wouldn't be fair."

"Didn't you get the memo?" I joke. "Life isn't fair."

Our convo is ended when the professor calls for quiet, but we go for coffee afterward and thrash everything out. I leave the coffee shop feeling happier than I have in days. I'm not watching where I'm going as I round the corner, and I collide with a hard wall of solid muscle. Pain spears me on my right-hand side, and I drop my bag, crying out as I sway on my feet. A meaty pair of arms holds me up.

"Shit!" a familiar voice says, and I look up. Brett has a concerned look on his face. "Are you all right?"

"I will be in a minute," I rasp, gently holding my sore side.

"Let's sit there," he suggests, pointing at a bench over the way. He takes my bag and helps me hobble across the road.

"What happened to you?" His eyes fixate on the bandage on my neck.

"If I tell you, you can't tell him." When Kal contacts me, I want it to be for the right reasons.

He rubs the pronounced stubble on his chin, looking conflicted. "I know you guys have, uh, shit to work through, but he'd want to know you're hurt."

"Please."

He leans back on the bench, resting one thick leg over his knee.

"You're killing me, Lana, but okay. If you won't let him help you, let me."

"I don't need help. It's not like that." I fill him in on what went down Monday night.

"You shouldn't have to deal with stuff like that."

"I made my bed, Brett. Now I'm lying in it."

"I'll be honest, I was hugely skeptical when Kal first told me about you. I struggled to believe he could forgive you, but I get it now. I know we don't know each other all that well, but I can tell you're not a bad person. Anyone can see that within ten seconds of meeting you."

"Thanks." We are both quiet for a bit. "You don't have to give me deets, but is he okay? How is he doing?"

He twists around in his seat. "He's trying to get his head around it, but it's a lot to take in."

"I know." I pick at a loose thread on the hem of my jacket. "I'm trying to be patient, but it's hard. I miss him so much." I look up at the sky, my eyes following the slow motion of the fluffy clouds overhead. "I always seem to be missing him. You'd think I'd be used to it by now," I add in a jokey tone, trying to lighten the mood.

"He misses you too, but you lied to him again, Lana, and he's pissed."

My heart bleeds at the confirmation. "He has a right to be."

I stand up. God, I'm sick of myself at this stage. If it wasn't for Hewson, I don't know that I'd have the energy to face the world every day.

"Do you have a picture?" he asks.

"What?" My brow puckers.

"Of Hewson." He grins. "Rad name."

"It is, isn't it?" I grin as I extract my phone from my bag. I pull up a cute photo and hand it over.

His grin softens into a more affectionate one. "Wow. That asshole's got good genes, got to give him that."

I clear my throat. "Ahem."

He barks out a laugh. "I'm just yanking your chain." He pats the seat beside him, and I sit back down. "Lana, he's beautiful. You two have created a beautiful little dude."

I beam with pride. "I didn't think it was possible to feel so much love. I've always loved Kal with an intensity that is borderline unhealthy, but this is different. I look at my son, and my heart floods with happiness, with a joy that's so pure and untainted and innocent, and it's like nothing I've ever experienced before. I want Kal to experience that too."

Brett hands me back the phone. "He'll get there, Lana. I know he will. He's good people."

"I think so too. That's the only reason I haven't been pounding on his door. I'm trying to respect his need to think this through. To give him space to figure things out. All I ask is that he includes Hewson in his life. I want him to grow up with a father. I want him to grow up with Kal."

"He'll be a great dad."

"I know."

He stands up. "But don't tell him I said that. I'm planning on getting plenty of mileage out of this one." He chuckles, and I shake my head, getting up alongside him.

"Thanks for being a friend to him. I'm glad he has someone to talk to."

"He's spoken to Ky and Faye too."

"I thought he might." And I'm guessing Faye is under strict instructions not to call me, which is why I haven't heard from her. I'm not brave enough to call her myself. Besides, it's not fair to put her in an awkward position, and I promised I wouldn't do that again. I touch Brett's arm. "I've to get ready for my shift at the center, but thanks for everything."

"No problem. Anytime, Lana." I move to walk away, but he holds onto my elbow. "Give me your phone again." I hand my cell over without question. "If you need anything, anything at all, call me." He inputs his number before handing the phone back to me.

"I will, thanks, Brett."

The center manager calls me into her office before I've even taken my jacket off. A weight of dread sinks to the bottom of my stomach like a lead balloon. I think I'm about to get my marching orders.

She spends a couple of minutes fussing over me, asking how my injuries are, and if I need anything. Once that's out of the way, she jumps straight to the heart of the matter. They don't want me volunteering here anymore. Now the word is out about who I am, it's no longer appropriate. Client comfort is of paramount importance, and she's worried victims will stop coming forward. The work they do is too important to take any risks.

I agree completely, and I won't stand in the way of victims receiving the support they need; however, it doesn't stop the anguish from chiseling a hole in my heart as I trudge home.

Chapter Twenty-Eight
Kalvin

"I just saw Lana," Brett exclaims, stepping into the room and shutting the door with his foot.

I'm lying spread-eagled on my bed, wearing a pair of sweats and indulging my new favorite pastime—staring at the ceiling. I've spent so much time staring at this ceiling the last week and a half I can tell you where every little bump and every little stain is located. I know that at the end of my bed is a black smeared mark that is the squished remains of some insect. My money says someone deployed Lana's old trick. Grab the thickest book you can find, jump on the bed, and throw it at the poor unsuspecting creature. At least it's a quick death.

"Did you hear me?" Brett asks, dumping his gear bag on the ground.

"Yep," I say, popping the P.

Just trying to pretend I didn't.

My thoughts are consumed with Lana and the baby, and it feels like my skull is going to explode.

Last week marked the first anniversary of the trial, and I've been in a pretty shitty mood since. When I returned to the dorm that night,

I found a package waiting for me with Lana's handwriting all over it. She sent me her manuscript. *The Story of Us.* I still haven't plucked up the courage to read it. Now, it sits on top of my bedside table taunting me. Hurling imaginary abusive comments at me. Words like coward, chicken, deadbeat dad, and other unmentionables.

Brett drops onto the edge of my bed. "Come on, man. I know you're hurting, but you can't hide in here forever."

"I'm not hiding. I go to classes and the track."

"And you're a hermit the rest of the time." He leans forward on his hands. "I can't fucking imagine how you're feeling, but you have to face up to things eventually. The longer you leave it, the more damage you're doing."

I pull myself into a sitting position. "Don't fucking pin this on me! If anyone's responsible, it's her!" I've undergone the whole gamut of emotions since I fled Lana's house that Sunday, but I can't seem to get beyond the anger and disappointment.

"I know you miss her."

"Of course, I fucking miss her!" I yell. "But that means jack shit. She lied to me for months. Lied to my face for weeks. I can't forgive her for that."

He rubs the back of his neck. "What about your son, Kal? What are you going to do about him?"

I flop back down on the bed, the usual wave of terror flooring me. "I ... I don't know."

Brett sighs. He's been earning his best bud accolade these past few days. He let me stew for the first week, but, slowly, he's been trying to coax me into talking. The tricky thing is I can't figure out the maelstrom in my head. I go around and around in circles, never reaching a solution. I've never felt so many conflicting emotions. Been so unsure of my own mind. Not even when I was a prisoner in my home awaiting trial for a crime I hadn't committed.

The fear I felt then pales in comparison with the fear I feel now. I've barely eaten all week, and nothing messes with my appetite.

My entire system is in flux.

And I don't know what to do about it.

How to pull myself back.

I sit up again, flattening my back against the wall. "I want to be there for him, Brett, honestly I do, but what the fuck do I know about being a dad? I'm not even eighteen yet, for fuck's sake, and I can barely manage to take care of myself!"

Visions of Hewson's tiny face invade my dreams at night. If I draw a breath in now, I can smell his smell. I may have only been in his company for a short while, but that kid sure made an impression.

"Dude, no one knows how to be a parent," Brett says, sounding suspiciously like he's quoting something he read in a parenting book. "It's a 'learning on the job' situation."

"What if I'm no good at it?" I vocalize another one of my fears.

"You won't know until you try."

"I can't treat my son like he's a guinea pig! He's not a test subject." A renewed surge of inadequacy swims to the surface.

"Dude, think of your own parents. Are you telling me they've never made mistakes, because I know mine did."

I snort, thinking of all the ways my parents have fucked up. "Dude, my parents practically wrote the 'how not to parent' book."

"And do you think any less of them? Love them any less? Hate them for anything they did?"

Well, shit. "No to all the above," I begrudgingly admit.

Brett's expression is smug.

I stick my finger up at him. "No one likes a know-it-all."

"You're just pissed because you know I'm talking sense."

"I guess there's a first time for everything."

"Ha, fuckin' ha. I can be serious when I need to be. And this isn't about me. We're talking about you, so stop trying to go off topic."

"It's a lot of responsibility. My life will completely change." My brutal honesty demonstrates my selfishness in all its ugliness, but it's one of the thoughts that has cropped up a few times since I found out. Babies are a crap ton of work and responsibility. I'm not sure I'm ready for that.

He glares at me, and I'm pretty sure he wants to throat punch me right about now.

"You want to hit me, don't ya?"

"So fucking badly, you've no idea."

"I know how it sounds. I'm just being honest."

"Thing is, Kal, the deed is done. That kid is your flesh and blood. That automatically makes him your responsibility. You don't get to pick and choose the timing." He pulls his knees up. "How do you think Lana felt? She had no choice in the matter, and all the responsibility has fallen on her shoulders, and, from the sounds of it, she's getting on with things because she has to. That little boy is depending on her."

Greta's words come back to haunt me.

"She's had over a year to come around to the idea. I've had twelve days. *Twelve!*" I climb off the bed, pacing the floor. "And she had a choice. She didn't have to carry the burden alone, she made that decision." Or allowed it to be made for her.

"Let me tell you a story," he says, patting the space beside him.

"Story time with Brett, yay," I deadpan. "Please, Unkel Brett, can you read me Pinocchio. That's my favorite stwory," I lisp, putting on a babyish voice.

He slaps me across the head, pulling me down beside him. "Dipshit. I'm trying to have a grownup conversation here, and that's difficult enough for me as it is. Stop being an ass. Just shut up and listen."

I put my serious face on and turn to face him.

"My brother Asher found out he was going to be a dad a week before his nineteenth birthday," he starts explaining. "Unlike your story, the girl was just a random hook-up. A girl he had gone to school with. He went on a bender for two weeks after he found out, trying to drink himself into oblivion. I should know. I was still in high school and the only one living at home. I was there for it all."

Brett comes from a large family like mine. He has four older brothers and one older sister. How he tells it, he was an accident, arriving unexpectedly when Asher was five. His mom gave birth to him when she was forty-four, and both his parents are in their sixties now.

"Man, it was the worst shit show. Genesis—the girl he knocked up—"

I hold up a hand. "Wait a second. Genesis, dude? Who the hell calls their kid Genesis?"

"It happens, bro. Get over it." He sends me a "shut the fuck up look" and I clam up. "Anyway, *Genesis* came from a bad neighborhood. Her dad skipped town when she was a kid, and her mother was a known alcoholic. She tossed her out on her ass when she got pregnant so she came to live with us. Asher had no choice but to grow a pair. Living with Genesis was ... interesting. At first, man, it was gross. All she did the first four months was puke. Don't know why they call that shit morning sickness, 'cause she puked nonstop, all day long. Then she seemed to perk up, if you catch my drift." He wiggles his brows.

"Speak English, dude."

"Her tits fucking exploded, man. Like, they were the biggest breasts I've ever seen to this day, and believe me when I say I've seen my fair share." I don't need convincing. He makes a cupping gesture with his hands, and his lips go all pouty.

"You were sleazing over your brother's pregnant girlfriend? Dude, that's some sick shit right there."

"Dude, I was fourteen, and she used to prance around the house in these tight tank tops with her tits on full display. I spent months jerking off just thinking about them."

My face contorts. "Dude, you have serious problems."

"Dude, do I look like I give a fuck?"

"Continue." I wave my hand in the air. "This is disgustingly entertaining so far."

He shoves his middle finger up at me. "It didn't take long for Asher to realize Genesis wasn't going to win any Mom of the Year awards. She drank throughout the rest of her pregnancy, and we worried the baby would come out drunk or a raging alcoholic, but Demi arrived all pink and healthy and utterly gorgeous."

His eyes light up at the mention of his niece. He's told me about her before, but I never knew the background. "I love my niece. She's the coolest, sweetest little thing, but it was difficult when she was a baby. The first few months were a fucking nightmare, not going to lie to you, bud. She had colic and she screamed all the time. Like, I mean, *all* the time. I couldn't go to sleep without ear plugs."

I have no idea what colic is, but I don't feel like educating myself either.

I'm in sync with that old adage—ignorance *is* bliss.

"Dude, that girl has a fine pair of lungs on her, I tell ya." He chuckles. "Genesis did a runner when Demi was four months old, and we haven't seen her since."

I curse under my breath.

"Honestly? Best thing that could've happened. Not that Asher felt that way at the time. He took it all on himself. Felt he hadn't done enough to help. To make her feel accepted. He felt huge guilt over the fact Demi was growing up without her mother. Our mom helped out a lot, but she was still his responsibility and he stepped up. Dropped out of Yale. *Yale.* Fact, friend." He wiggles his eyebrows. "Asher was always the smart one, the one designated to take over the family business, so no one was surprised when he got into Yale, but he had to give it up. He didn't want to be so far away from Demi, so he enrolled in a local college and worked his ass off to graduate with a business degree."

His expression turns grave. "He had a rough couple of years, but he did what he needed to for his daughter. I've never been prouder of my brother, and he's an amazing father. Demi dotes on him. Worships the ground he walks on. Asher works for Dad's company now, and he'll take over as CEO in three years when Dad retires. He started going out with Melinda two years ago, and she insisted that Demi was an integral part of their relationship from the get-go. She's been the mom Demi deserves. They recently got engaged, and they're planning to marry next year."

It's a nice story, and I get why he's telling me this, but the whole scenario still scares the crap out of me.

Brett's hand lands on my shoulder. "I know you're worried you won't be good enough, but you will be. It won't be easy, but nothing worth fighting for is. Everyone knows that."

"There's more to it than that. There's Lana, figuring out how we do this whole thing, and telling my parents and the rest of my brothers. There's a shit ton of stuff to figure out, and honestly, man, I don't even know where to begin."

"Asher was a fucking mess at the start. He expressed a lot of the same sentiments as you, but he pulled through. If you talked to him, he'd tell you he wouldn't have it any other way. I can set up a call for you if you think it'd help."

"Maybe. Let me think about it."

"I just want to say one final thing, and then I'll shut up. There are a couple major differences between your story and my brother's. You have history with Lana and you love her, I know you do. She's made some bad choices, but they're not insurmountable if you can find it in your heart to forgive her. And *she* loves *you*. She's loved you her whole life. You have a girl and a son worth fighting for, Kal. Don't do something you'll end up regretting because that may be the one thing you can't recover from."

Chapter Twenty-Nine
Lana

When the following day passes and there's still no word from Kal, I hit rock bottom. I've lost him, and at this stage, I'm also concerned that he's not going to be there for Hewson. I'm running out of ways to throw Mom off the scent, and I'll have to admit the truth if he doesn't man up soon. I'm also questioning my whole approach. *Am I right to leave him alone to work this out, or should I be more forthright?* I don't want to push him. *I want him to make this decision by himself, but what if he doesn't?* For Hewson's sake, I'll have to intervene. Kal can reject me, but I'm damned if I'm going to let him reject his son without putting up a fight.

I thought leaving him a copy of my manuscript for *The Story of Us* along with a handwritten note on the day of the anniversary of the trial might have sparked something in him, but it appears to have made no difference, which worries me enormously. While I'm talking a great game, deep down I'm scared I'm deceiving myself into thinking everything is going to work out when it's not.

I'll have more free time on my hands now I'm not volunteering at the center. It could be a curse if I don't keep myself busy, so I'm going to use the time to focus on two things—working on my book and researching options for college next semester. I meant what I said to Mom a couple weeks ago. I want all of us out from under my grandmother's influence. I've discovered there is family housing on campus and childcare facilities—Baby Gators—and I'm actively looking into it to see if it's a possibility for Hewson and me. I want Mom to be free to reunite with Dad in Connecticut. I know she'll put up the mother of all fights, but I'm prepared for it.

At the very least, I'll make sure Kal provides some financial support for Hewson, so I think I can make this work. The big issue is funding for next semester's fees. I'm due to meet with the administration next week to see if there is any scholarship potential. It's a long shot, but I want to do everything in my power to stick with my life plan without the need to rely on my grandparents' money.

I also have another idea which might help with the financial side of things, even if it's a long shot.

I'm one of the last to leave the library Tuesday night, and I'm bone-weary by the time I make it back to my dorm.

A form steps out of the shadows, and I scream.

"Shush, Lana. It's only me," Kal says, while I try to recalibrate my heart. His hands are shoved in his pockets, and he's staring awkwardly at the ground. "Can we talk?"

"Yeah. Sure," I pant out.

He leads me to his truck and we both get in. Tension is ripe in the air as I wait for him to start. He clears his throat, and I turn to look at him. Even in the dim light of the cab, I can see the strain on his face. Dark, bruising shadows linger under his eyes, and there's a thick layer of hair on his chin. It looks like he hasn't shaved in weeks. His mouth is pulled into a grim line, and his face is leached of all color.

He looks as bad as I feel.

"I'm sorry for running out on you. I shouldn't have done that, but I freaked," he starts by explaining.

"It's okay. I know you were in shock."

He frowns as his eyes hone in on my neck. Instinctively, I reach up, wrapping a hand around my bandaged skin. "What happened?"

"It's nothing."

"Goddammit, Lana! Hasn't there been enough lies? Enough omissions?" My stomach lurches sourly. Slowly, I nod and explain what happened. "You should've told me. I would've come to the hospital with you."

"You weren't exactly speaking to me, and I wasn't sure you'd want to know."

"Of course, I would have! Just because things are ... messed up between us right now doesn't mean I've stopped caring. I'm trying to wrap my head around it, Lana, but it's a lot to take in."

I gulp. "I know. I've been there, but if it helps, Kal, he's a sweet little boy and so easy to care for. He is sleeping through the night now, and he's always happy and smiling during the day. It's ... it's not hard to love him. Not hard at all."

"I don't think I'll be good enough," he whispers. "I don't know the first thing about being a dad."

Taking a chance, I shunt over a little, taking his hands in mine. "You just have to be yourself. That's all. I believe in you."

"How did you do it? How did you know what to do?"

I snort. "Kal, I was completely terrified the first couple of weeks. The enormity of it only hit me when I was holding him in my arms. To know this tiny little person was so defenseless and so utterly reliant on me was the proudest and scariest feeling in the world. Believe me when I say I know all about feeling inept. I would look at him sleeping in his crib at night and feel wholly inadequate." I bite the inside of my cheek. "But I was also determined." I eyeball him. "I was all he had, so I had to be enough. That gave me the strength and determination I needed. Well, that and the baby books I devoured." I laugh, but it sounds forced. "Between them and Mom and learning as I went along, I've managed, and you will too."

He rubs the back of his head. "Can I, uh, borrow those books?"

My lips tug up. "Sure. They're back at the house, but I'll get them for you this weekend."

"I, uh, was thinking maybe I could come visit this weekend? If that's okay?"

I can't contain the happy feeling, and a huge smile spreads across my mouth. "That'd be great. We could take him out somewhere so we don't have to be around the others. Maybe we could go to the—"

"Lana," he cuts in bluntly, removing his hands from mine as if he's only just realized our hands were conjoined. "I was thinking maybe you could show me how to look after him this weekend and then I could take him out, by myself, every Saturday."

Disappointment is a brutal kick in the gut. "Sure. Of course." I try to rein in my misplaced excitement.

He levels me with a sincere look. "You lied again, Lana, and I'm so angry with you. It honestly wasn't that hard to forgive you for the trial because that was hurt speaking, and I'd contributed to that, but this—this is completely different. You kept something hugely important from me. Denied me the chance to be at the birth of my child. Forced me to miss out on the first six months of his life. I will never get that time back."

He looks out the window, carefully planning his next words. Slowly, he turns around. "I want to forgive you, and maybe someday that forgiveness will be forthcoming, but how can I ever trust you again, Lana? How can I believe you're telling me the truth when I know you're capable of such dishonesty?" His voice cracks, and tears are clogging my throat, but I hold them at bay. I have no right to them. Everything Kal says is the truth.

"I came to UF to fight for a second chance. To prove I could be the man you deserved, but things have changed. Now you need to prove you're the woman I know you to be, because the Lana I knew didn't lie, and she sure as hell didn't allow herself to be manipulated into doing things she wasn't comfortable with. The girl I knew carried such quiet confidence with grace, she knew her own mind and had the strength to follow her convictions. But you're not her, and I can't believe in you, can't trust you, not when I know what you're capable of. And without that, there is no us. When I look at you, all I see is deceit and lies, and that's not a good foundation for a relationship, so, whatever we had, whatever we were reclaiming, it's lost. You and I are over. I'm here because I won't abandon my child, and I want the opportunity to get to know him, but that's it. That's all I can offer."

It's a miracle I hold the tears at bay, but I do, nodding my understanding.

But when I get back to my dorm, the dam breaks, and I collapse into a sodden heap on my bed, soaking my pillow, and only falling asleep after I've cried myself dry.

I don't see Kal the rest of the week, and it's for the best. My heart is broken, shattered into a million pieces, and I can scarcely drag my body out of the bed each day. It would be so easy to give in to my depression, to stay in bed, shutting out the outside world and giving into my grief. But I can't. I can't indulge my self-pity. I'm a mom now, and I've made a commitment to my son, and that's why I get up every morning and go to class and immerse myself in my studies and my book.

I promised Kal if there was anything to report regarding Hewson I'd contact him, and I meant it, but our son has had a placid, uneventful week, according to Mom. I travel to Earleton on Friday night, forgoing the usual social interaction. I haven't had much enthusiasm for parties these last few weeks. Anyway, I'm making great inroads with my manuscript, and I plan to stay up late tonight, writing on my veranda, looking out over the lake. If there's anything I'll miss about my grandparents' estate, it's the peace and quiet and the stunning views.

Mom has deliberately kept Hewson up a little later tonight so I can see him before he goes to sleep. He's fresh out of the bath, all soft and gorgeous smelling when I pull him into my arms. I give him his bottle seated in the rocking chair in his room and then tell him a story, watching as his eyelids grow heavy. I continue to talk in hushed tones, rocking him in my arms long after he's fallen asleep. I miss him so much during the week that, some weekends, it's almost impossible to let him out of my arms.

Placing him carefully in his crib, I slide the blanket up over him. I kiss the top of his head and sigh in contentment.

This right here.

This is why I'm doing everything.

Why I know everything will be okay, even if my vision of the perfect family life has come to a crashing end.

I tiptoe out of his room and make my way to the smaller reception room where I know Mom's waiting to talk to me. When I step inside, I startle at the sight of my grandmother, sitting stiffly on the couch across from Mom looking like there's a lamp pole shoved up her butt. My grandparents use the formal living room, and they hardly ever step foot in this room, which is why Mom and I have claimed it as our own. Mom's lips are pulled tight, and her eyes look shiny. My fingers dig into my palms. If grandmother has said anything to upset her, I won't be responsible for my actions. No matter how hard Mom tries, grandmother never praises her, and she's always quick to find fault.

Honestly, I can't get out of here fast enough.

"Ah, Lana. There you are," she greets me almost pleasantly, patting the couch alongside her.

My eyes dart to Mom's and she subtly nods. With mounting trepidation, I sit down beside my grandmother. She smiles at me, and warning beacons boom in my head. "I believe your young man is visiting us tomorrow."

"He's not my—" Mom's terrified eyes stop me mid-sentence. Understanding, I clear my throat. "Yes." I smile.

"Excellent. I look forward to meeting him. I expect he'll stay for dinner."

Over my dead body am I subjecting Kal to whatever she has in store. "I'll ask him."

Her smile turns into a grimace. "I expect you both to be there." Her tone is demanding, and I have a silly, childish urge to poke my tongue out at her. I stifle my giggle, merely nodding. She can go to hell. I'll have Kal out of here in plenty of time. I don't care how mad she gets.

Mom slumps on the couch after grandmother has left.

"What's that all about?" I get up and move to the table. I pour two glasses of wine and hand one to Mom as I sit down beside her.

"She was over the moon when I told her Kalvin Kennedy was Hewson's father and that he was coming to see him tomorrow."

"Ah, I see." I kick off my shoes and lift my bare feet onto the table. We hadn't told grandmother who the father was on purpose because Mom said she didn't trust her not to interfere. Not to contact the Kennedys and make them aware. We were worried she might do that anyway, even without proof. My trial testimony is a matter of public record, so it wouldn't take much to join the dots, to figure out he was my baby daddy. Grandmother is a total snob, and the fact Kal comes from such a prestigious family has clearly delighted her. Blood boils in my veins.

"It makes me dislike her even more," Mom admits, a little apologetically. Even though no one would blame Mom for saying she hated her parents, she has never once said that about them. My mother has more dignity in her little toe than my grandmother has in her whole body. "If your father had come from money, she would've been overjoyed that he wanted to marry me and accept responsibility for his baby, but because he was poor, she wanted to get me as far away from him as possible." She takes a big swig of her wine. "It hurts a little that she's willing to accept Kalvin just because he comes from money."

"I know, Mom." I rest my head on her shoulder. "But she's a narrow-minded bigot, and she's going straight to hell. I don't care that she goes to church every day, donates thousands to church funds and charities, and acts all pious in the community. Being charitable in your every thought and every action is what matters. It's why you'll be an angel when you get to heaven."

I'm happy when a smile lifts the corners of Mom's mouth. I deplore seeing her so upset. I know living here has been very hard on her, and I sense she shelters me from the brunt of it. My heart swirls with love and pride. "I love you, Mom. I don't say it enough, but I love you and Dad so much. I couldn't have asked for better parents." My words carry much more weight now I'm a parent myself, and I see how difficult it is.

"I'm proud of you, Lana, and we both love you very much." She kisses my temple. "I always knew you'd make a great mom, but you've surpassed all my expectations. I know things haven't been easy, but I admire your strength and your determination. I admire how you've pulled yourself out of that dark place you were in and how hard you're working to create a better life for you and your son. I genuinely hope things work out for you with Kalvin, but if they don't, you'll be fine. More than fine." She pats my hand. "Forge your own path in life, sweetheart. Don't rely on anyone else to do it for you."

I'm a complete Nervous Nellie the next morning as I wait in the lobby for Kal. The front gate confirmed he just arrived. After what feels like eternity, the doorbell chimes, and I take a step forward. I dressed Hewson in a cute blue-and-white polo shirt and shorts. He's been in great form all morning and is not due a nap for a little while. My heart is thumping so hard in my chest, I'm sure you can hear it echoing along the cavernous hallway. I open the door with clammy palms.

The sun has decided to grace us with its presence today, and thick beams of glorious sunshine bathe Kal in a golden glow. He's wearing snug-fitting dark denims and a white T-shirt under an open azure button-down shirt that brings out the blue in his eyes. Pristine navy sneakers adorn his feet. The scruff from his chin is gone, and some color has returned to his face. Looking slightly uncomfortable, he claws a hand through his thick, glossy hair, and a few strands fall over his forehead. He looks sinfully good, and my heart longs for him.

No measure of time will ever erase my attraction to him or how he makes me feel.

The woodsy, citrusy scent of his cologne swirls around me as he steps into the lobby. His eyes are fixated on Hewson, and expectation is ripe in the air. Tentatively, he extends his hand, curling his fingers around Hewson's. "Hey there, little buddy." Hewson wraps his fingers around Kal's and gurgles. Kal's eyes fill up.

The sharp *tappity-tap* of heels on the marble floor has me groaning. "Heads-up," I whisper. "My grandmother is incoming. She's a massive fan." His expression is disbelieving as he arches a brow.

"Lana, darling," Grandmother says, leaning in to kiss my cheek—for, like, the first time ever—"there you are. And you must be Mr. Kennedy. It's a pleasure to meet you." She extends her hand, and Kal shakes it while I resist the urge to run to the kitchen for some bleach to scrub her saliva from my cheek.

"Likewise, Mrs. Williams. You have an impressive home." My grandmother's smile is so vast I think it might split her face in two. I stare at the stranger in our midst with growing unease.

She pats his arm affectionately. "You're too kind."

"Thank you for taking Lana and my son in." He glances at me, looking a little apprehensive. "But, you should know, I intend to support them going forward."

That catches me off guard. And Grandmother. She's a little shaken when she replies. "That's very admirable, but Lana and Hewson are always welcome here." She leans in, pinching Hewson's cheek. I don't think she's cruel enough to deliberately hurt him—her assaults are more of the verbal kind—and she genuinely seems fond of our baby, but she clearly pinched harder than she should have. Hewson bursts out crying, and instant rage replaces the blood flowing through my veins. My motherly instinct roars inside me, and my hand is on the move before I think. Kal reacts fast, curling his fingers around mine and pulling me into his side, before I can raise my hand to my grandmother. His eyes urge caution.

Shucking out of his hold, I cradle Hewson to my chest, rubbing a hand up and down his back as I whisper soothing assurances in his ear. I gently rock back and forth until he's settled.

Grandmother looks a little sheepish, but she doesn't apologize. I don't think sorry exists in her vernacular. "If you'll excuse us, Grandmother," I say through gritted teeth. "Kal and I have a lot to talk about."

I urge him to follow me with my eyes. He trails wordlessly behind me as I head upstairs to my room. We need privacy to talk, and this is the only place I'm confident Grandmother won't impinge on.

Hewson has stopped crying by the time we close the door, but his face is splotchy and tear-stained.

"I wanted to slap her too," Kal admits, "but that wouldn't have been very smart."

I start pacing the room, holding my son protectively to my chest. "That pompous, interfering, snobby old bag!" I hiss.

Kal steps in front of me, holding my elbow. "Stop. Chill." He looks down at Hewson, nestling into my chest. "Can I hold him?"

My anger flitters away. "Of course. Here." Gently, I reposition Hewson in Kal's awkward arms. Lifting one of his hands, I place it across Hewson's back so he's lifted a little higher against Kal's torso. When Hewson wraps his tiny arms around Kal's neck and leans his head on his shoulder, a little whimper leaks out of my mouth. I can't help it. I've imagined it so many times.

Kal is standing rigidly still, a look of utter shock on his face. His eyes well up, like my own. My son looks so tiny clinging to his dad but so at home. It's all my fantasies come to life. Raw emotion clogs my throat, and I can't speak. Gradually, Kal relaxes, becoming more confident as he smooths his hand up and down Hewson's back. He looks down at him with so much love in his eyes, and I can't stop the joyful tears from falling. "You're a natural," I whisper.

"Lana." His tone is awed. "He's so beautiful."

"Of course, he is, Kal. He's a part of you." I shrug, trying to lighten my words even though they come from my heart and soul. "There's no way he couldn't be."

After Hewson has fallen asleep, I place him in his crib, and we head to the veranda of my room with the baby monitor. Mom has left pink lemonade and honeybuns on a tray for us, and I smile at her thoughtfulness.

Kal looks a bit dazed as he sits down. "My heart feels so full. I didn't think I'd feel so much, but holding him in my arms, damn, that was special."

"Every day with him is special." I pour lemonade into two glasses, handing one to Kal. "That's why it's so hard to be away from him all week. I hate it, but it's necessary. The reason I'm taking extra classes is so I can graduate as quickly as possible. I want to get a job and provide a proper home for him."

Kal takes a sip of his drink, looking thoughtful. "That's the real reason you're studying business?" I nod. He is quiet for a bit. "It's kinda one of the things I wanted to talk to you about today. I have no right to demand things of you, and that's not what I'm trying to do at all. Despite how things are between us, I still want what's best for both of you, and living here isn't it." He looks over his shoulder into my bedroom. "This place is not what I want for my son," he adds quietly. "It's ... stale, depressing, devoid of life." A little smirk crests his lips. "Comes complete with its own domineering tyrant." I can't help but smile. He's not wrong. "And I want my son nowhere near her."

Removing an envelope from his back pocket, he hands it to me. "This is all I have right now, but I'll get more." I blink excessively as I open the envelope, losing count of the amount of hundred dollar bills. "Will that help?"

"More than you know," I whisper.

Chapter Thirty
Kalvin

She clutches the envelope tightly in her grasp. "I get the first half of my grandfather's trust fund in January when I turn eighteen, and it's yours. You can pay your tuition and maybe buy a house or an apartment for you and Hewson. Something close to campus would be good so I can see more of him."

Tears prick her eyes. "A house?" she whispers. "How much is half exactly?"

"A mill or thereabouts," I confirm.

She blinks rapidly. "Wow."

I shrug. Money has never meant that much to me, but I know I'm lucky because we have plenty of it. All I'd have to do is call Mom or Dad, and they'd wire the funds so Lana could buy a house immediately, but I'm not ready to tell my parents quite yet. They're going to give me hell when they realize I sat on this, but I need to get comfortable with my son first before I bring the rest of the Kennedy clan down on top of him.

I need this time for me. For me and him.

Plus, I'm not sure how Mom's going to react to Lana. When we were kids, Mom had treated Lana like the daughter she'd never had, but all that changed after I kissed her in Nantucket. I don't know what she's going to think now. I may be all kinds of pissed at Lana, but I don't want her burdened with more stress.

Brett said something last night that struck a chord. He said a lot of girls would have put my name on the birth certificate if they'd just had my kid. Use it as an excuse to bleed me dry. Lana did the opposite, and not because she's never been into me for my money. She was attempting to give me back my life, and she mistakenly thought saddling me with a baby would interfere with that. She fucked up. No question about that. But her motives weren't entirely wrong.

I wish I could say it was enough to forgive her, because I want to, but I can't help how I feel. Something is broken between us, and I don't know if we can find our way back.

For now, I've got to push that aside. Ensuring she and Hewson are provided for is my number one focus. I want them out of this fucking mausoleum, pronto.

"I can't take all your money, Kal," Lana protests. "I'm glad you want to help support Hewson financially, and I'll happily accept, but *I'm* not your responsibility. I can't take your money for my tuition. I'll fix that myself, and I already have a few ideas."

I knew she'd do this. I put my glass down and turn to face her, blasting her with the full magnitude of my awesomeness. Her eyes, predictably, glaze over. I'm not going to apologize for blatantly using my charm to get her to agree. This is for her too, and I'll use whatever tricks I have in my arsenal to convince her. "I'm getting to follow my heart's desire, and it's only right that you do too. It's not too late to change your major. You can still pursue your dream, and you don't need to sacrifice your ambition anymore. I'm going to help you. I swear it. I won't leave you to bring our son up alone. I'm invested." Naked emotion clogs my throat. "I mean, I'm fucking useless, but I'll learn, right?"

Tears brim in her eyes as she nods.

"Promise me, first thing Monday, you'll go speak to the appropriate person and put the wheels in motion." I see the conflict in her eyes. The unwillingness to take something for herself. The belief that she hasn't done anything to earn it. I jump to Plan B. "If it makes you feel better, you can consider the tuition fees a loan, and you can pay me back once you are making millions from your books." My smile is honest. I've been reading her stories for years, and she's got a God-given talent. She's going to be a very successful writer. I feel it in my bones.

"Did you read it?" Expectant eyes meet mine.

Fuck. *The Story of Us* is still sitting unopened on my bedside table like a ticking time bomb. "Not yet."

"Oh." She averts her eyes.

I tilt her chin up with my finger. "I will read it, I promise, when I'm in the right frame of mind." It means a lot that she'd trust me with it when I know she had concerns about showing it to me.

"I ... okay. And thank you for the money. That's enormously helpful."

"You'll accept?" She nods. Thank fuck. A little bit of stress lifts off me. "I've spoken to Ky, and he's prepared to loan me whatever cash we need until my trust fund kicks in. He received his, this year, and he's hardly dipped into it." I reach out and hold her hands, because I know she's going to fight me on this. "If you want, you can start looking for a new place to live right away. I'll make it happen, whatever you need, whenever you need it."

Tears course down her cheeks. "You can't just swoop in and save the day." She half-laughs.

I smirk. "Why the hell not? I'm Hewson's father. It's my job to provide for him. And you're the mother of my child, and that means I need to make sure you're looked after too. I'm not going to take no for an answer, and we both know how stubborn I can be."

"Let's not forget impatient," she jokes.

"Exactly. Which is why you must say yes to everything before I flip."

She nibbles on her lip, and so many emotions skate over her face. I want to pull her into my arms and hug the shit out of her, but I can't. I can't forget what she's done. And it's hurt me more than I've let on.

"Okay," she relents, and I breathe a sigh of relief. "But the tuition money is just a loan. I'm going to pay you back every cent, and I don't want to buy a place, I already have something in mind." She proceeds to tell me about Baby Gators and the family housing on campus. Her name is already on the list for the next available unit. I make a mental note to have a word with the relevant person to see if I can do anything to bump her up the list.

I spend the rest of the day with Lana and Hewson. She shows me how to feed, change, and bathe him. We take long walks on the grounds, in between spouts of torrential rainfall, and we pore over a bunch of books covering every aspect of caring for babies and toddlers. She shoves me out the door at four p.m. before her grandmother can interrogate me during dinner.

On the drive home, I'm feeling less freaked out and more confident than I've felt since finding out. I pull out my cell and punch in my brother's number.

Over the next week, I throw myself into my classes and the track, texting Lana daily for updates on Hewson. She forwards me photos Greta sends her during the day, and I well up at each and every one. I still can't believe he's mine. That we created such a perfect little baby. I pepper her phone with texts as I progress through the baby books, and we laugh together over the absurdity of some of the advice. I enjoy the flirty nature of our conversations, but I'm deliberately holding back. We need to get along for Hewson's sake, but that's all this can be.

I tell Mom I can't come home for Thanksgiving, and I spend the day at a hotel with Lana and Hewson. I know if I went back to Wellesley I'd have to confess, and I'm not ready for that yet. I hate lying to my family, but I've got my own family now, and they have to come first.

Another week passes by, and I can't believe we're into December. My first semester is almost completed, and I'm doing okay at this father lark. I've spent the last couple of Saturdays with my son. Usually, I just hang around Earleton, but I make a point of taking him out on my own. It would be too easy to fall into a pattern with Lana, and I don't want to get her hopes up.

She handles it stoically, although I can tell by the long, wistful looks she sends my way that she wishes things were different.

Brett came with me last week, and he doted on Hewson. We had a hairy moment when Hewson detonated a stink bomb in his diaper. Man, shit was literally flying everywhere. At least Lana had the foresight to pack a fresh change of clothes for the baby, but the same couldn't be said for me and Brett. When I returned Hewson later that night, the smell of shit off me was puke inducing. Lana was in hysterics when I told her what happened, and I left the house with her laughter echoing in my ears.

I'm still smiling at the memory when my cell rings, dragging me back to the present. I pick up, offering my brother the usual greeting. "What's up, asshole?"

"Hey, douche. Just calling to check in. How's my little nephew?" Ky asks.

"He's great. Did you get the pic I sent last night?"

"Oh, we did. Dude, Faye has a whole wall dedicated to Hewson in the kitchen. My cell was out of my hand before I even had time to look at it." He chuckles.

"Bro, someone sounds broody," I tease.

"Don't fucking go there," he warns, and I drop it. "You booked your flight yet?"

"Nope." Stress undercuts my tone. Christmas is only a few weeks away, and I know I'm going to have to go home and tell the folks. The thought makes me want to submit for a full body waxing. It'd be less terrifying.

"You can't delay it any longer, Kal," Ky says quietly. "You need to tell them."

"I know. How do you think they'll react?"

"They'll be okay with it, bro. I'm sure they'll be shocked at first, but they'll be happy once the news has settled. You know how much Dad loves babies. He'll be all over Hewson like a rash." He pauses for a second. "Are you planning on taking Lana and the baby with you?"

"No." Lana's going to Connecticut to spend Christmas with Greta and John. A family unit has become available on campus, and she's moving in there with Hewson in January, so this'll be her last opportunity to be with her family before everything changes. There's no need for her parents to live separately any longer, so Greta is moving to Connecticut full-time. Everything is starting to fall into place.

"That's too bad," Ky says. "It'd be good to see them. I'm not sure how I'm going to break the news to Faye. She'll be devastated. She can't wait to hold Hewson in her arms."

"You're so screwed, bro." I prefer to joke than face the truth. He mumbles something incoherent. "When everything's out in the open, she can fawn over Hewson as much as she likes. I'll need all the help I can get when I take him home." A pang of sadness washes over me at the thought of going home without Lana.

Just then, my phone pings with a text. It's Riley. Strange. We're not that close. But I know he's still seeing Olivia, so I figure this must be something to do with Lana. A sudden panicky feeling causes all the air to rush out of my lungs. "Bro, I've got to go."

"Book your flight, Kal," Ky says before hanging up.

I call Riley immediately and he answers straightaway. Blaring music rings out in the background. "Give me a minute," he roars down the phone, and I hold the handset away from my ear. The noise mutes, and then Riley is speaking in a more level tone. "Sorry about that. It's loud as fuck in there."

It's Friday night and I don't need to be a rocket scientist to work out where he's at. "You at the frat?"

"Affirmative, and you need to get your ass here, stat."

Tiny hairs lift at the back of my neck. "Is Lana okay?"

"Look, dude, I don't want to get involved in your business, and I know stuff is awkward between you guys right now, but I figured you'd still want to know this. Chase is putting the moves on Lana again. Usually, I wouldn't be concerned 'cause Lana's got no interest in him, but she's kinda sad tonight, and she's been drinking. I'm worried she might be about to do something she'll regret."

Oh, hell to the no.

That asshat is not laying a finger on my girl.

I'm already pulling on clothes. "I'm on my way. Keep her away from him till I get there?"

"I'll do my best. Hurry the fuck up."

Chapter Thirty-One
Lana

A few hours earlier

It's Friday night and I'm lying face down on my bed, wallowing in self-pity. I had a late study session this evening—cramming for my exams next week—so there was no point going home tonight. Hewson would be fast asleep by the time I arrived. I'm not sure why today, of all days, I woke up so depressed.

It's all tied to Kal and the fact we don't have a future together except as co-parents.

He's been completely up front with me, and he's kept his word in relation to Hewson. That's all that should matter. He's spending time with our son and providing for both of us. He's paved the way for my parents to reunite. Things are slotting into place, so I should be ecstatic, yet all day I've felt like I'm on the verge of tears. Like the tiniest thing will set me off.

I've got to face facts.

I've lost Kal.

I've lost that dreamy vision of the future I had—the one where the three of us were a proper family. Where Kal was living with us and we were raising our son together as a couple. As a team. And it hurts so much. It hurts to see him collecting Hewson and going off by himself. If I'd told him when I first discovered I was pregnant, I would have that life now. But there's no point in crying over all the what ifs. I don't have a time machine. I can't turn back the clock.

And I shouldn't be so greedy. So selfish. Kal is doing more than I could ever ask of him. He's proving to be a natural father, and he's going out of his way to support my ambitions. I shouldn't want more.

The door opens, interrupting my pity party, and Olivia prances into the room. She takes one look at me and jumps on the bed beside me. "What gives?"

I lift my head. "Just ignore me. I'm having a bad day."

She leans back, tucking her hands behind her head and crossing her ankles at the feet. "Someone once told me I was a great listener." She smirks and I swat her with a pillow. That someone was me. And I meant it. She has listened to me whining about all my drama for months now and never once complained or sought anything for herself. "Come on. A problem shared is a problem halved."

I half-laugh and half-moan. "So cliché!"

I sit up, pulling my knees into my chest. "I'm having one of those 'woe is me' days."

"Let me guess? This is about Kalvin?"

I nod. "He's doing great with our son, Liv. Really great, and I shouldn't want more, but I do."

"You can't help loving him."

"I know, but I think this is it for us. I don't think he's going to change his mind. I've hurt him too much this time. And I deserve it, I do, but I can't help thinking what'll happen when he starts dating again. The thoughts of another girl hanging out with him and Hewson break my heart. And what about when he finds the girl he's going to marry and spend the rest of his life with? Will some other woman try to replace me as Hewson's mom? Maybe it's stupid to be thinking so far ahead, but I can't help where my head's gone, and these thoughts are making me ill, Liv. I don't think I can bear it." I bury my head in my knees.

She squeezes my shoulder. "It's only natural to feel like that, but I don't think you should give up hope yet."

I lift my head. "It would be easier if he wasn't so Goddamned irresistible, and I swear my ovaries have gone into meltdown since I've seen him with our son. That only makes him more desirable. I didn't think it was possible to love him any more than I did, but I do. The love I have for him is infinite. Whether he loves me back or not, it doesn't matter. He is it for me. I know there'll never be anyone else. I'll be this lonely old spinster, and he'll be married with kids, and Hewson will want to go and live with his dad, and I'll end up on my own." I pour every ugly, miserable fear straight from my heart, realizing how pathetic I sound.

"Wow. That's one hell of a pity party you got going on." She scrambles to her feet. "I know what you need. You need to get drunk and let loose. Just drink and dance and forget about all the stuff in your head. Riley and I are heading to the frat. Come with us." She extends her hand, and I let her pull me up.

I'm not convinced I'm in the party spirit, but it sure beats hanging around here feeling sorry for myself.

We've been here a couple hours, and the place is packed to the rafters. Now that exams have commenced, it's a much-needed stress reliever. I've had a few wine coolers and I'm nicely buzzed. "Hey, pretty lady," Chase says as he approaches. "I think someone's been avoiding me." His breath oozes across my ear, and I step sideways, away from him.

"You know I have been, and you also know why." I fold my arms sternly across my chest. Chase practically called me a gold digger the last time we spoke, revealing a side of him I didn't much care for.

He scrubs a hand over his jaw. "Look, about that." He leans into my ear. "I was way out of line, and I apologize. I know you're not that type of girl. Kennedy just gets on my fucking nerves."

"Apology accepted, Chase, but it changes nothing between us. Sorry."

Not sorry.

His face drops, and a twinge of guilt sparks in my gut. His hands land on my hips. "I respect that, Lana." He presses his mouth to my ear. "And I'm not hitting on you, I swear."

Says the guy with his hands on my hips.

"But I just need to know one thing."

Removing his hands, I step back, peering at him suspiciously. "What?"

"Not in here." He gestures toward the other room. The one Liv and I have affectionately christened the weed room. "It's quieter in there. I can hardly hear myself think out here."

I'm keen to get this over and done with, so I stupidly agree. I'm trailing Chase when Riley steps in front of me, blocking my path. "What are you doing?"

"It's not what you think." He pins wary eyes on me. "I'm not interested in Chase. This is my last conversation with him, and then we're done. I'm going to make sure he understands."

"You can't trust that guy."

I sigh, spotting Chase frowning over his shoulder at us. "I know, which is why I'm shutting this down now." I smile up at Riley. "Thanks for watching out for me, but I got this." I maneuver around him and head toward Chase.

He guides me into the cloud-filled room, and my nostrils twitch. I think I'll get high just breathing the air in here. Leading me to a little nook in the corner, he lounges against the wall, piercing me with a pitiful look. Every part of me goes on high alert. "I know who you are, Lana." His tone is deceptively soft. "Now that whole thing with Kennedy makes sense, but I want you to know that you aren't alone. You don't have to put up with it anymore. I can help you."

My eyes narrow. "What are you talking about, Chase?"

"You don't have to pretend with me. I know."

I scratch the side of my head, utterly confused. "Know what?"

"That he paid you off to withdraw your statement. Everyone knows he raped you and bought your silence." My mouth falls open. *What the actual fuck?* Before I can protest, he continues. "And I'm guessing he followed you here to continue tormenting you and he's got you right where he wants you. You can't let him get away with this, Lana. People like him, people with money, they think they rule the fucking world. They think they are above the law and that they can get away with anything. But he can't. He can't do this to you. My uncle is an attorney, and I've spoken to him about it. You can tell the truth, no matter what confidentiality agreement they got you to sign. There are ways around it. I'll help you." He moves to take my hand, but I swat him away.

If I thought that Chase genuinely cared about me, and honestly believed what he said was the truth, then I might feel differently. Might be touched that someone cared enough to want to intervene. Makes a change from the usual reception I receive.

But I'm not buying this.

Chase showed his true colors the last time we spoke, and the look of pity on his face is as fake as the tits on that brunette across the way he keeps sneaking glances at. He's got some kind of agenda with Kal. This isn't about me at all.

"I don't need your help," I clip out. "You are way out of line and way off the mark. Kal did not rape me nor did he buy me off. I retracted my statement because it was a lie, and I had only said it to hurt him. I retracted it in court because I wanted the public to know this was on me, not him, and I am pure sick of people like you trying to manipulate the situation for your own end. I don't know what your beef is with Kal, but I won't be a part of it."

Chase's lips curl into an unattractive snarl. "You're making another mistake here, Lana."

"Screw you."

"I know you wanted to," he sneers, his eyes roaming over my body in blatant disinterest, "but I'm not into Kennedy's sloppy seconds, even if I was prepared to take one for the team."

"You're a sick individual, and I want nothing more to do with you. Stay away from me." I push past him.

"Don't say I didn't try to warn you," he calls out. "It didn't have to be this way, but you've left me no choice." His words peter off as I stalk away, leaving him for dust.

When I reenter the main party area, I make a beeline for the counter. I've had enough of this, and it's time I did something about it. Most people know my real identity on campus now. I haven't missed the secret looks, the finger pointing, or the hushed whispers these last few weeks. No one has hurled abuse at me, at least not yet, but that doesn't mean they are oblivious to the rumors doing the rounds. I'm finally learning to ignore people's prejudice. It infuriates me to no end, though, that my sacrifice seems to have been in vain. People still think Kal did it, and I'm going to put an end to these new rumors once and for all.

I duck behind the counter and pull the megaphone out of a cubbyhole. Kicking off my shoes, I pull myself up on the counter beside the three other girls dancing their booties off. The crowd hollers when I stand up straight. Clearing my throat, I glance at the DJ in the far corner of the room as I raise the megaphone to my mouth. "Can I have everyone's attention, please." My voice booms out across the room. The DJ looks up. "Can you kill the music, please. I have something I need to say, and I want to ensure everyone hears."

My heart is thumping wildly in my chest, and a line of sweat drips down my spine. Butterflies are having a field day in my gut, but I'm glad my voice rang out confidently, that resolve zips through my veins spurring me on. I know I can do this, and it's the right thing to do.

I'm doing this for Kal. For Kal and Hewson.

Our baby hasn't been on this campus once for a reason. I don't want people finding out about him yet. But when we move in to our new apartment, the news will spread like wildfire, so, it's important I put this latest rumor to bed first. The last thing I want is other students believing our son is the product of rape. He was conceived in love, and I don't want anyone casting doubt on that.

The DJ mutes the music, and the crowd stills. Most everyone has turned toward the counter, giving me their undivided attention. Groups trickle out from the weed room, curious. "Most of you probably know who I am," I begin to explain, "but I want to state it for the record. My name is Lana Taylor, and I'm the girl who accused Kalvin Kennedy of rape."

A shocked gasp ripples through the crowd. Olivia and Riley push through to the front, and my friend gives me a big smile and an encouraging nod.

"I know there are all kinds of rumors floating about, and I wanted to help put them to rest. Kalvin Kennedy *did not* rape me. And he didn't pay me to withdraw my statement. I did that all on my own because I had falsely accused him of something he didn't do. Kalvin and I have known each other since we were two. I've been in love with him as long. I'm not going to delve into details of our personal lives, but our relationship has been difficult the last few years. He did things to hurt me, and I was hurting a lot, so I told a lie. The worst lie a girl could ever tell about a boy. It was a horrible mistake, and the guilt and self-loathing is something I will carry with me to my grave. I'm ashamed of myself."

I look around the room, and I have everyone's devoted attention. This feels strangely cathartic, and my heart opens wide as more words filter from my mouth. "I let myself down, because that girl you all read about is not the person I am. I let my parents down, too, but, most of all, I let Kal down. He's my best friend, first and foremost, and I treated him appallingly."

A loud snort from the side of the room causes a few heads to turn. I cast a quick glance at Chase, lounging against the wall with a jeering expression on his face. Ignoring him, I continue. "I confessed in court because I wanted the public to know the truth, so this wouldn't follow him around. It's sickening that it wasn't enough. That people still think the worst of him hurts me so much, because he doesn't deserve it. Kal's a good guy, a great guy, and I want you all to give him a chance. To know the truth when you hear it. To understand he's not the guy you've been led to believe." A layer of stress lifts off me. I sway a little on my feet, feeling drained and suddenly exhausted.

A few startled gasps emerge from the crowd, and people start stepping aside. "That's all I wanted to say. Thank you for ..."—my words falter as I spy Kal weaving his way through the masses, right toward me—"listening." I manage to get the last word out, although it is barely louder than a whisper.

Kal lifts his head up when he reaches the counter, his piercing blue eyes locking on mine. The look of fierce determination on his face has my heart skipping a beat. He holds my waist, lifting me clear off the counter. Ever so gently, he places my bare feet on the ground, keeping a hold on me. His head dips, and he never takes his eyes from mine as he lowers his face toward me. "I love you, Lana Taylor. I love you so much." His words are loud, and clear, and they seem to reverberate around the room. Then his mouth is covering mine, and he's kissing me like he's never kissed me before. The room disappears. The noise fades. It's as if it's just the two of us. Glued to one another, as close as two people can get without getting naked. His hands hold me firmly around the waist as his mouth explores mine. My hands are planted against his impressive chest, and the steady thump, thump of his heart vibrates under my palm. His tongue sneaks into my mouth, and I silently swoon. Our lips move against one another in perfect rhythm, and my body comes alive from his caress. My heart feels like it's going to grow wings and take flight.

A throat clearing breaks us apart. "Get a room for fuck's sake," Riley says, with a teasing grin. Kal wraps his arms around me, keeping me close against his body.

"That was frigging awesome, girlfriend. I'm so proud of you." Liv manages to grab me away for a sneaky hug.

Kal instantly tucks me back under his arm. "Thanks for the heads-up, man. I owe you." He high-fives Riley as Liv and I trade puzzled expressions.

Riley slings his arm around Liv's shoulders, kissing her cheek. "Anytime."

Kal looks down at me. His eyes are dark with lust, his lips swollen from my kisses. "Can we get out of here?"

I lean up on my tiptoes, kissing him quickly. "I thought you'd never ask."

I grab my shoes, hurriedly slipping them on before I give Liv one final hug and let Kal lead me out of the basement. People stare at us as we leave, but the reception is a lot less hostile than usual.

I have only taken two steps outside when Kal grabs me, pushing me up against the wall, pressing his hot body against mine. "I can't believe you did that." His lips graze the column of my neck, and I shudder as intense desire sweeps over me.

"It better fucking work," I pant, gasping as he sucks on my neck, right where my pulse beats wildly.

He chuckles, lifting his head, and I pout at the loss of his mouth on my skin. He grins, reaching up to tuck my hair behind my ears. "You're so beautiful, Lana. I don't think I've told you enough. You're like the brightest star in the sky, lighting my life in so many ways." He runs the tips of his fingers over my cheeks, and his feather-light touch sends delicious tingles all over my body. He presses a kiss under my jaw and then a quick one on my lips. His expression turns serious. "I forgive you."

"You do?" My breath hitches in my throat in hopeful anticipation.

He nods. "I read your book, and I heard what you said back there, and I can't stay angry at you anymore. Not when we love each other so much. Not when I know we are meant to be together." He twines his fingers with mine. "I want you, and I want Hewson. I want us to be a family. My life means nothing unless you are by my side."

I can't help the tears that slide down my face. "You really mean it?"

He hauls me into his chest, enveloping me in his strong arms. "More than anything."

I bury myself in his chest, inhaling his gorgeous smell and just reveling in the feel and touch of him against me. I didn't think I'd have this again, and my heart is so full of joy I wish I could commit this feeling to memory forever. "But from now on, there can be no more secrets or lies between us. Complete honesty, Lana. That's what I need."

"You have it. I promise. I love you, Kal. So much it scares the hell out of me sometimes." I peer up at him. "The older I get, the more my feelings intensify. I don't know if it's normal for an eighteen-year-old girl to have so much love in her heart for a boy, but my feelings for you have always run deep. There will never be anyone else for me. Never."

He pushes me against the wall with a growl, running his hand slowly up and down the length of my thigh. His hard-on strains against my core, and my ovaries start a happy dance. "My feelings run every bit as deep," he affirms, before smashing his mouth on mine in a wild frenzy. Our teeth clash, our tongues tangle, and we devour one another. My body vibrates with need, and I rock against his hips, gripping his ass and holding him firm against me. "Lana," he whispers, his voice thick with lust. "I need to bury myself deep inside you."

It's like music to my ears. Finally, we are on the same page, and there are no more barriers between us. "Your place or mine?"

Chapter Thirty-Two
Kalvin

"**G**et naked, baby," I demand the instant we step inside my dorm. Thank fuck, Brett is at an away game tonight. I need this connection with her. Need to immerse myself in her so fully that all she sees, all she hears, all she feels, is me. I need to worship every inch of her body, and I can't wait a second longer.

"Already ahead of you." Her tone is smirking. I look up, and my jaw drops. She already has her top and her bra off, and she's in the process of removing her jeans. Lana can come across as quiet and demure, but she's never been that to me. She's a private person, and she doesn't let people in easily, but I know the real her, and she has this steely, quiet confidence that is totally sexy.

When we first started making out, I was taken aback by how forthright she was. She wasn't nervous or shy around me at all, and that was both a surprise and a major turn-on. When we had sex—that one and only time—she was unashamedly responsive, sexy as hell, and she rocked my fucking world. I almost come in my jeans, such is my excitement at the promise of a repeat.

A lifetime of repeats.

Sauntering forward, she palms the bulge in my jeans, popping the top button. "Strip, dude."

I'm standing there like a mute, frozen, as she shimmies her jeans and panties off, tossing them across the room. She stands before me, utterly naked, and she's completely stunning.

"Fuck, Lana. You are so beautiful." My eyes roam hungrily over every curve, and she flings her hair back, never removing her eyes from mine, letting me drink my fill. "If this is what having a baby does for you, I want a whole football field full of kids."

She rips my jeans and boxers down my legs in one smooth move. Wrapping her hand around me, she strokes me in slow, sensual moves. "Let's not get ahead of ourselves," she purrs. "One baby is quite enough for now."

"Fair enough." I nip at her lips, my hand curving around one supple breast. "But that doesn't mean we can't practice."

I start walking her back toward the bed, but she places her palms against my chest, stalling me. "Oh, I want to practice." Her hand goes around me again, and a guttural moan leaves my mouth. She runs her teeth along my neck. "I want to practice. A lot." She looks up at me, and the lustful sheen in her eyes almost makes me come on the spot. "You make me so fucking horny, Kal, and I'm going to ride you like you're my own personal horse."

"Stallion, babe. Like your own personal stallion." I can't be having any fucking horse comparisons. I squeeze her breast before dipping my head and sucking her nipple into my mouth.

She groans, and her hand starts pumping faster. Suddenly, she pulls back, and I mourn the loss of her tit in my mouth.

But not for long.

When she drops to her knees and takes all of me in her hot mouth, I let a volley of expletives out. She works me expertly, her mouth and hand hitting all the right spots, and I'm dangerously close to losing control. The sight of her bent over me, sucking me off, is the most glorious sight in the world. My fingers thread through her hair, and I throw back my head, groaning as pleasurable tremors whip up my spine.

"Stop, baby. I don't want to come yet." Gently, I lift her up, carrying her to the bed. I lay her down flat, kneeling between her legs. Nudging her thighs aside, I lick my lips as I slide one finger inside. "You're so wet."

"For you, Kal. Always for you. I want you inside me. Hurry."

"Patience, firecracker." I smirk, adding another finger, pumping in and out, curling both fingers inside her in a way I know will cause her the most pleasure. I flick my tongue against her swollen nub, and she cries out. I work her quickly, bringing her over the edge in less than a minute. I fail to keep the smug grin off my face.

Grabbing a condom, I suit up and position myself between her legs. I kiss my way up her neck, sucking on her earlobe and pressing wet open-mouthed kisses all over her face. When my mouth presses against hers, I kiss her deeply. No tongue, just our mouths moving together as my heart inflates with everything I feel for her. "I love you," I breathe against her mouth, staring into her eyes.

She threads her hand in mine. "I love you, too. Now, make love to me."

I inch inside her slowly, unsure if this will hurt or not. The books she gave me said it can be a little sore the first time after having a baby. I watch where we are joined, easing slowly inside her even though my dick is screaming at me to pound into her hard, marveling at how flat and unmarked her stomach is. I press a reverential kiss to her belly. The place my son called home for nine months.

"Kal?"

I look up at her, now fully situated, holding myself intact inside her. My biceps quiver with the effort involved in holding myself over her. "Yeah, babe."

She rocks her hips up, and stars explode behind my eyes. "You aren't hurting me. If that changes, I'll tell you, but, please, for the love of all things holy, move! I need you to fuck me now!"

I start thrusting gently, but she grips my ass, wrapping her legs around my waist and pulling me against her with more urgency. "Harder. I need you harder and deeper."

"Your dirty talk is so fucking hot you're going to make me come in about two seconds if you keep it up."

"Don't you dare!" She glares at me, and I chuckle, increasing my pace, thrusting into her in long, hard strides. She moans, and her mouth suctions on my chest. "Yes! More, baby."

I increase the tempo, and she matches me thrust for thrust. My hands are in her hair, and my lips are tasting her everywhere, as I continue thrusting into her. A wave of pure liquid lust shoots up and down my spine, and a tingling sensation starts building. "I'm going to come."

She leans a hand down between us to rub herself, and it's the hottest thing I've ever seen. "Faster, Kal," she croons. "Hell, yes!"

We tumble into bliss together, rocking and writhing against one another until we're both sated.

I get up, toss the condom in the trash, and bring a cloth back to bed. After I've cleaned her up, I flop down beside her, pulling her into my arms. "Fuck, Lana. That was something else. That was unbelievably fucking amazing. Incredible." I peck her lips.

She props up on an elbow, turning to face me. Her hair cascades over one shoulder. I press a kiss to her bare shoulder, and she shivers. "Really?"

I frown, unsure where this lack of confidence is suddenly coming from. "Abso–fucking–lutely." I tilt her chin up with one finger. "Why are you doubting yourself?"

Her cheeks flush red. "Because you've been with lots of girls, and I've only been with you."

I hate that I've done that to her. That she doubts herself because I was an asshole who couldn't keep it in his pants. I still have a lot to do to make up for that. To prove to her that she is the center of my universe. The only girl I want from this moment on.

I sit upright, pulling her with me. I grip her face in my hands.

"None of those girls meant anything to me. It was just sex." I kiss the tip of her nose. "I have no words to describe what being intimate with you is like, because it's *everything*, Lana. You're everything. Making love to you is like nothing I've ever experienced because I never loved any of those girls."

I place her hand on my chest. "You own me, Lana, and your touch ignites the most insane feelings inside me. Seriously, I only have to look at you and I get hard. Being inside you is the most magical feeling in the world, and the way you move underneath me, the way you know what you want and aren't afraid to ask for it, it's hot as hell. Sex has never felt as good with anyone else because none of them were you."

"Thank you," she whispers, and I pull her into my arms.

"You may not have been my first, which, by the way, is something I'll always regret, but you are most definitely my last. I have eyes for no one but you, Lana. You're my entire world. You and Hewson. You are it for me."

The next few days are a whirlwind of activity as we take our exams and make plans for the holiday season. Lana agrees to come home with me so we can tell my parents together. We are going to spend a couple days with her parents first and fly to Massachusetts on Christmas Eve. We've been busy buying tons of furniture for our new apartment, and I've broken the news to Brett that he'll have a new roomie come January, but he was happy for me.

"Do it, babe," Lana says, jumping onto the bed beside me. I've been staring at my cell for the last twenty minutes, terrified to make this call. Not for me but for her. I don't know how Mom is going to react to the news, and I don't want anything to hurt Lana. She wraps her hand around my wrist. "I know why you're hesitating." I look up at her, melting at the sight of her gorgeous big eyes, so full of concern for me. "I'm not worried about your mom, so you shouldn't be either."

"You're not?"

"Nope." She smiles, scooping a large spoonful of chocolate ice cream. "Open up," she demands, and I obey. Because I'm completely pussy-whipped and wrapped around her every finger.

"Mmm," I murmur. "That's good."

"I know." She swallows a spoonful and then leans forward to kiss me, pushing melted ice cream into my mouth. I groan, and my dick twitches in my pants. It's a wonder I'm still able to get it up so easily. We can't keep our hands off each other, and we haven't spent a night apart since the frat party. "Make the call, Stinky," she purrs, suggestively licking the back of the spoon, "and I'll eat the rest of the ice cream off your naked body."

"Deal." My hard-on is now straining against my jeans. "You're a wicked woman."

She pushes me playfully. "Shut up. You love it."

I do. And her.

I wait a couple minutes for my excitement to die down before calling Mom.

"Honey, it's so good to hear from you."

"Hey, Mom. I wanted to talk to you about Christmas." I'm so nervous I just blurt it out.

"If you say you're not coming home, I'll personally get on a plane and drag you here if I have to. We haven't seen you for months, and we miss you." Lana takes my free hand, running soothing circles on the back of it.

"Don't worry. I'm coming home. My flight is already booked, but, uh, I'm bringing someone with me." Two someones, actually, but I can't let that cat out of the bag just yet.

"A girl?"

"Yes, a girl, and you know her."

"It's Lana?"

"Yes. How the hell did you guess that? Has Ky said anything?"

"Kyler knows?"

Ah, shit. I should've kept my big mouth shut. "Yeah, but from your tone, I'm figuring he wasn't the one to tell you."

"No one told me, honey. Did you honestly think I didn't know Lana was the reason you decided to go to UF?"

"You knew?"

"I had my suspicions."

She doesn't sound upset or mad. "It's okay if she comes with me?"

"If that's what you want."

"It is."

"Are you sure, honey?"

I know what she's asking. My family was hugely disappointed with Lana for falsely accusing me of rape, and they are bound to be a little cautious of her now. It's something else we'll have to overcome. "More sure than I've been about anything ever before." I'm conscious of Lana sitting rigidly still beside me. While I know she's put on a brave face, my mom's approval means more to her than she's let on. "I love her, Mom. We're together and that's never going to change. She's the only girl for me."

"You're still very young, Kalvin."

"I'm almost eighteen, Mom, and I know my own mind."

"Very well. We can talk about it when you're home."

"You have to promise to be nice to her. Everyone has to. She's my guest, and if anyone treats her disrespectfully, I'll leave." Lana is shaking her head at me.

"Sweetheart," Mom says. "Your brothers have always been fond of Lana, and she's welcome here anytime. You have nothing to worry about. Please give her our love, and tell her we're looking forward to seeing her again."

"'Kay. Thanks, Mom. See you soon."

I hang up and turn to Lana. "That went better than expected." I run my hand around the back of her neck, pulling her toward me.

"She doesn't mind?" she asks, as I lower my mouth to hers.

"Nope." I kiss her hard and then pull back, whipping my shirt off. "A deal's a deal, woman. Pay up." I start tugging at the hem of her shirt as a loud knock booms on the door. "Hold that thought." I wink, racing to answer it. "I'll just get rid of whoever it is first."

I swing the door open, and the mad grin on my face evaporates on the spot. I'm pushed roughly against the wall as the officer yanks my hands behind my back, cuffing me. Then he says some words I'd hoped never to hear again. "Kalvin Edward Kennedy. I am arresting you for the rape and sexual assault of Ms. Shelby Walsh."

Chapter Thirty-Three
Lana

I grab my purse and my keys, pulling the door shut behind me as I hurry outside. I call Grandmother from the back seat of the Uber, on the way to the police station. Her displeasure filters down the line as I quickly explain. "I need a good attorney. Can you recommend anyone?"

She is aloof on the other end, not that I'm overly surprised. She's disgusted we're moving out and that Mom is going back to Dad.

"Please, Grandmother. He didn't do this. This is all my fault for casting doubt on his character in the first place. Are you going to help me or not?" I'm not holding out much hope. Kyler is my next call if she refuses to help. Even though he's emancipated and his parents aren't legally required at the station, I don't know if Kal would want me to call them anyway, and I'd rather leave that up to his brother to decide.

I play my final card, saying the only thing that might convince her. "I'm sure his parents will be extremely grateful. I'll make sure to let them know how supportive you were."

"Fine." Her voice is curt. "I'll call my attorney and ask him to go to the station. Ensure Kalvin doesn't say anything until he gets there."

"Trust me, he knows the drill." The sour taste in my mouth grows more pungent.

When I get to the station, they won't tell me anything or let me see him. I'm pacing back and forth across the floor in the waiting area, deliberating my next move, when a stout man with ruddy cheeks and a mop of silver hair bustles into the room. "Miss Williams?" he asks, and I almost shake my head.

"I'm Lana," I say, accepting his handshake.

"I'm James Montgomery, your grandmother's attorney. Let me secure a room so we can talk. I would like you to explain what happened before I meet Mr. Kennedy."

A few minutes later, we are seated in a small room. The attorney extracts a pad and pen and takes notes as I tell him what happened. "Do you know Miss Walsh?" he asks, removing his suit jacket and hanging it across the back of his chair.

"I've only seen her a couple of times. From what Kal told me, he slept with her one time when he first arrived on campus. I've no doubt it was consensual." I explain how she threw his boxers in his face and how mad she was at his rejection. "This is purely vindictive."

He rolls up his sleeves. "That may well be the case, but at this juncture, it is her word against his, and his previous reputation will not do him any favors."

I slam my fist on top of the table in frustration. "That reputation isn't deserved. It isn't a true representation of who he is. The case was thrown out of court, and he wasn't charged with anything, so how the hell can they use that against him?"

"I understand how upsetting this is, my dear, but, unfortunately, that case received massive attention in the media. Whether he was acquitted or not doesn't really help. People know of him. They have their own opinions. To some, he was always guilty."

A messy ball of emotion builds in the back of my throat. My accusation has ruined Kal's life. The shadow of suspicion is always going to follow him around. My heart is heavy in my chest. "What if I gave a statement? Would that help? I can reiterate the facts and explain face to face how my accusation came about. I can tell them what I know of Shelby, confirm what she said the last time they met."

He stands up. "I'm not sure how helpful that would be." He eyeballs me apologetically. "I don't know how much weight your word carries."

I feel like bashing my head against the wall. "Because once a liar always a liar?"

He nods sadly, slipping his suit jacket back on. He pats my hand. "Try not to worry. Let me speak with Mr. Kennedy and find out exactly how strong the case is against him."

He leads me back out to the waiting room. "Sit tight. I'll update you when I can."

The next three hours feels like three years. Mom calls, wondering if there is any news, and I pour all my frustration out. My fingernails are chewed to the bone as I pace the room, growing more and more agitated. My finger hovers over the call button on my cell repeatedly, unsure if I should call Kyler or not. I've all but decided to do that when Mr. Montgomery reappears with Kal in tow.

I rush him, flinging my arms around his neck. "I've been so worried."

He rests his head on my shoulder, and his arms circle my waist. He holds me tight, and my heart is splintering in my chest. He doesn't say anything, doesn't move, just clings to me like his life depends on it. Mr. Montgomery disappears, returning a few minutes later. "You are free to go for now, Mr. Kennedy. My office will contact you in the morning."

Kal lifts his head, taking my hand in his as he turns around. "Thank you, sir. I'll await the call."

We leave by the front entrance, and I'm relieved that it's reporter free, but I wonder how long it'll remain that way. We go back to his dorm, and I order takeout while Kal grabs a shower. He's been unbelievably quiet since we left the station, but I don't want to push him.

He emerges from the bathroom, steam chasing behind him, in

clean sweatpants and no shirt. His feet are bare. He rubs a hand towel back and forth across his head, still not talking.

After we've eaten, he pulls me down alongside him on his bed. I rest my head on his chest, curling my body into his. His hand smooths up and down my spine. "I'm so sorry, Kal," I whisper. "This is all my fault."

"I can't believe it's happening again."

His words slice through me like a knife.

"What did the attorney say? What does he think your chances are?"

His chest heaves up and down, and he sighs, his hand stalling on my back. "There is no evidence to support her claims. Just her word against mine, but that's enough of a problem in itself."

"When is she alleging this took place? If you have an alibi—"

"She is claiming I raped her the first night we met. Apparently, she has a witness, someone who has said she didn't want to leave with me, and this person is prepared to testify that she was upset and crying the next morning."

"If she's claiming that's the truth, why the hell did she wait three months to report it?" I fume.

"She was afraid, apparently. Your name was mentioned, and the insinuation you were paid off as well as your treatment at the hands of the media were both cited as reasons for not coming forward sooner." He harrumphs. "You've got to admit it sounds plausible. All this because I rejected her." He shakes his head. "What a clusterfuck."

A horrid feeling washes over me, and I think I'm going to be sick. "Oh my God, Kal. I'm so—"

"Do not say you are sorry," he roars, and I flinch. "I am so fucking sick of hearing you say that! This is never going to go away!" I pull out of his embrace, fighting back tears as I swing my legs over the side of the bed. I start gathering up my stuff, putting it in my bag. Kal sits up, planting his feet on the floor. "What's to stop more girls from coming forward alleging the same thing?" He shakes his head. "I'm royally screwed." He buries his head in his hands, and my heart is broken.

I was stupid to think we could ever get past this. To ever believe we had a future. Now Kal is facing the prospect of jail again, and I won't survive if he goes down for something he didn't do. I've got to make this right.

I've got to, at least, try.

"I think I should go." I hate how my voice cracks.

"I think that's for the best," he agrees, and my lower lip wobbles.

I kiss the top of his head, but he doesn't make any move. With silent tears streaming down my face, I exit his room.

Back in my dorm, I'm pacing the floor like a crazy woman. Liv has already gone home for the holidays, so I'm left with my own thoughts.

I replay Kal's words in my mind, and it can't be a coincidence. It just can't.

I need to speak to Shelby, but I don't have a clue where she lives. I can't ask Kal because, A, he's not currently speaking to me and, B, I know he wouldn't want me to do this, but I'm damned if I'm going to sit around and watch while my mistake tries to ruin him again.

I pull out my cell and call the one person who I know can help. He picks up on the third ring. "Keven, I need your help."

Twenty minutes later, I'm standing outside the apartment block where Shelby lives. Keven Kennedy has unbelievable IT skills, and it only took him five minutes to locate her address. I made him swear not to tell Kal, but I have zero faith he'll keep that promise. He wasn't in favor of me coming here on my own even though I fully explained. I reckon I have a very narrow window of opportunity to do this before Kal shows up.

I've got to make every second count.

I rap loudly on her door, praying to every deity known to

mankind that she hasn't skipped town yet. I thump harder with my fist. "Shelby! It's Lana. Open up. I'm not leaving until you talk to me."

The door swings open a few minutes later. Shelby is dressed to the nines, as if she's going out. "What do you want?" she hisses. "You shouldn't be here."

"I just want to talk."

"Well, I don't want to talk to you."

She moves to close the door, but I shove my foot in the doorway. Removing my cell, I thrust it in her face. I'm taking a huge risk doing this, but I don't think I have a choice.

"What is this?" Her brow wrinkles.

"His name is Hewson, and he's my son. My son and Kalvin's. If you won't talk to me for Kal's sake, at least do it for his son's."

Unnamed emotion skitters over her face. She clears her throat, looking more closely at the phone. "I didn't know he had a son."

"We didn't want anyone to know yet. Please, Shelby. Please, let me come in." It's killing me to be polite to the bitch when I want to rip every strand of hair from her head and poke toothpicks in her eyes.

Indecision washes over her features, and I know I'm running out of time. Fuck it. I'll say what I need to say out here. "We both know Kal didn't do this. You're lying. I'm going to take a wild guess and say Chase is somehow involved." Her eyes twitch at the mention of his name. "I'm right, aren't I?"

Her mouth pulls into a grim line, and her pupils dilate. "I don't know what you're talking about, and the fact you have a son doesn't change the situation. He raped me. I'm not soft like you. I'm not going to let him bully me into withdrawing my confession. He's going to go down for this."

Her face is an impressive mask, and I know I'm not going to get anywhere with her. Whatever sliver of hope I had dies an instant death inside me. "You are going to ruin his life for something he didn't do. I don't know why you and Chase are doing this, but you should know that you are going to ruin a good man, and I'm speaking from personal experience when I say this will ruin you too. Whatever your motive is, this won't feel so good when the dust has settled and you've put an innocent man in jail for a crime he didn't commit. When you've deprived a little boy of his father."

A glint of emotion flickers in her eye.

"My son has only just found his father, and you are going to take that from him. You are going to ruin my life and my baby's too." The air is fraught with tension. "I hope you can live with that on your conscience."

She stands frozen in the doorway as I leave, my heart weighted down with fear.

Kal is getting out of his truck when I step out onto the pavement. "Lana!" he shouts, running toward me. "What the hell were you thinking coming here?" He grips my elbow, looking up at the apartment building as he tows me to his car.

"I was only trying to help. Chase put her up to this."

"What?" Kal comes to a standstill. "What did you just say?"

"She didn't confirm it, but I saw it in her eyes. At the frat house, the last time, he was trying to get me to admit that you'd paid me off. When I told him that wasn't the truth, he got mad, and he said something cryptic. I ignored it because he was clearly crazy, but now I'm wondering if he didn't set this all up."

"But Shelby didn't confirm it?" His eyes crinkle as his face turns contemplative.

"Not verbally, but I could tell she was lying." I swallow the lump in my throat. "I showed her a picture of Hewson. I thought if I appealed to her on his behalf that she'd drop it, but she refused to budge." I'm sorry is on the tip of my tongue but I manage to keep a tether on the words. "What if we asked Keven to find some dirt on Chase or her? There has to be something there. Some reason why they are targeting you," I mull out loud. "And we can tell your attorney our suspicions. Plenty of people can confirm Chase is a douche, and it might, at least, cast some doubt. Buy us some time to prove you're innocent."

Kal surprises me, pulling me into his arms. His chin rests atop my head as I tentatively slide my arms around his waist. "I'm sorry for shouting at you earlier. I didn't mean to take it out on you. It's not your fault. I know you're only trying to help, and I need that. I need you."

"It's okay." I don't tell him he's wrong, that it's totally my fault, because I don't want to fight with him anymore tonight.

And if he needs me, then I'm going to be there for him.

For as long as he'll have me.

Chapter Thirty-Four
Kalvin

My cell phone is vibrating on a continual loop the next morning, waking both of us up. I stare at the screen through groggy eyes. As my eyesight focuses, I curse.

"What?" Lana asks through a yawn.

"It's Mom. I'm guessing the news has broken."

"Oh no."

I answer the call. There's no point in delaying the inevitable. Mom is frantic on the end of the line, and I do my best to settle her. She's furious that we didn't call her yesterday, but I assure her that Lana had it all in hand and her grandmother's attorney knows what he's doing.

"Fuck," I groan, tossing my phone aside after I hang up.

Lana peeks out the window. "I don't see any reporters."

"Mom got a heads-up from a contact of hers in the media. A local paper has picked up the story, and they're preparing to run with it. Mom has Dan on the case. Hopefully, they can get an injunction in time to stop it."

There's a firm rap on the door, and we exchange worried expressions. "I'll get it." She presses a kiss to my cheek, climbing out of bed and heading to the door in her cute pajamas.

I grab my sweats off the floor and pull them on. Running my hands through my hair, I try to tame it. Lana returns with a sheepish-looking Shelby. I glance warily at her. "You've got some nerve coming here," I snap.

"I've just come from the station. I've withdrawn my allegation."

Lana rummages in her purse, as the sweetest sense of relief washes over me. The pressure in my chest eases, and I lean over, breathing heavily as I cradle my head in my hands. Lana drops down beside me, wrapping her arm around my back. I lean into her for strength.

"I'm very sorry, Kalvin. More than I can say."

"Why?" I lift my head up, eyeballing her. "Why would you do that to me?"

She shuffles awkwardly on her feet. "You didn't want me, and I was pissed. Then I hooked up with Chase a few times, and he wasn't a fan either. It was all his idea. He suggested we could blackmail you."

My lips curl into a sneer. "How?"

"I was going to approach you and tell you I'd withdraw my claim if you paid me off." My fists curl into tight balls at my sides. "Then we were going to split the cash."

I glare at her. "What if I hadn't paid up?"

She looks down at the floor. "Then Chase was going to testify that he saw you dragging me from the frat party against my will and that I broke down and confessed the rape to him the next day."

"Why does Chase hate Kal so much?" Lana asks.

She looks me direct in the eye. "It's not you per se, it's what you represent."

"Explain that." I grit the words out.

"Chase grew up dirt poor, and he has a major chip on his shoulder. He hates anyone with money. When you showed up on campus, he saw a way to make some fast money and a way to stick it to the rich at the same time." She faces Lana. "He knew who you were all along. At first, he was going to fuck you, take compromising photos, and force Kal to pay to keep them out of the media."

I growl, anger plowing through my veins.

"But he couldn't get close to you, so then he thought if he got you to confess to being paid off he could use that to blackmail Kal. When that didn't work either, he came up with a new plan."

"He was using you, Shelby," Lana says.

"I know. I was an idiot, but the thought of all that cash was so tempting. We didn't have much growing up either. My mom remarried last year, and my stepdad is stinking rich, but he's a complete tightwad. It would've been nice to have my own cash."

"Get out," I snap. "Get out and stay the fuck out of my face."

She gulps nervously. "I'm sorry, Kalvin. I didn't know you had a son." She looks to Lana. "My dad ran out on my mom when I was only a baby. I know what it's like to grow up without a father. I couldn't do that to another child. I was awake all night thinking about it."

Lana rises, nodding tersely. "I'll show you out."

She is smiling when she returns. "It's over." She throws her arms around me, and I lose myself in her touch, her warmth.

"That's if she actually withdrew her statement." I check my cell. No missed calls from my attorney. which is concerning. *Surely, he's been notified by now?*

"Well," Lana says, reaching behind me. "If she didn't, I have it all on tape." She waves her cell at me. "I recorded her."

I chuckle. "Oh my God, the irony!"

She laughs with me. "I know, right?"

I pull her onto my lap. "Thank you."

"For what?"

"For fighting for me."

Chapter Thirty-Five
Lana

"We're here," Kal calls out, ushering me through the front door of his family home. A home that's as familiar to me as it is to him. A swarm of butterflies lands in my stomach. Nausea travels up my throat, and I'm sure I've turned an unflattering shade of green.

Originally, we had planned on arriving yesterday, Christmas Eve; however, with the events on campus those last few days, we were a day late arriving at my parent's place, and Kal, being all kinds of thoughtful, didn't want me missing out on time with my folks, so, he cancelled our commercial flights and arranged for the Kennedys' private jet to collect us this morning instead.

Thankfully, Kal's attorney called just before we left campus to confirm Shelby had retracted her statement, and the police have dropped all charges, eradicating the last vestiges of stress. Alex managed to keep all mention of it out of the press, and it appears we're home free. I've never felt more relieved, and I can tell Kal feels the same.

However, my shoulders are currently tied in a million knots as a new layer of stress descends at the thought of the reception awaiting us. I think I might actually puke.

Hewson woke on the journey from the airport, and I gave him his bottle in the back of the Mercedes. Max—the Kennedys' personal chauffeur—almost keeled over when he first greeted us, me holding a baby in my arms, but I haven't missed all the cute glances he's thrown our way since. I can tell he's already enamored with Hewson. Our son seems to have that effect on everyone.

"We're in here," Alexandra hollers, and my stomach lurches.

Kal slings his arm around my shoulders, pulling me in close to his side. "It's going to be fine. I promise." He kisses my forehead and then our son's.

I grab hold of his arm, terrified. "Maybe this is an awful idea. Maybe we should have told them on the phone."

"It's bound to be a shock, but they'll be okay with this. I promise." He captures the back of my neck, lowering his mouth to mine. He kisses me deeply, and some of my stress dissipates. "You trust me, right?"

I nod. "I trust you."

"Then trust that I've got this. You and Hewson are my family now. You're my priority. If this doesn't go well, we'll leave. All you have to say is the word. Okay?"

I wrap my free hand around his waist. "I love you, Kal."

"I love you, too. Both of you." Hewson emits a small gurgle, nuzzling into my chest as Kal musses up his hair.

Kal keeps his arm firmly around my shoulder as he moves us through the lobby and out into the living area. All his brothers are here. Faye too and her dad, Adam, along with her half-brothers, Jake and Josh. I've never met them before, but she's told me all about them. Crappity crap. I didn't know they were coming. Didn't realize our welcoming committee would be quite so large.

All conversation dies in the room the minute we enter. Everyone is looking at us with similar dazed expressions. I'm trembling with fear. Kal notices, reeling me in tight and running his hand up and down my back. "Hey, everyone. You remember Lana." He turns to me, his eyes glistening. "And this is Hewson." He flips his chin up, looking his parents directly in the eye. "Our son."

You could hear a pin drop in the room. No one says anything. Everyone just stares, mouths hanging open, with shell-shocked expressions on their face.

Faye is the first to break the tension. Of course, she and Ky already knew, but Kal had sworn them to secrecy. She races across the room, giving me a quick hug. "You look great, and I'm so glad you're here." Dipping her head, she beams at my son. "But this little guy. Oh my gosh!" She kisses his cheek ever so gently, and tears fill her eyes. "I've been so excited to meet you," she whispers, cooing at him.

She grabs Kal into a smothering hug, never once taking her eyes off Hewson. "He's soooooo beautiful. I want to run away with him." A mischievous glint appears in her eye. "Clearly, he takes after Lana, considering you're pig ugly and all." She nudges Kal's shoulder, smirking. Her teasing tone is exactly what's needed to slice through the frigid atmosphere.

Then our son bridges that final gap.

I've heard Mom talk about the precious moments in life. Those special times when I was little and I did things for the first time. This is one of those times. A memory to cherish.

Hewson's lower lip trembles a little as he looks around the room at all the expectant faces. He's at the stage where he's starting to get nervous around strangers. He wiggles in my embrace, and his arms go out, reaching for Kal. Kal gathers him to his chest, his eyes shining with so much love. Then Hewson opens his mouth and utters his first word. "Dada."

My heart explodes with pride and sheer happiness. Tears leak out of my eyes when Kal starts crying, cradling Hewson in his arms and kissing the top of his head repeatedly, holding him so lovingly, like he's the most precious cargo in the world. "Say it again," he whispers, being totally greedy.

"Dada."

"That's my boy!" Kal smacks a loud kiss on his cheek as a sob erupts across the room.

Alexandra rushes toward us, tears flowing freely down her cheeks. The rest of the family trail behind her. "Darling, that was so precious." She wraps her arms around all of us, hugging us. "He's so beautiful." Easing back, she crouches over until she's eye level with Hewson. "Hello, darling. Welcome to the family." She takes his tiny hand, and he latches on, curling his finger around hers. She visibly melts. Then Hewson gurgles, smiling at her, no hint of discomfort at all.

"Oh, boy," Faye says, winking at me. "That one's going to be trouble." We laugh. "I can already see the girls lining up."

"Hey, Lanabelle," Keaton says, drawing me in for a hug. "I've missed you."

I can scarcely speak over the wedge of emotion in my throat, although, I shouldn't be surprised. Keaton has always been the most gracious, the most sensitive of all Kal's brothers, and we've always gotten on well. "I missed you too," I croak, holding him tight.

Then he looks at Hewson, and my heart melts at the look on his face. "Hey there, little dude." He wipes the sloppy dribble off Hewson's chin in a sweet gesture.

"He's teething," I explain, removing a fresh bib from my bag and replacing the wet one around his neck.

"He's adorable," Keaton remarks, staring at Hewson with a massive smile on his face. "Let's hope he takes after you and not jerk face." He gestures toward Kal.

"Hey, no bad language in front of my son." Kal shoots his brother a stern look, and Keaton cracks up laughing.

The others crowd around, and I soak up the atmosphere, my tense muscles relaxing with every laugh, every joke.

We are late starting dinner because each of Kal's brothers wants a turn holding Hewson. Kal goes to his room—where we're all staying—to make up Hewson's crib. I'm comfortably seated on one of the big leather couches, with Hewson dozing in my arms, while Faye and Alex set the table. James, Kal's dad, disappears for a while, returning with a sturdy, wooden old-fashioned highchair. "This was your daddy's," he tells Hewson, strapping him in.

When we are all seated, with heaped plates in front of us, James raises his glass in a toast. "To family and extended family." His eyes are soft as he looks around the table. "Alex and I are so grateful you are here with us today. Every person at this table holds a special place in our hearts." He glances at Adam, Faye's father. "Even you, Adam," he teases, and we all laugh. According to Faye, her uncle and her bio dad resolved their differences during their Irish vacation last summer.

"Wow," Adam jokes. "That's high praise indeed." He nods at James, and a moment passes between them.

"We are especially grateful to officially welcome Lana and Hewson to the family. Awesome name by the way." He winks at me, and I smile. "All any parent wants is to see their children happy. And I see lots of happiness today."

He clearly misses the eye rolling Kent's been doing at his expense.

We raise our glasses. "To family. To health, happiness, love, and forgiveness. To the future."

Kal is putting Hewson down, and I'm sitting with Faye, Kyler, and the rest of Kal's brothers in the game room. "Who would've thought a little baby would turn all the burly Kennedy boys to mush?" Faye says, smiling. "They adore him. *I* adore him." She looks wistfully at Kyler.

"I can tell." I take a sip of my wine, as Kal strolls into the room.

"All good?" I ask, straightening up.

"He's tuckered out." He chuckles, taking his beer off the table. "He fell asleep the instant his head hit the pillow."

Kent snorts, leaning forward and winking at me. "Taking after his daddy already. You'd want to watch that."

Everyone groans. You can always count on Kent to try to stir shit up.

"That reminds me." Kal hands me his beer and walks to his brother's side. Superfast, before anyone has even registered the motion, Kal's fist juts out, and he punches Kent on the nose.

The place goes crazy.

"Shh!!" I hiss. "Don't wake the baby!"

"What the fuck?" Kent explodes, prodding the sides of his nose for damage.

"If you ever touch Lana again, I will happily kick your ass all over Wellesley."

All eyes turn to me, and my cheeks heat. "Oh my God. Kal! Stop it!"

"Dude, she was *so* into me." Kent smirks, and I draw a sharp breath. He's not going to let this go. Standing up, he starts rolling his hips in a thrusting fashion. "She loved every second of it. Don't let her tell you different." Next, he starts humping the arm of the chair. "This cock is magic, baby." Faye snorts with laughter, while I bury my head in my hands, groaning. Trust Kent to totally exaggerate and Kal to completely overreact. He knows we only made out for a bit. That Kent's cock never came in direct contact with any part of my body.

But they're both idiots.

Kal lunges at his brother, wrestling him to the ground. They thrash about, swinging a few punches as the rest of the Kennedy boys watch the show.

Kaden—Kal's eldest brother—lands a hand on my shoulder. "And he's a father now?" His lips curve into a smile. "God help us all."

Kal and I are sitting in the conservatory, alone, drinking hot chocolate a few hours later. "Are you happy?" he asks.

"Couldn't be happier. I was worried they wouldn't accept us, accept me, but they've been very welcoming." I know it can't be easy for the Kennedys to forgive me. I put Kal through hell last year, but they seem willing to give me the benefit of the doubt, and I'm grateful. This has gone much better than I expected. I know how important this was for Kal, so I'm delighted it's gone smoothly.

"I knew they would be. Dad loves babies, and my brothers act all tough, but they're really pussies underneath." He cups the back of my head, kissing me sweetly on the lips. "Besides, you're practically family. You grew up with us, Lana, and I know my brothers all love you."

We wander back into the sitting room, and I smile at the sight of Faye softly singing to Hewson as she rocks him in her arms. "He woke up a few minutes ago. She didn't want to disturb you, or at least that's the story she's sticking to," Kyler tells us in a whisper. His eyes look suspiciously shiny as his girlfriend cradles Hewson in her arms, looking like a total natural.

Kal and I share a knowing look. Kyler hasn't taken his eyes off Faye for more than a few seconds all day. This is the first time I've been around them since they got together officially, and it's not hard to see how besotted they are with one another. It's a side of Kyler I'm not used to. As he gazes adoringly at her, it isn't difficult to guess his thoughts.

Alex obviously thinks so too. Planting herself directly in front of Kyler, she pierces him with a serious look. "Don't even think about it," she whispers. "Let me get to know one grandchild before you introduce another."

"Chill out, Mom." Kyler tucks her into his side. "I'm just admiring the view." Faye is completely oblivious to all this, totally wrapped up in Hewson, pressing soft kisses to his head as she continues to rock him in her arms even though he's already fast asleep again. "And hoping that'll be me, be us, one day. But not yet." He kisses the top of his mom's head. "I always wrap it before I tap it, so don't worry."

Alex turns pale, and Kal almost chokes. I attempt to smother my laugh. Alex puts a hand over her heart. "I'm sure I didn't need to hear that. We're being responsible would've more than sufficed."

From the corner of my eye, I watch Adam narrow his eyes at Kyler. Kyler straightens up, clearing his throat. "Apologies, Adam. That was insensitive of me. I meant no disrespect."

Kal buries his head in my shoulder, muffling his laughter.

"The twins are in earshot, Kyler. I'd appreciate it if you remember that. And I'm with your mom. I'm not overly fond of hearing details of my daughter's sex life."

"On that awesome note," Kal says, snickering, "we're heading to bed." He takes my hand as we say our goodnights. Faye reluctantly passes Hewson into my arms, and together, as the family unit I always wanted us to be, we retreat to our room for the night.

Alex asks to speak to me the following morning after breakfast, suggesting a walk on the grounds. It's freezing outside, but the air is crisp and dry. Smothering my nervousness, I wrap Hewson up nice and cozy and grab my coat. I push the stroller outside, with Alex by my side. We don't talk for a few minutes, and my anxiety is increasing with every step.

A short while later, just as we've entered the wooded area that borders the rear of their estate, she clears her throat. "I wanted to talk to you because there are some things I need to say." She looks over at me, smiling softly. "I don't know exactly what you think of me, but you should know I was never opposed to you, Lana. You're as much a daughter to me as Faye. I've always known how you and Kal felt about each other. You were inseparable from the moment you met, even when you were very little we could see the love shining between you. James and I always said you two would end up together."

I can't hide my surprise. For years, I've believed Alex disliked me.

"That day in Nantucket, I knew things had turned a corner, that your relationship was evolving, and I stopped it because I felt you were too young. I didn't tell Kalvin not to hang out with you anymore. I asked him not to take things further with you until you were a little older. I didn't realize the part I would play in what would end up happening, and for that, I'm truly sorry. I don't fully understand what happened between you, and I don't want to know, Lana. He's my son and there are certain things I don't care to hear. I'm sorry that you got hurt, and I'm unbelievably happy that you were able to find your way back to each other."

She stops, and I'm shocked to see tears in her eyes. She squeezes my hand. "I'm so grateful you've brought Hewson into our lives. I'm a firm believer that things happen for a reason."

"You're not upset? Because we're so young, and it's something else I kept from him?"

"Sweetheart." She hugs me briefly. "A baby is always a blessing, and I can already see how much you and Kalvin love him. Besides, I wasn't that much older than you when I got pregnant with Kaden. It'd be very hypocritical of me to criticize you."

"Thank you," I say quietly. "I was very worried coming here. I thought you'd all hate me because of what I did. I know I've hated myself enough for it."

She pauses momentarily. "It's time to forgive yourself, honey. You want to look forward to the future, not remain chained to the past. I should know." She peers into my eyes. "I spent years hiding a secret that almost destroyed us. I've only recently come to realize how that link to the past was holding me back from the things I wanted to do. I don't want you to make the same mistakes. I know you love my son with all your heart. You always have, and I know the person you are in here." She taps a finger against my chest. "And that's why I can forgive you. Why we've all forgiven you. God knows we've made our fair share of mistakes. Who the hell are we to judge?"

I don't realize I'm crying until she wipes her thumbs across the dampness on my face. She pulls me into a hug. "I wouldn't want anyone else for my son. You've always been perfect for him, Lana. My intention was never to keep you two apart. I just wanted to slow things down until you were both ready. All I want for my sons is that they're happy. That they find someone to love who loves them as much in return. Kalvin has that in you. You two are for life. I wish you every happiness, honey, because you deserve it. And I want you to know you are as much a part of this family as anyone. You always have been."

When we return to campus in January, we discover both Shelby and Chase have been expelled for conduct which brings the university into disrepute. One in five students on campus suffers some form of sexual assault which is why the authorities treat such incidents very seriously.

I'm now enrolled in the creative writing program, and I've a huge amount of work to catch up on, but hard work has never scared me. As we settle into our new apartment, and Hewson settles into the Baby Gators daycare facility, I feel a level of contentment that is unsurpassed.

Mom and Dad are happy in Connecticut, and while I'm sad that things didn't work out for her with her parents—my grandparents have resumed ignoring us and pretending like we don't exist—I can't say I'm losing much sleep over it. It's a shame my grandmother couldn't get over her aversion to my father, couldn't let the past stay in the past, and while I will always be grateful to her for taking me and Hewson in, I'm not going to allow her to cast a shadow on my future. If she wants to reconcile in the future, I would be receptive, but I'm not going out of my way to make amends.

Kal and Hewson are my priority now, and everything else takes a back seat.

As the weeks turn into months, we adjust to our new schedule, with the help of friends. Saturday night is date night and the one day of the week when Kal and I can focus on our relationship. Our friends take turns babysitting, even Brett who turns out to be the best sitter of all, and life is good.

More than good.

I'm living my dream, and the reality is even better.

Every day, I fall more and more in love with my man. Kal is everything I hoped he'd be and more. I couldn't wish for a better best friend, a better lover, a better cheerleader. And he's an amazing dad. Hewson is the apple of Kal's eye, and they are literally joined at the hip. On weekends, we go on family outings, and once a month, we take turns visiting our extended families. Mom and Dad were a little wary of Kal, at first, but thanks to his unwavering love of me and our son, they have since embraced him.

I walk around with a smug, happy look plastered on my face, and there is little to complain about.

Kal finally read my book, and I shared my plans with him. With his support and encouragement, I self-published *The Story of Us* two months ago. To my shock and delight, it was an instant bestseller. I'm distributing twenty-five percent of the profits to a rape support charity, and the rest is being saved toward next semester's tuition. Kal argues with me relentlessly over it. But, a deal's a deal.

And I'm a lucky bitch.

I know that.

As we prepare to spend the summer break together, I acknowledge how things could have turned out so differently and how happy I am with where my life is heading.

I couldn't ask for anything more.

Epilogue
Lana

August

I'm leaning over the ledge staring at the crystal-clear waters of the Atlantic Ocean, taking a moment to cherish the beauty that is my life. The moon casts magical shadows on the sea, and in the distance, the faint sounds of laughter can be heard. Glancing along the beach, I spot the telltale glow of a fire. The beach parties along this private strip are legendary.

When Alex and James said we could use the Nantucket house for the summer, I squealed with joy. Getting to spend every minute of every day with Kal and my son is a luxury we don't normally have, and I wanted to pack as much into our summer break as possible.

But it's more than that.

This house and this island have always had a special place in my heart. This is where I fell completely in love with my soul mate, and the memories I have of summers spent here will never fade. That we get to experience this again, and to make new memories with our son, thrills me in ways I can't even begin to explain.

We quickly settled into a new routine. I get up at five a.m. and spend a few hours writing outside, before the heat and humidity affect my productivity and before the two men in my life start making welcome demands on my time.

We eat a leisurely breakfast on the deck before heading to one of the public beaches. We stop in town on our way back, having a late lunch or early dinner. On lazier days, we stay here, using the private beach to chill out, kissing, touching, and making plans, as Hewson makes sandcastles and snoozes under the shade of the umbrella. Kal is teaching him to swim, and we spend hours every day in the water. He's running all over the place now, and, I swear, you need eyes in the back of your head.

Nights are filled with sipping wine, snuggling up outside, and making love until the early hours. Kal is adventurous in bed, and I still can't get enough of him. Barely a minute goes by without us touching in some shape or form, and I'll never grow tired of it. I crave his touch as much as I need air.

Strong arms slide around my waist, and a firm, irresistible body lines up behind me. "You doing okay, baby?" Kal asks, brushing my hair aside to kiss my neck.

I shiver as delicious tremors ghost over my skin. "I'm perfect. Just taking a moment to appreciate everything." I twist around, looping my arms around his neck. "Where is everyone?"

"Our moms are clearing up after dinner, and our dads are drinking whiskey in the study. Everyone else is ... around."

Both our families came out two days ago. I was nervous about it, but so far things are going smoothly. I know it's strange for my parents to be back here as guests rather than the hired help, but Alex and James are gracious hosts. Even though they are separated, they are a solid unit, and I know all the boys are holding out hope they'll officially get back together.

I tense a little in his arms. "Who has Hewson?"

He smirks. "Who do you think?"

"We'll have to check Faye and Ky's bags before they leave. I wouldn't put it past either one of them to try and kidnap him," I joke.

Kal draws me in flush to his body. "Neither would I. They are going to make awesome parents someday."

"I think so, too."

His Adam's apple bobs in his throat, and he looks a little green in the face, all of a sudden.

"Are you okay? You don't look so hot." My eyes crinkle in worry as I cup his face.

Michael Buble's melodic tones waft through the nighttime air as the sound of "I Believe in You" emits through the outdoor speakers. "Dance with me?" Kal gulps nervously as he extends his hand.

I place my palm in his, and he pulls me in flush to his body. My heart is thumping as I curl my hands around his neck. His arms encircle my waist. Then we're moving, softly brushing our bodies as we sway to the music. He's peering deep into my eyes, with so much emotion radiating from his gaze, telling me everything that's in his heart. So much love exists between us. It never ceases to blow my mind. To know I could love another person as much as I love him.

Our eyes remain locked, as we dance, while Michael sings about starting over, how good things come back to you, and about reasons to believe in love. As I listen to the lyrics, it's as if he wrote the song especially for us.

Kal starts singing, and then I'm twirling in his arms, spinning around and around, laughing as my heart and soul soar with everything I'm feeling.

The pitter-patter of little feet has me turning around. Hewson is running on his chubby little legs toward us. Our entire families are lined up at the edge of the patio, watching with happy smiles. Blood thrums through my veins, and a fluttery feeling starts up in my chest. The music quiets until it's a hum in the background.

"Come here, buddy," Kal calls out to Hewson. Hewson runs past me, and I pivot around as he barrels straight into his father's arms. I gasp. Kal has removed his button-down shirt, and now he's sporting an identical T-shirt to his son. Both of them are on their knees, peering up at me.

My eyes fill up automatically as I realize what's happening.

"From the moment I met you, my soul came alive," Kal says, his voice choked with emotion. "Every part of my life has been full of your presence, and I know that I couldn't exist without you. Your love lifts me up. It makes me a better person, a better man, a better father. You are the reason I believe in love. You are the reason I'm so unbelievably happy. That I get up every day counting my blessings. I'm so grateful you gave me another chance. That you've given me this unbelievable life. I don't want to spend a second without you by my side."

He stands up, scooping a wriggling Hewson in his arms. They move in front of me, both my boys wearing matching "Marry Us" shirts. Kal lifts the lid on the little black box. "I love you, baby. Make me the happiest man on the planet and agree to be my wife. Marry me, Lana."

Kalvin

I've never felt such abject terror as I do in this moment. My hand is outstretched, the massive diamond ring glistening under the glow of the outside lights. Tears flow down Lana's face, and I can't tell what she's thinking. She's shaking, sobbing, but she still hasn't said a word, and now I'm petrified. Damn my cocky arrogance. If she rejects me, my brothers will never let me live this down. Why I thought it'd be a great idea to propose in front of both our families fails me now. *What the hell was I thinking?*

I know we're still young, and I'm not suggesting we rush out and get married straightaway, but I want my ring on her finger. I want the commitment. I want the world to know she's mine. I want her to know she has my heart for eternity. That I'll always be here for her and Hewson. That I want more kids with her.

I think I've stopped breathing. Hewson is restless in my arms, not understanding the magnitude of the moment.

"Yes," she chokes out, finally. "Yes, I'll marry you."

My relief is immediate, my knees almost buckling. Over my shoulder, I see Faye move forward, and I let Hewson down, nudging him in her direction. Lana flings herself at me, crying and laughing, and I lift her up, spinning us around, my heart full to bursting point. "Thank fuck. You almost gave me a coronary."

The music starts up again, and I put her feet on the ground, sliding the ring on her finger. She can hardly see it through her tears. "Oh my God, Kal, it's beautiful."

"Just like you," I whisper, reeling her into my arms. "I love you, honeybun. So, so much."

"I love you, too. You've just made me the happiest girl in the world."

"My new mission in life is ensuring you're happy every day of our forever." I can't hold back any longer, needing to taste her, to feel her lips moving against mine. I kiss her long and deep and passionately, uncaring that we have an audience. She's my fiancée now, and I'm going to kiss the shit out of her every second of every day for the rest of our lives.

A not so subtle tug on my leg has us breaking apart.

"Up, Daddy," Hewson demands, not liking to be left out.

I scoop him up, and he wraps an arm around me and Lana. We dance to the music, laughing and twirling around as our son giggles. In the background, our families are chatting and smiling, and no other moment could be more perfect.

"Have you any ideas on a date?" Faye asks, a couple of hours later. Hewson is tucked up in bed, and our parents have retired inside for the night. Melissa and Keaton are snuggled up on the loveseat, while Kent,

Keanu, Kev, and Kade have wandered down the beach to check out the party, leaving only Lana and me, Ky and Faye, Faye's Irish friend Rachel, and Brad. Everyone is delighted for us, and this night can't get any better. Well, it can. Once I get Lana under me later. I can't wait to make love to her as my fiancée for the first time. I'm already hard thinking about it.

"We're in no rush," Lana says, having already discussed it with me earlier. "We're thinking just after we graduate."

"I can't believe you picked this by yourself." Faye takes Lana's hand in hers, admiring the ring.

"I might've had some help." My eyes flick to Ky's momentarily, and I smile at the secret we're keeping. I wasn't the only Kennedy choosing an engagement ring that day.

Faye's gaze bounces between me and her boyfriend, frowning a little. Ky pulls her in tighter to his side, pressing a kiss to her temple as he shoots me a warning look.

"You did good, babe," Lana says, kissing me softly on the lips.

I stand up. "Excuse us. We have somewhere we need to be." Taking her hand, I lead her around the front of the house.

"Where are we going?"

"It's a surprise."

I open the car door, nudging her inside. I've only had one beer on purpose. She slides in, staring at me in confusion. "Where—"

I silence her with a drugging kiss. When I pull away, I place one finger against her lips. "No questions. A surprise is only a surprise if you don't know."

I'm smug as I drive away from the house, heading southbound.

Ten minutes later, I stop at the high wrought iron gates, punching the code into the keypad. I feel Lana's eyes on me as I drive up the small entranceway, stopping in front of the one-story Spanish-style property. It's painted in contrasting shades of terracotta and cream, which are a bit gauche, but it was the stunning architectural design that caught my eye.

I hope she likes it.

That she isn't mad I purchased it without consulting her.

I was too afraid she'd say no.

She's a bit funny when it comes to money, but she's going to have to get over it. As my wife, she'll share everything that's mine.

I run around to open her door, taking her hand and helping her out of the car. "Why are we here?" I spot the nervous look in her eyes.

"I wanted to show you our new vacation home." My heart is in my mouth. "Surprise, baby. Happy engagement."

Her eyes are out on stalks. "You bought us a house?"

Carefully, I draw her into my arms. "I know how much you love it here, Lana, and I love it too. I wanted us to have our own home. For Hewson to spend every summer here with us." She's crying again. "Don't cry, babe. Please. On a scale of one to ten, how mad are you?"

She laughs, playfully slapping my chest. "Stupid, crazy, Stinky. Why would I be mad?" She presses her body against mine, her eyes darkening. "I can't ever be mad at you. Not when you love me as well as you do. You love me good, Kal. I don't know what I've done to deserve you, but I won't ever take you for granted. I promise."

She presses her mouth to mine in a feather-soft kiss that unravels every part of me. "I love it, and you. I love you so much." Then her mouth is on mine again; this time it's hot and intense and hungry. We devour one another, and my hand creeps under her dress, tracing soft caresses up and down her thigh. Ripping her mouth from mine, panting with the same desire I feel, she grabs my hand and starts pulling me toward the front door. "I have an idea." Her eyes glisten mischievously, and the bulge in my pants strains to the point of pain. "We need to christen our new home, and I can't think of a better time to start."

And as she pulls me into our new house, there isn't a single part of my anatomy that disagrees.

Brad

I'm surrounded by fawning, lovesick couples, and it's souring my stomach. Melissa and Keaton are kissing innocently on the loveseat while Faye and Kyler are kissing not so innocently on the couch across from me. Kal has taken his new fiancée off to show her the house he bought her. I'm happy for my friends, honestly, I am, but it only serves to highlight what an epic clusterfuck my life has become.

Everyone is moving on but me.

I knock back the remainder of my beer, reaching out to grab a fresh one from the ice bucket. Rachel eyes me over the rim of her bottle, and I stare back at her. Her eyes look as pained as mine. I only found out at the last minute that Faye's Irish friend was coming. Apparently, she's spending a few weeks on vacation in the States with her bestie. If I'd known she was visiting, I most definitely wouldn't have come here. I avert my gaze, not able to witness her agony. I can scarcely tolerate my own.

Why the fuck did I agree to come here? It's bad enough I've had to endure this intense yearning in my chest all year, without subjecting myself to it during summer break. I feel instantly guilty at my uncharitable thoughts. I'm a fucking shitty friend. The worst kind. The one that skulks in the shadows, bitter and seething, coveting the one girl he can't have.

I've tried everything to forget Faye, but nothing's working.

Every girl I've fucked in an effort to forget her has only served to remind me more of her. Every girl morphs into the Faye of my imagination while underneath me, and the guilt ratchets up a few notches. By the time we're done, I can't get the girl out of my bed fast enough.

I'm a mess, and I've no one to blame but myself.

I should never have allowed my heart to become invested.

I'm ruining everything, and there doesn't seem to be a Goddamned thing I can do to stop it.

Nothing is working. The only relief I get is when I'm numb from an alcoholic high and I'm too drunk to think coherently. Then my head is a blissful Faye-free zone. At least for a few hours, until reality comes crashing back down, reminding me I'm in love with my best friend's girl.

My gaze has drifted to Faye unknowingly. They've stopped kissing, and now Ky is glaring at me like he's seconds away from ripping into me. I wouldn't blame him, and I'd deserve everything he dished out.

I look away, inwardly cursing myself as I knock back my beer. The seat dips beside me, and a sensual fragrance tickles my nostrils, evoking memories I've long since buried.

"She's never going to leave him. He's it for her," Rachel says quietly.

"You think I don't know that?" I snap.

Fiery eyes meet mine. "Still an asshole I see."

I snort. "You didn't seem to mind last time."

Her eyes narrow. "I don't tend to discriminate much when it's a drunken fuck."

"Or at all," I reply nastily.

"You don't know me, so don't pretend like you do," she clips out.

My eyes roam her sexy body, remembering how good it felt being inside her. "That's where you're wrong," I reply, spotting the anguish and the pain lingering at the back of her eyes. "I know you're hurting and that you'll do anything, try anything, to blank the pain."

She glares at me, but there's a hint of fleeting vulnerability behind the heat. "You should know. Found anything that works?" Her tone is taunting.

I bark out a bitter laugh. "Nope, but I've only made my way around a fifth of the campus. There's plenty more girls to fuck next year."

She shakes her head sadly. "It's not the solution. You've got to change things up."

"Like you have?" I throw back at her, pissed for all sorts of reasons.

"I'm trying." She rests her hands in her lap, biting her lip, and damn if my cock doesn't twitch to life.

"How?" I ask, my mouth dry and hungry at the same time. I'm in desperate need of a lifeline, and if she's got ideas, I'm all ears.

"Didn't Faye tell you?" she inquires, arching a beautifully curved brow. She tosses her hair over her shoulder, and my mind conjures up memories of twisting my hands in the thick, silky strands as I thrust into her. Her long tresses are dark brown now, not the garish red she was sporting the first, and last, time we met. The first and last time we fucked.

She jerks her chin up. "I'm moving here permanently."

I sit up straighter. "What?"

She nods. "Alex helped me secure a place on the fashion design degree program at the Massachusetts College of Art and Design. Faye and I are going to share an apartment off campus this year." Her eyes sparkle with relief and expectation, and it's a different look on her.

Well, shit. That means another year of sharing living space with Ky. I had prayed and hoped that he would move in with his girlfriend this year and spare me the agony. I guess I'm in for a second year of absolute torture. I take an angry swipe of my beer. I could tell him I want to room on campus this year, but I'm not leaving my best bud high and dry. That would just be another shitty act to add to the list.

God, this situation is unbearable, and I feel like I'm walking on eggshells all the time.

"You know," she says, turning toward me, a softer expression on her pretty face. Her beautiful brown eyes light up, and her face semi-glows, enhancing her hotness. Rachel is stunning, and there's no doubt the guys will be lining up for a sample. "I'll need all the friends I can get, and maybe we can help each other. I ... I know what it's like to hurt so much that you can hardly breathe."

The look she gives me is the most honest one she's shared with me yet. I'm not sure why she's let her guard down, but this shit can't happen.

I stare at her as if she's insane.

I can't be friends with her.

One, she's Faye's best friend and an additional complication I don't need in my life.

Two, she's hot as all fuck, and I don't trust myself around her. Especially when I already know what a great lay she is.

And three, she's even more messed up than I am. I don't know what demons lurk underneath her skin, but I've enough of my own without adding hers to the mix.

Rachel and I can't be friends.

Rachel and I can't be anything.

I need to make that abundantly clear.

Sighing, I plant my feet on the table, working out how to do this.

The nice guy hiding underneath my exterior doesn't want to hurt her, but there's too little of that guy left in me. I'm killing him, slowly, one brain cell at a time. I pierce her with my most venomous look. "Why the hell would I want to be friends with you?"

A glimmer of pain darts in front of her eyes, but I ignore the remorse, pushing on.

"You're just some girl I fucked against the wall when I was drunk. If friends is code word for fuck buddies, you can forget it. I don't offer seconds."

Her nostrils flare, and her eyes narrow. She gulps, and I know I've hit my mark.

I feel like a worthless pile of garbage.

"Fuck off, Brad. For the life of me, I will never understand how either of them can call you a friend." She stands up, and I can't stop my eyes from drinking her in. From her sinfully luscious lips to the creamy swell of her breasts and down over her long legs, barely covered in her skimpy jean shorts, Rachel is temptation on a platter. Leaning down, she pins me with a vicious look. "And for the record, I wouldn't piss on you if you were on fire let alone fuck you again."

She stomps off, anger radiating from her pores, shaking her

delectable ass, while I try to disguise my begrudging amusement and my growing boner.

No, Rachel and I can never be friends.

Because friendship would never be enough with a girl like her.

And contemplating anything else is like tempting a hornet's nest.

Two damaged hearts plus two messed-up minds equals one motherfucking destructive clusterfuck waiting to happen.

And my life is enough of a clusterfuck as it is.

So, I add her to the list of girls I'm not allowed to touch.

And hope that this time I can stick to my resolve.

Saving Brad is the next book in the series. Available now and free to read in Kindle Unlimited.

If you need to talk to someone regarding sexual assault, please call the National Sexual Assault Hotline in the US at 800.656.4673. If you live outside the United States of America, please contact your local support services.

SAVING BRAD (The Kennedy Boys Book #5)

Brad

I'm in love with my best friend's girl.

She knows it. He knows it. **Everyone** knows it.

Faye will never be mine but try telling that to my stupid heart.

An endless rotation of girls streams in and out of my bedroom in a desperate attempt to forget her, but nothing eases the horrid ache in my chest. Rejection isn't anything new for me, but it hasn't gotten any easier.

Until **she** reappears in my life. Like an out-of-control tornado. Storming in, all fierce and angry, ready to steamroll everything in her path. Rachel is trouble with a capital T bundled in a gorgeous, sexy, Irish package.

She pushes all the wrong buttons, and I can't decide if I want to yell at her or kiss her.

I should steer clear.

But I've never been very good at taking my own advice. Especially when it comes to girls I can't have and shouldn't want.

Rachel

I need to escape.

To put as much distance between me and that monster so I can start living my life.

Yet, even the vast Atlantic Ocean isn't enough to sever the connection. To allow me to forget how he's ruined me. His hold is more than just physical. He has a vise-grip on my head and my heart, and I can't breathe, can't think, and can't function.

So, I do everything to blot it out.

Until **he** reappears in my life.

Brad McConaughey. So hot. So infuriating. So in love with my best friend.

Every word out of Brad's mouth makes me want to throat punch him or kick him in the nuts.

But he makes me feel, and I hate him for it. A part of me might actually love him for it.

I should keep my distance, but like destructive magnets, we are drawn together.

This isn't going to end well.

I know it. He knows it.

But we're powerless to resist.

Available now in ebook, paperback, and audiobook.

pain. Until Jared rocks up to the art gallery where I work, with his fiancée in tow, and I'm drowning again.

Seeing him brings everything to the surface, so I flee. Placing distance between us again, I'm determined to put him behind me once and for all.

Then he reappears at my door, begging me for another chance.

I know I should turn him away.

Try telling that to my heart.

This angsty, new adult romance is a FREE full-length ebook, exclusively available to newsletter subscribers.

Type this link into your browser to claim your free copy:

https://bit.ly/TITMHFBB

OR

Scan this code to claim your free copy:

Acknowledgments

Loving Kalvin was quite a different book for me to write, but I loved each and every part of Lana and Kalvin's story, and I hope you did too! I'm aware that a lot of readers dislike Lana because of her actions toward Kal in *Finding Kyler* and *Losing Kyler*. I understand that, and I am in no way condoning her behavior, but I wanted to explore how good people can make bad judgment calls and if someone makes the wrong choices should they be punished for it for the rest of their life?

While it was never my intention to delve into the sensitive subject of rape in this story, I felt it was important that Lana acknowledged how her actions might have affected rape victims and that she tried to atone for it.

As always, I have to thank a great team of people who work with me to deliver these books in the fastest possible time frame. Huge thanks go out to Kelly Hartigan, Robin Harper, Ciara Turley, my beta readers, and all the wonderful girls on my ARC and Street Teams.

Massive thanks to my family and friends for all the online posting and sharing, and I would be lost without the support of my husband and my sons.

Most importantly, thank you so much to all the readers around the world who have embraced the Kennedy Boys and who enabled me to write more stories in this world.

About the Author

Siobhan Davis™ is a *USA Today, Wall Street Journal,* and Amazon Top 5 bestselling romance author. **Siobhan** writes emotionally intense stories with swoon-worthy romance, complex characters, and tons of unexpected plot twists and turns that will have you flipping the pages beyond bedtime! She has sold over 2 million books, and her titles are translated into several languages.

Prior to becoming a full-time writer, Siobhan forged a successful corporate career in human resource management.

She lives in the Garden County of Ireland with her husband and two sons.

You can connect with Siobhan in the following ways:

Website: www.siobhandavis.com
Facebook: AuthorSiobhanDavis
Instagram: @siobhandavisauthor
Tiktok: @siobhandavisauthor
Email: siobhan@siobhandavis.com

Books By Siobhan Davis

NEW ADULT ROMANCE
The One I Want Duet
Kennedy Boys Series
Rydeville Elite Series
All of Me Series
Forever Love Duet

NEW ADULT ROMANCE STAND-ALONES
Inseparable
Incognito
Still Falling for You
Holding on to Forever
Always Meant to Be
Tell It to My Heart

REVERSE HAREM
Sainthood Series
Dirty Crazy Bad Duet
Surviving Amber Springs (stand-alone)
Alinthia Series ^

DARK MAFIA ROMANCE
Mazzone Mafia Series
Vengeance of a Mafia Queen (stand-alone)
*The Accardi Twins**
*Taking What's Mine**

YA SCI-FI & PARANORMAL ROMANCE
Saven Series
True Calling Series ^

---

*Coming 2024
^Currently unpublished but will be republished in due course.

www.siobhandavis.com